'A brilliant novel of adu[...]
[Cook's] portrayal of Baths[...]
mo[...]
seductress.   [...] remarkably approachable.'
          Sam Sacks, *[...]e Wall Street Journal*

'Full-throated.'
Elizabeth Buchan, *Daily Mail*

'Almost two decades in the making, *Lux* is well worth the wait.
Like its predecessor *Achilles*, it's an ambitious and compelling
novel, equally vivid in its conjuring of myth and history,
particularly striking in its portrayal of religious belief under
pressure, the nature of holiness and the sacred.
It's a remarkable book.'
Michael Symmons Roberts, author of *Drysalter*

'Quietly masterful prose builds a huge world, unsentimental,
numinous, and deeply moving ... A joy to read.'
Susan Hitch

'Cook's visual imagination is as sharp and gorgeous as any
Pre-Raphaelite painter's. Her psychological penetration
is deep and compassionate.'
John Drury, author of *Music at Midnight*

'Beautiful and complicated ... Here is the rare book
that functions on multiple levels, inspiring new ideas
and insights with each re-reading.'
Tara Cheesman, *On the Seawall*

'A remarkable interweaving of one ancient king's story
and his place as redeemer within and beyond Judaism.'
Rabbi Dr Aviva Kipen, *J-Wire*

LUX

Elizabeth Cook is an award-winning author, poet, librettist, and scholar. Born in Gibraltar, she spent her childhood in Nigeria and Dorset. She has been the British Academy Chatterton Lecturer and a Hawthornden Fellow, and has written for publications including the *London Review of Books*. She is the editor of the Oxford Authors *John Keats* and author of the acclaimed novel *Achilles* (Methuen and Picador USA), which, in a performance version, won a Fringe First at Edinburgh and has been performed at the National Theatre. She wrote the libretto for Francis Grier's *The Passion of Jesus of Nazareth*, commissioned and broadcast by the BBC. She now lives in London and Suffolk.

LUX

Elizabeth Cook

SCRIBE

Melbourne • London

for Michael Baxandall and Joseph Burney Trapp,
in grateful memory

Scribe Publications

2 John St, Clerkenwell, London, WC1N 2ES, United Kingdom
18–20 Edward St, Brunswick, Victoria 3056, Australia
3754 Pleasant Ave, Suite 100, Minneapolis, Minnesota 55409, USA

First published by Scribe in the UK, Australia, and New Zealand 2019
Published by Scribe in North America 2020
This edition published by Scribe 2021

Typeset in Janson by the publishers

Printed and bound in the UK by CPI Group (UK) Ltd, Croydon CR0 4YY

Scribe Publications is committed to the sustainable use of natural resources
and the use of paper products made responsibly from those resources.

978 1 912854 74 5 (UK edition)
978 1 925713 71 8 (Australian edition)
978 1 947534 86 5 (US edition)
978 1 925693 54 6 (e-book)

Catalogue records for this book are available from the
National Library of Australia and the British Library.

scribepublications.co.uk
scribepublications.com.au
scribepublications.com

How do you know but ev'ry Bird that cuts the airy way,
Is an immense world of delight, clos'd by your senses five?

William Blake, *The Marriage of Heaven and Hell*

PROLOGUE

Lukkes, my fair falcon, and your fellowes all,
How well plesaunt it were your libertie!

Thomas Wyatt

Those who knew nothing of what was about to take place saw
the crowds — they felt the pull that drew the capillaries of the
narrow streets into a central artery where the crowd surged
like a great and overflowing river. If you had just gone out into
the yard to scour a dish or air a mat you would probably not
have stayed, the tug of that mass was so strong, the current
caught you and pulled you on with it. Excited voices. What
festivity were they all pouring towards? Some were eating
as they hurried along, cramming dates into their mouths as
hastily as they walked, as if their excitement could be pacified
in no other way. There were men, and women too, some of
the women clutching children who were too small to leave
behind. There were also children who had joined the throng,
as eager as the adults to be where all converged. Eddies of conversations, news exchanged between neighbours, the thwack
and swish of cloth as determined limbs pressed against robes
in the hurry to advance. Some robes lifted for ease of walking.
Nearly running. A name, a woman's name runs through the
crowd, concentrating the sounds to make a rope, thickening at

1

the core of a strong current till soon this name is known by all.

Miriam. Repeated as information and as question.

The tributary streets meet in a wide street — the main thoroughfare — which pulls the growing crowd to the fringes of the town, to a place which is neither town nor desert, a place where travellers sometimes camp, where thin animals dither and the vultures gather like gossips. The gate they go out of is called the Dung Gate. It is the exit route of the town's effluent, and the sweet smell of the excrement, so valuable as fertiliser, fills the air and leads many to hold their headcloths over their mouths and noses. But they do not go as far as the dung carts go. The destination is near to the gate: a wide place where the sand is packed down hard.

Here the festive atmosphere is concentrated — traders have set up stalls selling fruit, hot bread, roasted corn. But this is not all. Near the centre of the arena there is a pyramid of stones — some as large as rocks to build a wall with, some smaller, the size that could fit in a hand. There are smooth stones but the majority of them are rough and jagged — the kind which a builder would reject unless he had the means to shape them. People are wandering over to this pile and helping themselves, lingering over their choice, weighing a stone in their hands, even turning it between one hand and the other in appraisal of its qualities, before moving away, their stone now concealed in the folds of their garment. Those who have already selected a rock or a stone stand around or sit on the ground, waiting for all to be ready.

Wailing and raised voices; seven men pushing and pulling by turns the shrouded figure of a woman. Her head is completely covered by her robe, and the rope around her upper body binds her clothes. But you can hear her cries, and the cries of the women who follow.

So that is Miriam. There. Under that cloth.

They lead her to the centre of the place where two planks of wood cover a deep hole. The wood is removed and the woman, still bound, is lifted into the hole where she stands, her body thrashing in protest, up to her waist. A man comes forward with a spade and shovels sand into the space around her, tamping it down with his feet until she is packed in tight. He does it with a practised neutrality, as if planting a tree.

A woman thrusts herself forward through the crowd — an old woman, far too old to be the mother of the child she holds in her arms. Her mouth is a gash of despair and she makes no efforts to protect the baby from the wet of her tears.

One of the men goes to her, takes her by the arm, and attempts to lead her away. But the old woman will not be deterred. She presses further forward till she is right by the edge of the pit in which the other woman is held.

'For the love of God, let her live. Let this child have a mother.'

There is a murmur in the crowd. A voice calls out, 'Stone the bastard too.'

This causes a stir; a protective protest. The woman holding the baby is restrained but not forced away.

The baby attracts sympathy. Sensing himself the object of too much attention he begins to grizzle and soon this becomes an unassuageable gasping cry, the single consistent sound in all the commotion of murmurs and jostling.

The old woman holding the child wraps a hand protectively over his head, jiggles him up and down in a mechanical way, but her attention is on the woman in the ground. She is straining towards her.

'Let her hold him. Just for a moment let her hold him.'

LUX

'If she holds him, he'll die too.'

Then an immense struggle from the figure in the ground. The dark mound of fabric which is the woman's swathed upper body twists and works itself into such a pitch of expressiveness the form is like a face in agony. A cry from the woman within, which the thick fabric can muffle but not stifle.

'Let me see my child again.'

The man who seems to be in charge goes up to her; crouches down so he can speak to her. He tells her that the cloth around her head is an act of kindness, 'so you will not see death flying towards you.'

'Take it away. I want to see.'

These last words pierce the fabric so that everyone near the front of the crowd hears them.

The man signals to another that the cloth covering the woman's head should be removed. The rope binding her arms to her body makes this difficult, so the fabric is cut away with a knife. The man doing the cutting is very careful not to let the knife hurt the woman, careful as he eases the fabric away from her face though the woman cannot keep still while he works.

It is her arms that need to be free. Though they are lashed to her body everything about her is reaching out, stretching towards the baby. Many of those who were to remember the scene — and most of those there did remember — would picture a woman half buried in the ground with arms outstretched. A woman with frantic, avid eyes that seemed to drink in what they saw: the sky, the high surrounding hills, the baby comforted by his grandmother, crying to be with the mother whose face he could now see and then crying to be away from her, the immensity of her pain too much for him to bear.

The girl Bathsheba is there in the crowd having been pulled along by the current. She has just begun to menstruate and her body feels awkward and unfamiliar. This new womanliness is a gift she is unsure of: what makes her fertile also makes her raw and open. The quiet time before purification only adds to that feeling. What enters her mind, as sight and sound and thought, sinks deep. It is as if she has become soft wax.

When the first stone is released into the air it is almost experimental. It lands wide of its mark and sits on the ground, a few inches from where the dug-in woman is. For a moment all eyes fall on this stone, half-expecting it to move, as if an animal had inexplicably stopped, dropped down to the earth to play dead. And then it begins in earnest. A large, jagged stone flies through the air with vicious force and smashes into the woman's ear. Bathsheba cannot see who hurled this missile but she can feel the deadliness that propels it and it makes her duck her head as if she were the target. Soon the air is dark with flung stones; dark and messy as when a flock of birds takes off as one and is buffeted and flung apart by a strong wind.

She cannot look. The woman's screams are her own. But even in the midst of this crowd it is a dangerous place to be; fragments of rock fly off, injuring those who are only there to take part in a killing at no risk. It feels to Bathsheba as if the frenzy and violence of the crowd is against herself. While the bloodied woman, one eye now crushed and useless, persists in seeing to the last, determined to die whilst she looks on her child and on the harmless sky, the girl Bathsheba cowls her cloth around her head to shield herself from the horror of what surrounds her.

ARK

1

When Eli, the holy priest who had first discovered and, after that, nurtured the vocation of the prophet Samuel, was told that the Ark had been captured by the Philistines — the people of the sea and plains — he fell from the wall he was seated on and broke his neck. It was this that ended his life, not the simultaneously learnt fact of the death of his sons, who had served the Ark so inadequately. The Ark, for which he would have given his life, had till that moment preserved his life. He had served its compacted holiness in a reciprocal relationship. When it entered into enemy hands, he fell with it, and his soul tumbled into Sheol.

The Glory had gone from Israel, yet the knowledge that the Glory had once been present remained. Like the tip of a fled lizard's tail, wedged between the rocks through which it escaped, that knowledge, that memory, handed down in words, provided proof that the Glory had been theirs. Even if the tail tip was a dry husk, the living creature far away, it was evidence of what might yet be again.

—

In the Land of the Five Lords — the land of the people of the sea and plains who had captured the Ark — the Glory proved a terrifying guest.

It had been in their keeping for seven months. This great, ornamented casket was a beautiful thing; a thing to wonder at. And all who saw it did wonder. They wondered at the workmanship, having not thought the Hebrews (unlike themselves) capable of such fine work in metal. Two winged men — angels — wrought in gold guarded the Ark, bending over it with a tender care. Their faces moulded with great delicacy and expressiveness, their fine-tipped wings, with realistic, overlapping feathers, nearly touching each other as they leaned across the precious object of their care. Had the wings touched, the delicacy would have been less, the sense of care less poised and perfect. Poised to defend and to revere. The Hebrews had carried it into battle with them like some kind of mascot, but it had failed to protect them from the superior skill and might of the sea-and-plains people, always better armed than their eastern neighbours.

They took it to Dagon, that great god whose thick scaly figure presided in the splendid temple that crowned the beautiful city of Ashdod. What better way to do homage to the fish god than to present him with this marvel they had captured? The Ark was a heavy thing. It required four men to lift it, once the carrying poles had been threaded through the four gold rings that hung from the base for this purpose. They struggled to carry it up the steps to the threshold of the temple, panting like men with a vast tray of bricks. There was nothing graceful about the way in which they set it down, but they recovered their balance quickly and walked backwards out of the temple, doing obeisance to Dagon.

They had set the Ark as a gift-offering before Dagon. In the morning, when the priests entered the temple, they found their god — the stout, fish-bodied figure — prostrate on the floor in front of the Ark. Kissing the ground. They had to employ a pulley to restore the figure to the plinth it had occupied for so many years without the slightest disturbance. They swept up the mortar dust and leaves that had scattered with the fall and left the temple as before, with the Ark, again in the place of offering, at Dagon's feet.

The following morning, the priest of Dagon entered the temple alone. He encountered the aftermath of a massacre. Dagon's limbs of wood and brass, the carved stone of his body, lay hacked, splintered, and shattered in every area of the temple. As if a great storm had picked the figure up and flung it against the walls of the temple which were now marked, as if with the blood of victims. The Ark was untouched and remained exactly where it had been left.

The priest had fled, screaming in terror. He was never seen in Ashdod after that day. Some said he fled east to learn how to worship the god of the Ark.

They left the Ark there in the temple of Dagon with the scattered parts of the trounced god littered around. No one dared do anything else. The temple of Dagon became the Ark's home, simply because no one had the courage to take the Ark anywhere else.

But its power leaked out beyond the temple. At first people noticed a few more mice than usual in their homes — they had to keep their grain jars sealed at all times. Soon the city was overrun; the whole place filmed with the faeces and urine of the mice that seemed to be hatching in the very gaps between walls, anywhere the mortar was loose. There were so many of them and they were so close together they formed a vast, shifting rodent rug. A sea of moving fur.

How to disencumber themselves of this terrifying guest

when no one wanted to go near it? The governors of the city found two men awaiting punishment and gave them the option of transporting the Ark to Gath as an alternative to the maiming they expected. The men obliged and were unscathed. But the suffering of Ashdod had not ended. While they swept up the corpses of the mice they had succeeded in poisoning, several people began to notice discomfort around their anuses and in their back passages. This grew until a large part of the city's population was suffering — some very greatly — with haemorrhoids that swelled, burned, and bled within them.

It was the same story at Gath; the same at Ekron. The Ark scorched the very ground they trod. They had wanted to keep it away from the Hebrews who seemed to gain strength from it, but they no longer wanted it anywhere near themselves. It did not like them, and they did not know how to appease it.

Once, they might have questioned Dagon, but he was less to them now that he'd been trounced by the terrifying god of the Ark. Ashtaroth? Her priestesses were invited to search, in all the secret ways that they alone knew. Indeed, few wanted to know their methods, for these priestesses — even the loveliest — carried a taint of death. Sorcerers too were consulted. Men who could examine the pattern that the sand made when it fell and there find an account of what was to be.

All were unanimous. The Ark must be returned, and with compensation.

It was a relief to think about making something at a time when their world seemed so much less secure than in the past. The best goldsmiths were consulted and they in turn were advised by Elders who had taken the counsel of sorcerers: they set to the difficult task of transforming the recent plagues into something of value and fineness. Using skills that had been handed down and refined over many generations they created golden mice — so life-like in appearance you would think their noses quivered. Five men collaborated over this, each trying to outdo the other in skill and accuracy in portraying the suppleness of the mouse bodies, the delicacy of the clawed feet, the suggestion of quivering whiskers. When they set them on a table together it was as if their golden mice were about to run together, scamper and breed.

But they scratched their heads over the haemorrhoids. How to replicate something so formless, so lacking in any structure other than a capacity to fill and swell with blood? In the end, they shrugged. They had seen — and certainly felt — haemorrhoids like small clusters of grapes. So be it. They would fashion such grapes in gold. One haemorrhoid grape for each of the Five Lords.

2

Following his father's instructions closely, but without any intervention by the watching elder, he had pushed the whole of one arm — up to the elbow and a bit beyond — into the straining cow. With difficulty, he had inserted his hand between the clasping wall of the cow's interior and the nervous, spindly bundle which contained the calf's forelegs. He'd pulled. Pulled with all his young might until something began to release and suddenly both calf and cow took over and the whole thing completed itself in a rush and soon the now-calm cow was dedicatedly licking the membrane from her child and that child was lifting himself onto thin legs and taking his first astonishing steps in an endless new atmosphere of air.

The boy, Gurion, was still virgin in the way of men, but this entrance into the living body of another creature altered him. That texture — smooth with some softness, charged with energy and purpose — was new to him. He could not shake off the memory of that clinging heat.

His father, satisfied that the boy was equal to the task, left him to deliver the next calf unsupervised. Gurion approached his second cow with the confidence his father had given him — he had, after all, known cattle all his life, it was only their interiors that were unfamiliar. He spoke reassurance to her, stroking her flank with his free arm whilst tugging with the other on the legs that were reaching out into the world. He tugged gently this time, for the resistance was less.

The calves were born only a few hours apart; their gravid mothers had grazed the same fields. Gurion felt that they were his calves — that they belonged to him since he had brought them into the world — and he watched over them with interest and concern. He watched the mothers as they licked their young with indolent solicitude. The calves stalled together — as if they were the siblings he felt them to be — and learned to lick one another, discovering their world through their tongues. But their mouths were busiest when suckling. When their mouths found their mothers' teats they clasped them, as if soldered, oblivious to all else.

The mothers liked to have their calves nearby. Even though they often appeared to find the relentless seeking out of their udders a nuisance — they would at times attempt to walk on regardless of the attached youngster — each mother would look anxiously around the field if her calf was away from her; return to calm chewing only after she had located him by smell or call. Gurion was as alert as the mothers to the lowings of the two calves: the different pitches, the varying pulses of urgency. He could feel the reassurance in the mothers' responses; the calls that said, 'I'm here.'

The mothers were both young, beautiful animals, and these were their first calves. Gurion's father had yet to put these mothers to the plough, having a great many other cattle for the purpose. These two were given the task of rearing young and producing milk. They looked set for placid, undemanding lives, and Gurion had begun to regard both mothers and calves almost as family members. Not exactly domestic pets (like the kid he had reared) but something approaching that. The feeling was personal, for he was aware of what each was like and they responded to him. It dismayed him when his father came to him and told him to prepare the cows for a journey.

'What about the calves? They're not weaned yet.'

'We'll have to feed them from skins.'

'But the mothers will never leave them behind. They'll never stop crying.'

(He was not sure whether he meant the mothers or the calves. Or possibly himself.)

'I understand that's part of the plan. To see if they do cry — the mothers — or if they'll go quietly.'

'What plan?'

Then his father told Gurion what he knew about the Ark.

'They want to give it back. It's been trouble ever since we've had it. Not that we've had anything to do with it here on the plains.'

'What sort of trouble?'

'Vermin — overrunning the cities. We're lucky out here, we don't get that. People have died. Thousands of them. And been ill — sores in their bottoms.'

The father allowed Gurion a moment of amusement before he went on: 'So they want to get rid of it. Give it back to its rightful owners. Good luck to them.'

'What's this got to do with our cows?'

'Transport. They think — this is what I've heard — that the mice and the sores have been sent by the Hebrews' god who is angry and wants to go back to his own people. That's what the sorcerers say and that's what most people think. But just in case it's only coincidence and the bad things that have been going on are nothing to do with anything — not that Ark at any rate — they want to test it. That's why they want our cows.'

'To test the Ark thing?'

'To see if they'll take it, in spite of having calves left behind and in spite of not having had any experience of yokes over their shoulders or carts to drag along.'

'Why ours? There are thousands of cattle out there. Plenty of other cows with young calves.'

'Someone must have put in a word for us. We'll be compensated. That's what they said.' He knew his cattle were among the best.

Gurion shrugged. He realised they had no choice. But he thought no compensation could make up for the loss of his calves' mothers.

———

He did not see inside the coffer, but the coffer itself was a thing of great beauty: olive wood inlaid with mother of pearl and buffed to a sheen. People talked about the things that were inside, but he knew that only a priest could handle them; that the content was dedicated to the god of the Ark and to the people who worshipped it.

The cart that carried the Ark and the coffer was made with as much care as the load it carried. Master carpenters planed and fitted the wood and threaded the wheels onto an axle whose gilded hubs would catch and mirror the sun's light. They created a kind of throne for the Ark and the coffer to sit upon. It was covered with a tasselled awning. There was no seat for a driver.

A small crowd had gathered around the laden cart when Gurion and his father led the two mother cows to the appointed place. They had made a loose collar for each and expected reluctance on the cows' parts as they were coaxed away from the place where their calves were sleeping. Yet the cows moved willingly and barely needed to be goaded, pausing only to release their streams of urine or to defaecate, swishing their tails and turning their heads in annoyance at the flies but apparently untroubled to be leaving their young.

The crowd made way for them as they approached the cart. One of the Elders stepped out and drew Gurion's father aside. He handed the father a package which the man inspected swiftly before tucking it away; the Elder spoke in a low voice and Gurion realised by the way the Elder jerked his chin in his direction and the considering expression with which his father looked towards him that he was being discussed. His father appeared undecided. Then the Elder said something that made the father laugh and the Elder clapped a hand around the other man's shoulders and the two, both of them smiling now, approached Gurion.

'He'd like you to travel with them,' said his father, 'Keep an eye on the cows while they make their journey with the cart.'

Gurion thought the Elder looked foolish, nodding and smiling ingratiatingly, towards him. He guessed he knew nothing of cattle. Might perhaps be afraid of them.

He looked towards his father for permission and saw, from the amusement in his eyes, that his father too guessed the Elder's motive.

'Go,' he said. 'I can manage without you for a day or so. I'll see those young ones won't go hungry.'

A sudden fear gripped Gurion.

'You won't kill them will you? Promise me you won't kill them while I'm away.'

How was this tender boy ever going to grow into a successful cow-man? Yet, for now, the father offered reassurance, 'Not those ones. Not yet, I promise.'

He hoped the responsibility he was giving Gurion now would help bring the boy to manhood.

———

It was unclear to Gurion what his duties were since the Elders were emphatic that the cattle must not be led. But he was allowed to be the one who placed the yoke across the cows' shoulders. They accepted it placidly, still chewing the hay they had just been given. He watched as the shafts of the cart were attached to the yoke. They were standing on the track that leads east towards the hill country. He looked that way too: towards Beth-shemesh, the city of the sun. High on the rocks that marked the boundary between the people of the plains and Judah, the buildings of Beth-shemesh would catch the light of the setting sun and glow pink with its reflected light. They seemed to bask in it.

This was where their small caravan appeared to be heading. No one led the cows, but there was only one track for them to choose and it led in that direction. The cows took it, dragging the beautiful cart with its important cargo along the rocky track. The fringe on the canopy over the Ark swung from side to side as the cart was jolted along, but the Ark itself remained largely out of sight.

The day was hot. Gurion wished that he had a fringed canopy to shelter him from the sun's force. At midday he would normally be resting from the heat under the shelter of a rock, eating a small meal of cheese and herbs with his father before falling asleep for an hour. The Elders walked with a shade over their heads but did not think to admit him. When they reached a brook he spoke up. The cattle needed water. The thirsty beasts did not wait for permission but lowered their heads and drank noisily. Gurion too scooped water in his hands; drank it, then splashed himself and the cattle. The others followed his lead — the lead of the cattle. They stopped, cooled themselves, drank from the stream, never taking their eyes from cattle and cart. Never taking their minds off the Ark that sat there, magnificent and, for the time, harmless. The harm it was capable of dormant.

Gurion was aware of another presence. He felt they were being watched. It was similar to the sensation he had when he was with cattle and a lion was near. Was it that the cattle heard the lion and that he, attuned to them, observed their unease, or that the lion's act of watching and listening was palpable? He didn't know. All he knew was that there was this active presence. He felt it, though he could not interpret it.

The cows were also aware of something. When they lifted their heads from the brook their ears swivelled to catch sounds. Their eyes were uneasy. They appeared to want to get away from something and, in unison, jerked themselves forward, pulling the stationary cart up with a jolt that threatened to endanger its cargo. To Gurion's surprise, no one reached out a steadying hand. Only he reached to pat the flank of the cow nearest to him before stepping back to allow the cattle to make their way unled, as had been stipulated.

The climb towards Beth-shemesh was steep. He was the only one to keep up with the cart while the cattle scrambled up the path. The Elders held back, either from exhaustion or reserve. But Gurion was only a few paces behind the cart as it made its way along the path, which is skirted on one side by a sheer rock wall, the rock and its vegetation at times overhanging the path, pushing the group dangerously close to the other edge, from which the ground falls away sharply. If you were to fall here you would fall a long way, tumbling through thistles and scree.

The cows began to low in protest; there was barely room for the two of them abreast, let alone the cart that they were pulling, effortfully, along the track. Gurion fell back a little further from them, fearful that the cart might roll backwards and run into him — he could see nowhere to climb to if he needed to protect himself from the impact, unless he could scramble up the sheer bank into one of the trees that were rooted in its crevices. The Elders were so far behind that he could no longer hear them, though he still had a sense of being watched.

The wheels of the cart had just, with difficulty, cleared a large boulder. In doing so, they had dislodged another, sending a small avalanche of rocks and stones flying in their wake. The cattle were terrified and, for the first time since setting out, attempted to buck off the yoke and rid themselves of their burden. They were too firmly attached to succeed and in their alarm they galloped straight ahead — the only direction available to them. Gurion pressed himself against the cliff wall and waited while the stones and scree rolled to a halt. Above him, a network of thick roots and shrubs.

The cattle were far ahead now and to follow them on the track would be difficult since the rubble loosened by their galloping would make his steps slide backwards. Better, if he could, to haul himself up to the top of the bank and onto the plateau above. The roots held fast as he pulled on them and he was able to make his way through the vegetation, getting scratched by thorn bushes as he scrambled, and stung by the ants dislodged from their nest in the shallow margins of the bank.

It took a while for his eyes to adjust to the longer view that opened to him when his head had cleared the ledge. The air was milky with chaff and this increased his sense of being in a strange new land. He was looking down an escarpment as steep as the one he had just climbed, into the territory of the hill people: the Hebrews who for so long had troubled his own people of the sea and plains.

He could see the cattle and the cart as they rounded a corner and entered a broad way between two meadows. They were a long way below him — it must be that a descent had followed their climb. They were no longer galloping but trotting. If anyone were to see them now they would think a driver had been thrown out and was lying somewhere, injured.

The Hebrews were binding their wheat at the end of harvest. The cropped fields shone tawny in the sun, like the pelts of lions. Gurion watched as his cattle, their white horns held high like lyres, made their way unhesitatingly between the two large fields, drawing the beautiful cart behind them. The men and women who had been stooping to their work in the fields stood up, put their hands on their hips or to their aching backs, or else shaded their eyes the better to watch this strange spectacle: the splendid cart with the gilt axles and no driver, but the two pale cows whose full udders swung beneath them as they trotted between the two fields and then turned, trampling the stubble, into one of the fields. A field with a huge rock at its centre.

3

The men and women who had been stooping to their work in the fields stood up, put their hands on their hips or to aching backs, or else shaded their eyes, the better to watch this strange spectacle: the splendid cart with the gilt axles and no driver save for two pale cows whose full udders swung beneath them as they trotted between the two fields. Then the cows turned, trampling the stubble, into one of the fields: the Field of Joshua which bears a huge rock, the Great Stone of Abel, at its centre. A rock which stands to this day though the land has changed hands many times.

It was a marvellous sight. All trained their eyes on the wagon, wondering what had become of the driver; perhaps he had fallen and lay injured by the side of the track. All who had been working in the fields put down their scythes and watched. A child had run back to the town to fetch her mother and soon most of the population of Beth-shemesh had gathered. Including the priests who were as curious as all the others. It was one of the priests who identified the Ark, first with incredulity, then with a spreading joy which made him tremble and weep.

He ran on shaky legs to greet the wagon, beckoning to the other priests who were looking on uncertainly. Together they laid hands on the cart shafts while two men held the cows by their horns. It was difficult to keep everyone back — priestly authority was a feeble quantity beside the strong lure of the Ark which all knew about but very few had seen.

Four of the Levites lifted the Ark from its mount, stooping so that the tassels of the canopy brushed their shoulders. Another two carried the casket that had travelled beside it. Both were carried to the Great Stone of Abel whose flat surface resembled an altar.

Meanwhile the townsfolk had set about the wagon, dismantling it, stripping it of its gold. One of the priests had said they should make a sacrifice and give thanks. Sacrifice requires fire and fire requires wood. The wood was provided in the form of the cart. Gleefully they set about hacking the wood into pieces to burn, peeling away as much of the decoration as they could. There was plenty of kindling to be found in the dry, stubble-filled fields — the danger was that the fire would spread too far and burn their homes. A space needed to be cleared in which the fire could be contained.

The working day — set to be long, as days are at the end of harvest — had turned into festival.

——

While the fire was being constructed, the Chief Priest unpacked the casket, laying its contents out in the way of a workman setting out tools in readiness for an intricate job. He weighed each object in his hand, puzzling at the weight which so contrasted with the appearance of lightness. The five golden mice so resembled their live models it was as if a sauce of molten gold had been poured over a family of mice while they were actively about their business, gilding them in all their mousey vitality. It was impossible not to smile at such accurate rendering — the sharp, busy claws, the fine filaments of whiskers, in appearance as restless and sensitive as those of living mice; the nose tips almost moist, as if sniffing out something to eat. At least these mice were continent — unlike their counterparts who left trails of faeces and urine in their wake!

The other golden objects, again there were five, were less easy to interpret. If he had not witnessed the skill with which the mice had been made he might have thought these golden blobs the work of an inept maker, or merely the congealed left-overs of molten gold. Mounds, each about the size of a great toe or a walnut. Then he recalled what he had heard about the plagues that had punished the sea-people. Golden haemorrhoids; that's what these were. He called his priestly colleagues over. They chuckled in spite of themselves — in appreciation of the exceptional workmanship which no one in this hill country of Judah could emulate and also (and this compensated for the inferiority they felt as craftsmen) in satisfaction at what the sea-and-plains people had suffered as a result of appropriating the Ark.

Perhaps it was the laughter — albeit low — of the nine priests gathered around the Great Stone that felt like an invitation to the others to crowd in. Soon there was jostling — enthusiastic and good-humoured, but alarming to the priests. Those who couldn't see were shouting to those with a view, and those with a view were shouting back, reporting what they could see, interpreting it as they could. Children were pushing through legs and one rushed forward before anyone could stop her and seized one of the golden mice.

For a moment there was silence. The Chief Priest stepped forward and held out his open hand to the little girl whose giggles had given way to open-mouthed awe at the tall priest's stern expression. She handed the mouse back, a little sticky now. The horrified priest hardly knew what to do with the sullied offering. There was no means of purification available to him there and if he were to leave the field he felt sure that the jubilation of the townspeople would swell into riot. He placed the golden mouse back on the Great Stone, companion to the other four and to the five golden haemorrhoids. He no longer felt like laughing. A cool wind of fear prised open a flap in his mind and insinuated itself there.

Elsewhere in the field the fire had already caught and was burning fiercely: the heat of it struck anyone within range, and those who had taken it upon themselves to tend it were streaming with sweat. Only the sacrifice was wanting. The crowd had at least held back from the priestly task of slaughter: the blood of the two pale cows might save them yet.

—

Gurion had kept his eyes on the cart and the cattle for as long as he was able. The Elders had struggled along the track in the cart's wake, but were too far behind to have witnessed its entry into Beth-shemesh. That had been something splendid that Gurion would never forget. The hill people too knew that they would never see anything like this again. Not just the Ark — which most of them had never seen before — or the wagon's fine workmanship. It was the cows themselves, heads held high as they trotted, acting as their own heralds, lowing, throats uplifted so that the soft folds of skin below flopped from side to side as they moved. It was they, not the wagon or the Ark, that had made the people in the fields stop their work, put down their scythes, and watch. That was how Gurion saw it.

By the time the Elders had caught up with him, the field was too busy for anyone from their distance to make much out. Gurion had pulled himself up to the highest safe point of an old tree that grew out of the rock wall. The tree, difficult to reach for anyone not agile, was heavy with unharvested olives, some of which fell under Gurion's weight. He curled his fist to make a tight tunnel through which to look, bringing the scene in the field closer. He saw the fire. He heard — though it was diluted by distance — the great commotion in the field; he heard the bellows of distress that came from the cows' throats as the priest put his knife to them. He did not need to hear or see the knife go in. At the start of this journey he had thrown his mind like a gentle lasso over the cattle and thus managed to stay close to them even while they were out of sight. He felt it when their lives ceased. The texture of the air changed.

—

The Chief Priest of Beth-shemesh did not long outlive the cattle he killed that day. The Field of Joshua, scene of such rejoicing when the Ark arrived, was soon a place of mourning. The few inhabitants of the town who had escaped the sickness struggled to bury the many dead. The raptors circling overhead prospered better. There was a complacency in their waiting, as if they knew that the able-bodied of Beth-shemesh were no longer able-bodied enough to dig graves that were sufficiently deep to escape the probings of beak and claw.

The little girl who had taken the golden mouse and put it into her mouth to suck before the priest could stop her was one of the first to die. Some thought the mouse was poisoned. But the priests — both those who survived and those who were dying — thought the deaths were a punishment: the holy thing, the Ark, had been returned to them and they had received it, not with reverence, worship, and due trepidation, but with undisciplined excitement, a prying curiosity, and a vanity which made them oblivious to the dangers. They of Beth-shemesh were no more equal to the charge of the Ark than the sea-and-plains people who had been at such pains to return it, with interest.

The Ark was sent to the house of the priest Abinadab, up in the wooded hills of Kireath-Jearim, where it stayed, feared and unclaimed, for more than twenty years. Only Abinadab, his sons, and the prophet Samuel himself dared to go anywhere near it.

4

The prophet Samuel had grown old. The black hole of his mouth, framed by no more than a few ragged teeth, seemed to reach right down into Sheol. The people of Judah and Israel wanted a king.

Why would you want a king when you can have a prophet? Why invite the dominion of a man, with all his greed, arbitrariness, and taking, when you could be directed by a prophet who consults with YHWH?

Samuel told them what a king is like:

He takes sons from their fathers and compels them to serve him. He makes them into his soldiers and places them in the hottest battles on his behalf for causes that are not theirs or yours. He requires your land and compels you to till it for him. He makes you hand over one tenth of all you have: your wheat, your barley, your corn, your olives, and your wine; your cattle, your goats, your asses, and your sheep. All taken — by force if you resist — and then distributed amongst his friends. He takes daughters too and makes them his pastry cooks and sweetmeat-makers; should they themselves be sweet, he makes them his concubines. He will take wives from their husbands. What he does not take into account are your wishes and the delicate bonds of affection

you have built up within your households and villages. He
does not listen to your cries.

In spite of these words they wanted a king; and (since nothing instructs better than the granting of a wish) YHWH instructed Samuel to give them what they wanted.

He chose Saul for them, and when Saul failed, as Samuel had promised he would, he chose David, though it was to be many years — and after Samuel himself was dead and buried — before David was made king.

5

When the Giant of Gath issued his challenge across the valley, first blowing a great war-horn whose noise resounded in the hills, no one had been willing to go and meet him. Not Saul, the King; not Abner, his chief warrior. Only David, the King's armour-bearer, offered. At the time, to David, this had seemed the most natural thing, and, since YHWH had so obviously tipped him to do it, there had been no difficulty. He, a young man, completely untried in battle but conversant with arms because he looked after them, to pitch himself against the giant that made the greatest warriors quake!

On this day, the two great hills that sloped to form the valley seemed to face each other in a rooted hatred of the opposing side. In the evening, when sun fell on the far side, the giant had shone in his huge armour, the pleats of his leather skirt clattering like a vulture's wings. The sun had glowed a furious red behind him and the sky appeared to boil with the giant's terrible, confident intent. The way the sun illuminated him from behind made him seem more huge, and, now, remembering the scene, David had a sense of the giant as part of the sky itself, looming above all of them.

He had risen early from a light sleep, untroubled by any anxious dream, but eager to be doing. Saul had insisted on meeting him before he left for the encounter, and when

David came to the King's chamber the King had been close to tears. He enveloped the young man in his embrace while David stood, separate and unleaning, unwilling to soften to receive this tenderness lest it muddy his clarity. Then Saul had unbuckled the wide sword belt that he was wearing and attempted to fasten it around David's waist.

What for, sir? he had asked.

I want you to slay the giant with this sword of mine; the sword that saved the people of Jabesh-Gilead will save our people when you wield it.

David, who had woken with his mind sharp and keen as any sword, now had a sensation of oppression and interference. Though he had handled Saul's sword many times, cleaning the blade, oiling it, keeping it honed and ready, it was not his to fight with. It was not a part of him and he knew, though he was not a warrior yet, that a warrior's weapon must be like another limb, supple to his mind's impulse. No sword in the world was that to him in those early days.

Sir I can't accept this honour. I've never fought with this sword. Let me use the weapon that I know.

When Saul asked him what it was, David had the sense not to tell him; only that it was a weapon he was perfect in. There was a wrinkle of annoyance in Saul's face when he said this. No one likes to see their generosity thwarted. But that wrinkle had soon smoothed itself into a look of dignified concern as he asked the boy to kneel for his blessing.

Once the threatened weight of Saul's sword and belt was lifted from him, David seemed to fly as he ran out of the royal house onto the terrace and down the many steps. Day was just breaking. He loved the coldness in the air at this time; it carried all the little moisture a fine day might hold.

There were a lot of people gathering on the hillside, waiting for their champion to encounter the Philistine giant. Some had camped out all night wanting to be sure to have a good view across the valley, to see the sun strike the giant's armour, to hear the thud of his feet and to feel the hills shake.

When David made his way through the crowds to the stream that ran along the bottom of the hill, the crowds instinctively parted for him. He carried such an air of purpose. But no one took any active notice of him — a small, agile young man who wore no armour, just the sandals and tunic he used for working. If they had noticed him they would have pressed him to go back and not contemplate the dreadful folly of meeting the giant in combat. But the crowds simply parted for him as the sea had parted for Moses.

He was aware of the mass of people, but also most marvellously free and alone; the air with its honey-breath of morning clasped him, mantled him. That morning he wore heaven on his back and found it supple. When he reached the stream he unbuckled his sandals and washed his feet in the cool water; he took the small drinking cup that hung from his belt, rinsed it, and filled it afresh.

Lord, whom the streams worship and adore, make my heart clean; perfect my aim.

Then he searched the stream-bed for stones and picked out five. He laid them carefully on the bank in a row and looked at each one, committing its qualities of contour and density to his heart. He would know these stones so that they were part of him. Then he scooped them up with one hand and dropped them into his bag. When he climbed the hill again, the crowds were murmurous with excitement. The giant had been seen. He was waiting.

The agitation among the crowd was palpable. Where was their man? Would it be Saul himself? No, surely he would send a deputy. As David entered the corridor of the parted crowd he felt the agitation and sensed how it could destabilise him. Quickly, he stepped out and made his way to a clear place apart. Yet how could he make himself heard in this hubbub? He would not shout, but he would call, using his voice as he had used it so many times to communicate with his brothers on the other side of a hill or to summon his scattered sheep.

Here I am. It is I, David, the son of Jesse the Ephrathite, who will destroy the Philistine dog who opposes the living God. I will cut him down as I cut down the lions and bears who worried my father's herds.

The crowd were quiet now. A hush of horror or fascination pressed down on them and they stood back, allowing their improbable hero to make his way.

Again he descended the hillside, but, strangely, it seemed to him that he climbed. The feeling was of going upwards. Perhaps, he thought, there were wings that bore him up. Down or up, he went to meet the giant who was now clearly visible on the opposite hill. Indeed it would have been hard to miss him.

—

The giant was big; prodigiously so. And he was noisy: the large armour, articulated by leather thongs, rattling as he moved. A sword hung heavily from his belt, sheathed in embossed leather. His face — rosy-cheeked where the sun had burnt — was leathery too. He looked as if he had been long baked, his hide well cured to repel all assaults. When he opened his mouth David saw the red of the inside. It was indecent, this revelation of a raw interior to the man who seemed all hardness, all outside. David had not wanted to see this, but he nevertheless watched the moving mouth as it pursed and stretched in time with the giant's insults. He did not listen to the words, waiting for them to stop.

The giant stood there, sword held slackly in his right hand, mirth on his face. He was waiting for David, but waiting in contempt, as if the lad he was about to encounter were no more than a tiresome insect he could swat away.

The giant was waiting for David to come and join him on the opposite hill. He was laughing; the horrible red lining of the mouth seemed to be inviting David in. Well, he could put a stop to that. He did not need to descend the hill any further to reach this laughing creature. He did not need to touch it. Without taking his eyes for a moment from the trembling rictus of the mouth he reached inside his bag and felt for a stone. With the same hand he fitted it into the little hammock of the sling which he had also kept in his bag. He set his bag down so that now he held only the sling, weighted by the single stone he had fitted there. The red mouth kept on jeering, making David's target wonderfully clear. He had only to continue watching it and his arm would do the rest; he had done this many times before when he had killed the beasts that preyed on Jesse's flocks — each of those beasts more noble than this oversized human with the obscenely glistening mouth. It was the mouth he saw as he aimed a short space above it and flung the stone that stopped the taunts forever. In death, that mouth sagged open even wider, and Goliath died with a look of stupid surprise on his face.

He wanted to walk away, disdaining even to touch the fallen fellow, leaving him where he lay, the round stone embedded in the brow like an ugly jewel. *As if God had showered his hail upon him*. He knew however that the head would need to be displayed and that he must cut it off himself.

Used though he was to handling swords in the armoury, he was not, at that time, accustomed to using one as a weapon. A knife, yes. A knife had always been part of his shepherd's kit. But a sword — particularly one as huge as the one the felled giant carried — was not easy for him to use. So he used his small horn-handled knife to sever the giant's head, just as he would have used it — and would use it again — to cut off the head of a lion that had worried his flock. The task was not much different. Nevertheless, he had unsheathed the giant's sword and waved it at the watching crowd while he held the big head up to them with his other hand. Then he was almost carried, swept along by the crowd of men and women, dancing, making music on anything they could find that made a sound, whooping and singing: *Saul has slain thousands and David has slain tens of thousands*. Accompanied by reedy notes of various pitches and the low penetrating sound of a blown conch.

As he walked, people reached out and patted him; children ran up and touched him and then ran away giggling as if afraid of the power that killed the giant.

Saul has slain thousands and David has slain tens of thousands. The chant became a roar, metrical and repeated until it seemed that this was the pulse which the air breathed in time to.

Saul did not like to hear that.

6

Abinadab was very old. He had heard of the young warlord, the giant-slayer who had once been the old king's armour-bearer and was now the new king. He remembered the days before there was any king at all, and his own life continued to be lived and regulated as if those old days continued. He was not a wealthy man and his compound at Kireath-Jearim was hardly different from all the others. But it did have a flourishing garden. An orange tree, crowded with fruit like small suns, stood, incongruously, just within the entrance. The dwelling itself was simple. Clean but faded woven cloths across the floor; some folded blankets. The old priest wore a jerkin made of sheepskin, the fleece on the inside, for cold winds blow in that high country and he had little flesh to withstand them.

He received David with the respect he would accord to any man but no more because that man was a king. Nevertheless, David did carry an air of authority and decision which made it clear that Abinadab had no choice but to surrender the Ark — that holy object to whose care nearly half his life had been devoted.

The Ark had been so long at Abinadab's house in Kireath-Jearim, people spoke of it as something that had gone: something from the days when YHWH ruled through prophets and spoke to them directly, His mouth pressed close to their ears. What better way for King David to ratify his power in his newly established centre — the City of David — than by the presence of the Ark? He'd set out with a small entourage of kinsfolk and followers. They would sing and dance the Ark from the priest's house all the way to its new home!

After providing King David and the men nearest to him with a little refreshment — a dish of dates and a beaker of sweet well water — Abinadab took David alone to a small building at the back of his compound. He had built this structure himself — a feat which now amazed him, for he could barely lift a single one of the stones he had once so skilfully set in place. Inside, it was dark and cool — lit only by a row of oil lamps that crouched like devotees before the Ark. The soft light of the lamps flowed over the gold of the Ark revealing the marvellous details of a structure that YHWH had described in minute detail to Moses, who had followed and carried out every instruction. It struck David like a blow to see for the first time this thing he had heard about for so long and known only in imagination. An instinct of reverence, as ungainsayable as lightning, flung him prostrate along the ground. Within the Ark, he knew, were the very stone tables of the Law that Moses had received on Mount Sinai. Not the originals, written by YHWH before YHWH had broken them in anger, but their duplicate — transcribed by Moses, YHWH's amanuensis.

Since the days of the Ark's capture by the people of the sea and plains no one had attempted to replicate the furnishings and the candelabra made by Besalel — that now legendary craftsman to whom Moses had imparted YHWH's instructions. They had vanished along with the artistry that fashioned them. Now all the skill in metalwork lay with the sea-and-plains people. The 'Philistines' as the Hebrews chose to call them.

There, as he lay across the swept earth floor of Abinadab's temple, David made a silent vow that he would build a temple worthy of the Ark. Skilled artificers would be found and others trained so that it would no longer be said that the hill people of Israel and Judah were inferior to the Philistines in this. Abinadab's building was simple: the work of reverent application rather than great artistry. David had no desire to slight what Abinadab had made; the reverence and care were unmistakable. But he longed to recreate the beautiful furnishings that Besalel had made when he constructed the Ark.

—

He watched as Abinadab and three other priests from the town threaded the wooden shafts through the carrying rings and lifted the Ark from the altar where it had stayed. They carried it out into the strong daylight to the platform of the cart that had been constructed for this purpose. A cheer rose up from David's followers when it appeared, but Abinadab's expression contained a caution. Rejoice by all means; but no rowdy irreverence.

Abinadab uttered a prayer of blessing for the journey and did reverence to the Ark for the last time. Then the oxen — who had refreshed themselves on fresh hay and water since arriving — were yoked together again and attached to the cart shafts. Abinadab had requested that his sons, Ahio and Uzzah, be permitted to accompany the Ark to its new home and it was they who drove the oxen forward. The journey to the City of David began, accompanied by music and psalms of praise.

Once the procession had wound out of sight, the old priest turned back to the building where the Ark had been. Only the row of lamps remained, the slight play — ducking and swelling — of their gentle lights made them companionable. He knelt in front of them as he had always done. As he prayed he sensed the forms of the two angels of the absent Mercy Seat; they were no longer made of wrought gold but persisted there as living presences. They prayed with him and at the same time protected his prayer.

7

It was wonderful, the music they made to accompany the Ark! New instruments made for the occasion, fresh turned from pinewood, pungent with the smell of resin. There were bowed instruments, blown instruments, skins stretched over hollow gourds; instruments to shake, beat, rattle, and bang. David himself led the music, sawing a bow across a two-stringed lyre and occasionally using the bow to strike it. His body too was a shaper of sound — whoops and ululations came from it. The Ark itself seemed to call forth these sounds.

It was the middle of the day. David and his dancing entourage hardly felt the heat of the sun nor any tiredness. Not so the oxen. The cart shafts chafed and the sun's heat increased their discomfort. With one mind they halted for a moment, and shook themselves to loosen the aggravating shafts. The Ark wobbled and looked as though it might slip. Uzzah, who was nearest, instinctively put out his hand to stay it.

It was the last thing Uzzah did. A little 'O' of surprise formed on his lips, then he fell. They buried him in a shallow grave not far from the road. All were full of fear. Even Ahio, who wept, feared to touch the body of his brother as he placed a cloth over the shocked face. Together they dragged Uzzah's body into the grave by means of its garments, barely looking as they spaded earth onto it; relieved when they could no longer see it.

—

They were afraid to touch Uzzah. How much more to be feared was the Ark that Uzzah had put his hand to. The Ark had acted from an entirely other kind of power from the one David had recently employed to found his citadel. David had been assuming that YHWH would continue to protect him in the way that YHWH had done till now. But the sight of Uzzah — a man who appeared so dedicated to priestly service — struck down and shrivelled, made him doubt.

He now proposed that the Ark required a more gradual journey to its new resting place. He said they had been too impatient to transport it (though it had been twenty years with Abinadab!). A new, temporary, home must be found.

Ahio looked up from his brother's grave mound where he had placed a stone. He regarded David with a look of weary and sorrowful patience. The Ark had been taken from their father's keeping. Their father had acquiesced in this, having no choice to do otherwise. Now Abinadab was bereft of both Ark and son while he, Ahio, had lost his brother. If, after all this, the plan to transport the Ark was to be altered, what had it all been for?

They were all surprised when David decreed that the Ark should now go to the home of Obed-edom the Gittite for his safe-keeping.

8

Obed-edom's eyes filled with tears of joy. Fear did not seem to be any part of his response. He had not expected such fulfilment in his lifetime.

He was a tall, dark-skinned man from Gath, whose regular life and modest habits had been swept upside-down by his first encounter with the god of the hill people of Israel and Judah. The people whose Ark the Gittites had captured. He had not fled when the streets of Gath had been overrun with mice and the back-passages of his fellow Gittites were inflamed and smarting. He swept his floors so the mice could find no scrap of grain to feed on, and he restricted his diet so his bowels would suffer no strain. He thought and he prayed.

When he did hear what had happened to the statue of Dagon at Ashdod — how the Ark's quiet presence in the same space had been enough to cause the statue to shatter, exposing its flaws so that it could no longer hold together — Obed-edom, the Gittite, had smiled. The silent authority of this Ark, its compacted power, spoke to him more than the beguiling, creaturely effigies revered by the sea people. He enquired among the metal workers whom he knew to trade with the hill people. What kind of god did the hill people worship? Was it just another god in the pantheon? If so, how did it appear?

He learnt that this god did not appear. Not any longer. This god spoke, though seldom and to few. This god had given laws and those laws were written, in words, held and carried in the Ark, but also, more importantly, in the hearts of those who worshipped. It appealed to Obed-edom that this god was more to be seen in the conduct of his followers than in extravagant carvings in temples.

He had learned the commandments by heart and practised them. Or rather, he continued to practise them, for, when he learned how they went, he realised that they described a rule of conduct which he had long ago chosen to live by. He had left Gath, a young man, soon after the Ark was returned to Beth-shemesh, departing his old city nearly empty-handed — carrying only his favourite short-handled hoe and a trowel — but willing to work and to learn, as well as to teach skills known more in Gath than the hills. When the Ark was moved again to Kireath-Jearim he followed it there and lived for some months with Abinadab who, at the Gittite's request, performed the circumcision which confirmed Obed-edom as a follower of YHWH.

All that had taken place long ago, during his enthusiastic youth. Now, twenty years later, he had settled in the hill-country. He had taken a bride from the region and cultivated his own land so that it could support him and his small family. He continued to worship YHWH, his chosen Lord, with all the zeal of the convert. In this he put most of his neighbours to shame. He had continued on good terms with Abinadab, visiting from time to time in order to be near the Ark again. Doing this, and enjoying Abinadab's company, reconfirmed his new-found faith. When Abinadab knew that the Ark was to be moved he sent word to Obed-edom. This is how the tall

Gittite found himself in the party that accompanied the Ark to the new City of David. This is how he was available to take the terrifying object off David's hands.

———

Obed-edom sent runners ahead of him to tell his family of the great honour that was coming to them. As he made his more stately progress to his house, accompanying the Ark in its cart at the same pedestrian pace as the bullocks, what joy shone from his face! It was as if he were a porous container of joy, an earthenware vessel not baked long enough to be water-tight. Joy simply leaked from him.

As the weeks wore on, the reports from Obed-edom's house were consistent: the goats and sheep yielded more and sweeter milk, the apricot trees fruited more abundantly, the grapes weighed down the vines, and the pomegranate trees bowed under their load. The livestock bore healthy young: not one was still-born. Obed-edom's wife conceived again. Before long, this man who had left land and religion to follow the Ark and its god would be the most prosperous man in the region.

If it occurred to David that the messengers who brought him news of Obed-edom's prosperity were laughing, he did have the sense to laugh with them. He acted as if Obed-edom's new wealth was what he had always intended in appointing him guardian of the Ark, and he travelled in person to Obed-edom's compound to retrieve the Ark and recommence its journey to the City of David.

Everything about the way in which he approached Obed-edom and his family spoke of princely generosity. Though he came to take the Ark *from* Obed-edom he did so in a way which appeared to honour the deprived man, who was, in any case, left brimming with blessings.

So when David danced and played the Ark into the City of David it was as if the three-month stay with the Gittite had been an intended part of its progress.

9

It begins so simply.

A pebble in his sling.

A taut weight in his balls as he watches the woman.

From where he stands on his roof he catches the gleam of her skin as she washes herself in a stream at the bottom of the hill. Rocks shelter her from the gaze of anyone below but not from him, peering from his high vantage. He sees her in her solitude and this adds potency to the sight.

She performs the loveliest of all gestures. She lifts her hair from the nape of her neck and bows her head forward so that the hair tumbles, falling over her eyes, while, with the other hand, she raises a small bowl of water, scooped from a larger bowl.

She tips the water over her neck.

He imagines how the water must separate and run in two equal streams down the little slopes of her collar bones to the valley between her breasts.

He imagines himself that water. Modest as water or as dust he is able to enter every small place.

Then she does a strange thing.

She tips back her head and empties a whole scoop of water — not into her mouth, but onto it — so that the water splashes over as she purses her mouth and seems almost to be kissing the water, playing with it. She is laughing. She reminds him of a bird who frisks its wings in a shallow pool, seeming to take a pleasure beyond the practical business of ridding itself of dust.

There is nearly always dust in this dry, desert place. It gets between his teeth and into the folds of his skin. As he watches the woman rinsing away all the dust of her day he feels how it would be if he too were near water.

There is a waterfall he sometimes goes to. He has noticed that the flowers growing on the little ledge of rock behind the waterfall do not get dashed by the torrent of water that streams in front of them. The flowers are sprayed and sometimes pushed by the small winds generated by the flow but they are not dashed down or destroyed. Could he be such water to this woman? Refresh her, bedew her, gladden her? Bend her a little to his will — but not destroy her? His huge desire fuels a tenderness that could delight in such a holding back. This it is to be a king: to have power, but to exercise it with restraint.

He sends a messenger to the woman, inviting her to his presence.

10

When the man from the King came to fetch her, her first thought was of her husband. Something had happened to him. The King's man communicated so little, beyond that she was to go with him to the King's House — she could not tell whether she was being summoned for censure or reward. Had her husband disgraced himself, spoken against the war and provoked a mutiny? Or had he displayed that rare personal courage of his in an act of shining magnanimity, turning events in the Israelites' favour? Given his extreme and absolute nature both were equally possible.

The man the King had sent was rough and curt. She guessed that he did not know any other way — a man used to being an instrument of others, reliable, incurious. Not capable of giving the reassurance she would have liked. While he waited, impatiently, beside her door, she readied herself by covering her hair with a dark shawl. Her hands were shaking.

So were her legs. She was grateful for the fact that the way to the King's House was up. The effort of placing one foot after another on the rough stones that formed a path through the terraces steadied her. She needed to feel the pressure and resistance of the ground. The back of the silent man who led the way moved on ahead of her and communicated nothing. He went fast and she stumbled at times to keep up. At one point, when the path led beneath a terrace planted with vines, he suddenly scrambled up over the stone wall that banked the terrace and tugged off a bunch of fat grapes. He tasted one, spat out the pips and turned to her with a surprising smile that showed a mouth with few teeth. He offered her the grapes on the flat of his hand, as if offering them to a donkey or a horse to muzzle up. She pulled a grape from the bunch and ate it. Thick and leathery outer skin but the flesh delicious. She smiled and nodded her thanks and the man signalled that she should take them all, the whole bunch, which she did, biting them off one by one as they continued their ascent. After this, the man never acknowledged her presence behind him. Though he climbed fast his wheezing suggested that he had no breath to spare.

She had seen the King's House from a distance. Everyone had. It jutted out over the rocks like a great lion, basking in the sun, unafraid of being seen but also alert, ready to unfurl a big paw and annul any small creature that threatened to disturb it. As they got near the house they fell under the shadow of the rock. The day's heat was replaced by a dank chill and a strong smell of urine. She held her shawl over her nose and mouth and took more care than before over where she placed her feet.

They came to a door cut into the base of the rock. A heavy wooden door with a grille cut into it, like the door of a dungeon. Bathsheba for the first time felt really afraid. There was nowhere to run to, nowhere to go except back down this track (which was not, she now realised, the principal road to the King's House but a back way leading to the dungeon and the kitchens), but an instinct to flee made her turn — whereat the man, who had gone back to seeming little aware of her, caught her with both hands and gripped her arms so tightly she cried out. She could no more go than if he'd manacled her in irons and that is what it felt like as he hammered at the door, still holding her in the iron grasp of one hand.

A piece of wood that blocked the grille slid back and a woman's face peered out. Then a bustling as the door was unlocked and opened.

It was a decent, middle-aged woman who opened it, plainly dressed in good cloth. She nodded to the man — 'I'll take her from here' — and, as the man reluctantly loosened his hold, took Bathsheba's other arm in a much more kindly way. A clasp of guidance rather than restraint.

Bathsheba felt it would be futile to ask questions. The only thing that was clear to her was that the man and the woman had been instructed about where she was to be brought and that they would fulfil these instructions without comment. Nevertheless, the close proximity of the woman, whose matronly face looked intent but not cruel, brought with it a bodily comfort and she did not resist the contact as she had the man's.

The woman led her through long corridors lit only by small lamps whose flames cast swooning shadows on the walls. At this level there was no natural light. Then a flight of stone steps, uneven and narrow, so that there was not room for the two of them side by side, and the woman pushed Bathsheba, not roughly, to lead the way.

The stairs led up into light: the body of the house, where daylight poured in through open windows. The woman brushed down the front of Bathsheba's clothes, clearing away any dust or cobwebs that might have clung from below, and straightened herself, seeming to assume some particular duty.

Curiosity now overtook Bathsheba's fear. Released from the obscurity of those lower corridors she could now begin to take in the extent and nature of the King's House. The scent of resin pervaded the whole place — the floors were wide planks of polished cedar and cedar beams supported the ceilings. The stone staircase had delivered them into a wide corridor — or was it a room in its own right? If it was a room, it had no clear function — there was no furniture or any kind of implement in it.

There were several doors leading off and the woman walked her through one of these, then up a further flight of steps which turned sharply to face another door. This opened on to a room with a wide bed in it.

'You are to wait here,' said the woman. 'There is water if you need to wash or drink.'

Then she left. Bathsheba thought she could hear a bolt slide to on the outside of the door, but she already felt too thickly contained to think now of escaping. She sat on the bed — a high, solid affair, not like the straw-filled mattress she and her husband were used to sleeping on. A small window looked out onto a courtyard. She could just smell the orange blossom that grew down there.

But why was *she* there? Her anxiety, which had grown to fear, had been suspended for a while as the sheer strangeness of her predicament and her surroundings absorbed her. Now it flooded back. Had she been mistaken for another? Not possible. The man had asked if she were Bathsheba, wife of Uriah the Hittite. But had the woman at the door mistaken her, been expecting the delivery of someone else — a family member, a distant kinswoman in need of protection? The King, she remembered, was known for his kindness. Everyone knew what he had done for Mephibosheth, the man who swung himself along with the anchor of two sticks since both his feet were lame — the man who now took all of his meals at the King's table. He was the old king's grandson, son of the present king's dear dead friend, Jonathan, the one whom the King had been known to love above all others.

There were other, more cynical, accounts of David's generosity to Mephibosheth. There were those who said that, by being seen to be so generous to Saul's descendants, the King discredited rival claims. Bathsheba had heard these voices too, but the idea of his generosity gave her more solace at the moment.

It occurred to her that there may have been no mistake — that the King had discovered what neither she nor her husband had known — that there *was* a direct kin relationship between them.

Footsteps outside, the bolt drawn back. He is in the room with her. The King. King David.

She makes to prostrate herself before him but, while she is still folding back the edge of her garment so it will not trip her, he takes her hands to stay her upright. He does not let go of her hands but keeps her there, bringing her close as if he knows her.

Who does not know the story of David and the Giant? It is shocking to see him at such close quarters, this man she has known as the hero of such stories and, at a distance, heard cheered by crowds. He is known for being small, but that is only in comparison with the Giant. Beside herself he is far from small. He is as old as her father was when he died but, where her father was worn and slack-skinned, this man shines. There is a sense of compactedness about his presence — as if the years he has lived have confirmed and filled him. Now that he has her hands in his she knows she could not pull hers away if she chose. She can see the film of sweat on his face, a little scar on his left cheek, see how full his lips are. The lips are like a small animal pulsing within his curly beard. Or like the still beating heart of a creature that has been ripped open by a predator. She can feel his breath on her and the meaning of it is unmistakable. It would be impossible to mistake it as he puts his hands against her back and presses himself to her.

Till now, no words.

'Why me?' she cries. And then, with more strength, with equal emphasis upon each word. 'Why. Me. My husband — he's fighting for you.'

His only answer, spoken into her hair where his mouth presses, 'I saw you. I saw you washing yourself.'

She does not understand. She has never met him before.

'I have good eyes and from the roof here I can see a long way. You were washing in the stream. Clothes. Then your hair, your body.' His voice thickens as he completes the sentence. The words 'your body' seem to draw on a depth of imagination and feeling; they are drenched with those depths.

In her indignation she forgets who he is — and if she remembered it would be no different. She ignores the fact that he's strong and could compel her. She only feels the insult of the intrusion. That she has been spied on! That a man whom she does not know has handled her in his thoughts.

'So you look down on women from your great height and pick them off if they appeal! How many others — girls — boys? Boys too? —' a rumour flashed through her mind '— how many have you dragged out of their quiet lives to please yourself?'

This is not a question to be answered. He does not let go. He hardly appears to be listening, just watches the way anger lights up her face, gives it colour and fire.

'Shhhhhh, shhhhhh,' he strokes her hair, her lovely hair, as if gentling a child.

ARK

But he does not for a moment let her go.

She feels stiflingly trapped, by this man, by his arms, by this room, by this building, and by the journey she has undertaken to get here. The revelation that he watched her when she had thought herself private and free has created an unbearable sense of intrusion. This, more than anything, is what threatens to stifle her and makes her cry out in rage. If her fury can have an outlet then she will have dislodged this foul sense of his prying eyes having filled her up, plugged her with their intrusive speculation.

'Shhhhh, shhhh, shhhh,' and on he strokes, holding her close, keeping her prisoner, ignoring her words.

'I want you,' he says. 'When I saw you I wanted you.'

She is quieter now, exhausted by her anger.

Still he strokes, smoothing her hair, quietening her. He holds her gently. If she wants to, she can move away.

'Will you sit? Take something to refresh you? There are grapes. Milk. Wine?'

She sees that there are plates, bowls, a jug — all set out, prepared on a table. Lying in wait. The thought that this has all been planned renews her fury.

'Am I free to leave?'

He does not answer her directly, but removes his hands from her and turns away; walks to the low table and tips wine into a vessel and drinks.

He seems scarcely to be aware of her. She watches his turned back as he sets down the cup and stands, hands on hips. The posture of a man who does not know what to do next. He runs his fingers through his hair in perplexity. Suddenly it seems to her that he is the one who is more trapped.

'I would like some milk.'

Her words startle him out of his private reverie. She is standing, calm now, a woman addressing a man.

He pours some milk into a bowl and passes it to her, timidly, as if this wild animal might start. As she drinks he watches closely. She feels that he can see the milk as it fills her mouth, as it travels down her throat to fill the other bowl of her stomach.

The fine hairs of her upper lip are beaded white with milk.

When she has drunk nearly all the milk in the bowl he comes close and covers with his own large hands the hands with which she cradles the bowl. He guides the bowl up to his own mouth and empties it.

They have shared this. Now she lifts a hand to his face and he buries his mouth in her palm, his mouth soft as a ewe's when it takes grass.

———

Afterwards he had wanted to give her something — not to pay her, but to thank her — a bracelet, a necklace, a ring. Each of them an enclosure. She refused them all, as she refused the offer of an escort back to her home. She wanted to walk free. She did not want the thoughts of others — the woman or the man with their prying guesses — to press in on her. She asked to be left alone while she washed herself and he offered her a new dress to put on when she had washed. This she also refused. After her one assent, freedom once more lay in saying no.

No one took much notice of the dark-shawled figure that made its way back down the narrow path between the terraces to the streets of the City of David.

11

In the days that followed, she worked in her usual way on the vegetable plot, tended her animals, ground flour, baked bread. Everything that she usually did. She spoke to no one about what had happened. No one she knew had seen the man arrive or the two of them leave together — if they had, they had not mentioned it to her or asked her about it. What had taken place in the room at the King's House was, in its detail, known only to the two of them. Herself and the man. Herself and the King.

It was so improbable, so entirely out of the course of what she knew or expected from her life, that she pocketed it away to examine later, when she had time. But she did not know how to examine it, what kind of thoughts she should bring to bear on it, so it remained in her pocket to be occasionally fingered but never completely extracted.

Her own conduct in it all was part of what she postponed thinking about. She could follow the process in her memory up to the break-out of her anger; she could even feel that anger again. That she should be fetched like a farm animal and expected to comply. But she *had* complied and she had not been forced. She could tell herself that she would have been forced if there had been no other way for him to have her, but she was not entirely sure if that were true. She had complied because it had suddenly, overwhelmingly become what she wanted. Not her mind — at least not her thinking mind — but her body's mind, had wanted the man's touch as deep inside her as it was possible for him to go. She did not just comply, she met him. She felt her womb shudder into a shower of stars such as sometimes occurred in a desert night. That was the gift which she'd hurried away to treasure, not some trinket of jewellery such as he'd wanted to give her.

It was months, getting on for years, since Uriah had touched her. When she had married him as a young girl they had assumed, gladly, that child on child would be born to them, and Uriah had set to the task of making this happen with the single-minded fervour with which he approached everything. The tenderness of the early nights when he had marvelled at the sweetness of her ripe girl's body, approaching her with reverence and kindness, gave way to an almost grim determination so that Bathsheba felt herself to be just an intermediary between Uriah and the child he wanted. But there was no child. Instead, each month, there was blood. The smell of her monthly blood seemed to hang around Bathsheba all the time. Even when she was not bleeding he sensed it — it caught the back of his throat with its rich reproachful sweetness. Just as the scent of a good rich goat stew will pervade the corners of a house so thoroughly that, even when the smell has long dispersed, you sense it there, so the smell of Bathsheba's blood seemed to have sunk into the fabric of their home. She would wash and wash to make herself and her rags free of any taint of it but her husband sensed it anyway. She blamed herself and he blamed her too. He kept away from her bed. The call to war with its other blood had been a relief.

She asked herself — in those moments when she fingered

the strange gift she had pocketed in her mind — whether Uriah's attitude to her had in any way freed her to turn to another man. Was this why, when she turned to David, she had turned with such a full and longing consent? She allowed herself only to glimpse these thoughts; she had no place to keep them other than in this pocket. She did not dare to spread them out in order to examine them in daylight.

She moved as if the air had thickened, as if it were weighty as water but luxurious to the touch. She felt as if she were carrying a large bowl, brimful; that she must be careful lest any spill. Everything about her became heavy and slow. She would sit or stand in her doorway looking out, watching the sky as it eased itself into daylight or folded itself back again into darkness. She tended the animals, watered the vegetables, and thinned out the new shoots. She did all this as before, but slowly and gently. The tenderness with which she trimmed her plants was almost an apology for her abstraction. She caressed them to make up for not thinking about them as she should.

It was no surprise when no blood came. The surprise would have been if this steady quiet sense of building had been ruptured by anything as violent as blood. Nevertheless, for days on end she did not think about this but allowed herself only to think about the requirements of the day. Every evening she went to the Horse Gate in the east and stood with the other women whose husbands were fighting. This is where the news from Rabbath-Ammon arrived first — news of hardship and hunger, of small victories, injuries, and deaths. Along with the other women, she contrived regularly to send small parcels of food — raisins, a cheese, bread baked hard into biscuits that would keep. The men might be hungry, but they were not half as hungry as those within the besieged city whom no supplies could reach. These supplies were conveyed by means of the runners — boys too young for battle but drawn to its smell — who made the journey between the worlds of peace and war on an almost daily basis.

The women come here as much to meet one other as to hear news of their men. Many have children with them, either hefted up to waist level or running around, forming their own small society at ground level. Approaching this daily group you hear the music of the chatter, little spirals of laughter or indignation issuing from the general hum. Bathsheba's friend Hannah came here, the youngest of her four sons not yet old enough to walk but an energetic weight in his mother's arms. The eldest, now nine, stayed home looking after the next two. Bathsheba never asked after them and Hannah never spoke of them out of delicacy for her friend's presumed barrenness. It surprised her when Bathsheba said, 'Pray that these wars will be over before your sons reach fighting age.'

Hannah had replied with a rueful shake of her head, 'They've reached that already. I tell Joseph that he's the man of the house now and must keep the other two in order. But as often as not I get home to some battle. Someone's kicked someone; someone's taken something and has to give it back. The same story every day.'

———

When Bathsheba did allow herself to understand the evidence of her body, she was simply not able to feel the anxiety which was due. Anxiety and fear, she knew, were the right responses, but her joy at having conceived was so great it cancelled everything that might qualify it. The absence of her husband felt to her like a puzzle that she would get round to solving one day soon. When she could be bothered to concentrate on such things. Not now. Now she was too busy facing this joy which filled her up.

But sometimes there would be a gash in this curtain of joy, and through it she glimpsed the bloody mashed head of the woman in the sand. Remembering Miriam, her heart and her womb would constrict with terror.

One part of the puzzle was clear to her, though that also led to fear. She should let the King know she was with child. She did not want to go to him again. The thought that she might appear to be asking something of him offended her pride; the idea that he might reject her or turn her away unseen was intolerable. Yet she did want something of him. It was essential that he know.

She could not entrust the news to a messenger. If she did so then the messenger would know and that must not happen. She wished she could write — perhaps one day her son would do so — but she could barely recognise a single written character, so seldom had she seen such a thing. Perhaps she could send him a drawing! In the dust of her courtyard she experimented with a sequence of elementary drawings.

1. a woman and a crowned king
2. a woman with a swelling stomach
3. a woman with a baby

Making the drawings gave her pleasure and again she imagined being with her child, instructing him, drawing with him.

But she could not carry the dust to the King and she had no Egyptian paper, no wax tablet. She considered making a simple clay dish and poking a series of drawings into it before baking it hard; but for the drawings to be clear the dish would need to be impossibly large and beyond her limited skill to make. And who could say that the King would read the images rightly?

12

She expected him to be an old man. How could knowledge of those signs — like the prints of bird feet in the mud — be acquired except through long years of patient application? Before writing there must be reading, and reading entailed reading the signs, paying attention to the shapes things made and to the small differences and deviations that signified. It was like tracking an animal's traces to discover where it had made its nest or den, whether it was breeding or had young, what food it favoured. Only once the marks of nature had been mastered could the deliberate marks of humankind be undertaken. Wisdom, borne of long living and study, must be the ground of such knowledge.

But the letter-writer recommended to her when she made enquiries in the market was a man younger than herself. Scarcely more than a boy, his beard a few dark silken threads, cultivated and stroked in an attempt to give a semblance of age. His dark robes appeared too large for him, giving the impression of a child dressed up. His air of impatient irritabil-ity — the kind which can be natural in an older man — seemed equally put on, as if in behaving so he gained an air of adult authority.

'I would like you to write a letter for me,' said Bathsheba.

'Yes, yes. That's what I do. I write everyone's letters for

them. Can you pay me? I charge so much for materials and after that, by the word. Do you know what it is you want to say? Half the people who come here don't even know that. I have to do that for them too.'

He fidgets frowningly among his implements, straightening the pots on the shelf behind him.

Bathsheba is amused by him; she wants to applaud his clever acting which so wonderfully takes off a certain kind of adult. But she knows she must gratify him by seeming to take these mannerisms seriously. And yes, she can pay him. She had had no idea what unthinkable sum so marvellous a skill as writing might command and had, with great resolution, sold a piece of fine pale woven wool, put away for her first child. This too was for her child.

'I know what I want to say. Just these words: *BATHSHEBA IS WITH CHILD.*'

There had been no need to worry about his discretion. A gossip and spreader of tales has at least the warmth of human curiosity — a desire, perhaps, to augment the smallness of his own life through a preoccupation with the lives of others. This clever young man, filled with a sense of his own sufficiency, had no inclination to speculate about any of his customers, though most had been driven to him by distresses and joys worthy of another's consideration. Bathsheba felt liberated by his unconcern. While the young man worked with admirable sureness and a speed she had not anticipated, she was able to take in the implements of his trade, the rolls of paper arranged in a deep shelf in a stack of tubes to resemble a large honeycomb; smaller wooden frames which were boxes filled with wax; jars like quivers, bristling with reed pens; a small sharp knife on the table; pot upon pot of coloured inks. The place smelled of these inks and of the wax in the tablets. Delicious, this smell of writing.

Her short message required only a small roll of paper (a reusable wax tablet would have been cheaper but she thought it too cumbersome to be discreet). She watched intently as the letters were formed, wet and shiny on the paper. Which ones, she wondered, spelled *BATHSHEBA*? She longed to know but did not feel able to ask this brisk person so absorbed in his task. It seemed to her that these glistening marks were in their own way pregnant with their contained pressure of meaning.

The letter-writer had asked to whom the letter should be addressed.

'No address will be necessary. It will be delivered in person and there will be no possibility of mistaking.'

She did not need to spend all the money she had brought with her. The brisk, incurious young man was not greedy.

13

Every boy in the land had been brought up on stories of the King as a child. 'Don't you want to be like King David?' a mother would ask a churlish or a lazy son. 'King David wouldn't have gone to sleep,' a father might say to a shepherd boy who had dozed on his watch at lambing time. King David was the most brave, the most honest, the most God-fearing, the most dutiful, the most strong, the most generous. He was also known to be the most musical, the most handsome, the most ingenious. A king, not only by appointment but by nature. His kindness would always exceed desert and any anger he showed would be just. Every child in Israel and Judah knew this, including the boy whom Bathsheba employed to deliver the letter to the King.

This boy, raised on the stories, had now reached an age when he was the one to tell those stories to his younger brothers, passing on an ethos of magnanimity and courage. Now, as he approached the King's House, he told one of them — the most famous — to himself. He was thirteen years old — nearly a man in those parts — close to the age at which the King had killed the Giant of Gath with a stone from his sling. *Imagine a man, tall as a mountain. Well the Giant of Gath was higher than the mountain at the back of the house. So was every member of his family. Together they stood like a range of mountains. But Goliath was the tallest. If he wanted a club he would take a tall pine and lop off the branches; a regular man's club he would use to pick his teeth.* That was how it might begin.

But now he has arrived at the King's House and there are other words to say.

He is received kindly by the guard at the gate. The King's special kindness to children is well known and the boy has wondered whether he would return with a new tale of some privileged encounter. He is taken by the guard to a woman who offers him a drink which he refuses, so primed is he to deliver his message and to say the words he has learnt:

The lady does not read, but if you have word for her, I will carry it.

He repeats these words to himself, frowning with concentration, hardly daring to take in the extraordinary scale of his surroundings, the tall corridor he is led down, pierced by high windows which let in light from the central courtyard.

They arrive at the room where the King is and the woman signals he is to wait while she informs the King of the boy's errand. He cannot see beyond the doorframe so he fixes on a bole in the wooden lintel. The whorls of it, like a larger version of those in his own thumb. He becomes so absorbed in this, so lulled by this absorption, that he jumps when, less than a minute after she had gone in to the King, the woman returns to him, touches him on the arm, and tells him to go ahead. The King will hear him.

Everything here so high, so large — except the King himself who is scarcely taller than the tall boy. What distinguishes him is not his dress — not even his physique which, though lean, does nothing to announce his prowess — but the ease with which he inhabits these surroundings: a large room with fine chairs piled with white and dappled fleeces; carved and polished stools on which are placed silver trays bearing silver bowls. A room set high as a hermit's cave and with a hermit's view over all the plain — but filled with all these comforts.

So this is what it is to be a king!

The King stretches out his hand for the letter which the boy is clutching. Even more tightly has he been clutching the words he has been instructed to say, and these now spill out, a little before their time:

'The lady does not read, but if you have word for her, I will carry it.'

The King, who has not yet broken the seal of the letter, nods, hardly taking the words in. The boy watches as the King breaks the seal and scans the contents before seeming to be pulled back to look at the letter again, more closely. He sees the King glance away, walk to a window, and look out through it. He stays there, his back turned to the room, for a long time, then he looks at the letter again, as if to see whether the contents had altered.

It is clear that the King is displeased. The boy guesses that he will not be taken to see the stables as he'd hoped. But he must wait, at least to be dismissed, if not for an answer to carry.

The King seems to have forgotten the boy's presence. He walks to another window from where he can look out across the descending terraces towards the east. There he stands a long time, occasionally lifting his head as if in acknowledgement of some thought, his eyes tightening at the outer edges in the way of a man tightening his focus. The boy, who feels able to stare unobserved, feels that the King is not looking out, but in.

The boy has the ability to stand very quietly — in such a way that a frightened animal will not know he is there. When his parents quarrel — which they have always done — he does not need to leave the room to escape his father's fury; he can simply do this thing of folding himself in to himself so that his presence disturbs no one. He does this now.

Suddenly the King seems to remember the boy's presence and turns. His face has changed. It has become pinched and wizened.

'Are you waiting for a response? Does the lady who sent you read letters?'

'She does not sir. But if you have a word for her, I will carry it.'

'Then say to her, "It is well, and shall be well."'

The boy repeats these words to show that he has them secure, '"It is well, and shall be well."'

The King nods, 'Now go.'

So the boy leaves, the words he has to deliver safe in his mind, but thinking that, in spite of the words, it is not well with the King.

—

The news put David into an evil temper. Why could it not be as if he had taken a perfect, on-the-point-of-dropping, apricot from a tree and, having bitten it open and spat out the stone, swallowed it in one? Pure, present delight, complete in itself?

After Bathsheba had left him he'd remembered it with a serious, savouring pleasure which included the possibility of a repetition. He had taken the encounter out of the casket of his memory as he might have taken a precious jewel, an amulet, from its silk housing to examine again. When he replaced the memory in its dark safety it was with the knowledge that he could return to it. Never, though the memory reliably aroused him, was he tempted to handle himself and trick himself to climax. He had a sense that to do so would dilute what had taken place and diminish its entirely satisfactory nature. It might also injure what might yet happen again. That time he had called her to him the strength of his wanting had conferred a perfection on the experience that he did not want to make ordinary. Every time that he had thought to call her to him again in the months since their encounter, he had postponed his summons out of an instinct that familiarity and ease were not what he wanted with her. To postpone — even indefinitely — would be to perpetuate the power of her separateness. He remembered how she had played with the water that she'd poured onto her face, laughing in her solitude. She had not needed another in order to be delighted. That was what he had wanted in her — the happiness and freedom he had seen. That was what had made him desire her so powerfully.

No one had been harmed, and no one else had needed to know. He had thought it would be without consequence. Part of the satisfactoriness of their meeting lay in this. That this was no longer so puts him in a fury at the unfairness of it. This time he does reach for himself, his anger finding expression in a stinging ejaculation that succeeds only in confirming his sense of something precious having been spoiled.

He has sent her word that all is well, that all shall be well. But how can that be so? By what means can that possibly be? He cannot own the child without bringing disgrace upon himself. Her husband — at the battle front for months — will know he cannot be the father.

Then let her bear the shame alone and suffer the consequences. He does not need to own the child. It is her word — the word of a soldier's wife — against the King's.

14

Fighting had begun early and treacherously that morning. A posse of Ammonites had dropped down on them where they slept, waking them into an instant, dangerous alertness, routing comfortable dreams of home, whetting their anger with a renewed sense of loss. Five men had been killed and Uriah himself had received a wound where a sickle-shaped blade had sliced into his shin. Not a serious wound, though he could see the white of the bone through it. He was angry at having relaxed his vigilance, to have felt himself secure enough to sleep unguarded. Now, after a morning of hot but inconsequential skirmishes, he and the other men in his hundred had withdrawn to a place a little beyond the city where rocks formed a natural circle and where, for hundreds of years, men had tethered their beasts and rested. It was a long while since any of them had eaten well. Hard-baked cakes of bread which they chewed to a softness were their staple food, supplemented by the eggs of desert birds or what little meat they could find and kill. It was a week since anyone had arrived with fig-cakes and raisins.

There was little talk between them at this time; each man had hunkered down inside himself into a place of endurance. Each knew how the others felt — wretched at the loss of fellows, a little afraid, a little relieved, and tired. Tired because there seemed no end to this fighting, no sense even of what a victory would entail. To get through a day a man had to make his mind as hard and narrow as the mountain pass he most dreaded, bounded as it was by sheer rocks, no one in it safe from ambush. They didn't dare long to rest their thoughts on their homes, the tender cooking and soft skin of their wives, the darting bodies of their children. They had to keep their purpose single and their weapons sharp. The loss of any one of them was bitter and experienced as shame which only courageous fighting could wash off.

The messenger brought fresh loaves. But the first thought of every man there when they saw him was that he carried bad news from home. They crowded round him, hungry for his words.

'I bring you greetings from David, King of all Israel and Judah. He wants you to know that, while his body remains in the City of David, his heart and mind are here with you, outside Rabbath-Ammon. He salutes you for the dangers you endure and for the comforts you forgo. And he has asked that one man — Uriah the Hittite — return to Jerusalem with me to provide a full and witnessed report on what has taken place.'

Having delivered these words, the messenger, whose name was Shimeth, unfastened his saddle-bag and delved into its darkness to draw out some choice gifts from the King's kitchen: soft cheeses wrapped in vine leaves, cakes of pressed dates, figs, raisins, cakes flavoured with honey and spices. The men stared at them uncertainly, unsure if the privilege of such delicacies was right in their situation. They felt awkward and loutish beside these tenderly shaped confections. Some spat on their hands and rubbed them on their tunics in an attempt to make themselves cleaner.

Uriah held back from the small feast. The messenger had named him, no doubt about that, no doubting that he was commanded to leave the place of war. But what had he done to be so singled out? He was not one to attract notice. He liked to be part of a team, a solid stone in a tight wall whose loss would be felt but whose presence went unremarked. Had Joab nevertheless mentioned him in his dispatches?

He knew he was a good soldier. Loyal, courageous, strong as an ox. What he did he did whole-heartedly and to the exclusion of all else. He could work at the same task for hours, disregarding the sun's heat, his own hunger or thirst. He had been like this when he'd dug the well on his land. The place he had chosen looked promising — a few trees confirmed that water was present — but the water level was far lower than he had anticipated. He had begun digging soon after dawn, hoping to complete the task before the real heat of the day began. It was after dark before his digging revealed water, and Uriah had kept on at his work, through the midday heat and the afternoon, receiving only the shelter from the pit he had created and which enveloped him.

His concentration was of a serial nature. In the first days of his marriage he gave Bathsheba his whole attention. No man could have revelled more in a woman or been more devoted to the task of creating the child they hoped for. It was not just the act that he attended to — he was in every way her lover and servitor. Then, when this course of action yielded no fruit, his attention moved on, not to another woman, but to another sphere of action entirely.

Shimeth, having delivered his message and the food gift, was anxious to be gone. Uriah rolled his few things up into his bedroll and was on his horse, ready for the journey to

Jerusalem. There was little conversation between them on this journey. During the first part both were on guard lest a party of Ammonites should fall upon them. They guided their intelligent horses, picking their way through the rocky terrain.

Uriah took no pleasure in the King's summons. To be removed from his duty felt more like a rebuke than an honour. This thought kept him sullenly preoccupied as he rode. Shimeth wisely left him to his broodings, congratulating himself on his own employment — so much more comfortable than that of a soldier.

15

Now that the King had sent word that her husband would be returning she set her mind on making their home a welcoming place — welcoming as her womb had been to the seed planted by the King. She began to feel as she had done when she had first loved her husband, recovering her early joy in him, thinking of him again with gladness and longing. It occurred to her that what had happened was the gift of a just king. Was it possible that YHWH, who loved David, wanted Bathsheba and Uriah to be childed and for the goodness of their marriage to be restored? Could He perhaps have chosen David to be the instrument of this restoration? She remembered how Abraham's wife Sarah had been given a child late in life, long after she had resorted to Hagar to bear one on her behalf. But then she thought, *Who am I to play a part in YHWH's purposes?* Sarah and Abraham were of another order: the great forebears who had known YHWH and so made Him known by all who came after. Had there been a time when Sarah was just an ordinary woman, living in ignorance, as she now was?

She would return to the extraordinary fact that she had been intimate with the King — something so far from any expectations she had for her life. If that was possible, all might be. She reasoned in this way for she could not, in her brimming contentment, perceive a conflict in her situation. To be with child at last, after all the years of hope and disappointment, was a thousand times more wonderful than the inconvenience of the child's not being her husband's was trouble. It was just that — an inconvenience. If she could turn her joyfully pre-occupied mind to other things it was to the thought that this inconvenience could easily be made right. Though she could, if she tried, recover in memory her real experience of being with the King, remembering her anger as well as her assent, she had reverted to a child's sense of the King as the benign figure of myth; the father of his people who could make any-thing right. Now that the King had sent for her husband she had this one enormous task before her: that of concealing her joy from Uriah at the outset. Somehow she must find a way to veil her brightness so that he might only know of her joy in a month or two's time when he might believe himself the agent of it and so its sharer. She needed him to come back to her bed and, in her need, she forgot how long it had been that he had kept away.

Her home seemed to her a perfectly satisfactory place. Though she had experienced the King's cedar-roofed rooms she wanted nothing more than this dwelling of hers with its packed earth floor, its cool walls washed newly white each year. Jars of grain stood in a line along one wall and on a shelf were all her pots and bowls and eating plates. She cared for each of them, its shape, its coloured patterns, just as she loved her cloths and would unfold them at times solely to enjoy and feast on the colours and textures of the thread.

She looked forward to Uriah's return; imagined the gentle goodness of taking a sponge and washing his tired, dusty body before leading him out into the night to rest her head on his chest as they stood beneath the stars. There were two orange trees in their small plot and the air carried the sweet scent of their blossom even at night. They would begin again, in gladness, he not yet knowing the greater gladness that would be his once she had confided that there would be a child. They would walk in the warm and fragrant night and hold hands and talk and he would want her again. What if it had been a great many months since he had joined with her in their bed? Surely — when so great a man as the King had found her lovely — he would want her now? She would lead him to the bed that she had prepared and there they would conceive their child. This child that she carried would become their child, made by them with love and longing.

It was a week since the King had sent word that her husband was coming home. For the first four days she assumed that he was preparing to leave or was in the course of travelling. For the next three days and nights she waited for him actively, her own longing growing with each hour. Though her happiness was almost unshakeable, a small insect of anxiety burrowed its way into her consciousness and led her to climb the steps up to the roof from time to time to cast her eyes in the direction that she expected Uriah to take. She knew he would report to the King first. The journey between the King's House and their home was burned into her mind and, though Uriah might not choose exactly the same route, the alternatives were few.

Surely the King would not wish to keep him for long. He could not, since his object must be less to see Uriah himself than to know him with her. Would Uriah be as anxious to reach her as she was to be reached? Why had he not come? Perhaps he never reached the King. Perhaps an enemy Ammonite had fallen on him while he was travelling. Or a common bandit. Or a snake. She tried to hold in her imagination the possibility of Uriah no longer breathing on the earth but she could not do it. She felt that if this were the case she would know it: that whenever it happened she would feel his ceasing as a shock interrupting the flow of her own being.

Yet still he did not come.

She could think of no way to go to the King's House in search of him without giving away the fact that the King had sent her a private communication. She had the idea of sending a messenger to the Front with fresh supplies of bread and dates — simply so that the same messenger would return after several days with word that Uriah had left for home. An elaborate and extravagant ruse on her part which accomplished nothing but the swallowing of the time taken to think it up.

It was hard for her to talk with her friends — she felt that her preoccupation would show. She decided to weave a shawl for the new child and the decision, with the need to act upon it, brought some relief. If Uriah asked who the shawl was for — he would know that the soft wool she chose could only be for a baby — she would say it was for the child of a cousin. What colours should the shawl be?

There was a woman she had known since she was a child who spun and sold wool and made all her own dyes. Her house was saturated in the smell of these dyes so that, when Bathsheba had been a girl, she had associated certain colours with the smell of the solutions that held them.

She made up her mind to go to this woman now. It was good to do something other than wait. If Uriah came home while she was out, he would stay, knowing she would not be long. She left a dish of apricots on the table to welcome him. Their bloom, like a baby's cheek.

16

The sides of the passes seemed higher and more sheer than he remembered. It was as if everything enclosed and restricted his vision. Not a bad thing with a skittish horse that needs to be brought to look straight ahead, but he was no horse and this sense of dark at the sides of his seeing made his mind ache and flinch. It distressed him to have been removed from the war. He adhered himself to his task with complete commitment and it felt now as if he had been unpeeled and had left some of his skin behind, stuck to the stones of Rabbath-Ammon. He felt he was moving against the grain of himself. Away not just from his fellows and their dangers, but from the Ark. He was more conscious of pain from the wound in his lower leg, as if leaving the Ark and his fellows had contributed to the injury.

The Ark was out there, with them in the field, holier by far than the person of the absent King. The Ark was the Israelites' guarantee of YHWH's presence and they in their turn protected and guarded it with the fierce tenderness of a mother towards a new child whom she has to shield from all the buffetings that come against it. Golden wings of cherubim were folded over the covering, the wing tips almost but not quite touching; like the fingertips of a prophet praying. They seemed to signify that holiness was not something that could be grasped or clung to. Not some *thing* at all — more a quality or an essence, to be cherished, sheltered, and guarded with enormous, delicate care. It must be stood back from, framed by apartness to allow it space for breath.

And what breath that was!

The Tables of the Law lived there. The very Word of YHWH as given to Moses. As close as you could get to YHWH's breath. Also within the Ark, a jar containing manna, the food YHWH saved his people with. They said of this manna that it dissolved like frost in sunlight. Impermanent as the men it fed. Stuff and spirit both.

Uriah knew that the Ark could roar. He knew the stories. It had roared at Uzzah with devastating power. The man had put out a hand to stay it when the ox-drawn cart bearing it home was jostled — the act, one might think, of a pious and honest man. Yet the Ark had roared and felled him in a single breath. There were all those men from Beth-shemesh — killed, although most had not even touched the Ark. They had merely looked at it with a curiosity void of humility and awe. Gazed hungrily and without reverence. And the Ark had trounced the fish-god Dagon, reducing the wooden idol to a mess of splinters.

Uriah thought of these things as he travelled back to the City of David. Though he was a soldier through and through, his considerable strength and courage were dedicated to the service of what he held to be true and holy. He had an instinct for holiness.

Immense human skill had gone into the making of the Ark. This skill was one of the ways YHWH showed His Presence: funnelling it through the hearts and hands of men, equipping them first with a sense of symmetry and splendour and then endowing them with the gifts to embody these in metal-work, carpentry, jewellery, embroidery. Of course Uriah had never touched the Ark or even been particularly close to it. But he had gazed at it, seen the gold of it flashing in the sun and the two gold cherubim that guarded it. He had not been near enough to see their faces but he felt he knew them, grave and beautiful. The faces of the cherubim expressed a perfection of purpose, a clarity of focus such as even the most committed mortal might only touch on rare, gifted, occasions. Their sharp, fine-tipped wings with overlapping feathers expressed an unimpeded alacrity. YHWH's servants are swift in their obedience. These strong angels gazed upon each other with clear eyes and Uriah felt that he had seen those eyes. The thought of their gaze clarified his own purpose; yet to be summoned apart, unable to fulfil his role in defending the Ark, caused him a physical distress which combined with the pain in his leg to make him wretched.

—

In other, ordinary, ways his arrival at the King's House brought welcome relief. The King's House was like a delectable mirage glimpsed in the heat but then entered and made real. His dusty feet were bathed and oiled, his head and hands were washed and kindly dried, fresh garments were provided, while all around, on low tables, were items of food — dried fruit, nuts, and small pieces of cheese — placed casually without the ceremony conferred by a meal. Ready to be eaten with barely so much as a thought.

Yet while his body consented to the offered comforts, Uriah could not feel himself at home. The sensation he had had during his journey, of a narrowed vision with blindness at the edges, persisted even after he had made himself known to the King: he could only see the road straight ahead, answer the questions put to him about the siege — what manner of weapons, what casualties and how they came to pass, what victories and how won. He had lost the power to speculate and imagine. He felt like an obedient dog who could respond but never initiate.

All the while that he was in the King's company he had a sense of preoccupation with something else; somewhere else. Even the novel fact of being in the King's presence failed to engage his interest. He answered the King's questions as well as he was able, ate the food set before him and drank the wine. All this he did resolutely, setting nerves and muscles in motion. He answered with the minimum that truth required — with neither embroidery nor expansion to make his tale come alive. If the King thought him lacking there was no indication of this. He listened courteously and seemed entirely satisfied with Uriah's spare responses.

When evening came it did not occur to Uriah to make the short journey between the King's House and his own. The two places were in different worlds for him now. His own home was a house of peace where peaceful practices like building and cultivation took place. Even when he and Bathsheba had felt estranged they worked together on their land, comfortable in their shared productive purpose. His present was in a time and place of warfare where food was fuel, rest what the body's strength required. Though he was in the King's House and seated on a splendid cloth it was to him as if he were still outside Rabbath-Ammon with spears and rocks flying through the air. He was here because the King required him to be here. It was a soldier's duty.

But he was still at war.

And so, on the second night, he again remained by the King's House, after the King had insisted that he drink wine with him and match him cup for cup. There was no question in his mind that he might pick his rather drunken way through the narrow streets that led to his home. In spite of himself he had welcomed the analgesia, but the drunkenness made him clumsy even while his mind and will were intact. Still the obedient dog, he would not leave his post until the war had been won and he had been finally recalled. When that time came he thought he might again turn to his wife and become her full husband again. The rigours of war would prepare him for that salve and draw a line beneath their time of estrangement. But he could no more bed his wife now than he would have fetched her to the battlefield. His loyalty was to the King, certainly, but in equal measure it was to the men who at this moment were facing the dangers that the King's summons had removed him from. Above all it was to the Ark that protected each one of them.

He had carried his bedroll with him to the King's House and on the second night, as on the first, he unrolled it on the terrace below — a place where several of the King's servants also slept. It was like a small village where men and women squatted down to cook and eat or carry basins for washing their clothes, their pots, and their bodies. Soft conversations continued late into the night, as did games, small bones cast down, scooped up, recast. The sound of someone hawking. The barking of a dog. All this business was soothing to Uriah and these sounds accompanied him into a deep sleep in which he dreamt that he was indeed home again, sleeping behind his wife and cradling her soft belly in his hands. It was a dream of infinite tenderness in which he felt again the dearness of the woman he had married. In his dream he entered her and had a sense, not of spilling his seed but of dissolving.

But when he woke the dream fled quickly and he wiped away the semen he had spent without any internal comment.

17

On the third morning she knew he was not coming home. Though at first she had firmly expected him, she now knew with certainty that he would not arrive. Could something have happened to divert him from his journey back to the City of David? If he had been injured — or worse — she felt sure the news would have reached her. Another thought began to work its way into her — at first nibbling at the edges of her consciousness, then hammering at it like a fist on bronze doors. The thought that he'd heard about her and the King. If he had, would he just walk away and never see her again? He might find that easier than to come home and confront her. It would be far more contemptuous. She would not lie. If he did confront her she was not sure whether anger or sorrow would be the stronger in him. Would he kill her, or expose her for others to kill? She doubted it, but she knew he had it in him to walk away.

What if he were simply to persist in his absence: prolong into forever the months that they had already been apart? That might be what was already happening. Forever might already be underway. She stood on her roof and looked out beyond the city, across the desert wilderness that seemed to go on without end.

She began to mourn what she now knew she had lost. The baby inside her — *their* child — grieved too. She felt it tight, scrolled up like a walnut; her own womb, constricted in pain, hard as a walnut's shell. The two of them wept together.

Uriah's absence felt injurious to the home that she had been so busily making ready to receive both husband and child. It now seemed an abandoned place; a place ransacked by an enemy tribe, all that was precious in it taken. She felt most terribly alone. In a corner of her mind was the woman, Miriam, buried up to her shoulders in sand, her terrified eyes. She could hear her cry which conveyed not just physical pain but all loss, all longing. For the first time since her pregnancy was known to her, she felt afraid.

Fear made her practical. She must dissimulate. If she were seen to grieve she would be pressed by her neighbours to explain. Maybe they had already found out something about her visit to the King? Could his messengers — and hers — have gone unnoticed? Was it their talk that had spread somehow to Uriah? Bathsheba's mother used to say that her face was incapable of concealment. Once, when she was about five, she had stolen something from the house of one of her mother's friends. What was it? Nothing of great value but something that had fascinated her. A sieve, yes, that was it: a small sieve through which that friend pressed curds and extracted a thin milk. The little girl had loved the transformation it effected. So, while her mother and her mother's friend were absorbed in conversation, she took it and later presented it to her mother as a gift, saying that she had found it. Her mother, without recognising the sieve as her friend's, saw the look on Bathsheba's face.

'You did not *find* it. I can see from your face that you took it from somewhere else where it belongs. Now put it back.'

Hot with shame, she had taken the sieve and left it outside

the door of her mother's friend, thankful not to see the woman and have to explain. From then on it had been a family saying that Bathsheba's face was as open as a sieve: it could hold nothing in.

Yet now it must.

She did not feel able to contact the King again. What had before been an adventure, a test of resourcefulness, now felt an intolerable exposure. She thought that he might eventually send word to her but even that no longer seemed certain. Could he not do as he chose? If she made a claim on him he could deny it, call her a liar, a slanderous, ambitious woman, attempting in the most outrageously bold manner to find a way out of the dilemma of a child conceived in adultery.

Unless and until the King sent word she had no recourse but to wait: to gather at the Horse Gate with the other women whose husbands were fighting and try, with them, to separate rumour from fact as the first reports of battles and skirmishes came in. She would be safe there amidst all the other anxious faces, the shouting and the tears. There wails rose up like smoke from the huddled knots of women, darkening the clear air. There her own troubled face would not stand out.

She cupped her hands over her womb and whispered to her baby.

'We're in trouble, you and I. I thought you had come to heal the rift between me and Uriah and that he would become your father. But you have no father. The one who seeded you is too high to own you. You and I will be alone, and when it's known that I've wronged Uriah, we'll be punished. We may need to run.'

She began to cry, stroking her belly to reassure the child in spite of her words. But the child had heard those words.

Little fish that he was, he caught on to everything his mother directed towards him. The taste of these words was bitter.

She was full of conflict and division. Angry too at having been woken from her sweetly dreaming state. Angry that this great promise of fulfilment should come in so dangerous a form as to undo all its own goodness. She was so *glad* to have conceived — she could not dissolve that gladness or even consent to unravelling her recent past. It was not what she had asked for: that sudden displacement into the King's House had snatched the flow of her daily existence into the shocking airless air of power. She had not wanted to be the King's concubine. But she also knew that he had not forced her — whatever might have happened if she had attempted to leave. As far as she knew, she had been free. Her body, untouched for many months by a husband who'd turned away in grim reproach, had met the man — the King — and been glad.

She felt wretched, alone and afraid. But she would not simplify the memory of what had happened to take away her sense that there had been good in it. There had been life in that encounter — not just the vitality of two people, but an experience of life at the heart of the meeting between them. To deny that experience would be to deny her senses, the flame in her own nature that was always alight and could flare up to be leaping and bold. The child she was carrying testified to this: a life had been made by the life of that encounter. But it was all shut up inside her and had nowhere to go. There was no home for her baby to be born into.

Sometimes the image of Miriam in the sand pressed in on her so much she felt she *was* that woman, the image having wrapped itself round her and sunk in. Then she would cry out, crying the cries of that poor killed woman.

She wanted to shield her child from the anguish in her heart but in the very act of trying to shield him she contracted her womb till the life in him was squeezed and threatened. She attempted to keep her thinking mind far apart from her womb, but her thinking mind thought terrible things: it thought that a woman can lose a child that she is carrying — that there are herbs that can provoke a womb to empty itself and that there are also midwives who know how to deliver an unfinished child by means of strong massage pressing down on the womb. These thoughts — the possibility they offered of injuring what was dearest to her — increased her isolation and misery as she attempted to prevent her child from overhearing them.

18

On the third night Uriah was again called into the King's presence and invited to eat. At one time such an invitation would have excited, even unbalanced him with the privilege it implied. He would have been at pains to conceal his excitement and would have pressed himself to take in every detail — what pots, what seats, what cups; the nature and spicing of the meats, sweetmeats, wines. But years of fighting had changed that. He had developed a closeness to his comrades he would once not have thought possible. This closeness, born of discomforts and dangers experienced together, nights spent huddled in cold damp caves where the only warmth to be had was from each other, small meals shared — always shared, however tiny the resulting portion — eaten with hands that had been caked with their own and others' blood (they would rub their hands clean in the sand, not wanting to waste one drop of precious water) — this closeness had made family of his fellows.

When he had arrived at the King's House his horse had been taken away to be watered and stabled while he was given the human equivalents. The cool of the King's House was delicious after the hot track and it had been marvellous to wash his head in water. But the noise of the war remained with him — the cries, the shouts, the smack and thud of missiles. The smell of it too — the horrible smell that had begun to issue from Rabbath-Ammon now that the siege had really begun to make itself felt. The smell of the death within, but also of all the refuse that they could not burn, not being able to go out to fetch fuel in. That smell persisted in Uriah's throat in spite of the sweet overlay of the oil he had been given. That and the persistent, worsening, throb of pain in his shin made the sweetness foul.

But the King appeared to have forgotten the war. His conversation — determinedly jovial — turned to anecdote. He told stories from his past — always (Uriah suspected) with the calculation of appearing to confer the favour of intimacy. Uriah was beyond the reach of such sleights — sleights directed as much towards an imagined audience as to himself. *The King told me about the time he shot a young gazelle who had wandered apart from its mother; how the mother had then appeared, grieving for it. And do you know — the King then shot the mother — not for sport this time but out of tenderness for her loss.* Or the King's seeming confidences about his commanders, or even about Saul and Saul's family; there was a time when Uriah might have relayed these to his friends in a way which seemed to take on the King's concerns — making it appear that the King had consulted him on some delicate matter. He might have done this had he been a man to find satisfaction in such postures, but if he had ever been such a man he was that no longer.

He respected the King as leader and warrior. David had — he knew well — performed great deeds of service to them all. But Uriah also respected and loved the men he had fought with and whose courage and humour he knew at first hand. Asoch, Ahaz, Misham, Aleakar. Their lives were this minute in danger while his and the King's were not. Why not? Why was this warrior king not himself at the forefront of the battle? He must have his reasons — indeed he had made much of certain 'pressing local concerns' that kept him at home. But why keep Uriah — whose value in the front line he had already fulsomely acknowledged — there in the King's House, away from that front line? All significant news of the battle had by now been extracted from him and was already almost certainly out of date. Uriah had stressed the need for more weapons and for reinforcements. No man could be spared. *He* could not be spared. The King must surely see that Uriah chafed to be back where he was needed; where it was his job to be.

It was hard for him to conceal his irritation when, on the third evening, the summons to dine with the King came yet again. Nevertheless he dutifully presented himself.

David wrapped an arm familiarly round Uriah's shoulders. Uriah could feel the heat from his body, smell it, so different from the scent of the jasmine oil on his hair. Though the King was less bulky than he, his embrace would have been hard to resist. Uriah was led through to a room where dinner had been set out, on a low table, for only two people.

What is this? What is this game that I have been brought into? Where are the counters? The knuckle bones? What are we playing for?

The King lifted a jug and poured wine into a large bowl which he then passed to Uriah. Next he filled another bowl for himself and raised it high, as if making a pledge. He laughed, in a comradely way and nodded to Uriah to raise his own bowl.

'To life. To all that is good in the life that YHWH sends.'

Uriah bowed his head in agreement and the two men swallowed their first mouthful of the night.

'And of those good things, among the best are our women. Let us drink to our women.'

For all the casual jollity of the toast, the King eyed Uriah carefully and saw him flush. Was it with anger? Embarrassment?

The soldier drank without word, bending his head over the bowl and avoiding the King's gaze. He was conscious now only of how different his circumstances were from the King's. He with his one wife — and what business was it of anyone but them if she was barren? — the King with his household of women, wives and concubines, whomsoever he chose to father his many sons and daughters with. He burned with anger and shame at the patronising way in which the King implied that they were the same; that they were equals in the matter of women.

The King forced a chuckle.

'You say nothing. You have a wife, I think?'

Uriah nodded his assent but remained silent. He would resist this collusive king until he knew what he was up to.

The King's next move was risky.

'By all accounts she's a lovely one. You must have been glad to lie with her again last night — I hope you've made the most of your recall. It wouldn't be fair of me to engross all your time. I know that what I've longed for more than anything — after days of fighting — isn't warm water or clean linen, but the touch of a woman. The ease it gives a man.'

And he leaned back, setting his legs a little wider apart as if experiencing that ease, letting the air circulate around his genitals. Uriah regarded this movement with distaste.

'Sir,' he said, 'the men of Israel have only makeshift tents for shelter. Our commander Joab sleeps in a field, not on a bed. The very Ark of YHWH travels under a temporary cover — we do all we can to keep it safe, knowing that it is our firm protector. But this most holy object endures the discomforts and roughness of the battlefield. How can I, removed from the battlefield where my comrades struggle — removed not by my own choice but by your command — how can I go back to my tranquil house, lie comfortably with my wife and eat the food she has cooked? I cannot do this. I swear it on my living soul. I cannot.'

His mind was contracted in a proud anger. He felt his own rightness and did not for a moment permit himself to remember the body of his wife or to know it could be for him again, should he but choose. The King would not guess how long it had already been since he *had* chosen. He looked squarely at his king as he spoke. His look said, *Why are you, our Commander in Chief, not there with us?* And the King returned his gaze with firmness. Yet there was a questioning in the King's eyes. The look of a man who has been matched; his escapes in the game they were playing cut off.

———

Still David would not let Uriah go. If the man would not go to the comforts of his home he would be obliged to stay with David; obliged to suffer the privilege of eating at the King's own table, of being served by the King with choice pieces of tender lamb, of having his wine bowl filled and filled again by the King's own hand.

This game was not to be a short one.

The King had more stories: offered intimacies about hunts, battles, women, children. He was at pains to reveal that his cares were the same human cares as another man's. He mentioned Jonathan and at this Uriah looked up, his attention caught. All knew the words in which David had lamented the death of Jonathan and his father Saul: every man in Israel had learnt those words, known as 'the Song of the Bow', and learnt to lift and notch a bow in time with the song's rhythms. It was as if Jonathan himself were his instructor and Uriah, a strong bowman, was conscious of the lineage of his skill. He could see that the tears that gleamed in David's eyes were real as he spoke of his dead friend. Something in himself had died with his friend he said and when he said this, he looked different. For a moment Uriah saw in front of him a man bereft. Less a king than a lost orphan.

Through the thicket of alcohol, David glimpsed, as if from the edge of his vision, something true in which he might rest. He seemed to see Jonathan, brother of his heart, standing with arms wide to embrace him, just as he had done when he'd tracked David down in the wilderness of Ziph and stood, laughing, at the mouth of the cave where David had been sleeping. Jonathan's laughter was without guile and this glimpse of his dead friend's dear, open face offered David peace and a respite from the willed course he was now set upon. It reminded David that he too could be guileless. He could choose to abandon the game he had embarked on with Uriah. He could admit that he had taken the absent soldier's wife and planted a child in her womb. Would he say he had forced her? To spare her shame and deepen his own? Even as he discerned these thoughts he veered away at the impossibility of following them. He took another deep draught of wine and returned to his project of propelling Uriah into his wife's bed (though if Uriah were as drunk as he was becoming, his ability to do the deed might be impaired).

David set about asking Uriah about his own escapades, his methods and instruments of hunting, what bait he used, how he made and set his traps. As the night wore on Uriah lost a little of his wariness; the man that he was relaxed enough to enjoy the good wine and the meat, the respite from pain. The more David spoke of the hills and caves that he knew, the more Uriah felt he was in conversation with one of his own kind: a man who knew his territory and the creatures who lived in it. He remembered that David had first been a shepherd and that it was through his own capacities that he had risen to be King. He began, grudgingly at first and then more fully, to appreciate the man who was so determinedly entertaining him. He allowed himself to enjoy the rare experience of this prolonged and inexplicable interview.

He let himself drink deep. What wine he had swallowed while encamped outside Rabbath-Ammon had been at best a dampening of pain. It was months since his body had experienced the comfort of a cushion. Now that his muscles had begun to relax he felt also the impact of their habitual tightness; as his creases softened, so a little demon of pain seemed to fly from each one and even his leg was quiet.

A numbness had descended on Uriah's body so that he had to take great care as he lifted the wine bowl to his mouth lest he tip the bowl awry and his blunted lips miss their target.

More jars were brought. The woman who carried them was discreet and modest in her movements, having long perfected the servant's art of anticipating and meeting the needs of her master — as if what she provided were simply the due dropping of ripe fruit. But her shadowy discretion could not conceal her beauty. David looked on appreciatively as she set down a jar — her movements efficient and sure, her lovely feet silent on the floor. As she dissolved back through the doorway David nodded to her in acknowledgement of her task, before turning again to Uriah with a look that invited him to comment on the woman's appeal.

'Not bad,' he prompted.

Uriah assented as wisely as he could with so much wine inside him.

The King elaborated. A woman like that excites the senses, he suggested. Her very reserve part of the excitement. He returned to his theme of the balm of a woman's touch after the harshness of battle. They were both by now very drunk, but it was only the King who spoke — with an increasing lack of reticence — of what a man may do with a woman. He could have been a coarse uncle, encouraging a young nephew to embark upon sexual experience. Trying to make him want it.

But as the soldier said farewell to his king, his one intention was to lie down as soon as was possible, not to go down the hill to the house where his wife still waited. He staggered under the warm weight of the night air, looked around him to where the King's servants had already found places to sleep, and spied an unoccupied corner. There he pulled his garment over his head, curled onto his side, and immediately fell into a deep and imageless sleep.

19

The King's sleep that night was deep and imageless too. After Uriah had gone he dismissed the servants that had been waiting outside in case they were needed. He remained in the room where they had been feasting. Though he had matched Uriah bowl for bowl his head was distractingly clear. He did not want to think about what the man had gone off to do. It was alright to speak, in a general way, about how soft a woman is and how welcome that softness after hardship. But he did not want to think of Uriah entering the softness of *that* woman — Bathsheba, whose shape had taken up residence in his mind. He could recall the exact resistance of her softness, what it took to make an impression in it. He could see her hand taking his own and the gold of her body laid out in welcome. He did not want to picture it welcoming another.

He continued to pour wine for himself, determinedly, ruthlessly shutting down the light of her inside him. He did it in the way of a man who cuts out the tip of a spear that had lodged itself in his thigh, wilfully overruling the body's objection. At the same time he shut down the light of his own nature, the light that showed him he had done wrong; that he was disobeying the sweet honesty that YHWH had found in him and which Jonathan had met and mirrored.

Shutting it down was a long task. The work of hours. By

the time a clenched sleep had cancelled David's consciousness and replaced it with the dark to be found in a fist, the sky was growing pale and the business of the day was underway elsewhere. A maid found him, wrapped in a rug which he'd cowled around him, his mouth open and not so much as a cushion under his head. His snoring breath exhaled a sour and ugly odour which filled the room. Gently, and with the same neutrality with which she would have brushed sand from a plate, the maid raised the heavy thing that was the King's head and inserted a pillow beneath it. The cool of the night was past so she left him with only the cover he had chosen.

He woke an hour later with the sensation that he had, in sleep, become stone. There was a terrible silence around him: the silence a man hears when he is operating in the wrong time and when he has not embarked upon the day as he should; when — if that man is king — those who usually wait upon him are getting on with their business as unobtrusively as they can. He woke to the sense that everyone had forgotten about him.

—

They had done no such thing. They were embarrassed. What they felt, knowing that their king had become uncharacteristically drunk, was not as deep a thing as shame but the perturbation of knowing what they would have preferred not to know. Some were old enough to remember the behaviour of David's predecessor, King Saul. The terrifying unpredictability of the old king had created an atmosphere of constraint and fear. His sour rages poisoned the air for days. Worse was the sense that a rage was brewing. Those times were like those when you felt and almost heard the shiftings in the desert: presage that the earth was planning to shake. Where, when, and how it would shake were unknown. All you could do was be afraid and ready to move as required.

But this king was not like the bruised giant who had ruled before him and whose life David had famously preserved. King David had not come wrapped in shadows. His sure-footedness and readiness for enjoyment spread to those around him. He noticed the men and women who worked for him in a way that went far beyond the calculation of a good manager. He did not expect them to do everything for him and still chose to exercise some of the skills he had acquired as a shepherd boy. He chose at times to milk his own flocks and he had a good eye for them. A further quality which singled him out as worthy of the respect of the herdsmen he employed: he was willing to learn. It would have been easy for him to perform the occasional kingly demonstration — shear a few pelts before handing the shears over to a servant to complete the task to which he had so magnanimously stooped. If Saul had done such a thing everyone would have simpered their admiration whilst concealing their impatience to get on with their interrupted work. But David, when he saw a young shepherd at work with a knife that was differently shaped to any he had handled — saw how efficiently the lad wielded it — would ask about it, try it, and then recommend that style of knife to others.

So the King, when he woke late in the middle of this morning, struggled to find anyone in his path. The entire household seemed to be engaged in invisible tasks elsewhere. When he woke he was still dressed in the exuberantly festive robe he had worn to feast his guest. He took it off, found a ewer of water, and poured some over his head, blinking at the shock this caused him. He twisted his neck from side to side and then took hold of it and rubbed it in an attempt to free it from the stiffness caused by his sprawled sleep. There was no fresh robe in this room where he received visitors, but he could not bring himself to resume the one he had slept in. Clutching it to him like a bundle of washing, he walked awkwardly, almost stealthily, to the room where he slept, glad now of the deserted spaces. From the chest where his clothes lay folded he took a plain wool garment, the undyed wool easier on his eyes than the bright weave of the night before. Dressed in this, he went out to the courtyard at the entrance of the palace, confident that he would find people there — members of the palace guard if no one else.

Bainoth, a young man whose confidence was at times close to insolence, came up to David and bowed. The King acknowledged this with a nod.

'What news today? Who comes? Who goes?'

'Sir, the soldier Uriah left three hours ago. He seemed anxious to return to the battle — he didn't even want to accept the food the women here pressed on him for his journey.'

'He came back here from his own house to take his leave?

'No sir. I don't think he visited his house. The other guards say that he spent the whole night here.'

David's brain was still curdled with the last night's drink and fumbled as it tried to understand the words it had heard.

'He left from here? Not from his house?'

'No. Not from his house, sir. He never went to his house.'

The words *never went to his house* sunk into his mind like a brand; as with any beast pinned down by hot metal, everything in him struggled to reject the brand, but no part of him could escape the pain it inflicted. He turned away from the guard abruptly and hurried to his private garden where he crouched behind a rock. His body was in revolt and he felt as if he might weep — with vexation or relief, he did not know. He began to retch and at the same time his bowels loosened and spat out the foul-smelling dung that follows an excess of alcohol.

Sweating with exhaustion he leant back against the rock. Something in him expanded and relaxed with the relief of knowing that the man had not touched her, that he, David, had been the last to do so before the gate of her womb was closed. Relief *that the child was surely his.*

Nearby a bird began to sing in little kissing notes. The repeated song comforted David. The bird had no interest in him, was neither pleased nor offended by his doings. The entire garden, walled and apart, contained a world of activity: the incessant crickets, snakes sliding and basking in the heat, the frogs — noisy these nights — the insects, the birds. Not one of them was ruled by him, and this knowledge expanded him, made him lighter. Flies had already begun to cluster on his vomit. He scraped up some earth with a sharp stone and heaped it over, making a little tomb of his waste. He badly needed to drink some water and he left in search of it. Some shit still clung to the edge of his garment.

—

After he had vomited he felt clearer and a plan came to him, ready-formed. He knew he needed to act fast if his man were to overtake Uriah.

As he composed the letter that Uriah was to carry to Joab it seemed to him that the man had invited his fate; that, when Joab had fulfilled the command contained in the letter, Uriah would have been justly punished for the ingratitude he had shown. Had he not been offered the opportunity of lying with Bathsheba? A part of David felt inspired and reckless with relief at the knowledge that Uriah had not been home.

During the weeks since Bathsheba's visit he had been in some perplexity as to how it could be repeated without scandal. How — he glimpsed this possibility — he could bind her, another man's wife, into his life. True, he had taken Michal, his first wife, back from her second husband Phaltiel. But she had first been rightfully his — removed from him by her father Saul in an act of deliberate humiliation. She and Phaltiel had grown to love each other — they told him that — but David had a claim to Michal which he'd needed to assert if he were to be respected as king.

He had no such claim to Bathsheba — only the power of a king to do as he willed. A power that he preferred not to exercise too conspicuously.

It had been perplexingly hard for him to contemplate Bathsheba being covered by another man. Even though he had contrived to create the opportunity, he had needed to exercise his will and great personal forbearance in the contriving. Then, after all that, the man had refused! Turned down the gift of fatherhood that David had attempted to fasten on him.

There was a satisfying neatness to his new plan: an economy in making Uriah the carrier of the letter that sealed his fate. The honourable Uriah! Oh how he had paraded this honourableness in a way that seemed designed to slight the King! He would never think to break the seal on the letter he would soon be carrying and read that letter himself. If he could read, which David doubted. But Joab could read and Joab would understand what needed to be done without asking questions. In Joab he had an excellent deputy.

He called for writing materials and wrote the letter with a dispatch that reassured the household that the King was himself once again. In a short time a messenger was galloping in the direction that Uriah — like many soldiers of Israel before him — had by now travelled between the City of David and Rabbath-Ammon. Fifty long miles of desert, river, and thickly wooded hills. David knew the journey well — he had covered those miles on foot as well as on horseback and was able to follow Uriah and the messenger in his mind's eye. He hoped the messenger would catch up with Uriah before he crossed the Jordan. If not before, then there. Uriah would certainly pause there to refresh himself and his horse. The river in which David had often washed and at times had forded; it was the boundary that divided his land from the land of the Ammonites.

Beyond the Jordan David felt his command to be more fragile. Would his voice be heard amidst the hubbub of other tongues?

Joab would hear him. Joab would know what to do.

In his mind he heard the low and spreading tone of the conch Joab used to hush his troops. At first you hardly knew you had heard it. So low the tone, so stealthy the sound, it seemed to be growing out of your bones and require you to be still because this was its source.

Imagining it settled the King.

20

Uriah was weary. The previous night's excess of drink had exhausted his body and depressed his spirit. When he had left the palace compound early that morning the alcohol had still been in his blood, creating a bright agitation which could be mistaken for energy. It had fuelled the first part of his journey. Apart from a certain queasiness, which he calmed with the bread that one of the servants had given him, he'd felt ready and fit for the long ride. As he put distance between himself and the City of David, the pain in his leg returned with more insistence. It made him more eager than ever to be back where his duty lay.

He stopped, dismounted, and sat on the ground before he began the descent towards Gilgal and the Jordan. From where he sat, he could look both east and west. It was pleasant to consider that no one knew precisely where he was at that moment. There were various routes he might have taken and he had passed virtually no one. He was alone with his horse — whose reins he still held lightly — and the birds, one of whom darted and pecked at the dry ground near his feet, hoping for some of the scraps that occur where there is human life.

His thoughts turned, for the first time that day, towards Bathsheba. He had so busily resisted the insolence of the King's suggestions that he had succeeded in shutting her out of his own mind while he was at Jerusalem. Now she seemed to him a very long way off, further even than the thirty or so miles he had already travelled. Thinking of her was like gazing at the moon and speculating about what kind of a thing it was, whether it was warm or cold, large but very distant, or almost as small as it appeared, but out of reach in the sky. It now seemed incredible to him that he had had the possibility of lying with her for the past three nights. All he knew was that the possibility had somehow not been real, however near she had been when the distance could be measured in paces. He thought of her now with great tenderness and something like kindness. He had not been kind with her for some time. Her barrenness had caused him too much pain and this had made him harsh. Now he saw what had been there to see all along: how his harshness had wounded her and dimmed her bright-ness. He remembered the glorious girl he had first known; how the sun seemed to break out from her laughter, from her gleaming hair, from her golden belly, and from the feet that he'd kissed. He saw that she was still that girl.

When he was a boy he had found a chrysalis. A lozenge of ribbed amber which he had prized for itself. But he also knew what it could be, what it was intending to be, and it was for this future that he kept it. He kept it in a small lidded basket and from time to time he removed the lid and saw that the chrys-alis was intact, the amber still glowing. Months passed, other interests claimed him, and he failed to check the progress of his treasure. Until he came across his basket one day in the course of doing something else. Remembering, and suddenly anxious, he hurried to take off the lid. What he saw inside was the most beautiful moth, wings spread wide ready for flight, each wing marked with a kohl-rimmed eye. The enormity of his crime struck his heart and he had knelt by the dead moth in tears of pique and penitence. He saw how it had struggled out of its sticky prison full of hope and purpose, entirely equipped for a life of soaring beauty. The crime of its murder weighed on him.

He had hurt his wife and offended her beauty by ignoring it. He had been so fixed on the idea of the children that were not there, he had failed to see what was. Now when he recalled the tenderness and delight they had found in each other — that ordinary miracle, given day after day — he wondered that he had ever wanted more than that. He'd heard men refer to their wives like livestock — good for bearing the next generation of labourers. Those men had not known what he had known, the gift which is not *for* anything, whose fruit is its own glory. He remembered the simplicity with which Bathsheba had said, 'But we have each other' and how he turned aside from these words, refusing to share her gladness, her sense that there was enough. He had become like those other men and thought of her as a cow that would not calf. A bad investment and a disappointment.

Why now, after spending three days almost within sight of the home where they had loved, never once exerting himself to be with her, did he suddenly see her again in all her luminous beauty? He saw it free of the sullying insinuations of the King on the previous night. Indeed, in his imagination, he rescued her from that taint. He remembered the welcome of her smile, her body, the velvety shadows that made her brightness brighter. He had turned away from it. Refused the gift. For the first time he saw the cruelty of his conduct towards her; how it had bewildered and then injured her.

He softened into a tenderness he had not felt for years,

there as he sat on the ground among the pine needles. Could he find her again — that radiant, welcoming girl — once he had returned from Rabbath-Ammon and laid down his weapons and his warrior's coat? He wished it with all his heart, yet found it hard to imagine.

He climbed back onto his horse and they picked their way down towards the river. As they drew nearer, the sounds of people at the river drifted up. The scent of human life, washing, bathing, trading. The horse was thirsty and he allowed her to drink her fill while he washed himself, washing away the film that clung to him from the night before. His lower leg was swollen and very hot. A thick pus was oozing from the wound and he realised that he would either have to cut the wound clean himself or find the man who acted as the camp doctor.

It was here that the King's messenger found him, ducking and rising from the water. He waited until Uriah had dried himself before handing him the King's letter to Joab. Uriah, glad to be useful in this way, stowed the letter safely along with his bedroll and carried it high so the water would not touch it as he forded the river on foot, leading his horse with gentle encouragement. As he made his way east his only thought was of work to be done.

21

Uzit found Bathsheba examining a small egg on the flat of her hand.

'There must be a nest nearby but I haven't seen it. This one must have rolled away on its own!'

'Tomer brought a bird home last week. Perhaps she was the one who laid your egg. He ate the whole bird. "Just a mouthful," he said, "not enough to share." That's men for you!'

Bathsheba smiled. She knew that Uzit would have called by with a purpose — to find something out or else to parade some piece of privileged knowledge.

Uzit was not a friend but someone Bathsheba had known for most of her life. There was between them the informality of friendship without any of the warmth. As children they had disliked one another — Bathsheba had found Uzit domineering and spiteful, always wanting to be at the centre of a group and happy to ostracise another child if that was the way to experience her own power. As they'd grown older Uzit saw that the mild Bathsheba had acquired a power of her own by the simple virtue of her beauty. This was mysterious and fascinating to Uzit who felt for Bathsheba a mixture of admiration and envy which produced an uneasy servility. It was not friendship.

'How is it with your husband Uzit? What news from the King's court?'

Uzit's husband Tomer was one of the palace guards. As she questioned Uzit Bathsheba was suddenly stabbed by a fear that he would have recognised her when she had gone to David. Recognised her and mentioned this to his wife who had now arrived in order to winkle out more. She felt her heart beat faster as she waited for Uzit's reply. If she had been observed but not suspected, then Uzit would soon mention it. But if she had been the object of gossip, the subtle hooks and suckers would come out in the course of a prolonged conversation.

Uzit was direct.

'Didn't you know Uriah was there? Tomer spoke to him. Said Uriah was in a hurry to get away but the King kept him for three nights. They all wondered about the King keeping him when you were so near — but a king can do what he likes can't he? Didn't your husband send you word? You could at least have gone to him there. Tomer said he slept in the courtyard with the servants — wouldn't even accept an extra blanket.'

She shook her head in disbelief whilst eyeing Bathsheba intently as she said again, 'I should have thought he'd have sent word to you.'

Bathsheba's face had been drawn and white but now she flushed as she tried to cover her discomfiture with a joke.

'I would have tried to find more of these eggs for him if I'd known.'

22

When Uriah was about five miles west of Rabbath-Ammon he stopped again. He was a man accustomed to lopping off the edges of his consciousness. He did it as regularly and instinctively as he would trim the branches of the fig tree that crowded in on their house. Yet, now he was again at the edge of a place of danger and death, the strangeness of what had just taken place overtook him. *The King had summoned him and he had gone.*

Who was he to be known to the King? He had the letter wrapped safe in the bundle strapped onto his horse — a letter from the King to his commander. Had he simply been summoned to act as a messenger? Where was the economy in that? The King could easily have sent a messenger direct to Joab without pulling Uriah out of the battle. It occurred to him now that Joab may have commended him to the King and that the King had wanted to see for himself before conferring the intended honour. If so, perhaps the King had been testing him, watching to see if he were worthy of this honour. He no longer regretted not going to his own house where Bathsheba waited. He had done right and spoken true. True to the unhoused Ark. True to his commander Joab.

Now it was clear to him that the letter he was carrying — and was unable to read, even if honour had permitted him to look — spoke of his own promotion. He didn't for a moment doubt that he deserved it but he gloried in the knowledge that he would no longer be one of the nameless ones. *URIAH THE HITTITE* would be recorded for evermore in the ranks of those who had served Israel.

He saw dark columns of smoke pressing up into the sky above the besieged city. They were starving in there: all the small animals long gone except for vermin and what could be plucked from the sky. No possibility of burying their dead outside the city walls, but inside there was scant earth for the purpose. Scarcely any wood to burn either. It must be that the stench of the decaying corpses had become unbearable. Anything to do away with the horrible smell of putrefaction, the sickening and grievous sight of piled-up bodies. They'd had to use precious fuel.

However harsh the conditions outside Rabbath-Ammon, the Israelites were in the better place. But, as Uriah and his horse picked their way down the hillside to where his fellows were camped, and to where the Ark itself had its makeshift shelter, he had the sensation of himself being walled in, surrounded by a darkness from which there was no escape.

The camp was as noisy as a marketplace. Sounds of sawing, beating, filing, sharpening. The slap of wet cloth flung against a boulder at the edge of a stream; flung and flung again to beat out the sweat. Small pockets of privacy, where a man would sit, cleaning his armour, sharpening a stick, thinking his own thoughts. It was as if he'd never been away. Uriah loosened his horse into a small corral and set off to find the commander. As he shouldered his way through the throng, a few nodded to him, but no one acknowledged that he had been away or came to enquire about his errand. His friend, Ahaz, attempting to shift a rock, signalled with an upward jerk of the chin that help would be appreciated.

'What's it for to be worth all the effort?'

'Wait till we get it to where I'm pitched and I'll show you.'

'No time now. I've got a message for Joab from the King.' This was as near to boasting as he would get.

Ahaz shook his head in disbelief, then crouched down again and returned to his attempt to prise the rock from the ground. Half kicking, half pressing, he eased it towards a hole which he'd dug and wanted the rock to cover. His personal store.

—

Life nearly always puts up a struggle. The strangling of a single creature — even one as small as a partridge — can be surprisingly difficult. Joab's task was the slow strangulation of a city. He and his men had to cut off the supply of all that was necessary for life within the walls of Rabbath-Ammon. The hold could not be relaxed for an instant, since the composite creature that the city was had teeth and fury to inflict great hurt. Death came so very slowly at first. Nothing but time and a sustained offensive could accomplish it. Sheer duration. There was something stupid about it. Keeping on and on and on. Stupid, tiring, unimaginative, cruel. No strategy to think through. Only pacing, persistence and a concern for the welfare of his men.

Throughout this process, the Ark was present. Though it neither spoke nor moved of its own accord, it was for some of the soldiers gathered there the true authority. Its presence reassured them. By its presence alone it prayed for them, guarded and sanctified them. Joab knew it was his duty to keep the Ark safe and that in its safety lay the safety of Israel. But he was wary of it. He was not a naturally religious man. He had no instinct for religion and if he prayed he prayed in public; his prayer was the act of a general who appreciated the need for a unifying concept, an authority beyond himself and beyond even the King. He protected the Ark by appointing guardians. He did not want to go near it himself lest it burn him.

He knew — they all did — what had happened to Uzzah when he put out his hand to steady the Ark. Joab knew Uzzah had died on the spot but he did not begin to understand why. Would he not have done the same, if something he had undertaken to protect was in danger? It was human instinct to reach out to prevent the precious cargo from falling. Supposing the Ark *had* fallen. What then? Should the men escorting it have picked it up and risked being struck down like Uzzah, or should they just have left it there where it fell for YHWH to sort out?

There was a line where priestly reverence deviated from natural respect and once this line had been crossed Joab was in an unknown, incomprehensible land. He also knew that the men of Beth-shemesh had been massacred for looking into the Ark. Fifty thousand and seventy of them. All dead. Because they were curious about this marvellous thing that had rolled into view, pulled into the field by the two pale cows who led it to them, seemingly of their own accord for no driver was ever seen.

When people spoke about the Ark in the old days they seemed to refer to a living being whose ways and wants they did not fully know. It had bided its time during its years of exile, in the coastal plains of the Five Philistine Lords, wretched but patient as it was shunted from city to city. Like Samson it had grown in power and ire, till the moment when it could break out of bondage.

Did Joab understand this holy thing any more than had those Philistines who'd set it in the temple of Dagon to square up to their fish-faced god? He feared he did not, yet he was charged to protect it with his life. He would much prefer to be running this war without the Ark to take care of. To him it was as dangerous as a city-full of Ammonites, armed to the teeth.

He could say this to no one and he was glad that the guardians he had appointed to protect the Ark thought otherwise. For these men prayer was not primarily a public act. Joab had the disturbing sense that these men actually listened to the Ark: that they were responsive to it in some way he did not understand. Rather they than he.

———

When Uriah found him, Joab was poring over a group of stones that he had arranged to form a model of Rabbath-Ammon. He was trying to identify the weak points in the wall and also the points where he and his army would have the greatest purchase in their assault. The wall had become the Ammonites' prison but it was also their chief protection. Any Israelite who attempted to scale it or get too close to it put his life in great danger.

'My lord Joab, I have a letter to you from King David.'

Uriah stood, feet apart, attempting to keep his mind neutral, while Joab cut open the letter and read.

His intuition that the letter referred to himself in some way was confirmed by the way Joab cast his eyes over him, weighing him up, speculating.

'Do you know anything of the contents of this letter?'

'No my lord. The letter was for no eyes but yours. In any case, I cannot read.'

Joab was silent for a while. Then he said, 'The King has singled you out for particular notice. Do you have any idea what it is you have done to warrant such attention?'

Uriah felt his chest flush with pride.

'I have always honoured the King and my lord Joab and would lay down my life to protect the Ark. This is no more than my duty.'

Joab again scrutinised him closely, as if searching for a chink in Uriah's honesty.

Then he folded the letter again and tucked it into the pouch that was threaded onto his belt.

'The King shows how he values your sense of duty. This evening I shall be placing the whole army in new formations. Have no doubt. There will be a special place for you.'

———

That night Joab addressed them all, summoning the murmuring troops to an attentive stillness with the sound of the great conch shell. This was the moment for them to overcome Rabbath-Ammon through ardour and fierce strength. The Ammonites were worn down and hungry; attrition had prepared the ground. Now was the time for the Israelites — stronger and fitter because better-nourished than the Ammonites — to strike like the Angel of Death.

As Joab had promised, so it proved. Uriah was given a special place. He was to lead a small division of fifty men to attack the wall. He would have to wait to deal with the wound in his leg, for treatment would temporarily lame him more. Pride at being so singled out made the pain easy to bear as he set about selecting his men. He chose them for their singular ferocity and unflinching commitment to any engagement. Men, like him, who would never turn tail.

Joab's words had rung in Uriah's mind throughout the chill night as he lay, sleepless and feverish beneath a sky that seemed to explode with falling stars. The words still possessed him as he made his way to the foot of the wall the next morning. Some of the men he was to lead were known to Uriah already. The others included those he might previously have overlooked or disregarded as brutish, lacking in finer qualities. Today he loved each one of them. They were his men and in each of their bold hearts he saw a reflection of his own.

Together they went to the wall — that place of horrors which smelt of the death and desperation of those within but which today, to their high hearts, seemed a hallowed destination. The smell was not just from inside the wall. The Ammonites, wanting to be rid of the stench of their dead and of their own ordure, threw the remains of the animals they had eaten, and emptied the scant, sour eliminations of their bodies into the dry ditch that ran outside. Joab — with breath-taking audacity — had assigned them to force a breach in the north-western part of the wall where the mortar appeared weak. But not far from this weak area and to either side of it were buttresses whose wide tops provided platforms from which the Ammonites could view their enemy. They were not the principal watch-towers of the city but they served a similar purpose. It would be almost impossible for Uriah and his men to attack the wall undetected.

They carried a battering ram made of a stout pine lopped clean of all branches, one end sharpened to a point. Eighteen of the strongest men — nine on each side — bore the tree on their shoulders, treading as swiftly and as lightly as if they walked empty-handed. When they were within feet of the wall they set it down carefully, almost with reverence, and awaited Uriah's command.

A great stillness. The exhausted city within the walls seemed to be asleep. Joab's army waited: they would pour in through the breach that Uriah and his men would make. Quiet enough to hear birds — those lucky ones who had escaped the Ammonites' catapults and traps — the barking of a wild dog in the distance. Uriah could see exactly where the battering ram should enter the wall: a place where the mortar had crumbled away and spilled like meal down the crevices between large dressed stones. Small plants had lodged in some of these crevices, finding enough for life in the dust and moisture that gathered there. One plant with tiny dots of flowers, the colour and brightness of coral, seemed to Uriah a feast for the eyes. YHWH was bountiful and good. At every turn He gave more than was needed.

Uriah took a small fledged dart from his belt and cast it so it landed silently in the gap in the mortar. He gave the men the signal to lift the battering ram in readiness; silently he mouthed the count-down — five, four, three, two — and then silence no longer: *CHARGE!* The great tree was rammed against the wall, its sharpened point nosing into the loose mortar. Uriah's men piled in, using the tree as a lever to dislodge more of the stones that formed the wall. Above them Ammonites who had felt the impact of the breach began to hurl down rocks and stones, while the weaker among them chucked their rubbish and their slops. Impossible for a man to survive long at the wall but Uriah's heart sang with the certainty of having been chosen for this essential mission. This was the moment he had been made for, the moment that Uriah the Hittite would enter the annals of Israel's greatness. He and his men had begun the breach and the Israelites would soon enter Rabbath-Ammon and take her. Even when the rocks rained down on them, darkening the air so they could not see their way, even when an arrow fell straight and with all the force of gravity upon the eye of a soldier who had vainly tried to shoot upwards, Uriah's heart was wide with the glory of his task. And, as the huge rock tumbled though the air to crush him into the ground, burying him where he stood, he had time to wonder what Ahaz had wanted to shift that other rock for, and then to see Bathsheba, in his mind's eye, waiting for him at the entrance of their compound, a dish of apricots held out to him.

23

It settled like slow snow: the knowledge that Uriah had been to Jerusalem and not seen her. At first so light she hardly noticed it, but as the days went by she felt a chilling weight. Once again her body had been waiting for him, waiting for his seed to claim and confirm what the King had begun. Waiting for the baby to be made his. This non-arrival of her husband felt to her colder than any of the rejections she had endured from him in the past as a result of her barrenness, though there had been many times when he had turned from her with an expression that suggested her desire for him was something she should have outgrown. She had come to know his back, turned towards her when he lay or when he stood at the entrance to their house, choosing once again to go out. Now, when she tried to summon him to her imagination, all she could see of him was his turned back, black where it blocked out the sun which he walked towards, resolutely away from where she stood. She felt that he would never turn towards her again.

The idea of a shawl was taking form. For as long as she could remember she'd teased the clumps of sticky wool from the bushes the sheep had blundered through. She always carried a cloth bag with her and when she walked she'd add sprigs of rosemary, juniper berries or myrtle if she found them. The wool went in there too and, though she was careful to wash and comb it smooth before she spun it, the wool often kept a faint scent of the herbs it had nestled with. She sorted it into strands of different shades: the rich earth brown she loved best, the creamy white and the near black. But she wanted another colour in this shawl. She wanted blue and blue was too costly for a soldier's wife.

Spinning soothed her. She kept her bag stuffed full of wool and carried it with her to the roof where she sat, twirling the spindle. She had weighted it with a stone that she'd found with a hole in it. Sometimes the stone would knock against her bare forearm, like a child's hand, importunate, annoying, and dear. It would remind her that while the strand of wool was being twirled and twisted into shape so was her child being formed. Then, for all the difficulty and danger of her situation, she wanted to clap her hands with joy.

But when she remembered Miriam, half buried in the sand, smashed to death by stones, crying for the child that had been taken from her, she felt her womb contract around her own child in order to hold him more closely, though it threatened his security to do so.

This child was now her only true companion. No one else — except the distant King — knew of his existence. If it were not for the fear, this deep, intrinsic relationship would have sustained her. When she tried to protect him from the fear, she shut herself off from that sweet conversation. At times the fear became terror. She *was* that woman Miriam, but without even a friend to mourn with her and comfort her.

She wondered again and again whether she could confide in Safi, her husband's cousin and the member of his family she loved the best. Safi had been betrothed to a man she had known from her childhood — a long betrothal, partly because the love between Safi and Hafiz was as calm as friendship and there was no need to scramble to secure what had been agreed, but mainly because Hafiz had a large family to support following the death of his father. It was felt that his sisters should find husbands to care for them before he took Safi into his home.

Then Hafiz was killed. A terrible accident in which he'd thrust his leg into the burrow of an animal — a fox's it was thought — and could not get it out. The ankle had swollen so much that he was unable to pull the injured leg free. He was far from any settlement. When his exhausted body had been found it was seen that he had used his knife to try to dig his way out of the root-clogged ground and then, more desperate, to cut his own leg free as a hare will gnaw through the bone of its trapped leg. The sand had drunk in his blood.

Now it was accepted that Safi would probably never marry, unless she were to become the young wife of an old man who had wives enough already and would ask little of her. She was best there, in the small community of an extended family, with those who loved her. And the one who loved her most was Bathsheba, who allowed Safi all the contrariness of grief, who would listen as time after time Safi tried to tell her the story of Safi and Hafiz so that it went differently to the story that had ended in such sorrow.

But how could Bathsheba tell Safi the story of her child? Safi who would never love another man now that her Hafiz was gone.

Sometimes the thought returned that if she had not given herself to the King he would have compelled her. Being fetched to the King's House underlay what had taken place, a layer of granite beneath soft soil. She might have told Safi this. But pride as much as anything kept her from excusing herself as the toy of a powerful man. Moreover she wanted to love her son, not hate him as the child of force.

So she did not tell Safi, in spite of the knowledge that her own condition would soon become obvious and that the simplest calculation would reveal that Uriah could not be the father. She knew that when this happened — before this happened — she would have to leave the compound where she was surrounded by Uriah's family. Would she have to go out into the desert and give birth to the child on her own, in a cave, among animals? She pictured herself a wild woman, crouching down on all fours, pushing out her baby and then receiving him wet and bloody into her hands. She saw her own triumph, how she would bite through the umbilicus and scrape him clean with her tongue before wrapping him in the shawl she had made and putting him to the nipple. The two of them, sufficient.

Alternate destinies presented themselves to her waking dreams. In one, she was a shrivelled outcast, her baby gripping onto parched dugs as she clung to the outskirts of human life in a constant search for food and water. In the other — outrageous in its presumption yet persistent and, against all odds, convincing — she lived plump and opulent. Gold flashed at the margins of that vision, her child, a radiant man. Each of these destinies could have induced panic if she had been able to contemplate either for long. But she was weighted down and absorbed by the new centre of gravity in her body. This smoothed the edges of her worry.

24

The assault on Rabbath-Ammon had been unusually successful and the wall had at last been breached. Not however without great loss of life on their side. This was the message. Included in the message were the names of the fallen: among them, Benaiah the Pirathonite, Hezrai the Carmelite, Shammah the Haratite, Uriah the Hittite. Upon hearing it David thought, *It is well*, and sent that word back to Joab.

For a moment he saw how it could be if man upon man were to be crammed up against the wall without regard to strategy or respect for their lives. He saw the heaped, mutilated corpses, their mouths open in indignation, their shocked eyes astare, their hands still reaching to defend themselves from the fatal blow. If he took no account of numbers, knowing there were more men where they had come from, would victory come sooner? He saw Uriah the Hittite who had so rebuked him with his righteousness, his righteous face smashed up. He, David, had made that happen. He could make it happen, not only to his enemies but to his own. As King, he had power over life and death; he was obeyed without question. He did not dislike this thought.

Saul has slain thousands and David tens of thousands.

That chant had risen up and carried him as he walked away from the dead Philistine giant — the first human he had killed. It had shocked and fascinated him then that he should have this power to cancel a life that resembled his own. *Saul has slain thousands and David has slain tens of thousands.* On the day they chanted this (the people who would one day be his people) he had killed a few bears, several foxes, a wolf or two; he had maybe scared off an eagle that was hovering over his lambs. In those days he could pluck a fish from the river with his hands; he had caught partridges in the desert and roasted them. But the only man he had ever slain at that time was the one he had slain that very day. Goliath.

With this kill he crossed a threshold. Like the first time with a girl — no longer the gorgeous dreams, but the real experience, his flesh in hers. That too had yet to take place on the day he shot Goliath.

On that day he did not even have blood on his hands, having aimed his sling from so great a distance. No blood at least until he'd hacked through the dead man's neck. But it was not long before he was to kill up close.

When Saul asked him for a hundred Philistine foreskins as a dowry for his daughter Michal, David had been eager to oblige. He could have used a bow and arrow but he found that he enjoyed feeling the impact of his wounding; the moment when the resisting body gave way and sagged. Saul had asked for a hundred so he had given him two hundred. He had enjoyed collecting them, discarding the men who had sported them. He had not been strictly fastidious when it came to separating foreskin from member. He had gathered them up into his bag once the slaughter was done. It was like gathering turnips from a field.

He still remembered the look on Saul's face at the moment he'd tipped them out onto the carpet in front of him. Some of them still soft and moist, others crispy and shrivelled having waited long weeks to be shown. Oh there had been a raw delight in that killing and cutting! He had assumed this was what Saul had intended: to give him an opportunity to revel in and display his warrior prowess. But Saul's undisguised expression of horror was not revulsion at the pungent offering. No. It showed that his plan had been otherwise. He had not expected David to come back. He had not *wanted* David to come back.

At the time it had been incomprehensible to him that Saul should have wished him dead. But what struck him now — for the first time — was that he had learnt from this act of Saul's. He had learnt that you can make others into your weapon and can delegate the act of killing your friend — the one who should be your friend — onto your enemy. That way you can appear innocent of the achieved death.

25

The journey between the City of David and Rabbath-Ammon, though not very long, felt like a journey between worlds, places occupied by different orders of being. Bathsheba had, as usual, gone to the Horse Gate for news. She had taken a small parcel of food with her to be carried to Uriah, but without any real expectation that it would reach him; it had been so long since she had heard word.

Such a jostle of women at the gate. Women and small children, many of the children carried in arms; a lot of talk — this was a meeting place where news was exchanged long before any messengers arrived — occasional flurries led by sharp voices — small local disturbances in a hubbub like the cooing of doves. The messenger did not always give out names — for that to happen every commander of every battalion needed to have named his own losses; days went by with little to report. But when a messenger did read out the names of the fallen, the waiting women attended, every pore an ear. Any child that annoyed or disturbed was sharply shushed. The long list of names read out on that particular day included the names that the King had heard in his earlier message from Joab.

Bathsheba looked round, startled. Was he here? Her husband? She had heard his name, 'Uriah the Hittite'. But the messenger went on reading names: 'Jabal the Bethlehemite,

Gareb the Ithrite, Shammah the Haratite …' She heard the cries rise up from the breasts of women nearby, rising up into the air in dark plumes like the cypress trees. She felt herself clutched, the air pressed out of her as another woman wailed in sympathy with her expected cry. Then Safi, who had heard the news which travelled swiftly from the cluster at the gate to all whom it concerned — Safi had pushed through the crowd of women to find her friend. Who knew better than she what it was to mourn a beloved?

———

Bathsheba did mourn Uriah with her whole heart. She forgot about the child she was carrying, the child that she and Uriah had longed for throughout their years together. Though at first she had thought of the child as his, her body knew it was not. In her grief and penitence she turned away from the child that the King had got upon her. The spinning and the weaving came to a stop. The child, lonely and uncontacted, curled in upon himself and clutched at the cord that tied him to his mother; he wished he could shake it to call her to attention, or else loosen it and so free himself.

Grief kept her too busy to hear her child. Just as she had sat with widowed friends and joined her own tears with theirs, so friends now came and wept with her. Hannah, Safi, family members, as well as friends from her childhood. Uzit, her spitefulness suspended, played her part. They understood that mourning is exhausting, demanding, necessary work, and they made sure that that was the only work she needed to do. They did not leave her alone for long but when they did, some-one had always left a pot of cooked food so that all that was required of her was to take off the lid and dip in some bread.

She was glad to be so carried. She felt as if she were on the point of drowning in a wide lake, all her garments spread out around her, their own buoyancy still — just — keeping her afloat as her body grew heavy with water and sank. The women who sat with her were those garments. If their buoyancy failed she would sink — as she did each night when alone — into a very thick darkness. Its thickness was composed of detail she was too exhausted to unpick. When she woke it was to another darkness through which she did not know her way. Uriah, his stocky, satisfactory body, was no longer anywhere where she could go. In the darkness of Sheol perhaps, but that was too dark, too utterly silent, to imagine.

Everything was changed. The silence that she woke to in the night was different from the silence of when Uriah was alive — however far away, however estranged. It was a silence without texture or structure. It could not be mapped. Once, very early in the morning, she attempted to go out on her own to the Horse Gate where she had first encountered the fact of his death. It was from an instinct to retrace that journey in the hope that it would help her to understand more fully what she had heard there. But she did not make it as far as the gate. Just a few turnings away from her home — their home — she was overtaken by beating wings of panic. She recognised nothing of where she was. The street where she had walked for most of her life seemed completely unfamiliar. She groped her way back like a blind person feeling the walls of a passage. But there were no walls. Nothing and nowhere was the same. It was not until she had reached her own door and closed it that the tight knot of fear in her belly relaxed and she knew herself to be — if not safe — at least provisionally sheltered.

Her baby, squeezed by the fear that twisted her belly, continued to grow in his own darkness, no longer contacted by the warm thoughts of his mother.

—

The moon had run its course, from nothing to full-bellied and back again to nothing, when she received the call to go to the King. She responded with sullen obedience. He was her king and she would obey. She made the journey alone and on foot.

26

He had waited, humbly and patiently as he saw it, for the prescribed days of mourning to be accomplished before he made any attempt to see her. He had congratulated himself on this discipline; on doing right. Any qualms he had about his treatment of Uriah had by now been buried. Uriah was not, after all, the only soldier to have lost his life at the wall. It was no more than any soldier might expect when he went to do battle. He himself had risked his life countless times. He also felt — though he did not care to examine the feeling — that Uriah had deserved to die. Had the man not made a display of his own righteousness and implicitly reproved the King?

His certainty that Bathsheba was only his and would be his now had steadied him over the past weeks. He would make her his wife and own their child. In this way he would recover whatever righteousness he might have lost. In thinking about her his desire for her had not gone away. It had lost the salt of uncertainty but in this case, with this woman, there was more satisfaction to be anticipated from a leisurely, uninterrupted unfolding of knowledge.

—

He hardly recognised the wrapped woman whose coarse dark widow's cloth concealed most of her features. The reality of this presence pulled him up short and made him formal.

'You are still mourning your husband.'

She said nothing, merely bowed her head in assent. She seemed to shrink into herself. It had never occurred to him that her mourning would be a matter of the heart.

He wondered — he would never ask — whether she guessed that her husband's death had not been an accident. Joab knew this. How many others?

'I will be your husband now. Our child will bear his father's name. You will be the mother of princes. Kings.'

He had imagined — expected — that when she came to him again that it would be as before. That he would take her and that she would consent. That from this time on she would always be his to take whenever he wanted. But this darkly swathed, grieving figure had its own centre of gravity which had nothing to do with him.

'Our child?' he asked. 'Does he grow strong within you?'

'I hardly know, my lord. He stirs from time to time.'

'Perhaps, if I feel your belly, he will know me.'

He asked this hesitantly. Everything about her seemed fenced off and apart. To reach out and touch her, though simple in muscular terms, felt a perilous enterprise for his naked hand to undertake. Gently, he laid his hand upon her and felt the hard, tight flesh; the little knot of the belly button, pushed out like a bumpy outcrop on the top of a hill. With his hand he tried to listen and to hear the other heart. He tried to shelter his child in the cup of his palm.

She hardly felt his touch but she noticed the gentleness of his action. She laid an answering hand on his. It was as much as she could do and all that was required of her for the moment. She could not begin to take in the changes that her life was about to undergo. All that she could see was that some dark, persisting complexity had found a way to resolution — like an underground stream that meets rocks and roots at every turn yet is determinedly drawn to where waters flow and gush in evident plenty. Her body as yet felt no relief or joy. It felt only the numb indifference of mourning. But her mind told her that it was well to follow the King's will. Especially when she had no real choice.

———

She packed her belongings with a sense of unreality. Now that she was leaving to live in the King's House, the simple building that had been home to her and Uriah seemed all that a person could ever need. The earth floor was swept, the hanging shelves cleaned of dust, and, ranged along them and the floor, were as many pots as could be needed for even the most festive and elaborate meal. But what would be the use of her simple earthen pots in a palace where all her meals would be provided for her? Yet she would cook for her child — for all her children. She would insist on this. Comforted by this thought, she set aside the two pots she used most; pots which her mother had used before her and which, though clean of the food they had held, were encrusted with years of love.

She went through her chest of cloths, each of them carefully folded with sprigs of lavender and rosemary laid between the folds to perfume and preserve them. Even the finest of them now seemed modest and plain, when thought of as the dress of a queen. The King — 'David', as she had yet to call him — had told her she would need nothing. But he was wrong; she did need something, and he of all men should know this. When she had heard stories of the King, in the days before she knew him, she had heard that he kept with him at all times the shepherd's crook he had used as a boy when he tended his father's sheep. He was said to do this so he would never grow proud and forget his birth. Perhaps the story was untrue — she had yet to see this shepherd's crook of his — but she was clear that she wanted something from her past to hold her to its truth. Not that she believed she would ever forget this life of hers. She chose a cloak of roughly woven cloth, striped in wavering shades of brown and ochre — the result of her first attempts at dyeing and weaving. She also took a small jar in which she mixed kohl for her eyes and, though she knew she might never wear them again, the bracelets Uriah had given her.

She had been all the wives and women he had ever known. Even when she failed to bear him a child and he had turned away from her, he never — to her knowledge — thought of taking another. Not even in the way of a soldier far from home finding comfort in the body of a foreign woman. She realised she could not know this for sure and that she might be wrong to think this, but she did think it. She knew Uriah, his stubborn virtue.

But David, who had liked what he'd seen and taken it, would see, like, and take again. She had no doubt of this. There were other wives whom she must join. They and their children. She must become part — perhaps a resented part — of the household they made up. She forced herself, for the first time, to think about them. How many were there?

There was Michal, Saul's daughter. But had not Saul taken

her away from David during the days when King Saul was mad with jealousy for the young man? He had — and Michal had found another husband and been happy. Then David got her back. Why? To show that he could? Or to strengthen his position by becoming once again son-in-law to King Saul? These new thoughts of David's calculation were troubling. Phaltiel — this was the name of the other husband — had followed Michal in tears, their loving household disregarded, shattered by David's assertion of power, Michal helpless to exert her will. Many had seen poor Phaltiel, heedless of his lost dignity, face wet with tears, his mouth a cave of grief, pathetically trailing after the carriage sent to fetch Michal. Michal, so they said, white, like a ghost, staring out from the back of the carriage. Michal would be there. Bathsheba would meet her. They would both remember the dear husbands that they'd lost.

Michal had been there on the day the Ark arrived in the City. Bathsheba had also been there, a small child at the time, hanging on to her father's hand in the surging, noisy, ululating crowd. She saw nothing of the Ark or of the King and held tightly to her father's hand so as to avoid being trampled. What she remembered of that day was how it had turned into a feast. King David had decreed that bread and wine and meat should be given to the whole population; distribution points had been hurriedly organised and everyone pressed towards the one nearest to them. She remembered clutching her small loaf, sucking at it, and being told that it was the gift of the King. Later, when she was much older, she had heard that Michal had stood apart from the day's jubilation, rigid and disapproving. Only now did Bathsheba wonder why.

Then there was Abigail. Strong, beautiful Abigail, her hair like a lion's mane and a mind that was in itself a lion, sinewy and decisive. Who did not know of her? She too had lost a husband, though Nabal of Carmel was not a husband many wives would mourn. As a child, Bathsheba had loved to hear the story of Abigail. How, in the days of King Saul, when David and his men had been living as outlaws, they — six hundred of them and hungry — had come across Nabal's men shearing Nabal's sheep. They had not assaulted Nabal's men as they might have done, but treated them courteously; guarded them. (*Who from? Themselves of course.*) Then, when they asked the wealthy Nabal for the provision they had not exacted under the duress they might have applied, they expected that Nabal would treat them as royally as they deserved. But Nabal, far from rewarding David and his followers for their forbearance, refused to give them anything. *Who is this David, son of Jesse the Bethlehemite?* was what he'd said.

David was poised to exact the hospitality that Nabal had refused: to exact it most terribly, with all the strength he had so far refrained from using. His hungry men were more than ready. Some of them had been baffled by David's earlier command to refrain from stealing from Nabal's store. Stupid Nabal — stupid like his name — not realising what or who he was up against.

It was then that Abigail — Nabal's splendid wife — had climbed onto a donkey and ridden out to where David and his men had gathered, preparing to descend on Nabal's household and slaughter every living part of it. Abigail would have been among the slaughter. They all watched her — this courageous, magnificent woman — ride down to the bottom of the valley, seated on a pale donkey, with behind her a troop of servants, laden with all the provision her husband had denied: food for a feast and plenty of it — bread, wine, sheep, corn, raisins, and fig-cakes. Those who had seen her riding towards them still spoke of this moment and those who had not seen always felt that they had.

The clever woman put a distance between herself and her husband. She addressed David using words as splendid and as supple as her form. It was not she who had met David's messengers and turned them away empty-handed; she would never have done or agreed to such a thing. She honoured David as one whose life was bound up with the will of YHWH and she believed it to be the will of YHWH that she prevent the bloodshed David now planned. She spoke with authority and David was struck both by the words and by their author.

The next day Nabal made himself drunk, feasting his own men as he had not David's. This was when Abigail — whose contempt for her husband was such that she could hardly bear to go near him — revealed to him what she had done and that David, son of Jesse the Bethlehemite, was a great warrior whose army was poised to destroy Nabal and all that was his. The nasty little man had shrivelled in fear. This fear and nothing else was the cause of Nabal's death that night. That is what they said.

David did not forget Abigail. Not her courage, not her eloquence, and certainly not her beauty. When Nabal's death was proclaimed (it being understood that David had no hand in it) David sent servants to Abigail to fetch her. She took five women with her and rode to him again. David made her his wife.

How small is the space between admiration and envy! Bathsheba had never even glimpsed Abigail, but she had long admired the woman of this story: the astute way in which she deployed her beauty; her self-possession, her independence, her wit. Abigail had not belonged to Nabal — no more than

Bathsheba would belong to David — her spirit was free of him. But now Bathsheba's admiration for the other woman was qualified by a fear; that when she met Abigail as a sister (for that was what a fellow wife might be) her own light would fade beside the Carmelite's strong splendour. Catching herself, Bathsheba resolved never to cross that small space which would lead her to envy. As a beautiful woman she had already known too much of that sour and joy-annulling force, so often directed towards herself. She would admire Abigail, appreciate her, learn from her if she could.

There were other wives too — Ahinoam of Jezreel whom David married at the same time as Abigail; Maakah, Haggith, Abital, Eglah. There would also be concubines. But he had not said, *You will be one of the several women to whom I offer my protection and from whom in return I expect submission and availability.* He had said, *You will be my crown, my perfecting.* She did not know what to think, only that she had little choice.

—

When she had cradled her womb in uncertainty and fear, two roads had shown themselves to her: the road of the outcast, the mad woman living at the edges of human life, scrabbling with her hands to find food for herself and the child no father would own. This road led to Miriam, smashed to death by rocks and stones, her child forcibly removed from her desperately clutching arms. Uriah's death had made this future the more probable. It had also made it more acceptable.

But now she was placed securely on the other road. Of course it was good that the King would make her his wife and own their child. But the reality was without the splendour that she had once only dared to glimpse. The reality was always the next action, the next encounter, the next small difficulty or answered need.

More difficult than the knowledge of existing wives was the thought that there would surely be more — for does not a king display his kingship in his garland of wives? How would she one day make way — and with grace — to the younger and lovelier woman who would surely supplant her? Might she be required to groom and instruct such a woman in the ways of pleasing the husband she would come to know?

These thoughts were luxuries. She did not forget that what mattered most was the safety of her child, and though she felt no gladness and much apprehension, the terror that had teased her was gone. She was going to take her place in a different family. The other wives would be her sisters. She would not triumph over them.

She gave Safi, sister of her heart, most of her cloths and blankets. It had hurt her to conceal the true history of her situation from Safi, but she knew it could not be told. Safi had marvelled that her friend was known personally to the King but she assumed that the King had met Bathsheba to condole her on her husband's death. She was not surprised that the King, having met her beautiful friend, should have wanted to gather her in marriage. Bathsheba felt the magnificence she was going towards as a chill weight from which nothing was going to rescue her.

PROPHET

1

It would be hard to estimate his age by looking at him. He could have been anything between thirty and ninety. A small and compact man, his face was lined with the fine lines that — especially in these desert parts — do not necessarily denote great age so much as habits of attention and far seeing. The lines at the outer edges of his eyes showed that he often looked into what lay beyond. The lines that fanned out from the corners of his mouth told that he was a man who could laugh.

David couldn't remember a time when Nathan had just turned up. Usually it was he who would either go to the prophet or send for him. He did this when he was unsure which path to take; when, having questioned YHWH directly through the ephod, he had received no answer. Then he would turn to the prophet whose access to knowledge of YHWH's will always seemed clear. That was the prophet's job: being clear about YHWH.

Nathan was no less a prophet than Samuel had been, but his demeanour was very different. If you met Samuel you could not think him anything other than a prophet or a mad man. Everything about him announced that he lived in obedience to laws others could only guess at. Nathan, by contrast, could appear an ordinary, simple man.

On the occasions when David had gone to Nathan, he

had made his way on his own. Travelling thus in solitude seemed a necessary discipline, adjunct to these consultations; on the return journey the solitude gave David an opportunity to ponder what he had heard. The prophet lived in the hills about half a day's journey away. There was a village nearby, but Nathan's house was a little apart, up a steep track into which stone steps had been set by Nathan himself. Each time he had occasion to visit the prophet David was freshly struck by the efficiency of this man who was so close to YHWH. Well-set steps and an orderly garden, arranged in neat terraces; those terraces draped with vines. A natural stream had been dammed and diverted to create irrigation channels and make the most of valuable silt for the crops. The vegetables planted there were always beautifully tended, orderly, and flourishing. This was not some transparent ascetic but a man confident in his handling of the world's stuff. The wine he poured for David was good.

It was a surprise to hear that Nathan had arrived, unsummoned. It must be, David assumed, that the prophet had reason to come to him now as petitioner. Mantling himself in benevolence, he asked his manservant to show Nathan into the audience room.

The prophet prostrated himself before the King.

The King tapped him on the shoulder to signal that he should rise. He pointed out a seat to Nathan, who ignored this and began instead to pace the length of the room. David kept silent, thinking that this restlessness on Nathan's part must be the prelude to prophecy.

I have a story which requires your judgement.

The King nodded; fidgeted for a moment with his robe, spreading it over the cushion he was seated on, admiring the zig-zag pattern of the cloth now it was smoothed from its creases. He turned to give Nathan his full attention. He liked a story.

'Tell me your story.'

There were two men who lived near to each other in the same city. One of the men was very wealthy — he had many flocks and herds and all were well-fed and sleek, grazing on the rich grasses of his land. The other man was poor: he had no livestock and no property from which to acquire wealth. All he had was one little ewe lamb whom he loved as if she were his daughter. This lamb was a member of his household and was fed at his table. At night he cradled her while he slept. One day a traveller arrived at the house of the rich man and requested hospitality. The rich man, who had the power that comes from wealth to impose his will with ease, not wanting to reduce his own stock by even a single head of sheep, exacted from the poor man his one ewe lamb. He took the poor man's darling from him; slaughtered her, and butchered her in order to feast his guest …

Nathan stopped speaking. He looked closely at the King who had risen from his seat in fury, not able to contain his indignation.

'Is this story true? Who is it? Bring him to me and I will punish him, this pitiless, arrogant man. He will be forced to make restitution, and then — then he must die. Such a man does not deserve to live.'

Nathan's gaze did not falter. The passion of the King's words seemed not to shake him. He remained silent until the King at last returned and held his gaze.

'Who is it?'

'The man is you.'

Nathan had spoken quietly, but with unmistakeable clarity. The only thing that was mistakeable was whether his words had been heard or merely thought. David continued as if he had not heard, as if the thought had been inserted into the flow of his own thoughts and he were attempting to muffle it.

His welling anger now turned on Nathan. Couldn't the prophet hear the justice in what David had said? That he was ready to do whatever it took to restore rightness? He would do it if it took a whole army to enforce it. Wasn't that enough?

But Nathan stood his ground, unmoved by David's bluster, and David felt a shaft of something like fear pass through him. He did not understand Nathan's meaning, but something of the prophet's intention reached into him and clamped his bowels. Nathan waited to see if there was a stirring of recognition in David but saw only a fearful incomprehension. The fear, however, was the beginning.

'I say again, that man is you. You are that pitiless, arrogant man who stole from the poor man his one and only darling. You are the man whom you have sworn to punish. You are the man who you say does not deserve to live. YHWH says this: I made you my anointed one, the King of all Israel. I preserved you in the wilderness, rescued you from Saul, established you in this place, and gave you Saul's wives. I gave you Israel and Judah and would have given you much more for the asking. Why, after I have done this for you, have you treated me with contempt? Why, when you had so much from me, did you steal from another man? You took the wife of Uriah the Hittite — the only wife he had — and got her with child. Then, as if this first sin were not enough, you killed Uriah, making the Ammonites your weapon. In consequence I say now: because you have done these things, the violence of weapons will always attend your house; and because you have taken the wife — the only wife — of Uriah the Hittite to be your wife, I will take your wives from you and give them to other men who will copulate with them on the rooftops, for all to see. All this shall take place in the full light of day. For you did what you did in secret, but I bring all things to light.'

David heard the words but did not yet absorb their weight. Was Uriah not his servant; his soldier, vowed to do for him whatever he, his king, decreed? Wasn't Bathsheba equally his subject? He had chosen her. He could have any woman he chose.

Nathan seemed to be reading his thoughts. His look said, *Yet you took Uriah's wife. His only one.*

Something in David sagged before giving way. As in a dream where he was on a ladder attempting to escape a burning house, he felt the rungs supporting his feet collapse, delivering him back into a hell of flame. All exits were closed to him. He was trapped. Powerless. Never had he felt so small. Not when, as the youngest child, he'd played under the table while his tall brothers ate, or when he'd hidden from them all behind a rock and they failed to find him, perhaps even to search for him. Now he was as small as an ant. Smaller. The hills that he loved crowded in on him, ready to crush him. His splendid palace was as flimsy as the papery cocoon of a wasp. He was barely aware of Nathan's presence; only of the vast condemnation that surrounded him where once there had been an almost infinite goodwill.

Nathan was silent. The great wrong that had been named filled the room with its presence leaving no space for speech. Now that he recognised it, David wondered how he could have avoided its crushing presence for so long. Beside the height, breadth, and weight of this wrong, Goliath of Gath was a crumb and he, David, less than the smallest particle of dust.

The moment when he had seen her first, washing herself by the stream, had been in daylight. There she had been, thinking herself unobserved, caressed by the sun and the water that bathed her. He had joined the sun and the water to examine, caress, and enter her in his thoughts. In his mind he had copulated with her there on his rooftop just as YHWH had said his wives would now do, with other men. From so easy an act of thought, all this had unfolded. He saw how his initial desirous thought had enlarged and grown progressively more dense: from thought to imagination to act. And then to another act; an act to undo the consequences of the first wrong act. Only it didn't. There was, he realised now, an uncontrollable multiplication of acts all issuing from his initial movement, the movement of thought that he had acted upon. The scene of his wives and the other men openly copulating on the rooftops was both the travesty and the direct consequence of this first thought. How could he not have seen it before?

At last, in a voice that hardly seemed his own — for who was he now that he was no longer righteous and beloved of YHWH? — he murmured, 'Truly I have sinned against YHWH.'

His lips barely parted as he spoke. Sweet singer that he was, a man whose voice could carry as far as the sound of Joab's conch, his words now were barely audible. Nathan, who had heard well enough, turned his head as if to catch what was said, requiring David to speak again, with more conviction than before.

'Truly, I have sinned against YHWH.'

Nathan bowed his head in assent. He waited.

The hills that had been David's home and his succour seemed to be surrounding him in deep disapprobation. If he flung himself onto their flanks they would no longer be merciful to him. If he crawled into a cave to hide, his sin would still have been found out and the world would be filled with the knowledge of it. Only in this truth, *I have sinned against YHWH*, was there any safety. From this speaking, and from Nathan's assent, a speck of peace. A speck so tiny it provided no island of rest and yet it made a difference. That tiny speck of peace, a dot of light in a great darkness, was not swallowed up. Instead, like the vibration that comes from the clapper of a great bell, sweeping clean the air it strokes, it created a clearing. A small safe place on which to stand.

Truly I have sinned against YHWH.

Nathan listened to the clearing and to the sweeter silence that these words ushered in. He waited while it swelled and grew; until truth occupied the room. The room had become dark during Nathan's stay. No servant had dared to enter it unbidden in order to light the lamps. Only a little light now came in through the windows, showing the dark outline of the hills. The two men faced each other. No one looking in could easily have guessed which of them was the King.

Then, with the air of a man who is putting the finishing touches to a piece of business and is in haste to move on to its realisation, Nathan said, 'YHWH says: You will not die because of this. But because you have dishonoured my name in the sight of my enemies, the child that Bathsheba is carrying will die.'

He walked out without formalities, not waiting to be conducted.

2

Bathsheba heard that the prophet had arrived. His arrival had caused a stir of anxiety. The end of the siege at Rabbath-Ammon had brought about a more peaceful situation, but prophecy often signalled trouble. The household was aware that the prophet was inside the King's House. While they continued with their usual activities all those who knew of Nathan's arrival were waiting for him to leave so they could begin to discover the purpose of his visit.

Bathsheba, her condition now very evident and her back feeling the strain, was resting on a low wall in the shade when Nathan stepped out. Though she was shawled and in shadow, he was immediately conscious of her presence and turned to speak to her.

'Not long to wait now.'

His words startled her. Though her body felt her pregnancy, her mind was occupied in adjusting to her new surroundings and situation. From the prophet — if he were to notice her at all — she might have expected reproof, not a neutral observation.

He continued, 'Your life is important. Don't forget that. Don't think that because you are young and a woman you are powerless. Send word if you need to speak to me. I will do my best to guide you. You and your child.'

Until this encounter she had known little about him. No one had seemed able to describe him. She'd heard someone say, 'You wouldn't think he was a prophet.' Compared with Samuel, Nathan was ordinary. You wouldn't look twice at him if you passed him in the market. Yet to Bathsheba, now she had met him, he was remarkable. Not so much in what she noticed about him as in his own capacity to notice. He had recognised her, as surely as if someone had introduced her to him by name. He had spoken of her child and, in doing so, reminded her in the gentlest way of that child's existence. She felt that he had called her back to her life and welcomed her into it. She had seen mothers seated or standing in a group, talking among themselves, seemingly absorbed, but all the time aware of the movements of their small children playing nearby; whenever a child deviated from a path of safety, the mother would break away from the conversation, lift up her child, and set it down again, turned now towards a new, safer, direction. This is how she experienced Nathan's effect on her.

———

No one was able to guess the purpose of Nathan's visit, but after it Bathsheba's new husband appeared to avoid her. The other wives, observing this, welcomed her more, as one who shared their situation. Bathsheba was content not to see David. There would be more years to come. She became curious about her situation and what it would bring: what satisfactions might be available to her in this new life. At last she wholly recognised that the baby she was carrying was David's and at last was glad this was so. It dawned on her that her child might be a king. That blue dye which she had wanted for his shawl

149

might now be within reach. She knew little about it other than that it was very very costly. She would ask the stately Ahinoam, who, though married to David after he had married Michal, occupied the position of Senior Wife. Had Ahinoam included blue in the cloth she had woven for her first son, Amnon?

Bathsheba had woken up and the others woke up to her existence. In spite of her smiles and inviting beauty she had seemed strangely apart, but now she was welcomed and included. Nogah, who had worked in the King's House from the beginning, made Bathsheba and the unborn child her special care. Each morning she would bring her a cup of almond milk from nuts she had soaked, pressed, and strained herself. 'Good for baby,' she said. Nogah's status among the household servants was like Ahinoam's among the wives. The sudden blossoming of Nogah's affection for Bathsheba had the effect of releasing a like concern among the others who lived and worked in the King's House.

She had been given a room not far from the King's apartments. Each of the wives had separate quarters where she lived with her children. The King would visit as and when he chose. Sometimes a wife would be invited or required to join him in his own rooms; to prepare his food and share it with him. Share his bed. The children, as they grew older, would come without their mothers and moved with great freedom around the buildings. To some extent the mothers acted as mothers to each other's children as well as to their own. Yet there was rivalry too as each was ambitious for her child.

The young men ignored this rivalry and crashed around as one, indulged wherever they went by their mothers, the household servants, and their father the King. They put Bathsheba in mind of a small herd of antelope and she brightened when she heard the clatter of their feet. Adonijah was a clown, forever making her laugh with his imitations and exaggerations. Absalom, handsome as his father and without the roughness of age, made her blush. The eldest, Amnon, was quieter, less ready to smile. There was an intensity about him which made her wonder what he was to become. Though he moved as part of the antelope herd, she sensed he would prefer to be independent of the others.

Then there was the girl, Tamar. Very beautiful in her early womanhood, but shy, surrounded as she was by so many exuberant young men. She was drawn to Bathsheba, so much younger than her own mother, Maacah. She found words difficult and hated the way in which her beauty seemed to proclaim her and shout. Her hair, with its burnish of deep red in it, was much bolder and louder than she was. She kept it covered as much as possible and withdrew in shame and torment when attention was drawn to her. With Bathsheba she often sat in companionable silence — the older woman providing her with a sense of safety. Bathsheba expected nothing of her but was glad to be a sister to the girl. Tamar liked to massage Bathsheba's feet and the feet, tired from their unaccustomed load, welcomed the kindness.

3

David could not face Bathsheba during the remaining days of her pregnancy. He didn't trust himself to conceal what he knew — that their child would not live; he flinched at the thought of her deluded gladness — deluded because of the wrong he had implicated her in. Most of all he flinched at the knowledge that while she would suffer, he would be spared; for what is more hard to bear than the love of YHWH?

His first knowledge of that love, of being singled out as one favoured by the Lord, was bound up in his memory with a sense of shame. It was the day that the prophet Samuel had emptied a hornful of oil over his head while his father and six brothers watched, silent and — so it had seemed to him — afraid.

He had run home from his work with the sheep in the hills, excited to be telling his brothers about a bird he had seen — a large, circling one that was not vulture or eagle or any bird he knew. He was looking forward to the meal they would eat together soon for he was very hungry. He had crashed into their home, yodelling his familiar, self-invented greeting and was met by silence. When he saw the strange man seated there and the whole family seated around, he blushed. The stranger had stood up and said, 'Here he is. This is he.'

The stranger had walked up to David and clasped his head

in both hands, making a cap of his hands and forcing the boy
down to the floor. The pressure could not be resisted for the
man's hands were very strong. David had felt a kind of darkness
coming over him, as if the hands were a cowl covering his head
completely. It felt like being compressed into nothingness, or
something so dense and so dark it amounted to nothing.

Then the oil. The man, still holding David's head down
forcibly with his left hand, poured oil over that head. So much
of it, it ran down over David's eyes, making them sting, over
and into his ears so he felt deaf. It ran down his neck, under
the opening of his tunic, tickling his chest.

At last the man let go and David was able to stand. His
father and all his brothers were still standing there, watching,
looking awkward. No one met his gaze, not even the man
who'd just been handling him. He felt wretched. In spite of
being hungry and looking forward to the meal, he wanted only
to run out back into the hills.

But the man was a guest. A meal — far better than usual
and requiring meat — must be served and all this would take
time. A calf had been slaughtered and was being butchered.
He was relieved when his father took their guest outside, but
even then his brothers avoided him. As soon as his father and
the man had left the house he went to the well and drew out
water to clean himself, but his hair remained full of oil and his
ears still rang with it. He shoved his forefingers into his ears
and waggled them to loosen the oil.

His mother, brittle with tension as she prepared and assembled the feast for their guest, appeared to be angry. But David
was hungry and didn't want to wait until the meat was cooked.
Barely looking at him, his mother jerked her head towards the
bread she had just baked. He took some of that and gnawed

on it, his mother's anger infecting him and becoming his own, mixed with the misery he felt at the sudden, inexplicable, change in the air of his home.

More hours passed before the meal came around. He sat with all the family, his brothers still refusing to meet his gaze. But the man — the Prophet Samuel, as his mother had crossly revealed — addressed him kindly now and passed meat to him in a way that indicated favour.

Nevertheless what he felt was closer to shame. To be so singled out and set apart from his brothers. Even Jesse, his father, seemed embarrassed by the incident. After Samuel left it was never spoken of at home and David, though he remembered the horror of it, had no way of thinking about it and went on with his life as if it had never occurred.

—

Awkwardness, confusion, uncertainty, an intense discomfort at being singled out as different. Nothing in the experience had felt like honour. Since then he had accommodated those singular events — now part of the story that was told of him — into a sense of himself that accepted his chosenness without difficulty.

This present singling out by Nathan, by YHWH, was different altogether. The wretchedness he experienced now was not born of ignorance, which would later be translated into understanding and something like pride. This time he had intended wrong, acted on the intention, and been found out.

He knew that YHWH loved him far more than He had ever loved Saul — this knowledge had strengthened his sense of freedom. Even when he was in grave danger, dodging Saul's

spear, hiding in a cave or in the wilderness of Ziph, a sense
of blessedness and deep safety clung to him. When Michal,
and then Jonathan, had helped him to escape their father
Saul's murderous rage, he had been aware of the urgent need
to act swiftly. It was not that the dangers were not acute and
real but that he trusted his choices and decisions to be good
ones. Within the freedom conferred by blessedness he danced,
knowing that his feet would always find firm ground beneath
them, that he would not twist his foot in roots or fox holes;
that, as he whirled and leapt, branches would not catch and
tear his flesh.

Had Saul done as he had done he would not have been
allowed to live. Saul got away with nothing. For each small
deviation from the will of YHWH Saul suffered and was punished. But David could no longer feel the comfort of his own
rightness. He had lost all claim to it. YHWH's love for him was
stronger than anything he could do to earn it or shake it off.
He must now learn to bear it. He had never lacked certainty.
The sureness of aim that had guaranteed his success when the
stone flew through the air to embed itself in the giant's brow,
had till this moment been present in all his purposes. His will
had not failed him.

Bathsheba's luminous beauty had so resembled blessing,
he had taken her in the assumption that this choice too was
blessed by YHWH; almost that his own will were an indication
of the will of YHWH. He never felt the blessedness leave him.

But YHWH had never said, *Do whatever you want and
I shall bless it.* He had said, *I will give you the discernment to know
what is right and always to be able to choose it. When you do choose
it I will further you in this choice.* Now that he thought about
it, David realised that these words had been there for him to

hear from the beginning, but he had not been there to listen. Now when he stops to listen, there is only silence. Not the full, clear, ringing silence of holy prayerfulness, but a silence that was nothing. Blank and without texture.

He no longer knew himself. How could he then be husband to his new wife Bathsheba who seemed to look to the birth of their child with so much simple happiness? It was as much as he could do to get through the days with a semblance of his usual demeanour. It was as if he were imitating himself, and not doing it well. He made sure he was away from the King's House as much as possible, travelling to meet elders in every part of his kingdom and leaving those elders honoured, though baffled, as to the motive for his visit, since nothing of substance had been raised. Throughout this period, he lived in dread of the fulfilment of Nathan's prophecy.

4

The labour went on for a day and a night. She had begun, squatting down, with Nogah and another woman, Sara, supporting her on either side. After several hours like this, exhaustion led her to lean back, supported by Nogah's wide thighs. But rest was impossible while the child pressed to be born. She struggled onto all fours and pushed against an unyielding wall. The child seemed unable to budge and Bathsheba, biting on a twist of cloth held out by Nogah, not wanting to cry out, thought she would surely die. The other women, who were trying to assist her assistants, crowded her, making what was already impossible more so, blocking her way, stifling her. Then Nogah, who had been standing behind Bathsheba, got a glimpse of the baby.

'He's coming. He's on his way.'

Then, after a long moment of good-natured perplexity, the woman interpreted what was before her eyes. It was not a head crowning, proudly announcing the arrival of a new person to the world; not a brave little head about to emerge from this first great journey into the light, but a pair of pinched buttocks.

'He's the wrong way round.'

I don't care what way round he is. Get him out of me. Get me out of here.

Nogah was speaking to Sara in a low voice. She was explaining something. Then more loudly, to the other women whose panicky whispers were infecting the room, 'We don't need you here. Sara and I know what to do. We'll see that the queen delivers her son.'

Bathsheba caught the words 'her son' and was able to lift her head and say, 'A son? You can see?'

Sara giggled, 'Yes madam. You have a son for sure.'

It was not clear to Bathsheba who was trying to rid themselves of who. It was both of them together. She was pushing with all her strength. Her heart was pushing, pressing up against a wall that would not yield. The pain was more than she had ever known.

Nogah asked Sara to take over the role of supporting the queen's back, and Sara took the straining weight, occasionally wiping Bathsheba's brow with a cloth dipped in water. Nogah was attending to the emerging child.

'This is good,' she said, 'the buttocks have come through together. It is harder when one leg comes on its own. Now push, madam. Push harder than you have ever pushed in your life.'

Bathsheba did not know how to push any harder but she maintained the effort and something seemed to yield. She no longer had the cloth between her teeth and as she pushed she cried out. Her throat seemed to expel a living creature, a cry such as she had never made before which seemed to float free of her and fly from the room.

'Well done madam. Now we have the shoulders. Now I can safely pull a little.'

At last he was out. Poor parched, crumpled thing. Nogah handled him robustly, and with a practised familiarity. When she gave him to Bathsheba, laying him on her belly, still soaked with the sweat of her labour, Bathsheba experienced the exhausted satisfaction she had seen and envied in other new mothers.

5

He received regular reports during the long labour. When he heard that the child seemed not to want to be born he had settled into expecting a stillbirth. Every child he had fathered so far had lived, but he was familiar enough with stillbirths among sheep.

When eventually a woman came to him with the words, 'It is accomplished,' he understood her to be referring to Nathan's prophecy, as if she too were a prophet. But the woman had gone on, 'Do you want to see your new son and your wife? Your wife is asking for you. They are both very tired.'

It was then that he realised that all was still to do.

Or else, could Nathan have got it wrong? Was it possible that YHWH had granted him a reprieve? Could he, after all, get away with it? Yet when he went to Bathsheba who passed him the small wrapped thing that was his son, he saw how small the child was. The little body was all bunched up, as if the effort of pushing himself out, buttocks first, had concentrated the whole of his being into his upper body where it threatened to stifle him. His legs seemed to dangle, bloodless when compared to the dark birdlike chest, the fragile box of the ribs where the small heart worked. This hot little fist of flesh, summoned into independent life by the two of them, made him think of a baby bird, gasping for life as it lay on a slab of rock where it had fallen, the great mouth widening and narrowing with each beat of the heart; mouth big, eyes big, but body just a flimsy sack. A bird on a rock or an aborted animal destined not to survive. On the many occasions when he had tugged a new lamb into the world he was always struck by how fast the slippery bundle struggled onto its feet and began to make claims on the new environment. The few that couldn't just lay there, panting and exhausted. These he would leave out for the vultures.

He could do the same with this child: set him out on a rock for the big beaked birds to devour. Had he not done something like this with Uriah? This scrap of hot, incompetent flesh was an image of the man he had put in death's way. He had set him out for the vultures, making them — the raptors of Rabbath-Ammon — his instruments.

But the man he saw, limbs flailing, helpless on a rock under the sun, helpless before YHWH, was not the child Bathsheba had borne him, nor was it Uriah, brought down at Rabbath-Ammon. It was himself, naked and resourceless before YHWH. This sense of himself seemed to crush the breath from him. How could he breathe, how could he move, if every particle of air, every grain of dew that the winds carried were part of YHWH, pressing in on him?

For a moment he wanted to destroy the child who panted with such a remote determination, like a stranded fish. He could have picked him up and wrung or slapped the life out of him and there would have been an end to it. He himself would see to the fulfilment of Nathan's prophecy and get it over with.

He turned away from this image of his own murderousness, his face twisted in the effort to squeeze this knowledge of himself from his mind. Bathsheba mistook this look of pain and covered his dangerous hand with her own.

'If he will only take enough milk. With YHWH's help —
and all the help I have here — we will make him well.'

Her smile, so confiding, so proud in her achievement of
motherhood, felt an additional reproach. It was the look of
thorough gladness he had been wanting from her since he first
saw her in her solitude. Now, when she was ready to meet him,
he could only turn away, ashamed. All he could give his child
was his absence; the lack of his death-dealing presence.

6

Clumsily, crashingly, he fled the palace, moving like a bird that has flown indoors, bewildered by the obstacles it meets, desperately and almost blindly seeking the free air. When he got out of the palace he did not stop but plunged on into the hills, running as he had not run since boyhood, taking the tracks the animals had made (these being the best), making for a high cave which he had often used as a shelter in his shepherd days. A great slab of rock jutted out over the cave, the rock sparsely populated by the parched and delicate flowers that were able to root in the shallow earth that lay there. No one standing on that rock would guess that its dark underside provided a cool awning for a cave. A cave whose only access was through a round hole through which a person would need to lower himself, feet first. It was as if a large bird had pecked this hole to find a way out of a stone egg.

Someone was making his way briskly towards him. David stood on the rock and saw Mathur, his man, loyally following. But David experienced his presence in this, to him most secret, place as a rude intrusion. Anger welled up. He pushed it down.

'Leave me here to fast for the child. It may be that YHWH will grant him my appetite. I know where to find water. Tell no one where I have gone.'

He heard Mathur's departure across the dry grass; the

sound of his bare feet and his robes whisking down the hill side.

A small breeze carried the scents of the mountain herbs — juniper and thyme; the comfortable smell of animal dung. The day was sweet. He alone was not sweet. He carried his own poison within him. It would be consoling to think that the poison had been sucked out of the baby and into his own body — he did this once when his father had been bitten by a snake; he'd made a cut just above the swelling from the bite and sucked till his mouth was full of the bitter foulness and his father's flesh wrinkled and white. He had spat out the poison and rinsed his mouth and neither he nor his father were the worse. This time he knew that it was a poison in and from himself that had caused the baby's sickness: the baby had taken it in. If the baby died, would the father's guilt be buried with him, bundled up cleanly in the poor guiltless creature he had so carelessly begot? The baby would then become the scape-goat, innocent repository of another's sin. But it was clear to David that, though the baby had taken the poison into his small body, he hadn't, in doing so, removed it from the father.

He had found the cave by accident, years ago, in the course of searching for a missing lamb. The dark, just-large-enough-to-wriggle-into, entrance, irresistible to the young man he then was; an opportunity to try his body's prowess. He had found it empty, except for a few pieces of rubble that had tumbled into it over the years, and dry. Wonderfully dry. It would make a marvellous, secret store. Not that he had stored much there — just a bedroll and a simple two-note instrument he'd made from wood and sinew. This cave had once been like a place in his own heart, but he had not ventured into it for years.

Had kingship made him too fat? He pulled off his bracelets and then his robe. For a moment he stood, looking back in the direction he'd come from, down at the rooftops of his city, the cloths laid out to dry, the King's House with its green courtyards. Then up at the endless sky above him, a kite riding on a wind he could scarcely feel, looking down at the small life in the scrub. What had been instinct, to come here, whether to hide from the wrath of YHWH or to encounter it more fully, now became decision. He sat on the edge of the hole, his legs hanging down into it, feeling themselves already clasped by the cool darkness; then he dropped down, finding even now some small satisfaction in the fact that his body could still manage this.

It took time — it always had done — for his eyes to become accustomed to the darkness. For a while all he could see was the circle of light he had dropped through and the pale shaft, like a fat pillar, which descended from it. But gradually the sharp contrast between light and dark softened into something with texture, grain, gradation. The shadows contained contours which defined substance. The bedroll was still there where he'd left it, several years before. And the instrument, propped against the cave wall, waiting for him. The placid waiting of these inanimate objects was a surprise. It would have seemed less strange to him if they had been changed in ways that matched his own alteration from the boy he had been.

He lay himself down on the earth floor, inhaling its satisfying scent of dark spore. He lay there, face down, panting in relief to have got there. This now was his altar, this earth, this darkness. And in the cool of the cave his hot thoughts might quieten. His prayer might become something other than a cry. But for now, *Lord, hear me when I cry to you. Listen to my prayer: I have done great wrong.*

Naked he lay; a child before his father. His whole longing was for that father to reach out to him again — even if only to punish him since this would at least involve the touch of the father's hand.

7

The other wives knew how difficult the birth had been. The woman who had arrived at the palace overflowing with beauty, as if a golden light continually spilled from her soft plump skin, had become pale and drawn from exhaustion and loss of blood. Seeing her like this made it easier to be kind to her. She was not Ashtaroth, glowing with the light of the moon. She was not a goddess. The other wives — all, save Michal, experienced in motherhood — offered Bathsheba advice, showed her how best to stroke the baby's abdomen to help the milk stay down. They showed her how to hold him, how to lay him down to help him sleep. Tamar stood quietly by, ready to do Bathsheba's bidding, holding the baby rather awkwardly when permitted, rocking him in a rapt, determined way. When Bathsheba was alone with him she would feed her eyes on her son's eyes, delighting in the way the little red fist encircled her finger, watching the tiny tongue push forward to the entrance of the mouth, dabbing stickily at what lay beyond in search of food. He would gaze back at her with solemn, dark eyes; mother and son sufficient to the other.

—

When she had turned to her husband and passed him the small weight of their child Bathsheba had looked for an answering gladness. She had never borne a child before and the fact that she had now done this wonderful thing was thrilling. In spite of her exhausted appearance, she felt as vigorous and bold as a lioness. If her earlier days here at the King's House had been marked by her timidity, she now felt entirely within her rights to command whatever was needed. Ahinoam had told her that the blue dye she craved for her son's blanket was indeed fabulously costly — the product of rare specific seashells and much labour. At the time Bathsheba's natural humility had led her to dismiss the possibility of asking for this. Now she felt almost imperious. It was as if the intimate blood she had shed during the long hours of labour had mixed itself into the mortar of the walls and established her there. She had massaged the buttery vernix that coated her new baby, loving the smell of it on him and on her hands. If her husband had come to her at that moment she would have smeared him with it too; she felt boldly, ambitiously lascivious — in sharp contrast to what the other women had led her to expect.

But when David had come to her and held the bundle that was their child his expression was taut and joyless. When he smiled at her it was with his mouth only, not with his eyes which could be so luminously expressive. It checked her joy somewhat that he seemed anxious to be away. When she heard that he had gone into the hills to pray for the child's welfare and was not expected to return for some days she was angry at what felt like a rebuff. But she could wait. She had the child. She would invite Safi to the King's House. Perhaps Safi could find a home with them here.

The child needed a name. A name would strengthen his life. Though she could not name him publicly without his father's presence, the name she whispered to her child in secret, pressing her mouth against the fine skin that covered his head, was Abimelech, for his father was the king. What if that father was absent? She was exhausted. An exhausted lioness. She had not absorbed the extent to which Nogah and the other more experienced women feared for the child. To her, who had never before succeeded in producing any child, he was perfect. With him (expertly swaddled by Nogah) in a cradle near her side, she slept a triumphant sleep.

8

For David, weariness and the gradual quietening of distress that came from lying still. He pulled himself up from the earth and settled with his back to the cave wall. His thoughts returned to what he had recently left. It seemed to him that the child was a banner announcing his guilt. It had burned him to see his wrongness so written for all to read in the faulty flesh of the little mangled thing that had been born.

But the child was not after all dead. The thin life that panted in him might yet enlarge and grow. David had expected a dead child and YHWH had confounded this expectation. Might it be that YHWH had changed his mind and would spare the child? There was all the difference in the world between life — any life at all — and the silence of death. He resolved to do all that was in his power to preserve and support that life. To earn its preservation if he could. By prayer and fasting. The old way. No tricks. No techniques. Only a hunger to meet his Lord again without this disabling shame. The vitality he denied himself, fasting here in the dark of this cave, would be dedicated to his new, unnamed, son. He would pray that this new boy could take his place amongst the healthy, boisterous herd of children he had bred.

It had been instinct rather than plan to make for this cave. It was where he used to go when he wanted to hide. This time, he had come in order to make himself — if possible — able to bear being seen again. Now that it was his dwelling it felt different; its qualities held another weight. As his eyes accustomed themselves to the dim light he thought he could see the beginnings of colour in the stone that enveloped him. The cave's high opening tipped towards the east and tomorrow the morning sun would again lay a narrow carpet of light upon its floor. At this time — late morning — he could see the pinks and the yellows of the rock walls, the layered gradations of colour, the dark streaks of ore and the places that shone where water seeped through. When the sun moved on, it left him in a shadowy place in which he was not sure if the colours he discerned were remembered or seen.

He would acquaint himself with the interior of this cave. It was just one small part of his land and he resolved to know it well. A patch of rock no wider than the span of his hand — full of distinctions, changes of texture, grittinesses, and whorled smoothness. Here was a feast for his attention: if he could learn the contours of this temporary home, his capacity to know would be expanded. He could never know all that belonged in his kingdom of Israel and Judah, but he could put himself in the posture of learning, could teach himself a manner of attending so that in the future he would be apt. Nothing was of no account, nothing negligible.

He began to investigate the rock walls with outstretched palm and finger pads. He investigated with the kind of listening sensitivity he would employ to caress a loved body or wait to know where to place his fingers for the musical note to sound true. There was so much information here and he had ample time to be informed. One area of rock was pitted with crevices. Caves within the cave; an infinity of worlds, such as the sky offers.

He could not attempt to hide from YHWH — there was no doing that — but here perhaps he might meet Him unobserved. He knew — though how had he come to forget? — that everything he did was in the sight of YHWH: YHWH had made him wondrously — sinew, bone, cartilage, organs. His speaking tongue, his lively, headstrong penis, his glistening kidneys, seat of the conscience that had slept for all those driven months, his bowels that spasmed with remorse and pity. Many many times he had seen a man cut open; had been the one to do the cutting. He had seen the mess of a man with his guts spilled onto the earth. It still had the power to turn his stomach. But the big birds were always pleased; they would pick a man as clean as they would a sheep that had rolled onto its back and been unable to right itself. YHWH made use of fallen men.

It would be easy to get lost in his troubled thoughts and allow the cave's darkness to dissolve the grammar of distinction. In order to train and somewhat contain his attention he began to collect some of the small pieces of rock that had fallen into the cave. His eyes had by now adapted to the diminished light and he was able to examine each piece quite closely as he set it down at the base of the pillar of light that poured down from the cave's entrance. He worked with the grave purposefulness of a child gathering together materials for play.

He knelt to go over his pile of stones. He had seen traders do the same when they had emptied their pouches of gems; the rough restless way the experienced hands would sort out dross from value, clearing away what was chipped and flawed with the side of a hand, scooping up the rest to deliver it to the cloth that displayed the wares. Here there was no cloth of contrasting colour to set off the stones, only the disc of light where the sun fell; but there was a formation of rock within the cave that suggested a table or an altar. This is where David set his stones.

—

Not one of them was large; a few were smooth (though what winds or waters could have rubbed them so was a mystery); most were faceted and jagged. He did not know how long he would need to be here or how he would know that it was time to leave, but he decided to select a minimum of seven stones, so there would be one for each day of YHWH's week. He would arrange them in a circle. His criterion for selection was that each stone should look as if it had been formed with intention. It did not need to be beautiful or symmetrical, but it did need to be a thing complete in itself. He rubbed each one between thumb and forefinger, gauging its quality and fitness for his purpose. He took the weight of each in one palm and then in the other, tipping it from palm to palm several times, experiencing the different ways in which right and left palm could appraise. He was good at this. All those years of selecting stones for his slingshot had given his palms a knowledge he could never have put into words. Whilst he handled the stones the turbulence in his mind quietened. He felt a return of the clarity by which decision translates into action and was able to select seven stones without difficulty, discarding the others. If necessary, he would choose more later but for now he would use the stones he had selected to stimulate and to carry his prayer. Perhaps the stones would even do some of the prayer-work for him.

He would begin with something tasty. A stone that resembled a cut kidney: a kidney still nestled in protective fat. The cut face was smooth to the touch except that at its centre — which in a kidney would contain a knot of tubes — there were the contours of something that had lived. It might even be that the once-living thing was still there, encased in a lustrous mica. It was raised like a scar, but symmetrical. Beautiful. He could not make out what kind of a creature it was — an insect perhaps or a fish. The way in which the stone held this delicate creature suggested protection. Only in this dark and private place could the stone be split as it had been, the veil drawn aside and the jewel at its heart revealed.

He returned to the place where he had sat before, noticing as he did so how quickly he had become attached to this area of the cave. It was not where he had tended to sit on previous occasions. He shivered. It had been instinct — as well as practical — to enter the cave naked, but it would distract him to be cold. He had more to think about than how cold he was. He pulled his robe over his head and wrapped the woollen cloth securely around himself.

Fingering the welted stone settled him. He had leisure here not just to review the last year when he had so lost his footing — but the years before. Was there a moment when everything had changed? As it had changed for Saul. Yes. *Think of Saul*. He seemed to have been thinking about Saul for most of his life. This split, partly beautiful stone could stand for him.

—

Is that you, David my son? Are you there? He was suddenly ambushed by the memory of Saul calling to him. The exact tones of Saul's voice, its depths, and the cracks within. A voice as dark and fissured as the cave he sat in now. How is it that the voice — that least substantial part of a person — can persist in the memory long after the image of the physical presence has faded? The memory of that voice, those words, as sharp as if he were actually hearing them, washed over him and brought tears. It was a part of him, threading round his heart like a marbling of veins. He could no longer quite recall — except in dreams — the tones of his real father, Jesse, but Saul's voice never seemed far from him. Now it came like a hand on his shoulder to offer a father's comfort.

There had been two occasions, during the long period of their enmity, when David could have killed Saul easily. He was that close. If he'd done so he would have killed the father of his dearest friend. Reason enough not to kill Saul, though Saul had regularly wished David dead. But David had made quite sure that Saul knew that when he'd had the chance to kill him, he'd chosen not to.

You could cut Saul down the middle and find in one half all magnanimity and fellowship and in the other a wild mistrust. Even those he loved best, like his son, Jonathan, could arouse that distrust. But David had been no more able to cut away the fearful, unlovely part of Saul than he could dismantle the stone he was fingering now.

He remembered the day he first came to Saul, on the donkey that Jesse had loaded with bread and wine and a beautiful white kid. Gifts for the King which left not much room on the donkey for the boy he was — he'd had to wedge and wriggle himself into the saddle. It had not been many weeks since Samuel's terrifying descent on the family at Bethlehem, singling him out, marking him for a distinct but unspecified destiny.

He was placed in charge of the King's armour. What a job for a boy! When Saul first showed him round his armoury he had barely been able to suppress a gleeful grin. He had been biting the inside of his cheeks to reform his face into solemnity while the King introduced him to the spears that lined one wall, the great leather shields that hung on another, the wide swords and the small daggers. All gleaming — and his the task of keeping them so — all breathing out that dark and spreading scent of metal and leather and warfare. A little later he was shown the rooms on rooms of weapons for foot-soldiers; the enormous enclosures where the chariots were parked. Rows of lances, dormant and bristling.

He loved his job as Saul's armour-bearer. He liked to rise early and go down to the armoury to make sure all was in place, all clean, blades sharp. The stone he was handling now had an acute edge. He rubbed it with a calloused thumb, recalling how he used to test those blades. *Readiness — the first rule of warfare. Remember that.* Saul's words. Not to be anticipating trouble at each instant but, when trouble arises, to be able to move fast and to lay your hands on whatever is needed. Soon David had no need to be told which weapon to select. He would pick out the axe, the knife, the bow as the King required it. Saul had only to reach out a hand for David to supply what was needed.

Music was the other side. He had played for his own family. In the evenings, when it was cold and they made a fire under the stars, David would take out the first of the many instruments he'd made and sing them a story as he plucked the notes. Sometimes he would rock between two low notes, sometimes he would pluck them together in a chord. He could stroke a note so gently that his hearers did not know that they heard, only that they felt a deep soothing of their being. His father Jesse used to say that if they'd had fur David's playing would have stroked it the right way till all lay smooth and comfortable.

Remembering this, David laughed with happiness that Jesse had, after all, made himself heard there in the cave. There was the instrument — one of his first — propped up where he had left it years before. The strings were slack of course, but the horn pegs were in place to tauten them into tune again. He had composed his first psalms to YHWH on this rough instrument, never doubting that he was worthy to sing to his Lord.

The times when Saul had most needed David's playing were exactly those times when the most natural response was to keep clear of him and leave him to his dangerous wretchedness. David had had no more desire than anyone else to stay close to him on these occasions, but time and again it was his music that turned Saul's mood. Other members of the household would seek David out; beg him to come and play. Sometimes he sang — not words but sounds — developing his song from the shepherds' calls he had improvised in conversation with his charges, sounds which the animals would respond to though many hills away. Saul responded to these sounds. The troubled creature he had become seemed to recognise a voice that called him home.

It struck David that it was his ability to anticipate and meet the King's needs and moods as they occurred that had led to a situation in which Saul assumed that David's entire existence was dedicated to him. This perfect service was, to Saul, a sign of perfect love. How could David have failed to fail in this?

David had always accepted love easily. His own brothers might have resented the fact that their youngest sibling could hardly do wrong in their parents' eyes, but he had also been *their* plaything when he was a child; their object of apprentice parenting to teach or indulge. When he eventually worked out that the Prophet Samuel's visit meant that Samuel had discerned the seeds of future greatness in him, he found it acceptable. Astonishing, certainly. But *acceptable*. In the same way, for as long as Saul's love lasted, David had drunk it in, unquestioningly.

It had never been so for Saul. David guessed that Saul had never assumed himself loved and when love did come to him, he distrusted it and withered it with that distrust. David had often been the recipient of Saul's fitful generosity. *Here. Take this cup*, he might say after David had soothed him into peacefulness after one of his terrifying fits. The cup that he parted with so casually might be of wrought gold. A king's treasure. Or he might give a robe or a spear or a bow. Always something valuable. When Saul made these gifts it was as if he'd opened up the cupboard of himself to reveal, behind the ranked knives, a store of sweetness.

A jewel at his heart, like this stone, he thought, rubbing its raised surface with his thumb. He scratched away with his nail at the creature embedded in the stone — wasn't that how gems were recovered from the earth? But there was no shifting the creature from its stone casing.

9

In the first hours after her son's birth she could see nothing but his loveliness and perfection. It was astonishing that he was here with her and nothing could diminish her secret revelling. But she knew that the chequered moods of her pregnancy, shifting between gladness and terror, had affected the formation of his flesh. She should have been more constant; she had abandoned him in her thought until it was possibly too late for him to thrive.

He cried so, and even his crying lacked force. This lack of force extended to a difficulty in suckling. Her breasts were taut and heavy with milk, they leaked and ached, but the baby did not seem to know how to attach himself to the nipple placed at his lips. He cried ever more hopelessly while she held him to her. She knew it should not be like this.

The other wives sat with her and took their turns at holding him, each hoping to be the one with the knack to soothe him. Dalia, who had been wet nurse to many of the children and whose breasts had never dried, was permitted an attempt. Perhaps she had a way that the novice mother had not. But nothing availed. They bathed him, massaged him, swaddled and rocked him. As they rocked him, they sang to him; they stroked his cheek and his tiny sternum. But his eyes were elsewhere; he seemed unable to notice or respond to all this attention. It was as if his weak but persistent screams were addressed to another order of existence, in another language in which he had no hope of being understood by the women who handled him.

Bathsheba barely slept during her first days of motherhood, keeping the sick child close at all times, sometimes dozing off, knowing she had slept only when she realised that what she had just dreamt — that she was shelling beans for instance — could not have taken place. Safi, who had gladly arrived on the day of the birth, had taken up residence and was with Bathsheba at all times; but she was no more expert in these matters than her friend. Tamar also wanted to be there. She wanted to help and, judging that her friend must be exhausted and sore, would lift the baby from his mother and cradle him with the shy intensity she brought to all she did, her long hair spilling down, obscuring him from view but doing nothing to lessen his cries.

The other wives came and went without so much as requesting whether their presence was wanted, as did most of the female members of the household. Now that David was known to be absent, the atmosphere in the household was different. There was a sense of greater freedom, of spreading out. The private world of each woman's personal quarters — a world of textiles, scents, and colours — began to extend and spill out over other parts of the King's House. Bathsheba began to feel that her own rooms had become public spaces where women came to eat and stitch and chatter. There was a litter of orange peel and nutshells on the floor. She was grateful for the help and advice that the older women could offer but increasingly she longed to recover her solitude; to be alone with little Abimelech with perhaps only Safi near, for Safi could be with her without chatter.

But it seemed she was not allowed to be alone. She was forever being cajoled to eat — chickpeas mashed in oil, almonds dipped in honey, soups to make a nursing mother strong. Not that she was nursing with any success.

She saw that Abigail and Ahinoam worked closely together. They were a team of two, not the rivals that Bathsheba had thought they might be; their time together with David during his outlaw years had ensured that their bond was strong and warm. A beautiful, confident pair: Ahinoam tall, straight-nosed, and dark, incapable of a graceless movement; Abigail with her mane of tawny hair, an opulent figure with an exuberance that could not be contained. A natural mimic, with the gift of making people laugh, so when she came into Bathsheba's apartment and took up an appraising stance that everyone recognised immediately as David's, the tension in the room dissolved into enjoyment. But the laughter only made the baby cry more loudly. Ahinoam swiftly took over and carried him to the outside step, jigging him up and down all the while. She held him up to face the country beyond.

'Don't cry darling. Or if you must, make sure your Daddy hears you. He's somewhere out there, thinking of you we hope.'

10

David's legs were hurting. He got up and moved around the cave. He needed water and had not thought to bring a full skin with him. But there was a stream not far from the cave. He could easily climb out to drink.

It was harder climbing out of the cave than he remembered. He had to pull himself up with his arms and then, bracing them and gripping a ledge at the top, bring up his legs to walk up the wall of the cave. He was not as agile as he used to be.

When he had managed to scramble out onto the hillside he found the light dazzling, but his eyes adjusted quickly and he saw that the sun had almost gone down. The clouds overhead were rosy and plump — almost quilted. They lay like a blanket above the hills whose profiles had become dark. He did not have to walk far to find water. Some soft-footed person — it must have been Mathur disregarding his words — had placed a skin of water and a board with fig-cake and cheese on it a few steps from the cave mouth. Ants had already discovered the food and were crawling all over it. They could keep it. But the water was welcome. It would be useful to have a skin to fill again. He drank thirstily from the skin and then walked to the stream to replenish it. Standing here, he looked towards the north where the City of David and his splendid house continued independent of his presence. And the child?

That hot piece of living flesh with dangling legs and flailing arms? He could imagine the bustle around him, all the women of his household united in their concern and interest in the baby. Was he able to thrive the better for his father's absence? Would Bathsheba know what to do? Recollecting himself, the task he had set himself, he walked back to the mouth of the cave and let himself down into it. He was grateful for its earth scents and its darkness.

He stretched himself out, face down along the cave floor. Prostrate before YHWH he prayed that the child might be spared; that his present penance be enough. Occasionally he banged his forehead against the earth, not to cause himself pain but to keep himself alert. In spite of this, he woke hours later, his open mouth against the earth floor, saliva gluing it there. He was in a place of utter blackness.

He knew instantly where he was and why. This recollection, though not exactly comforting, helped to calm an impulse of fear. His mouth tasted of earth, some of which still clung to the inner rim of his lips. His open mouth was itself a dark cave, opening into the labyrinth of his body that eventually became his bowels. Those bowels wanted to empty themselves but he would not foul this place, his temporary home, nor would he risk climbing out in this dark. He clamped down on them, the very discomfort of doing so was a real feeling that held him back and preserved him from pitching into the surrounding void. The pain gave him something to grasp in all the nothing-ness. He would eat earth in the grave. In Sheol there was only darkness. Only nothing.

No voice, no sound, no light, no pain. Only absence.

No mind.

In Sheol he would have no mind with which to remember his Lord. He thought, *I am in darkness but not in the darkness of Sheol. I remember you Lord. Do not let me forget you.*

Again, he might have added.

——

When he next woke it was morning. The sun poured in through the mouth of the cave, forming a beautiful column of light, like a waterfall. He took off his robe and walked over to bathe in it, as if it were actually water. He opened his mouth and drank in the light, cleansing himself of the earth taste of the night. He stretched out his limbs and turned them so that each part of his skin was exposed. Only then did he haul himself out into the open to defaecate and then wash himself with water from the stream.

Out on the hillside he made his habitual morning prayer of thanksgiving. The words of his praise spilled out of him, almost independent of thought. When, minutes later, he returned to the dark of the cave it was with the deliberate intention of pursuing the task of prayer and recollection that he had embarked upon the day before. So habitual was his morning praise he hardly knew it had taken place.

He surveyed his small collection of stones with a view to selecting one as the focus and irritant of his prayer that day. He knew that Saul would continue to perplex him, but for now he had laid aside the scarred, sliced stone he had handled so thoroughly the day before. He wanted something smaller; something more smooth. He picked up the single rounded stone in his collection and rolled it between his palms. The baby? Could it help him to think about the baby? His mind refused to stay there.

He continued to roll the stone for some time, but nothing came to him, no spark of prayer or thought. It was just a dull stone — good only for rolling in a game. He put it down. Another stone claimed his attention. Flat and narrow, a dark, flecked granite. The moment he picked it up, Michal came to mind.

He had noticed how Michal, alone among his wives, had stayed aloof from Bathsheba. Her manner said that Bathsheba and her condition had nothing to do with her; they did not touch her. It would be hard to know what did touch her these days as she drifted about the King's House, upright and apart, like those old sticks of widows, shawled in black, whose very look suggests reproach and long-suffrance. The reproach was directed at him. It had become a condition of her life, as had the low hum of anger it provoked in him. But he did not feel that anger here. The image of the young Michal stood before him in all its slender beauty.

She had been his first woman. No other woman — however longed-for, however ardently embraced — could displace her from that position or expunge from him the special wonder he had felt on acquainting himself with her lean brown body. She was little more than a girl at the time, and her body was not so different from his own young man's body. But where it was different, it thrilled him. The soft buds of her breasts; the exciting mixture of hard and soft. She had been a fierce little thing, determined to show him she was woman enough to be his wife. David had first wanted to marry her older sister, Merab — before Saul changed his mind and prevented it. This made Michal burn with shame. She was keen to show herself the Rachel that David truly desired — let Merab play the Leah he had so fortunately leap-frogged. He had laughed at this and agreed that yes, she was his Rachel. Her hair had been a marvellous dark cloud. He'd loved to bury his face in it.

The obedience that had once shown itself as attachment to her father was transformed into an absolute devotion to David. It was as if she were a garment, taken down from one peg on a wall to be placed later upon another. It could not hang from two pegs at the same time; wherever it hung, and only there, was where it was. Saul, accustomed to Michal's obedient love, grew jealous. He did not want his children to love anyone but himself. The knowledge that both Michal and Jonathan loved David caused him agony.

Saul hired assassins to kill David in his bed but Michal saved him by chasing David away and stuffing a goat-hair bolster to take his place. She even laid a hank of her own dark hair on the pillow so it would seem that her husband had snuggled down deep under the covers, burrowing into the scents of her body. She had patted the bolster in a motherly way and kissed it good night. She'd giggled at this, then burst into tears at the prospect of the inevitable separation with David once he'd fled.

Oh Michal. What a girl you were!

Her life had been a sequence of fierce attachments — moving from peg to peg, from father to him and then, once Saul had taken her from him, to Phaltiel. Then, simply because Saul was dead and David had the power to do so, he took her back and removed her from the life she had settled in. He could see Phaltiel now, following Michal at a distance, with the shuffling, broken steps of a captive, careless of the tears that streamed from his face. Why had he not seen this before? He could see it all in his mind so his body's eyes must have taken the sight in. But he had not attended to it that day. His gaze had been directed to Michal, straight-backed, rigid with hurt and anger, and a proud desire to conceal both. Everything about her was held in, except for her hair — that great explosion of soft black curls, dark and soft as ever.

When Saul took her away from him and gave her to Phaltiel, David had not mourned. He had had other, more exciting, women by then. Ahinoam and Abigail were the moon and the sun to his life in the desert. But the removal of Michal had made him angry at the slight. It lessened his position to be no longer son-in-law to the King. But he hadn't been sorrowful, as Phaltiel had been when Michal was taken from him. Michal, re-attached, clearly loved her second husband. It occurred to him now that she had lived what amounted to a complete life with Phaltiel. A life he had not begun to imagine but had caused to end because of a legal right to her and the power to exert that right.

A deeper motive for reacquiring Michal had been the hope of fathering a child on her. What better way to quench a Saulite rebellion than to father a grandchild of Saul? Now that would never happen. Since the day she had laughed at him, dancing before YHWH when the Ark was brought home, he had not once shared her bed. How could he? He had seen her disappointed, childless body lose its lustre. These days her hair was streaked with grey and she wore it bound. No one would father a child on her.

He had never considered her sadness till now. Not allowed it any weight. Neither her sadness or the sadness of Phaltiel, the husband with whom she had made a home and expected a future. She had been Phaltiel's only wife. Just as Bathsheba had been the only wife Uriah had ever known. This was what Nathan had shown him: the poor man's one, beloved ewe lamb, casually taken and slaughtered by the rich neighbour who already had flocks in abundance. Bathsheba was not the first wife he had removed from a loving husband. Was Phaltiel even alive? He knew nothing about the man.

11

Bathsheba knew well the shame and wretchedness that came with barrenness. That Michal felt this preyed on her. Michal was the only woman in the household who seemed to have other things to do than sit or fuss around in Bathsheba's quarters. But she had made one appearance — an almost silent visit during which she left a small dish of almonds as a gift for Bathsheba. After that she had slipped back into her shadows.

Did the older woman feel she had little or nothing to offer — not more than a few fresh almonds, newly shelled? Bathsheba crammed the almonds into her mouth. She was ravenously hungry and her room was littered with emptied vessels and orange peel. She would seek Michal out. Those almonds had been the first utterance in a conversation yet to develop.

Already in her two days of motherhood she had become more confident about handling her baby and she moved easily with the tightly swaddled child held close. She walked purposefully, knowing that any vagueness in her manner would lay her open to interruption since everyone seemed to think that she and the baby were their business too.

The door to Michal's apartment was open but there was no sign of her inside. Covering her head with her shawl and tucking the baby's head into its shelter, Bathsheba went out to where the King's trees grew. There she saw Michal, squatted down under a fig tree, scratching away at the earth with a small hoe. She had no covering for her head.

Michal looked up but did not stop her work. Bathsheba thought Michal was like a tree herself, gaunt, sinewy, brown. But it surprised her to see the daughter of King Saul working with her hands like this — as Bathsheba used to do before her present splendour overtook her.

'It's wonderful what a difference it makes stirring up the earth like that. Then when you come to put the dung on, the earth can take it in and use the goodness. Otherwise the dung just sits there. I got it wrong when I first tried to grow things.'

Now Michal straightened up and almost smiled. She dusted her hands down and then wiped them on the sides of her gown, more peasant woman than queen.

'My husband showed me how to do this,' she said with some pride.

It took Bathsheba a moment to realise that it was not David that Michal meant, but Phaltiel, the husband David had taken her from.

'You must miss him.'

Michal replied with a tight, grateful little smile. Her eyes filled with tears which she tried to conceal by crouching down again and resuming her work.

Bathsheba stayed, knowing that the sheer fact of someone's speechless presence can comfort. But she refrained from trying to suggest that her situation was like Michal's in that she too had lost a dear husband. If there was any truth in this, saying it would only make it false.

The next time Michal straightened up Bathsheba offered the swaddled parcel of her baby, 'Would you like to hold him?'

Michal looked surprised but glad. More vigorously than

before she rubbed her earthy hands on the sides of her garment, inspected them, found them wanting, and spat on them before rubbing them again. Bathsheba laughed, 'I wouldn't worry. It's only a bit of earth.'

Michal laughed too and Bathsheba saw that the aloof, censorious figure that Michal had always presented was someone hurt and lonely. If she seemed to exude disapproval it was because she herself felt rejected.

'Here he is. A bit of sun on his skin may do him good. Something has to.'

Awkwardly Michal received the small bundle. The expression with which she gazed at the baby's face was one of great tenderness and humility.

'This is your first?'

Bathsheba nodded, smiling at the two of them under the dappled light of the trees.

'But probably not your last.'

With those words, which might have been offered as consolation for the sickliness of this child, Michal handed the baby back to his mother. At the same moment her own sense of irrevocable childlessness seemed to fall on her like a shadow. She became distant again and Bathsheba knew that this short interlude of friendliness between them was over, at least for today. When she returned indoors she carried with her a sense of the weight of Michal's unknown life. Something delicate and tender had opened between them and might yet grow.

12

David paced the interior of the cave, back and forth, back and forth; restless, unseeing of what lay outside but searching and searching within himself to catch something that persistently eluded him. Why was it that his mind could not rest on the child he had come here to pray for? He paced in an attempt to drive into himself a space, a groove, of attention. That groove could be a cradle for the child.

It was what he did when he was looking for the right words for a song — when the right words were at the same time searching for him, wanting to make themselves known. The act of pacing helped. The psalms he had made and sung to the Lord were born of the beat of his heart, his breath and his gait. His even steps broke up the silence and revealed a greater silence at their edges. The space between one step and the next contained an emptiness through which something might be known.

Still he was not able to hold the new child in his thought. Either the child would not enter that emptiness and stay there or he, the father, failed to believe in the life of his son. By repeating words he knew already — *Lord though I flee you I seek you* — again and again, David found himself led into a different darkness: a mantling darkness of great comfort, for it lapped and caressed his body and his mind with unopposing intimacy. It felt like tender concern, like being known and not rejected. Was this what YHWH's love was? Not admiration for His creature or confidence in him? Deeper than either, more exacting, more intimately accurate, was a known-ness he glimpsed now: it lay in his bones and met him at the beginning of his being. It had allowed those bones to form him in the womb of his mother, Nitzevet. It had also allowed each shoot of grass, each leaf, each ant, each star in the great sky to exist in its own perfection.

He could see Michal, not as Saul's daughter, not as his wife, but as a woman with hopes that could be disappointed; with a warmth that asked to be met and a mind whose workings he would never know. He could see that Phaltiel had loved her in a way that he had not begun to do. Loved her in a way that had never occurred to him as a possibility. Perhaps he had received such love, but he had never given it.

Along with this glimpse of Michal as irretrievably separate from himself came a new discomfort. It was such an unfamiliar sensation he needed to think about it before he discovered the truth of it. The mantling comfort he had so recently touched was still there, but it was not enough for him and it no longer comforted him. It did not single him out. If he was not exceptional, he was invisible. He would disappear and no one would find him.

He felt lonely. Lonely as a little boy who has no one to care for him. Who is lost and does not know how to get home. He heard himself whimpering; snivelling. If one of his sons had done so he would have been bracing and stern, but now he sought comfort and there was no one to provide it but himself and no one to witness his ignominy. He pulled the fabric of his garment towards him and folded it into a pad which he pressed against his face. It was soon damp and warm from his tears. Its creatureliness was solace. Still clutching it, holding it close, he fell asleep.

13

When he climbed out the next morning he was aware of a new leanness. Once again, food had been left. This time the faithful servant — having perhaps seen the destruction the ants had worked on the previous dishful — had left it covered. Almost as an act of courtesy — for he had no intention of eating — David lifted the lid. The scent of cooked goat meat rushed up into his face. This was his third day without food and the temptation to take at least a morsel of this stew was almost overwhelming. What had the man been thinking of? It was not as if he'd asked for food. Rage suddenly gripped him — a fist squeezing his stomach — and he picked up the covered pot and threw it as far from him as he could. The sound of the earthenware shattering against rock set off the protests of startled birds. Juices from the thrown stew had run down David's arm leaving a smell as pungent and inviting as the stew itself. Lest he succumb to licking it off his arm he went to wash it in the stream, already ashamed of his outburst. The peace he had touched the previous evening was far away. His head hurt every time he moved and the inside of his mouth was hot and fetid. He did not like the way it tasted. His stomach felt squeezed and raw. He was not in pain — nothing so strong as that — but every inch of him was uncomfortable. Nothing lay easy.

Back inside the cave he did not feel better for having hurled the dish. It was the sort of thing that Saul would have done. Saul was a hurler. Whatever was to hand — sponges, cushions, pots, plates, drinking vessels, stones. Usually with him it was a spasm, a reflex of extreme impatience, or as if there were something horrible inside him he needed to expel. Some people did the same with words — a discharge of bile which might leave the hearers wanting to wipe themselves clean but left the speaker purged.

But David had not thought of himself as like Saul in any way. In the early days of knowing one another it had been David's task to be whole. When he played for Saul and sang he had the impression he was conferring something of his own sleek and golden health upon the cracked but noble being of the older man. It was as if Saul were sheltering under a rough pelt and David had been able to lift the pelt and reveal — at least for some moments — the suffering man who crouched beneath. He cared for that suffering man whose household he'd entered, who was father to Jonathan. If Saul had addressed him — at times — as *my son* it was because in many ways he had been a father to him. Entering into Saul's service had changed his life in ways he could never repay. It had grieved him to see Saul suffer, and injure others in the process. But he was never able to forget the danger in Saul's nature and had ducked a great many flying objects before the occasion when Saul threw a well-aimed javelin at him. That throw altered their relationship for good.

David saw the movement of Saul's arm before it released the weapon; he guessed its inevitable trajectory and swiftly removed himself. Had he not done so he would be dead. The throw had been full of venom. Concentrated, deadly venom.

—

Samuel had turned away from Saul and Saul had tried to stay him, grabbing onto the hem of the prophet's shawl, ripping it. *See*, said Samuel, *YHWH has torn Israel from you today and given it to a better man.* He, David, was that better man. Must he now relinquish the comfortable, bolstering assumption that this was so? Saul too had been YHWH's Anointed. Saul too must have felt the holy oil crawl across his head and through his hair till it ran, while the Prophet Samuel's strong hands clasped his head in prayer, as if packing the holiness in. It was well known that Saul did, on occasions, feel filled with God's power and, acting on this, had himself prophesied — incomprehensibly but fervently.

14

Nathan had been so certain of when the baby had been due, and so kindly in his manner of speaking to her, that Bathsheba — hoping that someone would tell her what this baby needed — decided to send for him. It was a bold action, but he had encouraged her to be bold and she was determined to do everything she could for her son. Nathan was not slow in coming and his arrival had the additional benefit of dispersing the women who were in the room with Bathsheba. It was not just courtesy on their part. They were afraid of him and his uncanny gifts. Bathsheba thought she should invite him more often.

He walked over to Bathsheba and held out his hands for Abimelech whom he cradled with the ease of a many-times father.

'You have given him a name?'

She looked around to make sure they were alone before replying in a low voice,

'Abimelech. Son of a king. He and I — and now you — are the only ones to know this name.'

Bathsheba blushed. She had admitted to Nathan what no one dared to speak out loud: that this was indeed (as most secretly believed) the son of a king — not of the soldier who had been her living husband only five months earlier. Nathan appeared not to notice, occupying himself instead with smiling at the baby, placing his own little finger near the small mouth, encouraging him to suck.

'That's right little man. Like that.' Then, turning again to face Bathsheba, 'Every life has a purpose. Remember that, whatever the future holds.'

'Do you know what it holds?' she asked.

He bent his head and avoided giving a direct answer, browsing the baby's head with his mouth and murmuring, as if to the child, 'No, no. We don't need to know that.'

Bathsheba enjoyed watching this man with her son. She felt easy with him, partly because of her relief that he clearly knew the whole of her situation and did not judge her, but beyond that, his own naturalness permitted hers. After he had passed the baby, no longer crying, back to his mother his eyes lighted on a dish of oranges. He picked one up, along with a fine knife, and peeled the orange neatly. Then he tugged the segments apart and passed one, on the flat of his hand, to Bathsheba. They shared the orange in pleasant silence.

Bathsheba tried again.

'What makes you a prophet? Did you always know?'

Again he seemed to be more focussed on the baby, to whom he seemed to repeat Bathsheba's question, slowly, 'Did I always know?'

He shook his head as if puzzled.

'Sometimes I knew because what I spoke was not what I intended to speak. I heard my words and they were not my words. I learnt by listening to myself. At other times something prevents me from speaking.'

'I heard it said that Saul was a prophet once.'

This made Nathan laugh as he remembered the story.

'It wasn't so much Saul as the place. Ramah was where Samuel lived. He'd been pulled towards it because it is one of those places where the wall separating YHWH from His creatures is full of holes. The place is drenched with holiness and Samuel felt at home there. It strengthened him and deepened his knowing.'

'And Saul?'

'For Saul it was different. He went to Ramah — where your husband was then — intent on injuring David, who he saw as his rival. But as soon as he got to Ramah all the rage and malice he'd set out with simply vanished. YHWH's presence drowned them. It was as if he'd stepped into a lake and been enveloped by the flood. His mouth was filled with what felt like water forcing itself in — he even took off his clothes to drench himself more thoroughly. It was obvious to everyone who was there (and I was one of them) that the sounds that came out of Saul's mouth came from a frenzy of joy, obedient to something beyond anything he knew. But no one could understand a word of it. Not even Saul himself who remembered that it had happened but went on afterwards exactly as before. It didn't change him in any way.'

'So he wasn't a real prophet, like Samuel. Or you?'

Samuel had been feared. Not just for his gifts of insight — as Nathan was — but for his rage and violence. She was too young to have known him but she had heard the stories. It was Samuel who chose Saul to be king, Samuel who anointed him. And it was Samuel who chose David to replace him. She knew that Samuel had hacked the dainty king of the Amalekites to pieces when Saul wanted to spare him. Nathan did not look like he would have the strength or the appetite for such a thing.

'I know you're a prophet but I don't think you're much like Samuel.'

'No. I'm not much like him.'

Nathan smiled and again shook his head, as if perplexed by the question.

'Different times call for different prophets I suppose.'

'Is there something I should be doing to help my son?'

'Nourish yourself. And be peaceful with him if you can. He understands far more than he can show you.'

It reassured her that Nathan was so calm about the situation. Still holding the baby, she got up, holding him confidently as if he were as robust as she would have liked him to be. She carried him to the step where the room looked out over the city and the hills beyond. She could see the rooftops picked out in the sunlight, glimpse human activity on some of them. She could see the rock beside the stream where she used to bathe — the rock that sheltered a person from prying eyes; as long as those eyes were not looking down from above as she was now. That was where all this had begun. With David watching her while she bathed, thinking herself unseen.

Nathan interrupted her thoughts.

'How are you getting on with the other wives?'

'Much better, since this one has arrived. They hardly leave us alone.'

'Well that's better than them being against you. You see this little fellow has already done some good.'

Just then, Tamar put her head around the door and just as swiftly withdrew on seeing Nathan with her friend. Bathsheba smiled at the retreating swish of auburn hair.

'Maacah's daughter I think?'

Bathsheba nodded.

'She's found a good friend in you. Look after her. She's one of those for whom the world is almost too strong to bear.'

—

Almost as soon as Nathan had left, Tamar returned and seized Bathsheba by the hand, tugging at it. She didn't speak (at times it seemed she had forgotten how) but her eyes pleaded with Bathsheba to come with her. The baby was asleep — Nathan's cradling had worked wonders — and Bathsheba willingly left him where he lay, supported on cushions covered in pale linen.

'Just for a moment?'

Tamar nodded and led Bathsheba outside to an old almond tree which had been allowed to continue growing away from the main orchard because it thrived where it was and fruited well. But it was not the tree which had excited Tamar. The angle between one of the lower branches and the trunk had been filled by a most beautiful spider web. The two of them watched in silence as a soft breeze ruffled and swelled the fine fibres but did not break them. Bathsheba had never seen such a large web before. It was perfect.

Tamar was exultant, almost as if she'd created the web herself, and returned Bathsheba's grateful hug.

'We'll never weave anything to match that,' Bathsheba said, and remembered she had yet to complete her baby's shawl.

15

David had been there to see Saul arrive at Ramah and be over-come by the ability to prophesy. And he had seen the power leave him just as suddenly. It showed him it was possible to lose the sense of the presence. The smooth rounded stone that had held no interest for him yesterday now spoke to him of separa-tion. The smoothness he stroked allowed him no purchase, no access. *The Strength of Israel is not a man*. Samuel had said these words to Saul and Saul had repeated them to David. Samuel had told Saul that YHWH was not a man to change his mind and yet He *had* changed His mind about Saul. He might do so again. YHWH is not a man to be second-guessed, cajoled, deceived, or appeased. Men calculate and are calculable. Not so YHWH who might be as secret, separate, and unavailable as the heart of this round stone. Within this stone he guessed were worlds on worlds. Every one of them shut him out.

—

How calmly he'd accepted the idea that he was the better man to whom YHWH had given Israel. Did Saul doubt the truth of Samuel's words and hope that he and his sons would continue to rule Israel, as indeed they did for several years? Did he think that only the reality he could touch was real and ignore what

YHWH said, either directly to him or through the prophet Samuel? On those occasions at Ramah, when the irresistible thinness in the air led Saul to prophesy, Saul surely did have a direct experience of YHWH. But those prophesyings — incomprehensible to others — arrived as strange interruptions to the usual course of Saul's life and remained separate, unincorporated into Saul's understanding as if they had occurred to someone else. The everyday man had no access to whatever revelation they held.

David's mind darkened at this point. The ache of loss and sorrow he felt was too deep to be experienced in thought. He pulled his knees up towards his chin and wrapped his arms around them. There was comfort in this contact with the warmth of his own flesh; his mouth welcomed the saltiness of the skin it met. He felt wizened and small. His head throbbed horribly and his eyes ached in the darkness. His three-days-unfed stomach had not yet learned to be without food and was working hard on its small ration of fluid to squeeze out poisons. He unfolded his aching legs and knelt again in prayer but that prayer seemed to collapse into his sour and aching body; the very tongue he moved in prayer was a sick, sticky, struggling creature stirring with difficulty in the rank pit of his mouth.

—

He'd lain down to sleep, clenched and grim, but in the course of this sleep he dropped down into softer depths. He woke refreshed and hauled himself out of the cave with muscles that were becoming accustomed to this effort. A low mist hung over the hills and during the night spiders had clothed the bushes with white: little nests and hammocks of silk lay in wait. He drank in the clean morning air and let the light bathe his body before he washed himself in the stream, filled his waterskin, and drank from that too. Out there in the early day he prostrated himself before his Lord, grateful for this life and for this morning. For this body with which to experience them. The gratitude welled up and pushed through him; it demanded expression in sound, in song.

Lord you are my light, my life, my whole goodness.

He sang out these words with unquenched gladness.

When he climbed back inside the cave he picked up the smooth round stone that he'd handled the previous day. His God stone. This morning it did not evoke in him the sense of exclusion it had carried for him earlier. It was a perfect thing in itself. It carried with it a sense of keeping its own counsel. It would not speak unless it chose. *The strength of Israel is not a man.*

16

Nathan's age was a subject of much speculation at the King's House. There were those who put it at over a hundred. He was not like other men they said. Magicians such as he are not subject to natural laws — they can live for hundreds of years if they choose — and they don't need food or drink in the usual way of mankind, though they will often eat and drink with you to keep you company. Some said he could speak the language of dumb creatures and that to him no creature was dumb.

Others said, 'No. A prophet is not a sorcerer.' Saul had made strong laws against sorcerers, forbidding them to practise their grimy arts, forcing them to scuttle into the dark places where only those desperate for a spell that would make their beloved love or their child live would persevere in seeking them out. Some, unable to accept the silence of their dead, wanted sorcerers to converse with them in Sheol. It was rumoured that Saul himself, having outlawed such practices, was driven in his last unhappy days to seek out a sorcerer for this purpose.

Bathsheba asked Nathan if he had known King Saul.

For someone so direct, Nathan was evasive.

'Samuel could be difficult, even to his friends,' is what he said.

'So the King consulted you instead of Samuel?'

'Not always. But I was easier to find.'

She imagined Samuel living in retirement during his last years, deep in conversation with YHWH. He would not have welcomed interruptions. As if reading her thoughts — could he do that? — Nathan said, 'Let me tell you about Saul's last meeting with Samuel.'

Bathsheba fidgeted for a moment, adjusting the shawl that covered her head so that it was also tucked around her baby, binding him more closely to her. She wanted to be comfortable while a story was told to her. She nodded to Nathan to signal that she was settled and ready.

'It was at the very end of Saul's life. When he and his sons were battling the Philistines on Mount Gilboa. Saul was exhausted. Spent. Too many of his men had been killed — the Philistines, as you'll know, always had the best weapons. It was rumoured that the present king — your husband — was fighting on the side of the enemy. Saul had long felt threatened by David and had sought his life many times — he must have known in his heart that David would be the next king — but to think of David fighting alongside the Philistines filled him with despair. Samuel was dead by this time — in any case, he had already turned away from Saul and ceased to help him.

'Saul, you must understand, was one of those who can't trust themselves or YHWH. Such people are driven to lean on another — and then, when that person fails them, as inevitably they do, on yet another. Each leant-upon person becomes suspected, driven to fail, the brief gift of trust withdrawn. In Samuel Saul had an advisor he could rely on completely, for Samuel had direct knowledge of YHWH's intentions (at least at those times when YHWH allowed these to be known). But there were times when Saul simply could not trust even Samuel and went against Samuel's explicit advice — or rather, against YHWH's commands.

'Samuel turned away from Saul because Saul wouldn't listen; but as soon as Saul was left on his own he longed for a conduit to YHWH. As King he had consulted the Urim and Thummim before. Those glowing stones on the high priest's breastplate used to speak to him. You can go a long way with "Yes" and "No" — and Saul would thread a way to knowing the right course of action by asking the stones. But after Samuel turned away, the stones refused to answer him. Neither one nor the other would flash. Both were dulled. It was as if a film of dust covered their surface and nothing could wipe it away. The stones became milky, like cataracted eyes.'

Bathsheba shuddered. She felt Saul's isolation keenly. It was not long since she had pictured for herself a future in which she too was friendless. She drew her child closer in to her body, protecting him from the chill.

'Was this when he turned to you?'

Again the prophet ignored her question.

'He became desperate. There at Gilboa, with the terrible noise of battle surrounding him, all he experienced was the silence of not being answered. Samuel dead, the oracle refusing to utter, and not one dream from which he could squeeze an augury. That was when he decided to consult the witch.'

At her highest pitch of fear after Uriah's death, Bathsheba had momentarily thought she might seek out a clairvoyant or medium to direct her. The idea had flashed in her desperate mind, only to be discarded when she recalled the punishment that such an action might bring.

'But I thought it was Saul who had banished the witches and sorcerers —'

'It was. He banished seers, diviners, clairvoyants, anyone

who could speak with spirits, all prognosticators. He banished them because he longed so much for their knowledge and he knew — *he knew* — it was wrong to obtain knowledge in that way. You see, a king can do that. If there is something in himself he does not like or want, he can go and create a law against it as a safeguard. Then, if after all he is unable to keep that law, he can go ahead and break it. That's what Saul did.

'You must understand, he was close to despair. He could not bear to be so cornered and so completely without guidance — of course he thought guidance would be reassurance! For someone so desperate, he was hopeful.

'He made enquiries. It was hard for him to obtain the information he needed when he himself had outlawed what he was looking for. He had to disguise himself — his voice as well as his clothing. You may think this strange but he did not have to wait long before he learnt of a woman who could help him. That damp hankering in his soul to know what lay beyond the hard contours of the present drew him towards the seer woman. It was as if he'd flung a grappling hook into the undergrowth and found it lodged in that one place where the seer hid.

'She was good, the woman he went to. An honest woman. She could not help the fact that she saw further than most. It was nothing she cultivated. She was one of those women that people turn to for advice, to heal the pain of their thoughts as well as their fevers and seeping wounds. She did not ask for the dead to come out of Sheol and speak to her, but sometimes, unasked, they did so, and if they then contributed some insight into a situation, she would receive it and report it. Most of the time, in my experience, the dead have nothing worthwhile to say.'

Bathsheba looked up at him enquiringly. He returned her gaze with a look that said, *Don't ask more*, but then he added, 'It takes more than dying to make a stupid person wise.'

He continued with his story.

'She lived at En-dor. Not wealthy, but with livestock of her own — people have always rewarded such people with gifts of produce and livestock, it is all that they can do. She didn't recognise the King at first — it was dark, he was disguised (and anyway she had never seen him before that day), but she suspected a trap when he asked her to summon a spirit from Sheol.

'Saul swore to her — on the name of YHWH — that no harm would come to her if she did what he asked. He asked her to summon Samuel.'

Bathsheba's eyes filled with tears. Even at this great remove of time and place, Saul's terrifying request had the power to appal. The tears came before any thought or feeling that might warrant them. It was her body that wept. With pity for Saul? For the woman? Or for Samuel, routed from his rest? She could not tell, but, even at this distance from the events, she could hardly bear to contemplate the scene.

'The woman was accustomed to dealing with spirits. They were her daily companions, unsummoned, familiar, and at times annoying. But she felt terror — as you do now, only more so — at what she saw. Divine beings poured from the earth, glowing like fire. They cleared the way as Sheol was unstoppered, releasing the old man, Samuel, wrapped in a dark shawl to protect his eyes from the light of the living which dazzles even at night.

'Samuel — disturbed from his rest in Sheol — could not be appeased by Saul's deep bow. "Why have you dragged me back?" he asked. Saul told him: he was cornered by the Philistines and no living prophet, no oracle or dream would show him a way ahead.

'This made Samuel more angry still. Yet he did give an answer. He told Saul what was about to happen to him. He told him that YHWH had turned against him for disobedience and had given his kingdom to David. He told Saul that he and his sons would die the next day.'

'Did they?'

'Yes. That is what happened.'

'Who told you this?'

'Would you believe me if I told you it was Samuel?'

Bathsheba shivered.

'I'm not sure I would want to. How dreadful for Saul to go into battle with no hope in his heart.'

'It was. He died without hope. A messy, bungled death. But he was brave. And his sons — all of them killed — were near.'

Nathan had become so absorbed in the events of that day, he forgot for a moment that he was talking to a young woman with a sick child. Rubbing his beard to bring himself back to the present, he searched for something to say that had to do with life.

'You know Mephibosheth?'

Bathsheba nodded. She had noticed that handsome and reserved man who limped to the King's Table to eat each evening.

'Jonathan — your husband's friend — was his father. The boy was left fatherless at five years old. Since then the King has been a father to him.'

'A good father?'

'He *is* a good father. You'll see.'

'And Jonathan. What was he like? Was he really so different from his father?'

'Very different. He didn't really want power. He'd probably have been happier away from all this —'

Nathan gestured towards some of the splendid trappings of wealth that surrounded them and Bathsheba grimaced, remembering her own simpler life before.

'He was full of life. A warrior when he had to be — a wonderful archer as you'll have heard — and generous. He didn't think overmuch about himself. Your husband loved him. Jonathan's death was harder for him to bear than anything else has ever been. I'm not sure he knows himself, how much he lost with Jonathan. No one has ever replaced him.'

Bathsheba looked up, a question not quite formed. Nathan got there first.

'No. No one can replace Jonathan. But it's not just your beauty you bring to your husband.'

—

The King's newborn son Abimelech had slept through the whole of Nathan's account. Bathsheba had listened closely to the story of Saul on his final day on earth, but she had not for one moment been distracted from the baby she cradled. He exerted a gravitational pull far in excess of his small size.

Her extreme anxiety had receded. Nathan had led her to understand that it would not be wise or helpful to know what was to come. This knowledge returned her to the present and to the living child in her arms. A small world, its heart beating fiercely. Now that none of the other women were there, silently comparing him with the healthy children they had nursed, she was able to recover her sense of his perfection. His eyes no longer slid away from hers but could return her gaze. She felt them to be pouring into her a wisdom that could be received without language.

Nathan had fallen silent, making way for her absorption.

'He knows you now.'

Bathsheba looked up and smiled her agreement.

'You are everything to him. Nothing you do for him will be lost — don't think the others know any better.'

But now she was smiling at her son, drawing little circles across his sternum with her finger and laughing, as at a shared joke.

Nathan got up.

'I'll be back to see you tomorrow — and to have a word with my small friend here.'

He bowed. He did so without any trace of mockery but nevertheless with a sense of lightness and humour. Bathsheba was left wondering how she could ever have been afraid of this man who seemed to know all about her and, in spite of that, to like her.

—

'Has he gone? We didn't want to interrupt.'

Safi was back, leading a bashful Tamar by the hand.

'Tamar has something for you. Go on, show her.'

Tamar came forward. She thrust a small skein of bright blue wool into Bathsheba's lap.

'Tamar. How beautiful! What a colour! How on earth did you come by it?'

Tamar shook her hair away from her face and beamed at the pleasure her gift had given.

'Abigail knew you wanted some blue. She had just a tiny amount of the dye left over in a sealed jar. She didn't even know if it would still work so she gave it to me to try. Nogah helped me. It was very smelly,' she giggled, 'There was just enough for this much wool.'

It was the most words Bathsheba had ever heard her say. And then Tamar spoke again, 'I didn't think it was working at first. The wool didn't look blue at all. But Nogah said it had to dry in the sun. That the sun would make it blue. And it did!'

Tamar laughed at the magic the sun had performed. Safi spoke now, 'There'll be enough for a whole blue stripe.'

They all looked at the small loom that was propped up against the wall where the first width of a fine shawl stayed unfinished, abandoned.

'If you like,' Tamar was bolder than ever, 'I can do some weaving. It would be a pity not to finish this. It will look lovely with a bit of blue.'

17

The women of the household, including the other wives, acted as if the baby were their common property, bustling in and out of Bathsheba's apartment with presents and suggestions. They would pick him up without asking for permission, leading Bathsheba to carry the child close to her more often than she might have otherwise. Michal alone lacked this sense of entitlement. After the gift of the almonds and the brief conversation in the garden, she had not been near Bathsheba or the baby, but Bathsheba could not put out of her mind the awkward humility with which the older, childless woman had held the baby. The very fact that Michal was disregarded in the household made Bathsheba wish to know her more.

She found Michal outside among the orange trees. She was about to twist one from its branch when Bathsheba arrived. She turned with a look of apology, as if she'd been caught stealing.

'Not quite ready on this one.'

Bathsheba looked at the cloth on the ground which already held several fruit of varying size.

'Could you spare one? I love the smell of them when they're just off the tree.'

Michal nodded and, with the swaddled baby Avi securely against her left shoulder, Bathsheba helped herself to an orange and perched on a low wall while she peeled it and tugged it into segments.

'Here. Please have some.'

Michal joined her on the wall and the two women ate companionably.

'When my first husband was alive we had just two orange trees. Imagine that. Two oranges, one apricot, and a fig tree. They all did well. We worked hard to make sure they did. And now — all this,' Bathsheba's gaze took in the extent of the orange grove, 'It's hard to get used to.'

Michal nodded. 'My father's house wasn't like this, even though he was king. As long as he had food he didn't care about how it came to be there. He thought farming and cultivating were for others, though of course he'd done that kind of work when he was young.'

Now that Michal had opened the subject of her childhood another thought came to Bathsheba.

'Your brother Jonathan. Was he like your father? I know our husband loved him very much.'

Michal answered by bowing her head, unknotting her hair, and raking her juice-stained fingers through it, shaking it free. She growled with rage as she did so.

'Loved him! A strange way of showing it! He very nearly killed him. All those wonderful words he spoke can't change that.'

Bathsheba had heard that David, in his outlaw years, pursued by Saul, had had the chance to kill Saul and not taken it. But Jonathan? When did he nearly kill Jonathan? Who was this man, her husband, who had been instrumental in changing her life so entirely? Was he capable of killing his friend? She pulled her baby more closely in to her body.

'I expect you've heard about Ziklag,' said Michal. 'Ahinoam and Abigail are always talking about it — David left them there, the two of them, more or less in charge, while he and his men were away.'

Bathsheba nodded. She'd guessed that the special closeness between the two women had been formed at the place they referred to so often.

'Did you know how David got Ziklag?'

Not bothering to wait for Bathsheba's answer Michal went on.

'It was given to him. *By Achish of Gath!* By an enemy of Israel and Judah, an enemy of my father and his house. Achish gave Ziklag to David to thank him for his help. David didn't just defend himself against my father, he fought on the other side. He fought brilliantly — which was why Achish rewarded him. It was just luck that kept him from killing my father and his sons.'

'Or YHWH's will,' suggested Bathsheba.

'Luck. I spit on him.'

18

He rolled his God stone across his palm, savouring the new sensation of liberty that came from accepting his own ignorance. Not only did he not know all that was knowable, he didn't need to. Was his new child still alive? This flesh of his flesh — who had no name — what could he know of him? What if Uriah had lived and gone home to his wife that night and done the thing that David had intended him to do? Would Bathsheba have gone on to bear a healthy child that only she and David would know not to be Uriah's? The thought of it made David contract in a protective sadness. This boy was *his* son. He'd come here so his prayers could alter YHWH's intention, but he knew at the same time that it was utterly beyond his power to do so. *The Strength of Israel is not a man.* If YHWH changed His mind it would be none of his doing.

This thought lifted a burden. He had made the mistake of thinking his prosperity belonged to him; that his own cleverness and ability had created it. He thought about that cleverness and the times when he'd been pleased about it: that neat trick of making Uriah the ignorant bearer of the letter that doomed him. How elegant he'd thought his ugly scheme. He'd met a man of radiant integrity and poisoned him with a wizened turd.

Another occasion when his own cleverness had delighted

him was in the early days of his double game with Achish of Gath. That led him and his militia to join an army dedicated to destroying his own people of Israel and Judah. What reckless presumption! He could only have embarked on that course if he'd felt invincible. He tried to remember what it had been like for him then.

It was during his outlaw years when Saul would have killed him if he could. David and his men lived where fugitives might, in caves, often on the move. When David had the idea of offering their services to Achish, one of the Five Philistine Lords, the Gittite king had been thrilled. It was well known that Saul sought David's life, so Achish could not doubt that David and his militia would fight against their own Hebrew people. His good-natured face had shone with gladness when-ever David appeared (and David and his men had laughed about this in private). As a small recompense for the joy of having such an ally, he had given David Ziklag. Just a small settlement of single-storey buildings on the edge of the desert but the first place David could call his own.

Many of Ziklag's native inhabitants had fled at the news that David and his men were to occupy it. They remembered the old song, *Saul has killed his thousands and David his tens of thousands*, and did not want to put those words to the test. Others gambled on staying and made themselves useful to the outlawed Israelites who erected new buildings — including a fine one for David and his two wives, Ahinoam and Abigail. The men became cooks, plasterers, vintners. Some of the Ziklag women became bed-companions to the outlaws, and thirty-eight children were born to men from David's band within eighteen months. The place became home, and some of the dwellings began to show the first signs of cultivation.

After years on the run, scuttling from cave to forest to cave again, stealing or compelling food where it could not be hunted or picked, he and his militia enjoyed their first taste of security. He concentrated on amassing what a military ruler and man of substance requires: livestock, cloth, weapons. Whilst Achish remained under the illusion of David's support, David and his men raided towns in the west towards Egypt — Geshur, Gezra, Amalek — and took everything of value from them, slaughtering all the inhabitants. He told Achish his raids were on southern Judah. There was no one left in Geshur, Gezra, or Amalek to say otherwise.

His double game gave piquancy to his satisfaction. If his success grew from seeming to be a friend of the Philistine enemy, his duplicity did not trouble him. When Achish, at the head of a large Gittite regiment, joined the other Philistine lords at Aphek to do battle against the Israelite army, he included David as the head of a battalion formed of the outlawed Israelites.

The assembled Philistine army was a brilliant sight, stirring together like a liquid about to break into a boil. The many-coloured crests on their helmets bristled with confidence — a throng of cock birds primed and ready. And such weaponry! All the weapons he had ever known had been taken or traded from these clever sea people from the west. Every item of metal, every arrow-head and spear was a prized acquisition. Now to be part of an army for which metal armaments were standard issue, skilfully plied by experienced soldiers — it was thunderously exciting.

He'd thought that by being close to the heart of the Philistine force he might find an opportunity to strike at that heart and turn the battle in the Israelites' favour. How grateful the Israelites would then be. And if he had no such opportunity, he would, at the least, have gained inside experience of the Philistines' methods of war.

The other Philistine lords did not share Achish's delight in the presence of David and his men. *Why are these Hebrews with you? What place can David have here, the man of whom they sing, 'David has killed his ten thousands'? What fine trophies our heads would make! What better way for him to wind his way back into Saul's favour than by betraying and killing us all!*

Achish could not reassure them. Brimming with apologies, he sent David and his battalion back to Ziklag. He said that he knew David intended him nothing but good; that David was to him an angel of God.

David had smiled. His God was YHWH.

—

There was no Ziklag to go back to; only its charred and smoking remains. An old man, dreadfully wounded, nursing the bloody stump of his right hand with the left, sat on the ground outside the burnt remains of his house. He flinched when one of David's men approached him.

He and a few other old people remained. They had been asleep when the Amalekites came. One or two deaf ones slept through the raid. Others had attempted to hide, and in doing so had lost their lives in the flames. Nearly every living thing — human and livestock — had been carried away by the Amalekites. Abigail and Ahinoam among the women. All the children. Anyone with enough health and strength to be useful. Gone.

When the realisation sunk in that each of their wives and every one of their children — even the babies — had been taken away into slavery, David and his militia abandoned themselves to grief. They had only recently been rejoicing together, whooping with gladness at the spoil amassed in their raids. David had been carried on the shoulders of his men, arms and torso dancing in time with the men's feet. Now there was only sorrow and desolation. His sorrow was as theirs — his wives been taken — and he had no idea at all what he might do to end it.

His men had been primed to fight when they'd set out to join the Philistines at Aphek in the north west. The adrenaline that had pumped through their bodies in readiness for war now thundered for an outlet. They turned on him. David alone was responsible for the decision to leave their families unguarded while they travelled north to a battle they did not even fight. David was responsible and David must pay the price. The men who for so long had fought with David, loyal to his command, were about to stone him. There were plenty of stones around from what was left of their homes. Large, dressed stones, the size of a man's head. Some of the men got as far as selecting and weighing in their hands the first stones they would hurl.

How could he have forgotten how frightened he had been as the men who had been his friends closed in on him? The fear was with him now; remembering it, he tasted it again.

He could not appeal to his fellows — he no longer had any. Every one of the men whom he had counted as comrades, linked in a common cause, faced him with an expression of obdurate hatred. Met with a wall without one chink of sympathy he was returned to himself, to his fearful heart that could just — and only just — remember to pray. A prayer that was no more than a cry. *Lord, help me!* Only YHWH could help him and be his strength.

His cry cleared the way. The energy of his prayer had the immediate effect of reviving his shaken confidence. Realising he must act fast in a way that would recover his authority he called for Abiathar, the priest. He commanded Abiathar — who so far had neither condemned nor defended him — to fetch the ephod without delay. The priest fetched it and, refusing to be hurried, spread it out across a rock with proper ceremony. Taking his cue from the priest, David too took his time. He held the attention of those who only minutes ago had wanted to kill him. He would maintain their attention and restore their respect, not by rushed acts that spoke of desperation, but by steadiness, ceremoniousness, and due reverence. Only when he had composed himself, intently watched by the recently murderous eyes of his men, did David ask YHWH through the oracle if he should go after the Amalekites who had sacked the town. The light danced across the gemstones of the ephod and declared God's YES.

We will recover everything and everyone. And we will take home more.

Did he believe it when he said it? He heard the words come out of him and the men were able to believe them because they needed to. Some sent up a ragged cheer, others maintained a sceptical and weary silence. All were exhausted and humiliated by the journey to and from the muster at Aphek. They had returned, hoping for comfort, and been met by desolation. In spite of all this, most were able to find in themselves a pocket of strength sufficient to follow David once again. Hope was preferable to despair.

—

You could almost touch it: the moment of cessation and alteration. The mind drops down like a bird into a valley where there is a river. It plunges down, whizzing as if to its doom, only to have its fall broken by water, its progress altered, to rise up clean and refreshed. Maybe a fish in its mouth. David listened to his breath — moments ago it had quickened at the remembrance of his fear — and noticed that place of change, the moment of stillness before the in-breath expired. There, in the smoking ruins of Ziklag, surrounded by six hundred or so bereaved and angry men, he had reached in and come into contact with that river. When he came out an alteration had taken place. A conversion.

A trail of detritus told them which direction the raiders had taken. He led them out — all six hundred — as far as the wadi at Besor where they stopped to water the animals. Many of the men waded into the water, attempting to revive themselves with cleanness. Here some of the men — about a third of their number — broke down from weariness. Once he would have pushed them, chivvied them to show their manhood, not to let their fellows down. He might have disputed the reality of their exhaustion, reminded them of other times when they had performed the nearly impossible. But he knew better. The very real terror he had recently experienced had affected him. He knew that he too could be weak; that his resources were finite and that you can push a man too far. *Wait here. We'll come back to you*, he said. *We'll bring you your wives and your children. And your war spoils. Wait. Rest. Soon you'll be rejoicing.*

They had galloped on. He was convinced they would be led, for YHWH sends His angels in many forms.

They found their angel in a field. Wandering unsteadily between rows of wheat, rubbing the unripe ears in search of grain. Grey-skinned, shivering with fever, the young Egyptian was brought to David. The man was faint with thirst and hunger so they gave him water from a skin and fed him with fig cake and raisins. Wonderful how quickly he was restored. Servant to one of the Amalekite raiders, he had been left behind to die of his fever, a dead weight that no one wanted to carry on their flight back to safety.

David asked him to take them to the raiders. The man made him swear — by his God — that if he did so the Hebrews would not kill him nor return him to his former master. David swore and helped the man up onto his own horse to ride, seated in front of him, to point out the way.

—

They heard the Amalekites before they saw them. Heard their music, their laughter, the bells that shook with their dancing. They could smell the roasting meat from the many fires they had built on the low plain where they were camped. Meat from the animals taken from Ziklag. How secure they were, dancing, carousing, shouting in that wide open space, framed by hills on every side. Did they think they had conquered all? Their lack of care, their obliviousness to the possibility of threat from the overlooking hills, was flagrant. Offensive.

For the first time in all his years of warfare, David had felt a pure, surging, quite personal hatred. It was monstrous, like a giant looming over his shoulders, pressing down on him and into him until the giant had become him and he could breathe a giant's fire. Ziklag had been their home, a place of stability where bread was baked and shared, where children were conceived and born to run around and congregate in happy safety.

After years of being fugitives, bandits in the eyes of some, making camp in inhospitable terrain, they had been given a home in which to spread out and build. For the first time since King Saul had chased him into exile David had been able to do more than survive. He and his men could begin to prosper. Then, in their absence, the Amalekites came and burnt the place down. Now David breathed an equal fire. The fire with which Ziklag had been torched returned to burn those who lit it. Somewhere down there — in a tent, bound and chained — were Ahinoam and Abigail and all the wives of his men, along with their children whose laughter and shouts used to irrigate the paths of Ziklag.

He thanked the young Egyptian and made sure he was comfortable and safe (he was too weak to fight with them and in any case, no fighter); then he ordered his men to surround the plain as silently as they were able.

The sun was going down when they began their attack, but the many fires lit by the Amalekites showed them their way. The Amalekites, drunk and unarmed, defended themselves chaotically. Some even thought that the strangers had come to join in their celebrations and began to dance with them. They were swiftly disabused. The slaughter was relentless and efficient. While the majority applied themselves to killing, others went systematically through the tents, cutting the womenfolk and children free. A safe corridor was created, an alley lined with men, to allow the rescued families to pass to safety and wait till the battle was done.

Everything and everyone that the Amalekites had taken was recovered and nearly all of the Amalekite raiders were killed. Those who got away — the sober ones — did so at the outset — galloping swiftly on slender-legged camels, in a cloud of sand.

A pity to lose those camels, but the spoils David and his men carried back to the wadi were more than enough to rejoice in.

Four hundred men had ridden away from the wadi. What they brought back resembled a small nation in caravan — carts with families clasping carpets and cooking vessels and birds; wagons loaded high with jars of grain. At the rear, noisy herds of cattle, sheep thwacked along the way by triumphant soldiers. All had been on the edge of exhaustion when they set out, but they returned, after a full day of battle, vigorous in triumph.

Those who had stayed at the wadi, having been too tired to go further, greeted the soldiers gladly and wept with relief at the return of their children and wives. But some of those who had travelled with David and taken part in the attack said, *Why should we share this spoil with these ones who had no part in it? They can have their women back, and their children. But not the riches we have taken.*

This was ugly, and as a principle, dangerous. David spoke, *When we have made raids — in Geshur, or Gezra, or Amalek — the spoils have been for all, not for the private enjoyment of the one who entered the tent. We are a people who support our women and children — our widows and orphans — and also those men who, for whatever reason — sickness or weariness or extreme distress — are unable that day to be strong.*

He laid down a rule, once and for all, that whatever was won in battle was for the benefit of all. When he said this, he had felt himself to be a king.

Then — how could he have forgotten this? — he had knelt and prostrated himself on the sand. He gave thanks to YHWH for the great restoration that had been granted them. His men followed him, bowing in thankfulness, remembering that all they had recovered had been YHWH's gift.

Ziklag was too far to be within reach that night, neither were they ready to face the rubble that their homes had become, so they set up camp where they were by the wadi Besor, which at that time of year was no more than a trickle. After the initial elation, exhaustion had set in. There was no dancing. No whooping or playing of instruments. But David did not sleep. Long after the last flurries of talk and laughter had died down, he sat beneath the stars — stars so numerous and close there in the desert sky they formed an almost uninterrupted fabric of variegated light. He had given thanks again, unseen this time by all but YHWH and those desert creatures who were awake. He had salvaged something — much — from the devastation, but the devastation was the direct result of his vanity. He should have learnt from this.

19

When David awoke on the fifth morning, light had already spilled onto the floor of the cave. His sleep had been dense and dreamless, but it had carried him somewhere. He woke with the image of a body pinned to a wall. Not his own but Jonathan's.

Might he have saved Jonathan if he had not been busy with Ziklag?

He had not been there to see Jonathan's body, dismembered and dishonoured by the Philistines at Beth-shan. They had pegged it up on a wall beside the headless bodies of Saul and his other sons. But the people of Jabesh-Gilead owed Saul their sight and they never forgot this. They never lost their gratitude to Saul, who, in the days of his greatness, had rescued them from the Ammonites whose leader Nahash had threatened to put out their right eyes. After the deaths of Saul and his sons at Gilboa, the men of Jabesh-Gilead had made their way to Beth-shan under cover of darkness and taken the bodies down, wrapped them tenderly in cloths, and removed them to their own city. There they washed the remains and cremated them, before burying the ashes ceremoniously under the shifting shade of a tamarisk tree. That took courage. After that, for seven days, the people of Jabesh-Gilead had fasted in honour of Saul, their departed saviour, and his sons.

Seven days. That was what he planned for himself now. But in whose honour did he fast? For Uriah? For the sickly, unnamed child he found so hard to think about? For YHWH? Why not dedicate a portion of this fast to Jonathan, brother of his heart?

Had he and his band stayed with Achish to march with the massed Philistine host to encounter the Israelites at Gilboa, would he have been in a position to save Saul and, above all, Jonathan? He would — he was quite sure of this — have been obliged to kill many of his own people if he'd wanted to maintain his cover. Could he have been the one to kill his friend? Unknowingly, in the mess of warfare? This appalling thought struck him like a blow. His double game — thrilling in its danger at the time — had been nothing but vanity and folly.

—

It was a young Amelekite who had brought word to David of Saul's death and the deaths of his sons. He told David of the terrible rout of the Israelites at Gilboa and of how Saul had turned his own sword on himself, asking the young Amelekite to finish the job. The young man was expecting a reward from David and presented him with a splendid golden torque, pulled from Saul's arm. *Were you not afraid to kill YHWH's anointed?* David asked, and ordered one of his men to kill the Amelekite, not wishing to soil his hands with the deed or to dignify the man with knowledge of his name.

He sent gifts to the people of Jabesh-Gilead in recognition of their courage in retrieving the bodies; and to secure their support for himself. He mourned his friend in words — beautiful words, words framed to move all those in Israel who had lost their king and his sons. Words that had proclaimed the beauty, the strength, and the sanctity of Saul and of Jonathan; words that imagined the participation of the mountains of Gilboa. He had forced all his sorrow into the words. But he had not stopped to hear those words as he spoke them.

Now he spoke them again, slowly, not to people whose hearts he hoped to win over, but to himself, shocking himself with the truth they carried:

> *You mountains of Gilboa, may no rain fall on you*
> *nor dew fructify your fertile fields,*
> *for you brought death to Saul and Jonathan,*
> *YHWH's anointed and his brave son.*

He had unfurled these words as a banner over a bereaved land but had been too numbed by shock to hear them. Now they spoke to him of an intimate sadness.

Without even being aware of it, he had taken a sharp piece of flint from his altar stone and closed his hand over it. While he spoke the words of the Song of the Bow, his public lament, aloud to himself he squeezed the flint in time with the beat of the words. It was the stickiness of his own blood seeping from his fist that drew his attention to his action. The death of Jonathan was a long unattended wound which had now re-opened.

He examined the bloody palm, the lines in it now stained into greater distinctness. Then, without thinking to clean it, he clasped the flint again more tightly, and allowed the pain in his hand to release tears for his friend.

I am distressed for you, my brother Jonathan. Your love to me was wonderful.

Jonathan had always been the more energetic partner. He made sure that David was never lost to him — even when his father Saul had forced David into exile. He'd pursued David as doggedly as Saul ever did. More so, love being more resourceful than enmity. The last time he'd found David was at Ziph — David an outlaw in that wilderness, acquainted with the honeycomb of hiding places that those hills held. Why wasn't he surprised when he saw Jonathan there — peering in at the mouth of a cave, not unlike this one — laughing at his own initiative, arms wide for an embrace? David had been glad, yes, very glad, but at the time he didn't even consider the difficulties that Jonathan must have overcome to reach him.

You will be king and I shall sit next to you. Our families shall be one.

This was Jonathan's cherished dream, a dream in which there was no more enmity between the house of his father Saul and his friend David: all the contrary forces gathered into a single, smooth, glistening braid. It was as if he and David had been children together, play-acting their bold visions of adult life, mimicking the postures of power and submission. David always played the king — they were agreed on that. But Jonathan's role was fluid: sometimes the royal consort, sometimes the king's chief friend; at other times, his son. Then they grew into men with real wives, wives who bore them real sons.

But at the heart of their parodies of married love was something truly offered. David had looked away from what Jonathan had offered him, reluctant to admit it in all its breadth and steadiness. The uninterruptedness of Jonathan's love, the readiness to surrender all in David's favour, made him almost ashamed when he contemplated it from the distance of years. There was a peaceful assurance between them such as he had not yet found with a woman.

Did Jonathan love him as a lover loves? Would he have been glad to anoint his friend's body with his kisses, touch him and enter him, be entered by him? He had never allowed himself to see it before, never permitted himself the leisure to contemplate what had been offered. How could he not have seen that all their laughing charades of king and queen could easily have led this way? Jonathan did not press it, but a cue would have led him forward. Why had he not permitted it? His body told him now that it would have been an expansion, not a transgression.

He allowed himself, for the first time, really to dwell on the beauty of his friend's body, so different in its strength and firmness from a woman's yielding flesh. Bracingly, hearten-ingly different. In his mind he caressed the long thighs, kissed the beautiful collarbones along their slopes to the dark salty well between them, took the reaching stem of the penis into his mouth. Why never while Jonathan lived?

His climax was easy and ushered in a deep, undisturbed sleep.

—

When he woke, the angle of the light that funnelled into the cave had changed and the light itself was fainter. He had slept through the greater part of the day. He woke feeling well, clarified, as if an ancient knot inside him had dissolved. But along with this sense of wellbeing came a further shock of loss.

I am distressed for you, my brother Jonathan.

Their real farewell — their most conscious parting — had been in the field of the stone called Ezel when Jonathan had communicated with David through the medium of archery. Only a man unerring in his placing of an arrow would think of this means — by which Jonathan made it clear to David that he should flee from Saul who wanted him dead.

Jonathan had said, *Hide where you have hidden before, behind the stone named Ezel. I will come into the field with a young boy, and shoot three arrows in the direction of the stone — as if I were aiming at a target. I will say to the boy, 'Go, fetch the arrows.' Now listen. If I say, 'See, the arrows are on this side of you, fetch them,' then you are to come to me, for no harm is intended to you. But if, on the other hand I say to the boy, 'Look, the arrows are far ahead of you,' then you must flee. YHWH will be telling you to go.*

David had heard the tread of feet on the dry grass of the field; he'd heard the low voices as Jonathan selected arrows from his quiver; the quiet as he notched the arrow. And then the whirr as the arrow flew far over his head and Jonathan's voice, unnaturally loud and with a strain in it that was new to David's ears, *Go, fetch the arrow. It's far beyond you.* Then, *Quick now! Hurry. Move on!*

He'd heard Jonathan tell the lad to gather up the arrows and carry them back to the city.

David had waited until he was sure that the boy had gone before coming out from his hiding place. He'd prostrated himself three times before YHWH. After that he and Jonathan had embraced, both of them weeping. They had affirmed their vow that YHWH would be present between them and their lineages for ever. Then, without looking back, he had left the field of the stone named Ezel. Danger lay all around and there was no more time for grief.

That had been their real farewell. In the short privacy after the boy had gone, before the urgency took over, it had seemed that no one but they existed in the world. That had been Jonathan's dream.

Your love to me was wonderful.

———

For the first time since Nathan's visit — the first time in many years — David gave himself over to weeping. He wept for Jonathan and saw him with arms held wide, always offering more love than he himself returned. He wept for his own loss of that love, but also for Jonathan, for what he had suffered. His dreadful death on Mount Gilboa; the shameful way in which his body had been dismembered and displayed. That dear, beautiful body. The tears came spasmodically at first, painfully, as if pushing out dry plugs from unaccustomed eyes. Then they took over, spreading and filling the darkness of the cave: an immense storm. Whenever it began to subside and quieten, another wave came to renew it until the darkness of the storm seemed absolute. At first the wildness of it was terrifying, but after a long and exhausting time, it began to soothe. It was as if a mother's hand had passed over a child abandoned to grief, running warm and kind through his hair to rest there, not denying the sorrow or hastening its end, but assuring the child of her presence; assuring him that he was not alone. *Lord, your darkness wraps and covers me. I am safer here than when I was in your light and fled you.*

The passage into the interior of this darkness was slow and variegated; punctuated with resting places — shelves in the smooth rock. But the shelter they offered was short-lived, and the nature of these places changed to become violently inhospitable, the blackness suddenly disclosing sharp-beaked, clawed, and angry birds that seemed to clutch and restrain David while he struggled to escape. Then he would be in flight once more; until again he would pause, recover strength, discover the ability to distinguish qualities within the blackness.

The sense of his failure could not be experienced all at once lest he drown in it. Not failure in conquest, survival, mastery — abilities to which he had dedicated much and for which he was widely admired. He had failed in qualities that were expressed by all around him — as much by the ewes he used to tend as by the men and women who lived with him. Did he love the children those women had borne him? He thought of them and, for a few minutes, forgot himself as he pictured them, the boys — men now, the elder ones — careening round the King's House. His household army he called them. And Tamar, the beauty! So shy, always hiding behind that curtain of hair; these days a consciousness of womanhood increased her shyness, even with him, her father. But he had carried her on his shoulders when she was young — called her his own lamb and laughed at her bleating.

All he had was one little ewe lamb whom he loved as if she were his daughter.

Yes, he did love them. Though not yet the new mite, so thoughtlessly conceived.

Then Nathan's voice.

You are that man who stole from the poor man his only darling.

The tears returned: the squander and ruin which he knew he had committed had been acted against himself, his truest, tenderest part. He felt his own, too-little-exercised capacity for love, and the different pain it brought. He did love Jonathan.

How greatly he loved him at last he knew. But how lazy and greedy he had been, always letting Jonathan seek him out, always allowing Jonathan to serve him.

Your love to me was wonderful.

Had he ever done anything for his friend? They had loved each other's company. Was that enough? He could think of nothing — no deed, no gift, no sacrifice he had ever made for Jonathan's welfare. All he could think of was that he might easily have been the instrument of his death.

He glimpsed how much smaller he was than those he had subjected to his will. Uriah — loyal to the Ark, Phaltiel — who loved Michal and grieved for her, careless of what others might think. Michal. He felt a rush of affection for the admonitory, disappointed figure she had become. He'd treated them as lesser, insignificant people to be shunted around like counters. He was the small one.

He tasted it, retreated, advanced again, then fled: a long exhausting dance of embrace and denial. There were intervals of utter contrition. He was nothing. He was water spilled onto the floor of the cave. Would that the floor could drink it in and he have no existence.

He fell into an exhausted sleep.

—

Whatever small peace he'd gained fled his mind as soon as he was asleep. Dreams of pursuit, of being pursued; of being pinned down by Saul's spear; of being dead, his own spread-eagled body fastened to a wall while his wives — all of them, Michal, Maacah, Haggith, Eglah, Abital, Bathsheba, Ahinoam, Abigail, all the concubines as well — ignored him as they copulated with other men or else surfaced for a moment to taunt him with expressions of wide-eyed provocation before returning with renewed zeal to their task of fornication; the naked backs rose and fell in a struggling tangle like fish closing on feed.

He woke to his sixth morning in the cave with the ash taste of shame in his mouth.

20

For the first time since the birth of her child she had slept well. She had passed her swaddled baby to Nogah, knowing he was in safe hands, before letting herself sink into a sleep so deep her dreams scoured the furthest reaches of her life. She was a child again, with her father in a crowd, receiving the cake that was handed out at the Ark's return; she was still in a crowd, being pulled along and unable to turn back from the place where Miriam was caught in the sand, waiting for the stones to kill her; then the crowd became a marching army, she caught up in the tight file, unable to get away though she wanted to cry out, *I should* not *be here. Can't you see. I'm a woman. I don't belong!* Until at last the close mesh of marching men cast her out — like an object carried forward by a hurtling river to be deposited onto the quiet of a shore. Only this was no valley but a high place. She alone there, looking out. She could see as far as the great sea in the west and the Sea of Salt to the east. She could see desert below and the green pastures that flank the River Jordan in the north. In her dream she had the sensation of being shown something — as if there were someone standing by her, pointing out not only landmarks but events. She was not able to comprehend them and yet she had the feeling that all was perfectly clear and as it should be; she had only to see and give her assent. This terminus of the dream was marked by a sense of trust and contentment, as if she herself were cradled at the heart of her own family.

She was lying, her eyes still closed, basking in this long-missed sensation when Nogah rushed in to her.

'Come quickly. His breathing has changed.'

The comfortable heaviness of the dream was gone; Bathsheba was with her baby, holding him, gazing at him with an expression which implored him to respond. His eyes were listless, they seemed to be focussing nowhere, his gaze just slid away, unable to fasten on any object.

They unwrapped him from his swaddling and saw that his small chest was sucked inwards into a hollow above the abdomen which seemed swollen and was pumping in and out very fast. Bathsheba cupped his head in her hand the better to keep it from rolling. Even so, the baby's eyes remained out of focus. The whole of his attention was taken by his breath, trying to find satisfaction in it.

Bathsheba thought of a fish, just landed, thrashing on the shore, unable to grasp the element it needed for life. For an instant she had the mad idea of submerging her baby in water — as if he were a fish indeed. It was only an instant. She banished the image in horror lest the very thought of it injure the child.

He was hot too. There was a breeze through the room created by two strategically placed openings. The walls were thick and the heat of the sun was kept out. But he was burning. Nogah fetched cold water from the deep of the well and, with the uttermost gentleness and care, Bathsheba bathed his brow, then turned him over and sponged his straining back with steady, even strokes. As if there were all the time in the world.

She spoke to him, soft endearments, telling him how she loved him, how precious he was to her, what gladness he had given her. She coaxed him to be well, telling him of all the adventures they could have together, all the things she and his father could teach him. All the stories of her own family she could tell him; about her own childhood.

Nogah came and went with fresh bowls of cool water and removed those that had been emptied. Once or twice she bathed Bathsheba's brow but Bathsheba hardly noticed, so fastened was her attention on her child.

No one else had been awake when Nogah had come in with the baby, but the urgent haste of her footsteps, in spite of her light tread, penetrated the sleep of others. Safi, whose sleep was thin, ever alert to the needs of her friend, hastily flung on a garment and went into the room where lamps were already lit. She did not need to say anything. She kissed the top of Bathsheba's bowed head and then settled herself by the loom. She picked up the shuttle and calmly resumed the work where Tamar had left off the previous day, weaving in the stripe of blue.

21

There was nothing arousing about his dream despite the avid, heaving copulation it contained. The dream did no more than present to his mind what Nathan's prophecy had said would be. Except that Nathan had said the wives would fornicate in full view of many; whereas in the dream he was the only spectator of a show that seemed laid on expressly for him.

Laid on for him but also very decidedly excluding him. The sight of Bathsheba's long, creamy back arcing in pleasure as she straddled another man: a sight he had not wanted to entertain in his waking mind on those nights when he'd attempted to direct Uriah towards her bed. Now he saw it anyway.

David had exulted in the fact that she was his and only his. He had seen her, wanted her, and then had the power to translate want into get. The fact that her body had so clearly and actively met his that first time led him to feel that they had acted together. Yet he knew that he would have taken her whether she had consented or not. He could not have resisted if she had been within reach. The punishment for adultery was death — her death, not his — and he had knowingly made her guilty and placed her in danger. The repugnance he'd felt just now as he'd watched his wives in energetic copulation was what Uriah might have felt had he been a witness to what he had done with Bathsheba. When he took Michal from Phaltiel it had been a cold exaction — not obviously forcing her into adultery but asserting the claim of his prior marriage. His taking of Bathsheba had not been cold. But that did not make it right.

He looked at his collection of stones and wondered if there was one for her. But none suggested her: nothing hard and defined could represent Bathsheba. She was light, a play of altering light, shifting between the soft rosy warmth of early sunlight and the glittering cool of the moon. He would not handle her here. Instead he took the largest stone from his collection: a grey rectangular slab. There were a few ridges on its surface, pleasant to his thumb, but not much differentiation to encourage the mind to grip it. Uriah. Of course, Uriah. Obdurate. Steadfast. Uncompromising.

The very Ark of God travels under temporary cover and endures the discomforts and roughness of the battle field. How can I, removed from that place where my comrades are fighting — removed not by my own choice but at your command — how can I go back to my tranquil house, lie comfortably with my wife and eat the hot food she has prepared? I cannot do this. I swear on my living soul, I cannot.

How offensive David had found this display of piety at the time. How the implied rebuke about the King not being with his army at Rabbath-Ammon had stung! How distasteful to feel that a man whom he commanded behaved better than he. Distasteful and irritating; to the extent that he had amplified it into a capital offence. The pious Uriah died for his piety.

As he ran his thumb along the Uriah stone he was sorry with all his heart that the man was now no more than this thing. The stone made him think of reserve, discipline, obedience. It reminded him of the wall at which Uriah had died. It could have been a small piece of that wall.

The Ark is with Joab now. The Ark is at Rabbath-Ammon.

He almost heard the words — as if Uriah had spoken them again. They came to him as a surprise though he knew the facts already. The Ark remained with Joab, bringing victory to the Israelites. But why was he not there, alongside Joab, leading his own army? Why, until less than a week ago, was he sleeping on soft fleece in a building roofed with cedar while the Ark was exposed to the horrors of battle with only a goatskin tent for shelter? If he had been there, as Commander in Chief, he might never have seen Bathsheba lift the hair from the nape of her neck to pour water across her shoulders, making them gleam.

Why had he not been there at Rabbath-Ammon? Was it simply because it had been much pleasanter to stay at home? After the years of hardship, camped out in caves, tents, dried-out wadis, dancing around the threat of Saul, it was good to experience domestic comfort. Seven years as King of Judah: seven years at Hebron, contending against the House of Saul until at last — and without his known contrivance — the last of Saul's sons was killed and every tribe in Israel turned to him as his own bones and his own flesh saying, *We are you. We are yours.* He had rewarded himself with a period of unaccustomed ease.

When a loved and admired person dies, the one who mourns will attempt to take on the admired qualities that the dead person can no longer embody. Might the reverse also be true? That at the death of someone not admired — in contrast with whom a person might have defined himself — those despised qualities, liberated from the dead one, may find another to take them on. Saul's conspicuous wrongness had been useful to David when it came to ordering his own conduct. But David's triumph had ushered in a complacency and an unwarranted comfortableness about his moral choices, no longer defined in contrast to Saul's. Once Saul was dead and David, the new King of Israel and Judah, surrounded by acclamation and approval, he had slid, inexorably and steadily. He was here, a fasting penitent, as a direct consequence of that slide. The child, its hapless fruit.

The thought of the child came as an interruption. A shocking recollection. Was he still alive? He had barely remembered to pray for him over the last two days, so little claim did he make, as if accepting that his role in the world was to make only a brief appearance, then leave, taking with him as much of the trouble that had surrounded his conception as so small a creature could carry.

Two stones remained on his altar. Two not yet assigned a role. One was a beautiful stone, shot and flecked with pink, its structure accreted like billowing cloud. It was far too splendid for his son. The other he had placed on the altar almost as an afterthought: a small piece of gravel — scree dislodged by his movements in and out. He picked it up now and thumbed it. He didn't even know if the baby had a name: that was how little purchase the boy had on life. But he was a king's son; acknowledged to be that, even if he intended it be thought to be by adoption rather than by blood. By making Bathsheba his wife he had given this honour to the child who, whether he lived or not, would always be the first-born of their alliance. Whatever — whoever — might yet be born to them, however healthy, fortunate, wise, or far-seeing he was — would always be the brother of this poor scrap. This thought led to a true prayer: *That a child of this lineage will be born who will pity the weak and fatherless and be their brother*. He desperately wanted to salvage some good from the wrongness. As he prayed he felt weak and dependent as the child — more brother than parent.

How little he could do. His sorrow could effect no difference.
It fed no one, healed nothing, brought no one back to life. His
penitence was powerless to make the child live. *The Glory of
Israel is not a man.* Not a man to be bargained with, or cajoled
into alteration. Nevertheless he prayed that good would come.

He knew about Saul's visit to the seer at the end of his life
and shuddered to think what it must have been like for Saul to
be informed by the dead Samuel that he had only one day left
to live. Samuel had been a figure to fear even when alive —
even he felt this, and the prophet loved him. A dead and angry
Samuel was frightful, even to the imagination.

Might it have been different if Saul had obeyed his own
law which outlawed all seers, all witches and magicians? The
law of a king should confirm the Law of YHWH. To honour
the King's law was to honour Law itself. If the King broke the
law he had made, what then?

David was perplexed by the question of whether Saul
visited the seer at En-dor *because* he had been forsaken —
something he could not have done had YHWH been with
him — or whether his action exacerbated YHWH's anger and
led to his utter rejection. At what point did it become fixed and
immoveable that Saul and his sons would die the next day? And
what of Samuel's role in what occurred? Did he compound
Saul's fate by naming it — *did he make it?* — leading Saul on
to despair and failure in battle? A prophet is close to God's
purposes, but does YHWH speak through him as through a
trumpet? Or as an underground river breaks out into brooks
and streams and thundering, smoking waterfalls? Had Samuel,
and now Nathan, simply opened their mouths for God's judgement to gush out? He didn't know what the answer was, either
for himself or for Saul.

Certain it was that the child had been alive when he left. That fact allowed him to glimpse the possibility that YHWH might alter His purposes; or that a prophet, in the process of framing those purposes into language, might colour, and so change, their bent. Either possibility left a little room. Room not to be futile.

What if he were to be told, as Saul had been, that he would die the next day? How would that alter things? Would he still find room in which to frame and direct himself during the time that remained? The odd thing was that he was almost bored. But could boredom be a possibility on a known Last Day? He picked up two stones from his improvised altar. Flat-faced stones. He clinked them together, flat face to flat face. They happened to be the stones that had stood in for Michal and Uriah — for a moment, he wondered what an alliance between the two of them might have been like. Loyal for sure! He clinked them together again, pushing away the thought of Uriah and Michal. The stones made a pleasant sound on meeting. A sound that contained both dryness and liquidity.

It didn't take much to make music: two surfaces, a hollow reed, gut stretched over a sounding board. The day he killed the giant — after the killing — the air had been thick with the sounds of makeshift instruments. Hollow things banged, slapped, or blown. A bruit to wake the gods and rout them. He clinked the stones together again. *Ta ta-ta*, *Ta ta-ta*, *ta-ta ta-ta Ta*.

He returned the improvised cymbals to the altar. A table of sorts. If it were set with a meal instead of stones and if this were his last day on earth, would he be able to eat? It was said that Saul had not wanted to eat with the seer woman. That was no surprise. His instinct would have been that of a trapped beast who flails and rears, plunging ever more deeply into the dead end and its unyielding undergrowth. But the men who were with Saul that night were hungry. They and the woman herself pressed Saul to stay. At least one of them had lived to tell this story since it was now well-known.

Did those men help the woman to butcher her heifer, gather wood and build up the fire it was cooked on? Was Saul able to forget or disbelieve what was to come and join in? Every boy — every man — enjoys making a fire, watching it kindle, and hearing the snap of lit kindling, following the sparks as they climb the sky. Could Saul have ignored, even for a moment, the horror of what he had just seen and what he had been told was to come, in the ordinary business of preparing a meal? Was he able to rest in the base of that cleft, the only place where life lives? How delicious that roast meat surely was, each gout of flavour framed by the nevermore of Sheol's black jaws. How soft and fragrant the new-baked bread.

22

She knew how long a death can take before the process is complete. When her father was dying he had panted for days and nights on end, neither moving forward into Sheol nor back into life with the family who watched and tended him. Yet there had been a moment when it became clear to her that death was the only possible outcome. With that clarity had come peace and a change in the direction of her efforts. Whereas before she had experienced a desperate urgency, as if she were attempting to restrain a headlong animal, she began to feel easy; spacious even. At one point, to the consternation of her mother and aunts, who hung over her father as if he were fed by their breath, she had stood up and announced her intention of going outside to water the vegetables and then to take a walk. She knew that there was time for this and also that there was something she needed out there in the sunlight which would help her.

She was right. There was time. Her father waited for her. Though his eyes were tight closed he recognised the moment of her return by extracting his right hand from the weight of the bedclothes and holding it, palm open, for her to clasp. She continued to clasp his hand during his final hours. She marked how his breathing changed and had the sensation of the breath being scooped from him as wind scoops sand from the desert to frame it into new shapes. It was arduous, this labour of dying, but she felt she knew about it and knew how to be with her father as he accomplished this work. For it was work.

So it was now. It was clear that the baby — her son, Abimelech — could not live much longer. What mattered now was not to save his life — an impossibility — but to notice and cherish as much of the varying elements of his being as she could. His hands were clenched but it was not hard to open them and kiss each small palm. Some could see the future in the lines of a hand but she did not need a seer to explain his fortune. She was comfortable and newly sure, no longer needing confirmation from those more skilled in baby-rearing. She asked to be left alone with her baby. Only Safi to remain.

'Keep on with that blue stripe. He might know you're making it for him and stay to wear it.'

Bathsheba was reassured by Safi's calm, regular movements as she passed the shuttle to and fro, pressing each new row of yarn firm before threading the next. They had often worked together, spinning and weaving. This, even more than her mother's old cooking vessels, linked Bathsheba to her previous life; told her that her life was one, in spite of the great changes that had occurred. Stroking her baby's cheek with an infinite gentleness she began to sing in a low voice,

A young camel, the youngest in the herd,
set out with his mother across the desert.
They travel far, without any water
they ask all they meet if they have seen water.
They ask an antelope, they ask a crane,
they even ask a hyena, though they're not to be trusted …

This was a song her own mother had sung to her. It changed every time, different animals and birds would come in and the length of time it takes to find water would vary according to the time available.

23

David woke in darkness. It was as if he had descended to a lower shelf within the labyrinth of caves. No light came here. No warmth from the sun. Was there life, other than his own? Small creatures, mining, eating, and excreting the dust? He listened; listened for the sounds of life, and heard only his own breath, regular and somehow comforting in the way that the breath or the heartbeat of another can be. Often he had soothed an orphaned lamb or kid simply by cradling it next to his chest and sensed how the creature had been calmed from its distress as its own rapid, skittering heartbeat slowed to match his own. Listening to his own soft breathing he became more aware of the gradually changing qualities of that breath as it moved deeper into his body: the airy space of his nostrils which led upwards into the chamber of his skull and down into the damp and narrow passage of his throat. From there, widening, filling his chest with life and power, mingling his own spirit with the sweet air he had taken in before returning it, mixed, to the atmosphere. The more he attended to this breathing, this marvellous process that would carry him to the end of life, the more interesting and wonderful it became. He listened, as if to the breath of another, and was filled with a kindness towards this breather and the air that he breathed.

A disc of paler dark had appeared at the cave mouth. The

cloud that had covered the moon must have cleared. As the
week had progressed, so the moon had thickened to give more
light and David felt confident enough to climb out of the cave
into the night. It was easy for him then to find his way to the
stream to fill his waterskin. He would not wash until the sun
had come up and could dry him, but he wanted on this, his
seventh morning to wait for the sun and welcome it. This
was the best time; the time when creatures were beginning to
wake. A few night birds were still about, their spreading airy
calls so gentle on the air, ruffling it no more than did their
feathers. They were about to hand over their watch to the day
birds, now stirring in their nests and roosts.

He settled himself onto a rock, facing towards where
the sky would soon, visibly, lighten. The City of David was
also to his east, but he did not want to thrust his mind into
its busyness yet. That would come soon enough. The moon
was by now barely visible, its contours drained from the sky.
This infallible process of the day dawning — a process towards
which he could contribute nothing beyond his superfluous
witness — supported the calm he already felt. When Nathan
first exposed the extent of his sin he'd felt his own littleness
against the crushing weight of YHWH's presence. Now,
though his sin had not changed or been cancelled in any way,
he'd begun to see himself again in relation to YHWH and the
world that YHWH had made. His own smallness was a relief.
He had used his power wrongly and that was ineradicable. But
the limits of his power were very near. He could not accelerate
the dawn or prevent its coming by one fraction of a second. He
had sinned greatly but even that sin was small compared with
YHWH, his Lord's, greatness.

The sun was making its first appearance. Contours that, a

moment ago, looked hard and forbidding, now appeared soft. Then it became like a sea, lapping, galloping, taking everything under its cover. Annihilating or making new. Which was it? It was both and he had not the least power to oppose either. He was nothing. He was entirely known.

He stood up on the rock and stretched his arms out towards the sun. It was not the sun he worshipped, but YHWH who made it. But the sun already was so much greater than he. He felt a rush of power rising from his feet to his bowels and from them through his belly and into his throat. Sound came out. Pure sound. No words. Just full chords of praise. If words had come from him, the bare act of naming — *Stone, Sun, Earth, Water, Light, Breath* — would have been acts of praise.

Even as these sounds issued from him he was aware that they were new. The cries that herders used to call to their goats were various and surprising. He'd had his own, used different parts of his throat and mouth and tongue to form them. But this great *Halleluja* used more of him than those had. His whole body had become an instrument of praise. Praise and nothing but praise. It was the only impulse, dwarfing into insignificance every smaller urge to placate or plead.

He did not know how long it lasted and when his body had stopped making these sounds he had the sense that the land and the sky, the water in the stream and all the creatures who lived there continued to express this *Halleluja*: that this was what they always did, though he had never heard it before.

He sat down on the rock, dizzied by what he had just been shown. Not once this week had he played the old instrument that he kept in the cave, though he had handled it affectionately and even tightened the strings so they would sound. What music he could make in that way seemed small beside

the utterance he had just been a part of. But it was not worth-
less. Saul's prophesying — and that of all the others who fell
under the spell of Ramah — could mean nothing to anyone
else. The meaning was incommunicable. What he could do
with his music and with the psalms he would compose was try
to embody a small piece of what he had just been shown. He
could approach it in notes and words and — though the words
would never be adequate — they could be dipped in the honey
of what he had experienced so that others could at least have
a taste.

—

The day he'd danced the Ark home there had been no decid-
ing. The dance — like his song just now — came through
him; all he had done was allow it. He'd twirled like a top set
spinning by YHWH's finger. It had felt as if he *was* YHWH's
finger, his whole body a scribe, writing a sacred script. He had
not seen the stone tablets that lay inside the Ark but he felt that
another kind of revelation took place that day: an experience
of YHWH which was more about His nature than His Law.

It had to do with music, sound, movement — all of which
contained intelligence of YHWH. It had little to do with
behaviour — the conduct prescribed by the Law — unless
perhaps it was its generative source. Less about conduct than
about a principle of order; a principle of binding and dissolu-
tion. The walls of Jericho shook themselves free of their mortar at the sound of the trumpet and the shout of the people.
Before that could take place, YHWH had commanded that the
Ark be carried around the walls for seven days: the circling
both prelude and part of the impetus to dismantle which the

sound of the trumpet sealed as if dealing a sudden sharp blow to a fragile vase.

He was sure that what he had experienced on that day he danced the Ark home was a true, if incommunicable, insight into the nature of YHWH. His whole body had been sure — as if dance were in some way an expression of the Ark, as if his movements originated there and so manifested something of its nature. The two stone tablets within, unseen, seemingly inert as stone is inert, but breathing, pulsing with the force of their meaning. On the outside, the two winged sentinels; angels so beautifully carved you could almost feel the air whirred by their wings, the winnowed light. Everything about the Ark and its sacred burden tended towards the movement that had seized him.

Of course Michal had seen none of that. All she could see was that he was naked apart from the inadequate covering of the ephod. She saw the bare genitals that she would never again touch with love and made it clear that the sight was ridiculous to her. Her shrivelling contempt had nothing to do with his dancing. The power to reject and pour scorn was all the power she had.

—

His plan had been to spend a week apart in the cave. A complete unit of time, the time in which YHWH had created the world, in which even a man might accomplish something. He had tried to make a shape of his penitence, even if it could not, should not, be contained. He had intended to pray ceaselessly for the child, but he had failed in this; for much of the time his thoughts had been elsewhere.

He re-entered the cave with a feeling of affection. It had been his home; it had held him in physical safety while his thoughts had often been far from safe. The little altar rock, laid with its collection of stones, like pieces ready for a game; or to assist in the planning of a military strategy. When it had been a matter of thinking about troop movements, the nature of the stones or sticks or torn-off bits of bread was immaterial. They were simply there to represent a mass or a man. But these stones were more than that. They had accompanied and enabled his thinking, partly by virtue of what was distinct about them, their unlikeness to the objects of his thought provoked him to think with more clarity about those objects.

There they stood: a stone for Saul; one for Michal; one — not for YHWH, but for his own apartness from YHWH, his self-exclusion; one for Jonathan; and another for Uriah. A poor piece of gravel for the sickly child. Only the white, rose-tipped one remained. Looking at them set out on his altar he was reminded of the Artefacts. The Artefacts that he — and very few others — had seen, created by the Philistines as an appeasement-offering when they returned the Ark. Unlike his stones they really did look like what they stood for — mice as close to living mice as gold could become and golden haemorrhoids which made his bowels wince.

He knew about the deaths at Beth-shemesh when the Artefacts had arrived there along with the Ark. He had been taught that the Philistines — the people of the sea and plains — were misguided to think that these golden replicas could buy their way out of trouble and improve their standing with a god whose name they did not know. These men from the west with their grubby practices of divination and magic — practices of a piece with an undoubted mastery in the manipulation of metals — had no idea who YHWH was or how to revere Him. How haughtily — so he had been told — the priests at Beth-shemesh had received these gifts on behalf of the Israelites. But hadn't they, if even for a moment, been amazed? Hadn't the boys they once were wanted to play with them?

Even now he marvelled at the artistry that had made those objects. Was there not something about their making which, by virtue of the skill and care devoted to them, spoke — albeit unknowingly — of YHWH? Aaron had made a golden calf out of melted-down bracelets and earrings. He did this to pacify the people while they waited for Moses to come down from the mountain. But *was it any good*? As good a piece of modelling as the Artefacts? He thought of some of the animals he had carved for his children — barely recognisable as the cows or sheep he said they were.

YHWH forbade the making of images in case they become objects of worship like the Philistines' beloved statues — or like Aaron's golden calf. But there had never been any danger that the toy sheep and cows he'd carved would be worshipped — he had no ability in that way. What he'd liked was the process of cutting, shaping and smoothing. Even if the finished product could have stood for any four-legged creature, he'd spent time thinking about the animal while he carved and that thinking had helped him to know the nature of the animal better. Was that wrong?

The teaching was that the golden calf was so beautiful the Hebrews worshipped it instead of YHWH. That was why YHWH condemned it. They had *asked* Aaron to make them a figure to worship, since they thought Moses might never come back to them from the mountain. They lacked confidence without something to gather their focus. Some object.

Had they, without realising, been worshipping Moses before that? At what point does complete reliance become worship? It could, he knew, so easily turn into hatred. He had learnt this at Ziklag.

After he had melted the calf back down into liquid, unformed gold and restored it to a state of pure potential, Moses had made a powder of that gold, mixed it with water and forced the people to drink it. Was this punishment or medicine or both combined? Moses had carried another kind of gold down from the mountain: the gold of Law, direct from the mouth of God. Was that the gold he had forced down the throats of his ungrateful people?

No images, that was Law (which surely did not extend to hand-carved toys). But the skill, the quality of attention, the dedication required to make an image as full of life and beauty as those golden mice — images that *showed* the beauty of life — must, he felt, be born of YHWH. *God saw that it was good, and it was good.* When the world was first made, good making and good being were one thing: beauty, fitness for purpose, and virtue all one.

YHWH chose Besalel to build the Ark and the now-lost Tabernacle that housed it. He was chosen for the marvellous skill he'd developed in handling and shaping the stuffs of the world: its woods, its stones, its metals, as well as the textiles and dyes derived from plants. Besalel — a figure of legend now — had made the angels that covered and guarded the Ark. How could human hands have made faces that gazed with such great sweetness combined with terrible severity? Had Besalel seen an angel (in which case the figures he made would have been representations of the outlawed kind)? Or did he act from an inner knowledge which permitted him to create figures that would demonstrate to all who saw them what an angel might be like?

He thought again about his music. His ability to make it came from a lifetime of experimentation and practice. Some children learn about their world by tasting it. They put everything into their mouths unless prevented by a vigilant parent. David had learnt by listening. He listened to the texture of a voice to know the nature or condition of a person; he could tell from the sound made when wind meets rock and sand what weather would ensue and how the animals in his care would be affected. He heard the calls of those animals and knew if they were combative or protective or alarmed, and he learnt early on how to call to those animals so that they would trust him and not fear his approach. It had made him a good trapper and butcher, as well as a soothing midwife.

He picked up the old instrument and twisted the horn pegs until the strings were taut again. As he plucked them he placed the instrument against his cheek to feel the vibrations of the chord in his brow, his cheekbones, in his teeth. He wanted to make sound and to shape words that every cavity in his body would feel and test for truth. Searching sounds. Words could grow from them, but they must begin here. In his emptiness.

He had used words wrongly, making them act as weapons. He had felt so satisfied with his own cleverness when he wrote that letter to Joab, amused by the economy of making Uriah its bearer. *That* was an occasion when fitness for purpose led far from virtue. It had been a neat, clever, and efficient plan. Good in that sense, but very far from goodness.

Sun. Earth. Water.

Light. Breath. Sound.

He could name these without duplicity or calculation.

He ventures further: *Lord, my desert soul is thirsty for you.*

Can he be as lacking in calculation as the desert: as patient and open to mercy as the desert is to rain?

The unfamiliar sensation of loneliness has returned. He feels lonely and small. Mathur stopped leaving food for him after the second day and it occurs to David now that Mathur might have been watching from behind a rock when David hurled the food away. Was Mathur stung by his ingratitude? Since then no one has bothered with him. Perhaps no one would notice if he were to stay away and never return. Life would just go on without him; the City of David could become a place with a name whose origins would eventually be forgotten. *David?* someone might say, *Wasn't he a bandit, or a warrior, or maybe just a shepherd who played a good tune?* The City of David would carry its name but the man who gave it the name would be gone. There would be a story linked to the name — as there were stories behind the names of every brook, valley, wadi, rock, and cave. Some of the stories would be remembered and re-told whilst in the case of others, the name was the only trace. He thought of the marks he had found in other caves. Marks by which someone said, 'I was here'; though who it was that made them, no one any longer knew.

Into his mind came the image of his father Jesse, at home in Bethlehem, basking in the presence of the various grandchildren at his side. Not requiring anything of the children beyond that they should exist. He could see them all — his brothers' children, his own — laughing, fidgeting, quarrelling, charging around in the course of a game. He saw their bright, distinctive faces and ways of moving — the way Adonijah had of walking around with hands stretched out in front of him, fingers spread wide, as if to explore the space beyond. The way shy, beautiful Tamar dipped her head, making her hair fall forward. Tall Absalom's wide smile. Each one of them was present to his mind, themself and dear.

He longed to see them again and to hold the little nameless one if YHWH had granted him life. He should have held him for longer on that first day, one week ago, when Bathsheba, exultant with her achievement, had shown him the new child. His son. However sickly, however weak his grasp on life, nothing could make him not his son. Nor could any human fashioning — of golden calves, mice, angels, songs — come close to equalling the marvellous forming of a living creature, even one that failed to thrive. He wept again; gentle tears of tenderness and pity for the child whose existence had kept eluding him these past days.

Could he sing for him? He picked up the instrument and stroked the two strings. Only two were needed to make a chord and create a depth of sound. This particular instrument belonged here in the cave. If he came back, it would be waiting. In the meantime he had others — beauties of polished wood, with ten or twelve strings apiece. In the room at the King's House dedicated to music he would continue making the psalms whose first words and notes he had begun to hear. Out of the depths they would cry.

But for now, all he wanted was to be with his family and experience the ordinary comforts of affection. Extraordinary ones too, for there was Bathsheba, so shockingly beautiful, now his acknowledged wife. It was impossible to regret that.

The sun fell on the cave's altar, illuminating the seven stones. They had served their purpose. He scooped them up and tipped them into the cloth of the garment he would wear again once he was out in the open. But he kept the little piece of gravel back and put it in his mouth for safe keeping while he climbed out, resolving to bind it into a cloth once he was home and to keep it there, to handle and feel. To remind him that he was the man in Nathan's story.

With his improvised bag in one hand, he eased his way out of the cave. He left the waterskin behind — for himself or anyone else who would find the cave in the future.

24

There was a moment when there was no more breath. The last small sip of air had been taken. The nostrils, flared while they'd fought for breath, were still; the lips, no longer taut, relaxed.

Bathsheba looked up at Safi without in any way changing the way she held her baby. Safi began to move towards her friend but, with a very slight movement of her head, Bathsheba asked her to stay where she was. Without speaking she said, *No movement please. Let us just be here. Let us watch with little Avi while his soul adjusts to its new condition. We need to be quiet and still.*

Tears ran down Safi's cheeks and she fought to control the sobs that were moving through her chest. She wanted to give Bathsheba what she had wordlessly asked for. Bathsheba moved just a little, to stroke the fine dark hair on the child's head. The head lolled and the contrast between its inertia and her own capacity to move threatened Bathsheba's calm.

Then something surprised her and made both her and Safi smile: a white egret had landed on their window and was looking in, completely unafraid and at home. The bird reached out its neck, unfolding it to its full stretch, the better to penetrate the room and look, turning its head so each eye could see what was there. If it were on a rock, by a river bank, they would be the movements of a bird who has spotted a fish. Safi and Bathsheba watched, at once delighted and a little afraid at this encroachment into their human space. The bird, its neck feathers lifted and fingered by the breeze outside, remained completely unperturbed and continued to peer into the room as if to ascertain whether all was in order. First one, perfectly round, eye and then the other would be turned towards them. Occasionally the bird would lift up a foot and replace it in the same spot, not in the least impatient to leave.

Safi's wide eyes contained a question. *What does it want? Do we need to do anything?* Bathsheba read the question and framed the silent reply *No, let's wait and see what happens.* There was still a faint smile on her lips.

The bird had enchanted them and continued to hold their gaze for many minutes as it peered and turned its head. Sometimes the long beak would open a little way but there was nothing there for it to eat or catch. It was probably a young egret — smaller than the many they had regularly seen, perched on the backs of sheep and goats, frisking them for ticks. Its elegant form, framed by the window, was startling against the blue of the sky. It made the women more conscious of what lay beyond, as if the bird, with its softly lifted feathers, brought the outside — the endless sky — into the room in a way that the window itself did not.

Bathsheba did not for a moment forget that her dead baby was on her lap, but the bird seemed to have something to do with him and there was comfort in the knowledge that the fact of Avi's passing was an event recognised by the wider world. She was waiting for something to be accomplished since she knew that more is needed than the mere cessation of breath for the soul to leave the body. The bird seemed to know it too. It was in no hurry at all.

But eventually, in the rather ungainly way of a man dislodging his legs from the mud at the edge of a river where he has been fishing, the bird turned round, first one leg and then the other so that its back was turned towards the watching women and the dead child. It stood there a while longer, looking out, before, in one fluent movement, reaching out and diving off the sill, lifting itself up into the air with slow, strong beats of the wide wings. It was a leisurely movement.

25

No one noticed David as he entered the King's House. It was the middle of the morning and the household servants were occupied with their usual tasks of food preparation and cleaning. One woman, seated by the quern where she ground the day's flour, looked up for a moment to observe a wild-looking figure enter the compound. She did not think it her business to challenge him and went on with her work. David wondered if he had indeed been forgotten. Only when he entered his own private quarters did Mathur, ever-faithful presence, greet him with a start of surprise before recollecting himself and bowing low. He offered to fetch water and fresh clothes for the King and only then did David realise how rough his appearance must be.

He washed. He combed his beard and the hair of his head and saw how much grit the comb raked out. He had removed the small piece of gravel from his mouth and placed it on a table, reminding himself that he would bind it into a cloth. But first, he must find his new son, if he lived, and greet him. That was why he had been away all this time and his sense that all was well gave him hope. He must go to Bathsheba. He put on a fresh garment and walked through the unusually empty corridors to Bathsheba's rooms.

She was there, with the young woman, Safi, and Tamar. Safi got up and went out as soon as she saw the King enter.

Tamar went up to her father and took his hand. He embraced her gladly and held her close while she bent her head to rest on his chest. Then she extricated herself, shook her hair free, and went out as Safi had done, leaving him alone with Bathsheba. She had not stood up when her husband, the King, entered the room. Now she did, lifting the small parcel of her child's body, wrapped in a fine piece of cloth with a thin stripe of blue. She had no need of words.

He cradled the lifeless body of his child in silence and looked at the crumpled brow, the flared nostrils of a nose slightly squashed, the tiny, closed, mouth. He felt into the cloth that wrapped the body and extricated a hand. It was still soft, death had not yet done its stiffening work, and he unfurled the hand and kissed the palm.

'My son,' he whispered, speaking only to him. 'Such a little life.'

'You missed most of it.'

Bathsheba, suddenly furious, flew at her husband. She wanted to punish him for everything she had endured over the last months. For her months of torment and fear; for Uriah's death and the death of her son; for her husband's desertion of them. David did not try to defend himself or insult her grief by the promise of future sons. As she hammered at him with her fists she reminded him of the spirited woman he had first encountered, even if he was no longer the man who had compelled her. He could not clearly taste how it might yet be between them but there was something — elusive as a bud of moisture in the air — that suggested a different terrain or season.

When her tears of rage had subsided, he said simply, 'We must bury him. We two alone. There is a cave near here which will be his tomb.'

It was not the cave where David had lived during the previous week but a much smaller one. It made Bathsheba think of an oven, her child a small loaf placed there to bake. The idea was surprisingly comforting. As far as her husband was concerned the child that they placed in the tomb was nameless. David had not thought to give him a name and, knowing that it was not for her to do so, she kept secret in her heart the name she had given Abimelech. He knew he was the son of a king and so did she, and so did Nathan. She remembered the prophet's words, that every life has a purpose. Could that purpose have been to change her into who she was now? If so, what was she for her life to be more than her child's? What, with her knowledge, could she give? Would she live to bear other children — children whose own lives would in turn have purpose? The cloth she wound around his body was the one she had begun and that Tamar and Safi had continued so tirelessly, cutting it down from the loom when the life it was destined for had ended so early. It was narrow for a shawl but wide enough to bind this baby's body. The narrow band of blue was like a ribbon of sky.

POET

1

Greenwich, England, the spring of 1528

A bright spring morning. A brisk and merry breeze is tickling the Thames so that the surface has become thousands of sparking, dancing spangles and quicksilver puddles. It is not yet warm: there is still dew on the grass and, where the ground has been churned by horses, the contours are hard. Later they will subside into sloppy mud.

The tournament will begin in the afternoon, but the grooms have slept here with the horses and have been busy for hours preparing them then clothing them with the cloth and armour that have been made for this occasion. The armour is so heavy, the smaller grooms struggle to lift it and have to make use of the pulley designed to hoist an armoured man onto his mount.

But first they must go indoors and become part of the audience to a pageant. The pageant is in celebration of the King's great new acquisition: a series of ten magnificent Flemish tapestries depicting the whole story of King David and his inamorata, Bathsheba. The cost of this is rumoured to be huge. A proportionate degree of admiration will be required of all who are assembled.

To the left of the timber stage sits a crowned man on a throne. On his lap, a harp, and, when he mimes the playing of it, the musicians below the stage strike up. The crowned man opens his lips and, as he does so, another man, standing at the side of the stage, begins to sing in high, silvery tones, the words of the twenty-first psalm:

Domine, in virtute tua laetabitur rex, et super salutare tuum exultabit vehementer.

The Latin words are familiar to Wyatt, yet, by way of pastime, he experiments with Englishing them, making them his own. This weighing and turning of words is ceaseless in him.

O Lord, the king shall be glad in your virtue, and will rejoice most vehemently in your safety.

'Virtue' or 'strength'? Which was better? Time was when 'virtue' — the quality of manliness — could not fail to be strong. But the *virtù* that Machiavelli had recommended to his Prince was not quite virtue. Not the virtue the psalmist rejoiced in.

O Lord, the king shall be glad in your strength then.

But the crowned man on stage has ceased to sing. He has put down his harp and is sat there, the embodiment of regal power.

Wyatt has a professional curiosity in what he is about to see. He knows the story of King David and Bathsheba — who does not? It is a story particularly close to his heart on account of the psalms written by the penitent David. He knows no poems that reach so deep. Though he has never, knowingly, written words to be performed on such an occasion, being too high-born to write for hire, he is interested to see what the journeyman rhymster was able to piece together at short notice, the King being so overjoyed with his tapestries he cannot wait to make them known. The pressure of urgency can at times force out good language. Though not, it seems, in this instance. He sits back to watch as, on the other side of the stage, a couple enters: a man in soldier's gear and a slim boy, veiled, wearing women's skirts to signify that he is the soldier's wife. The soldier has his arm draped over his wife's shoulder and she inclines her head to rest it on his arm. The man speaks:

Dear wife, I must away to war.
Keep thou our bed-truth ever dear.
While I the Philistine do slay
Slay thou each thought that might betray
Our faithful love, the single heart
That binds us two, e'en while apart.

The woman replies:

Husband, my fear is all for thee.
Wear thou this cross that all may see —
Sign of a Saviour yet to come
Who'll banish death and shun the tomb.
And yet — alas — why must we part?
To do so splits my very heart.

There follows much dumbshowing of grief at parting. The wife climbs into a tower (constructed of wood and paper, and painted) and waves her husband off with her handkerchief. He waves back, then returns his hand to the hilt of his sword as he strides away to war.

Now the stage king climbs a tower — a little higher than the one the wife occupies — on the opposite side of the stage. He makes a show of surveying his kingdom:

> *I look about o'er all my land*
> *Secure from any tyrant hand.*
> *A shepherd once, I guard my sheep —*
> *My people — who can safely sleep.*
> *To lands afar my soldiers go*
> *Bravely slay the Philistine foe.*

The woman has by now climbed down from her tower. A bowl and jug have been fetched onto the stage. She mimes pouring water into the bowl and then, after first removing her real cloak, goes on to mime the removal of all her clothes. What this entertainment lacks in verbal sophistication is more than compensated for by the abilities of the performers. The boy actor is so skilful that the spectators feel they can see it all: the untying and the rolling down of the sleeves; the unbuttoning of the heavy skirts, the stepping out of the same; the unfastening of the bodice and the subsequent freeing of the breasts which — to appreciative chuckles from the audience — the boy appears to weigh in his two hands. The unrolling of the hose, slowly, from the left leg and then from the right. Soon it is as if the woman stands before them all in a beguiling nakedness which makes the women in the audience blush to see their inviting ways so accurately displayed. The beautiful actor — he cannot be more than fifteen — proceeds to show the woman washing herself. In mime, she empties the pitcher of water into the bowl, then takes a smaller, shallow one and dips it in the larger. She appears to pour water over her head, down her back, between her breasts. She seems to wash her private parts.

Wyatt chuckles at the skilful comedy of the performance which more than compensates for the roughness of the words. The boy actor suggests a Bathsheba well aware that she is observed. Calculating her effect. Wyatt, who has long pondered the story of David's degradation and the great psalms of penitence that resulted, had never thought of Bathsheba as complicit. Now he wonders, could Bathsheba have set out to ensnare the King? She would not have been the last woman to act in such a way and David was surely not the last king to be so ensnared. Is Ann, seated now next to King Henry, conscious of any resemblance? He will not look her way to see.

The stage king, in his high tower, no longer surveys his kingdom. He watches, riveted, the woman while she washes, an expression of shameless lust on his face.

That damsel there, so dazzling fair,
I want to clip her body bare.
Whoe'er she be — maid, wife, or widow,
I'll nuzzle her upon my pillow.

He shouts into the audience:

Holla, servant — yonder dame —
Go enquire for me her name.
Nay — fetch her to me — say the King
Commands. His will is everything.

A tyrant king; a knowing lady; a loyal and honourable spouse? Reshuffle those ingredients and there are many present who might feel they are being spoken to particularly. Not least himself. In his mind, Wyatt casts himself in the role of Uriah the Hittite, devoted servant of King David and of the Ark. Stalwart soldier. While his wife …

He feels a clenching of his stomach as he thinks of her. Constraint and sourness. She had done it *in his own bed*. He hears himself tell the story of her betrayal to himself, for he cannot see but find words for the sight; always words tramping through his mind, pressing what he has seen and felt into their shape. How stupid the man had looked, surprised in the act. Tugging the stained bedclothes to his body to protect his wilting member from Wyatt's gaze. Trembling.

And she? His wife, Elizabeth? She had climbed sullenly out of the bed, letting her chemise fall to cover her thighs. *Her flushed thighs*, he corrects himself, needing the stream of language in his mind to represent truth as closely as possible. Sullenly, insolently, she had gathered up the garments she'd earlier cast to the floor and made as if to barge past her husband to reach the anteroom. He caught her by the shoulders, preventing her exit. He did not hit her — he would not. *One moment madam*, he said, and dragged from beneath the bed a chamber pot in which slooshed the dark urine of early morning. He tugged a chain from his neck and flung it in. *You would be so kind as to dispose of this rubbish with the rest*. He had passed the pot to her. He had bowed.

Then he had gone out, and made straight for the stables where he'd impatiently required a new horse to be saddled. The groom, busy with the tired horse his master had so recently arrived upon, hurried to comply. Once mounted on a fresh horse Wyatt had ridden away, he hardly knew where. The lover? He had made no impression beyond that of being ridiculous. Wyatt's mind did not give him the honour of house-room.

A man emerges from the spectators, doffs his hat and bows to the stage king:

> *Sire, that lady's Bathshebee,*
> *Wife to your general Uree*
> *Who does your will, eschewing wine*
> *And wife to kill the Philistine.*

The stage king appears to listen attentively.

> *Uree at war? Then fetch her now.*
> *(While the boar's away I'll mount the sow.)*

The servant crosses the platform to the base of the woman's — Bathsheba's — tower. He bows to her and shows her a summons. The woman looks alarmed, wraps a shawl about her head, and then, with little steps that make the short journey of crossing the platform seem to be a good many miles, arrives on the other side of the stage to approach the stage king, to whom she bows.

The servant departs.

The stage king makes to embrace the woman, who seems to implore him to desist. The king brandishes his sceptre and the two embrace.

Bathsheba departs.

Two children cross the stage. Each carries a sign of a new moon in one hand and of a full moon in the other — to signify the passage of months.

We see Bathsheba writing, and the servant takes her letter and delivers it to the stage king.

The king reads the letter with an expression of horror:

The dame with child! Uree away! Alack, all will be known.
He must return and bed his wife to think the child his own.

(*Why has the verse moved into fourteeners here*, thinks Wyatt. *Do they signify a quickening of feeling? A line of fourteen syllables needs skilful handling if it is not to sound clumsy and over-crowded. Yet perhaps here they are effective in conveying the king's panic.*)

The servant is dispatched to summon Uriah to the king's presence. Uriah returns, trudging across the stage in what appears to be heavy armour, dark battle scars painted across his face.

The king welcomes him; hands him a large goblet which he fills. When Uriah has emptied it he fills it again:

Now after feasting take delight
And comfort in your wife all night.

Uriah:
Nay sire, till done is all the war
I'll keep my loyal body pure.
I mean to sleep here, by your gate —
Those nuptial joys I miss must wait.

Uriah lies down in his armour to sleep. When he wakes he buckles on his sword and returns to the war.

King:
Uree must die. I'll send my word
That he must go and plie his sword
Where hottest, fiercest battle strife
Ensures that he will lose his life.

Horrid sounds of battle follow. Uriah staggers onto the stage, clutching his breast. He collapses onto his knees:

I'm wounded sore. My life I yield
Here upon this battlefield.
Serving my king, I lived, and die
His servant still, and shall be aye.

Bathsheba receives the news in her tower. She drags clawed fingers down her cheeks to signify her grief, her mouth an O of sorrow. She winds a black shawl around her head.

The king approaches her; makes a show of comforting her, and removes her shawl to replace it with a white bridal veil.

Next, the king is seated on his throne with Bathsheba — her belly bulging — in an adjacent throne.

Enter Nathan the Prophet:
Once was a man, humble and poor,
His one white ewe he did adore —
It was his onely, dearest deare —
On her he lavished all his care.
Another fellow lived nearby
With flocks and herds in great supply,
Yet when he had to feast a guest
He spared his own and stole the best —

Nay, onelie — ewe of that poor man
And slaughtered her. What think you then?

The king grips the arms of his throne and rises in indignation.

King:
That man was false and wrong and greedy
To make demands of one so needy
And take his all — tis worse than stealing.
Cruel. Heartless. Quite unfeeling.

Nathan:
Sire, thou art he. You had wives aplenty —
For Uree's dear one, you had twenty.
And yet you stole his onelie own.

King:
Alas, Alack, what have I done?
Sense of sin scorcheth my heart.
With scalding tears mine eyes do smart.
My long penaunce doth here begin.
But nothing can erase my sin.

The king tears off his royal cloak and replaces it with one of rough homespun. He takes up his harp again and, at the same time, a musician beneath the platform plays a real harp.

The king says the words of Psalm 130, the sixth of the Penitential Psalms composed by David in his contrition:

De profundis clamavi ad te Domine; Domine exaudi vocem
meam.

The familiar words never failed to touch him. *Out of the deep I have cried to you O Lord, Lord hear my voice.* He loved the repetition of *Domine.* The way in which the words touched each other like billiard balls, the second instance bouncing off the first with renewed force. *O Lord: Lord.* There is importunacy in the repetition but also, comfortingly, a sense of being answered. A confirmation that the voice *is* heard.

The music — played by the concealed harpist and mimed by the stage king — is played in a minor key, the notes slide and stoop in semitones: the sound of a soul feeling its way and whose range is constricted. Creeping up the dark stairs; up from the lowest dungeon pit. *De profundis.* He is moved to think that a cry, issued from the deepest depths, can pierce distance and reach a listening God. In his mind — not for the first time — he tries a version of his own:

From depth of sin and from a deep despair,
From depth of death, from depth of heart's sorrow
From this deep darkness …

Something like that. Every repetition of *deep* digging deeper.

But now a different sound breaks through and shakes him from his thoughts. The clamour of trumpets pierces the sounds of lamentation. Twenty young men in green rush onto the stage, each with a flaming brand in hand. And now the real king, King Henry himself, rises from his seat. He is dressed in cloth of gold. Diamonds stud the borders of his robe and catch the light of the brands so that all is sparkling. The stage king bows to him with reverence.

The stage king speaks:

My penaunce found end fortunate
When Jesus came to end our debt.
And now a second David reigns,
Who shows my virtues, not my stains.
People of England, be joyful still
For your great King does Heaven's King's will.

Wyatt, who has kept his own gaze resolutely expressionless while he watched the spectacle of his king being made into a figure of allegory, observes the complacency with which the King accepts the final compliment. He also sees how the King's eyes — like little currants in his wide face — dart about the room as if to ascertain that there is no trace of mockery in any other eye. Finding none, finding nothing but looks of bland encouragement, ready at any moment to break into smiles of delight at what King Henry would do, he settles to the real harp that has now been moved to the stage, and begins to play.

He plays a tune of his own inventing. A tune with a sprightly grace that is more pleasing than otherwise. Of course there is nothing new in it; the King has simply shuffled around certain sequences of note and rhythm that other, truer, musicians had originated. But Wyatt knows well enough that to do even this requires a good ear and much application. He himself learnt to versify through aping the art of his predecessors and masters. Copying, appropriating, translating. *Trans latio*: to carry a freight of meaning home across the seas and into his own English body and mind to be refashioned. But when he takes up a musical instrument his ability is limited — indeed the King far surpasses him in this. It is surprising how delicately those strangely plump and featureless fingers are able to pluck the strings. Wyatt's rudimentary skill on the lute consists of strumming a note or two to accompany a song. For him it is the song that matters. The words.

It is in verse — song of a kind — that he most hears himself. Even when he has Englished other poets and tried most closely to adhere to the lineaments of another's words, his own voice — very different from that of Petrarch or Boethius — would breathe through with the rhythms of his native speech. He would hear the weight and cadence of his own, as yet unvoiced, truth. In that narrow space between the song found and the song made lay the shape of his nature. There he heard the grain of a voice, as inseparable from him as his shadow.

But now everyone is rising to their feet. They are to follow the King — the real King — into the banqueting hall where they are to marvel at the new tapestries.

Wyatt has heard that they have been acquired from the Emperor's aunt, the Archduchess Margaret. Her palace at Mechelen employed its own team of tapisseurs. It was, he knew, a place of high cultivation. Its cultivars — such as Ann, who had lived there some years — showed its glittering trace as surely as the tapestries that flashed with gold thread.

Ann is here now and the Queen is not. He knows better than to look towards her as he takes his place in the moving sea of courtiers who make towards the banqueting hall. Yet he cannot hold back from thinking about her. Her strangeness compels that.

He thinks she is the wittiest woman he has ever encountered.

He thinks she may be slightly mad.

He has never known a woman more delicate and graceful. With her large eyes and high, slender neck she reminds him of a deer — one of the fragile roe deer he likes to feed with scraps from his breakfast when he is at his father's home in Kent.

He thinks she may be as tough as the fine filigree steel that curls so gracefully round his dress-sword's pommel. He thinks her not pliable.

Love is not what he feels for her. But she disturbs him; ruffles the calm waters of his heart in a way that is both casual and indelible.

However, she is not for him. Nor — and he wants everyone to be quite clear about this, for it would spell danger for him if they thought otherwise — has she ever been.

—

Ann and the King have led the way to the Banqueting Hall. All the guests follow, making their way through the connecting corridors as quietly as they are able — as if they are about to enter a chapel. They know that rapturous appreciation will be expected and are busy preparing their responses to what they have yet to see. Yet how can they see in this mêlée? How can they quieten their thoughts enough to take in such a density of depiction as is here displayed?

Soon Wyatt hears that some of the gasps from those who reach the hall before him are real. The chatter has changed tone; there is a focus to it. He gently disengages his arm from the gentlewoman who had asked him to accompany her (he had led her through, that would do) and pushes his way on, suddenly hungry to see what life the Flemish tapisseurs have breathed into the story that has just been so woodenly told. A story he has pondered so often and so long.

He has walked past miles of tapestries in his time, often without beginning to take in what they represented, their improving fables of vice and virtue unnoticed. As a boy he had sometimes amused himself by imagining himself inside one of the hangings at his father's home in Kent. He could not remember what the subject was supposed to be. It might have been Daphne turning into a tree or the Miracle at Cana for all he cared. What interested him were the animals at the edges: the birds perched on the open flowers, the butterflies, the frogs, the dogs — some splendidly collared, others free, ready to hunt — the rabbits — would they run away in time to escape the dogs?

The figures here are large as life, and the first figure he sees, on the extreme left of the first hanging, is a man writing a book. He looks closely to see how written words have been depicted in thread, hoping to read the story. But of course he can't. The 'writing' is made of tiny black cross stitches. Words of illegible wool. The narrative is told through the sequence of hangings — though you'd need to know the story in the first place before you could recognise it here.

A young man stands by him with a laden tray and Wyatt takes a glass. The woman he thought he had escaped is back, touching his elbow.

'They are fine, are they not Sir Thomas?'

'It would appear so. I have scarcely begun to look.'

He says this with a small bow and gratefully catches the eye — the *one* eye! — of his friend Bryan who is looking at him, rather than the hangings, with amusement.

Bryan walks over, drink in hand, and nods to the woman.

'Forgive us. Wyatt and I have a matter to discuss.'

'Do we?'

Wyatt is smiling, now the woman has slid off.

'Look solemn. As if we were discussing matters of State. I saw her attach herself to you like a clam and thought you might need rescuing. What is it about you, Wyatt? They won't leave you alone.'

'They want me to write songs for them. To them. And they know I'm already married which makes me particularly safe as a plaything. And you? What's your secret?' Bryan was known for his numerous conquests.

'Being an ugly bastard. They like being frightened.'

Wyatt laughs.

'A little perhaps. Fear can be wisdom, but too much is best avoided.'

Did the King overhear this? He made no comment as he placed avuncular arms around the two men and offered to expound the hangings to them. His wide face was shining with happiness, his little eyes sparkled with it. The happiness that comes from possession.

'You see here how it begins with the Ark. There's Uzzah, there, dead on the ground — you remember, he dared to touch it? And there's David,' he said, pointing to a bare-footed figure, apparently dressed only in a thin slip of a garment.

Sure enough, beneath the figure whom Wyatt had taken for Christ — perhaps Christ on His way to the flagellation — was the word δαvιδ. This name was spelled out in more than cross-stitched cyphers.

Wyatt thought it safe to say, 'I had taken that to be Our Lord.'

The King was delighted.

'You're wrong, but I see why you thought it. It must be intended. For David was Our Lord's ancestor. On the human side. So there would be a resemblance. And in some sense — you might say — David is entering into his own time of trial at the start of this story. His wife Michal is laughing at him.'

There indeed, now it was pointed out, was a woman whose expression could be seen as disdainful, looking down at the holy man. The name Michal resolved any doubt. Wyatt thought you had to know the story to know that the expression on the woman's face was disdain and not — say — modesty.

'Of course Michal was barren,' the King continued. 'It was a curse. As much so in those days as it is now.'

It must have pleased the King to understand childlessness as a sign of God's disfavour — at least it would have pleased him if he thought he could end that disfavour by means of a new marriage. He might also like to think that he suffered the disdain of a wife, though all Wyatt had heard suggested that indignation and sorrow were more apt descriptions of Queen Katherine's state as Henry's determination mounted to have their marriage annulled. But it must have been gratifying for Henry to find a way to feel that he was the one aggrieved. Christ-like in this.

As if aware of the immodesty of his tacit identification, not only with David but with his great descendant, Jesus, the King began to talk about the artistry of his new acquisitions.

'See here. Pure gold thread. And silver. I don't think the ladies of this court are any more splendidly dressed than these!'

The King had let it be known (without himself committing the vulgarity of saying it) that the hangings had cost him over one thousand five hundred pounds. An incredible sum. They were made of valuable stuff which had then become even more valuable through the skill that employed the stuff. Henry was making quite sure now that he was getting his full money's worth in admiration.

Others were pressing in now, eager to be included in the King's personal exposition. Ann had joined them. Now, laughingly, she said, 'Can you say with confidence that none of the ladies of this court are depicted here? Or gentlemen for that matter? I feel sure I recognise some of those faces!'

It was true. The faces depicted in the hangings had the look of portraits. Real living people were shown here, whether or not they knew of it. Wyatt was reminded of those carvings found on bench ends or under the misericords in churches. Some were purely fantastical but others — he would wager on it — depicted friends or enemies of the artist. Old scores were settled, affections recorded. He smiled at what she said but turned away. Their once-easy rapport was no longer safe to enjoy. She could meet him in wit as very few could, but his pleasure in her cleverness would be too evident and suggest a dangerous level of intimacy.

While the King continued to expound the narrative sequence and Ann to pass sharp remarks about the throng of courtiers portrayed (*but from whose court?*), Wyatt was at leisure to peruse the hangings and form his private thoughts. A virile man, he was interested to observe the depiction of Bathsheba bathing. But scan the tapestry as he might he could see no image of a naked woman — only the image of David looking out. The image of someone seeing without the person seen. Was this to respect Bathsheba's *pudeur*? Or to distinguish the viewer from David? Then, to his amusement, he saw that Bathsheba's nakedness had been transposed onto the figures on the fountain beside which she herself stood, fully clad, with her companions. The little naked women adorning the fountain spurted water from their breasts. There were three such figures, each holding one hand over their genitals whilst using the other to squirt water from a nipple!

And there was Bathsheba — *bersabee* — beside the fountain. And there she was again — even more splendidly dressed than before — presenting herself at David's court in response to his summons. At her feet were two tussling hounds but they did not fascinate Wyatt now. Bathsheba's lovely face did.

Who was she? She of the beautiful mouth, strong chin, and lovely straight nose? She was no idealised beauty — too distinct a person for that. Wyatt was sure she must have been known to the artist behind this work. It was a face worthy of the mother of Solomon, ancestress of Our Lord.

> *A face that should content me wondrous well*
>   *Should not be faire but lovelie to behold,*
> *With gladsome cheare all grief for to expell;*
>   *With sober lookes so would I that it should*
> *Speake without wordes, such wordes as none can tell;*

Clearly even the dogs on the ground were scrapping over her!

Wyatt moved from scene to scene following that one lovely face. He saw the tears with which she clasped Uriah's hand as he set off to war. Uriah, unknowing, having just been handed by David the letter that secures his death. Bathsheba's grief looked real to Wyatt, her compliance with David a matter of submission rather than will. Each one who tells this story must decide on the truth of the matter. These were not the first tapestries of David and Bathsheba that Henry had bought. How was the narrative tilted here? How were we to think about this new Bathsheba? This Bathsheba was not the knowing seductress portrayed by the boy in the interlude. The loveliest image of her, to Wyatt's mind, was the one of her arriving at David's court after Uriah's death. The scene showed a court thronged with attentive observers. Gossips. Back-biters. So it would surely have been, then as now, though then they would not have been dressed as courtiers from a modern court.

She was not in every tapestry. Her last appearance was after the death of her child, at the end of David's penitential fast. She was depicted serving her royal husband with a meal: three bread rolls and a fish, with David seeming to be in the act of blessing what they were about to eat. Was this again to suggest David's Christ-like nature — a reference to the miracle? Wyatt couldn't recall how many loaves and fish there were in that story.

In the hanging before that one, you could see Nathan the prophet hearing the shameful truth direct from God. (*How might that be, to know with such certainty, with no shadow of ambiguity? Did God speak to Nathan without words?*) Then you saw Nathan telling David of his sin. David was seated on his throne with Bathsheba by his side. Her hands were raised in horror while David's were lifted to heaven. As well they might be. Above them both, a frieze of winged beings: Contrition, meekly downcast; the Wrath of God, wielding a sword; Mercy and Justice trying to resolve the matter between them, while Wisdom holds out a skull and a mirror. *Thus shalt thou be.* It is wisdom to know this. Then Penitence, sword in hand, chases away Luxury; Luxury with her hair unbound, making away with a large coffer. There was only one dog in this hanging, well-behaved and standing to attention with a wide golden collar round his neck.

Bryan was at his shoulder.

'Recognise anyone? Ann's been making some shrewd guesses.'

Wyatt shook his head. He didn't want to be talking about Ann here, he feared the fascination she had once held for him was too well known for safety, though Bryan, as her cousin and his friend, knew the truth and limits of the matter. Bryan was not to be silenced. He went on, lowering his voice a little, 'I'm sure all those gossiping, disapproving faces at David's court look familiar to her!'

Wyatt merely made a small bow of assent. Certainly Ann was not a favourite of many, save the King, whereas love for Queen Katherine remained strong. Nor did Ann go out of her way to make herself liked — which was one of the qualities Wyatt admired and enjoyed in her. But now he wanted to change the subject.

'What do you make of those winged virtues?'

He pointed to the figures named *contritio*, *ira dei*, *misericordia*, *justitia*, *sapientia*, *penitentia*.

'Not a bad prescription for a virtuous life?'

Bryan scanned the figures.

'I like the look of Luxuria myself. Now that is a woman I might follow.'

He would too, thought Wyatt. Bryan was not called the Vicar of Hell for nothing. But beneath all the bravery, the venery, the gaming and profanity, there was something in the man he valued. Bryan was fearless, even in this climate of fear; and he knew what he was. That was it. You were on steadier ground with such a man than with one (he had not to look far) who had the idea that he was good and thought himself to be God's vice regent on earth.

'I think I prefer Lukkes, my falcon, to your expensive-looking Luxuria. Mice and mutton are all she asks of me — and freedom to spread her wings.'

'Freedom?'

Bryan's question was not a question. The word hung in the air.

2

Kent, England, 1528

He has longed to be here, far from the brackish joys of court;
the pressure of rumour and intrigue. The constant anxiety.
Here, along with his bird Lukkes, his mind can soar and stoop
untrammelled. Lukkes: his *luxe* in contrast to Bryan's *Luxuria*,
but more importantly, named for her luck and for his — as
if luck played any part in fortune. She was also his *lux*, the
light that pierced the clouds, the light that the darkness could
neither comprehend nor put out. The light that would always
return.

From where he stands, the land ascends gently to a summit
topped by a group of trees. Earlier that day he and Lukkes
were out hunting on open ground — ground that smells marvellously fresh for it has rained and rained. This time, for once,
the bird does not come to the lure. She has flown into the
trees, jesses dangling like torn and ragged tendons.

He has followed, insofar as he can without wings. From
his pouch, stiff and seamy with rotten meat, he takes a slab of
flesh, its red browning and softening with age. It tears easily
when he takes a thumb-sized lump in his hand. Now he takes
the lure and tucks the meat into one of its pockets so that a

little piece of it pokes out, enough to be visible to the falcon's keen eye.

'Ho! Lukkes, Ho!'

He begins to ply the lure.

His eyes are keen, though nothing compared to the bird's, and, as the lure circles and swoops and performs figures of eight, Wyatt seems almost to have an extra eye located in its weighted end; it becomes an extension of him, exploring the air, reaching out towards the trees, the fields, the sky. Plying the lure gives him a sense of ordered freedom: as if he were dancing a loose-limbed dance, footing the airy maze. He pays out the string of the lure inch by inch until it circles high over his head in a fluid, leisurely orbit. When it moves like this — the mouth of the funnel it makes so wide and inviting — it suggests only the sweetest, most gentle dalliance. Time after time he and Lukkes have played this sweet game, the bird discovering and responding to the invitation of the lure as if she had never glimpsed it before, as if it had never before teased and evaded her. Then, when she has returned to his gloved hand, jesses secure between his fingers, he will pluck a reward from his pouch — a mouse perhaps, or another gout of mouldy meat — and feed it to his wild friend.

'Lukkes, come back.'

Only this time she does not arrive. She must still be in the branches of that great oak — if she had flown from it he would have seen. Surely he would have seen. But if he turns his back now she might fly away. He is under no illusions about her loyalty. To her he is a regular and reliable provider of meat. Nothing more. If he keeps her always a little bit hungry it is his hope that she will turn to him; return to him for the food in his pocket. She is governed by appetite.

Knowing this, he delights in her. He would even say he loves her. At the beginning, when she was new to him, he sat vigil with her three nights in a row. All day, all night, for three days and nights, so that she would become accustomed to his presence and the nature of his movements. At that time, when he was in a trance of weariness and only the cold and his will kept him awake, he pictured himself a knight of the old days, doing penance for his lady.

Lukkes, my fair falcon.

His lady? He has seldom lacked one. He cannot forgive his wife and has refused to see her since the day he rode away from her after surprising her with her lover. But he never claimed chastity for himself — even before his separation from Elizabeth. He admits to himself that the cold disdain he felt at her adultery was the growth of a loveless soil.

All the talk of love. The game of it. The trouble of it. It is as with the waters of the Medway he has so often watched — watched its steady flow and the little vortices of currents that withhold themselves from the general direction of movement — where the flag irises set up their own centres of gravity, where fish rise or the long-legged, delicate, water-boatmen land. If a light wind catches an already-ruffled surface, the small waves will grow into little peaks and gradually, as the intervals between them increase, mount up into considerable waves. So with the heart's waters: once disturbed they may also, little by little, accrue force and mount up into a dangerous, romping storm. There is a storm brewing, for the King believes that he must have what he wants. He wants Ann, he wants a legitimate son, and he wants a divorce from the Queen. The case for annulment is being argued in Rome. The resulting waves can be widely felt.

POET

Ann has set the country in a roar and he has wisely stepped back, disclaiming any interest he might have had in her. In truth, the turbulence that the King's unquenched desire for her has created — not just in the nation but throughout Christendom — is like an exaggerated image of the small disturbance she once caused him. But it was no more than that: disturbance. Not a ramping need. Though she still retains that power to disturb. *Recede in te ipsum quantum potes.* Retire into yourself as much as you can. *Good counsel, Seneca! And how much, I wonder, were you able to retire into yourself with Nero on the rampage, wanting you under his thumb whilst displaying his respect for you as a sign of his probity? Did you, Seneca, also know that other tyranny? That of desire, with her raptor's beak?*

An evening chill has descended onto the hill where Wyatt still waits. Little flies have begun to climb the air to form a transparent, shimmering tower. This will attract the small birds, and they in turn are likely to draw the falcon's attention. If they do so, he will have to prevent her from taking one. If Lukkes falls upon a bird her hunger will be satisfied and she will continue to disdain the lure.

He lets the lure fall onto the ground and twitches it on its leash so it skitters in the grass like a mouse. *Come on Lukkes. Mouse for you.*

At last, a movement from the trees and she is nearly upon the lure. He whips it up into the air so that it eludes her and stuffs into his gloved hand an extra gob of good beef. She comes to his hand and he takes the jesses again as she eats, worrying away at the meat's fibres. Gently, he hoods her; strokes her feet.

Lukkes, my fair falcon. So you haven't deserted me.

He talks quietly to her, respectfully, not knowing whether

she understands any of it, but sure that, if she is his confidante, she will never betray him. *In friendship and in falcon I have been most fortunate.*

A fourteener, with all the *f*s. Worth pursuing?

Fourteeners can easily sound clumsy — as they did in that court interlude about David and Bathsheba. They make a kind of clatter, are childish, over-eager, and boisterous — rather like Hector, his lion pup. He wants voice in his verse, not rampage. But fourteen *lines*: that was another matter. The fourteen lines of a sonnet were the beams with which to build a house in which a man's words might live.

What matters is to build a home that no one can take from him. Allington? The castle his father so proudly acquired and where he stays now? A fine place and a familiar (*the fs again!*). It is where his son Thom was born, the boy whom he thinks of as all his own and none of his mother's. The girl Frances too. It is where they live — apart from their mother — during his frequent absences. It is where he has spent many pensive hours and also where he, with his father, has entertained ambassadors, knights, and a prince. But it can be taken. Home must be that which can never be taken from him.

—

Remembering his children, whom he so rarely sees, he knows that this love, his love for them, is inalienable. Yet, when Thom had wanted to go hawking with him today he had refused him, saying he was too young. The truth was that Wyatt had wanted to be alone. Alone with Lukkes, who leaves him free to think; alone with those thoughts that are closer to feelings than thoughts, thoughts that have taken up residence in him, that occupy his heart and sit within his mind, making their impressions in the way of rumps on cushions. He is ever in search of a language with which to know them.

As he walks back to the mews with Lukkes on his fist he resolves to spend time with both children the next day. He will read to them. Or rather he will tell them some of the stories they love best from the Bible in readiness for the time when they might read the Latin themselves.

———

Jesse said to his son David, 'Take a measure of this parched corn, and these ten loaves, and run to where your brothers are camped and give them the food.'

Fran pipes up, excited to be remembering this story, 'Because he was at home looking after the animals.'

She is straddling her father's thigh while pretending to ride a pony. Her legs are swinging rhythmically.

'Didn't I say *no kicking*? That's right. He was looking after his father's sheep in Bethlehem. Can you remember what else happened in Bethlehem?'

Young Thom, sitting on the floor where he has been playing with his new cup and ball (he is infallible at catching), looks up, pleased to know more than his little sister.

'That's easy. Jesus was born in Bethlehem. Everybody knows that.'

'And do you remember what happened next? When David had carried the food to his brothers and the cheeses to the captain of their garrison. What then?'

Thom likes this bit. He thinks that Fran should like it too, as she is his younger sibling. Sure enough, she is the first to speak, 'His older brother told him he was naughty.'

The legs start swinging again. It is exhilarating for a younger sibling, this promise of revenge.

Thom takes over, 'David talked to the soldiers and they told him that the Giant had asked for someone to fight, and his brother told him that he should be looking after the sheep and that he was naughty because he just wanted to see the fighting.'

'But he wasn't naughty, was he?' says their father. 'Far from it. He said to the soldiers, *Who is this uncircumcised Philistine, to stand up against the armies of the living God?* And his older brother didn't like it. Why do you think that was?'

'Because his older brother was frightened of the Giant and was too scared to fight him himself,' says Thom.

'Because David was brave but his big brother wasn't so brave.'

Saying this, Fran slides off Wyatt's knee and pushes at Thom to show that she can be a brave little sister. Thom, gratifyingly, wrestles her to the ground. Straddling her wriggling, supine figure, he bellows, 'But David didn't go and fight his brother, did he, Little Frannie? He fought the Giant.'

With that, he springs up and strides around the room, his chest puffed out.

'So you're the Giant now are you?' says Wyatt. Can you remember what the Giant was called?'

Both children shout in unison, 'GOLIATH!'

They had played the game of David and Goliath before and each time they did so they encountered the same problem: Thom, the elder and larger, was obviously more suitably built to play the part of the Giant, but it was clear — even to little Fran — that the role of the Giant-slayer, David, was the better one. Was it right that she — smaller, younger, and a girl

— should take this all-vanquishing role? Young Thom could allow it only if he did so in a spirit of being the magnanimous elder brother. Even so, while playing the Giant — stomping and puffing himself out with great relish — he would interrupt his giant-ness to remind Fran of the nature of her role.

Fran's face shines with ardent identification. 'He hasn't even got any armour on. He's wearing the breastplate of righteousness.'

Wyatt notices her pride in her ability to quote from what she does not know to be William Tyndale's Englished Letter of Paul to the Ephesians — a text perilous to own, but safe in his mind. Fortunately she is ignorant of her source. Reminding herself of the armour of righteousness she would, every time they played this story, revise her posture and stand very still, frowning with concentration as she summoned the spirit of righteousness.

Wyatt watches with tender amusement as his little girl puts on the armour of God. He is impressed by her instinct for this. (*Despise not one of these little ones. In heaven their angels always behold the face of my father.*) She presents herself ready-clad in this armour. He loves her valour, her confidence in virtue. Seeing her so makes him ache to protect her from the assaults that will surely come, when her armour of righteousness may not suffice.

Then they arrive at the bit where King Saul insists on equipping David with his own gear: *Saul armed David with his armour, and he put a brass helmet on his head; and then a coat of mail.*

The children beg him to bring out some genuine pieces of armour and a real sword for them to use. With more indulgence than wisdom he trudges out to his father's small armoury and lifts an old mail vest from where it hangs. Though Thom is already longing for his first full suit of armour, a helmet is out of the question for either of those small, silken-haired heads. But he does select a light broadsword — one of several ranged there — and returns to his children with sheathed sword, belt, hanger, and a small mail habergeon.

The children are thrilled. Now they both want to be David — not in order to clothe themselves in the armour of God and wield the Sword of the Spirit that is the Word of God — but so that they can look like real soldiers. The sight of Frances trying to heave the mail vest over her head is comic and pitiful. Her small hands are soon smeared with the oil that has been wiped over the mail to keep it from rusting (fool that he was, not to have thought of that!). The game must stop here or he will have to answer to her nurse. What had he been thinking of! But Thom has already pulled the sword belt round his boy waist — twice as tight as on the tightest notch — and is lifting the broadsword with both hands to attach it to the hanger. The sword, longer than his length from hip to heel, drags upon the flagstones but does not hamper the boy's delight as he struts and parades.

'Enough! I'm taking these back to the armoury now. When you're older, Thom, you shall have armour of your own to wear' (what pride and pain he felt at once conceiving this) 'but little Fran, you must content yourself with paper swords and habergeons. A lady has other weapons in her armoury.'

Wyatt decides that, for now, it would be wise to place more emphasis on the young shepherd's lack of armour: *David said to Saul, I cannot go with these; for I have no experience of using them. And David took them off and set them aside.*

'What did he have to fight with once he had given Saul back his armour?'

'A stone,' shouts Frances.

'A catapult,' says Thom, more quietly, enjoying his superior precision.

Wyatt notices that his son takes pleasure in the word itself. *Catapult.* Thom had tasted the word and let it fill his mouth. Wyatt recognises this sensation.

'Imagine,' says Wyatt, 'the sight of the young man, without a scrap of armour — maybe just a sheepskin on his back — standing opposite the Giant of the Philistines.'

'How big was the Giant?' asks Frances, her eyes cast upwards in awe and fear, as if at the hem of the imagined Giant's skirt.

'Big as a windmill!' says Thom.

'Big as a church!' says Fran.

'Big as the Tower of London!'

'Big as a mountain!'

They are giggling now, topping each other as they heap up bignesses.

Wyatt smiled with them, but the mention of the Tower was sobering and he felt an inner seriousness as he reined them in.

'I don't think even the biggest giant that ever lived was as big as a mountain. It says later on in the Bible that Goliath's brother had a staff the size of a weaver's beam. That gives you an idea. Think of the biggest man you've ever seen.'

'That's easy,' said Thom. 'The King.'

True enough. Six foot three in his stockinged feet, broad and getting broader, the calves widening as if pressed out by the weight of the rest of him.

Wyatt nodded a rueful assent and Frances, sensing that something unlawful was in the air, smirked and fidgeted as if she had been caught in a naughtiness. Even she knew — or sensed — that that line of thought would not be pursued.

Wyatt wondered if, for ever after, his children would picture Goliath as King Henry. He trusted that they had wisdom enough never to say as much. For himself, the association was now indelible, and secretly satisfying. This King, who liked to think of himself as a modern David, the sweet psalmist clothed in righteousness — why else would he have spent such a fortune on those tapestries? — was closer to the ogre-giant of Scripture than to the boy who killed him. A child could see that.

How had that lovely child, the young David (as lovely as his Thom and more practised with a sling-shot) coarsened into the tyrant who helped himself to what and who he wanted, regardless of justice? How had repentance then reversed the process? Those psalms were more than lip-service. They were the work, the difficult work, of deep contrition.

3

The man was a master-dyer. Wyatt had recently been granted a licence to import valuable Toulouse woad and he was here — at this dyer's near Maidstone — to observe the process of blueing at first hand. This new licence might prove lucrative (and God surely knew how he needed money: it poured through him as if he were a sieve and it water) but it interested him to see the work and action of this woad. He watched the man as he pounded the dark and brittle balls of dried leaves before macerating the broken stuff in urine.

He was led to a bath in which the dye was already in service. Wyatt watched as a white chemise was lowered into the bath and turned around with a paddle until every fibre was saturated. When the garment was lifted out, the greenish water streamed off it. No one wrung the garment; a wooden bar was threaded through it and the garment was suspended. Wyatt watched as it changed colour: from yellow to green and finally to blue. The extraordinary thing was that, as the yellowish dye-water drained from the garment, the colour became deeper rather than more faint.

Il faut que je ne me trompe pas. I must not make a mistake.

Il faut que je ne m'en trempe pas. I must not soak myself in this.

The monitory gifts of language!

The man was watching Wyatt as Wyatt watched the fabric grow a deeper blue. *Getting deeper and deeper in it.*

'I can see you find it curious. Not what you'd expect, is it!'

'It makes me ask where all that blue was buried — it's not there in the growing plant — at least not to the eyes.'

'You might think it's not there in that ball you're holding either.'

Wyatt had not been conscious of his action when he'd picked up one of the woad balls — *cocagnes* they called them in Toulouse — that filled a large basket by the wall. He had been rolling it idly round his palm throughout the demonstration. Now he opened his hand and sniffed at the ball. The scent he inhaled was deep and satisfying — unlike the rather nauseating smell that came from the vats. But there was no blue on his hand. He tossed the woad ball back into its basket, walked over to where the shirt was still dripping from the cross-bar, and inspected it by holding a section of it taut between his hands. He smelled it too; that earth-drenched smell he would evermore associate with blue was fainter there but still present. When he let go of the wet fabric he saw that both his hands had been stained by it, the left rather more than the right, a deep blue. The lines in his palm appeared etched in ink. If there'd been paper there he could have made a print of his hand upon it.

He laughed — from a childish pleasure in being so messily coloured. Then stared more at his marked hand.

'There's them that can read your fate from those lines,' said the man. 'And I can tell you for nothing that May will be bad for you.'

'How so?'

'It may be in your hand as well for all I know. That's not

the way I'm given to know things. They just come to me, in words, fully formed. I pass them on. Like just now, "May will be bad for you." This May or every May, or just the one May in ten years' time maybe. I can't tell you.'

Wyatt rubbed his blued hands on the sides of his dark breeches, though it would take time for the colour to fade. What was he supposed to do with the dyer's unsolicited pro-nouncement? *Thank* him? For what? What was he supposed to do with this piece of words that had been thrown to him — like a motto inscribed in a confection at a Christmas feast?

He did not like prognostications or prognosticators. Though they sometimes called themselves 'seers' they never seemed able to see that they were unwelcome. He had never sought one out, not even when reckless in drink. But, rather as he had noticed the way a cat will insinuate itself onto the lap of a person with an aversion to cats, these seers seemed to nose him out and attach themselves to him like burrs. Julius Caesar — whose image he kept ever near him on his ring — had been told to beware the Ides of March. A warning that did nothing to help him. If anything it would have unsettled the man, making him less safe. And now — equally uselessly — he had been advised to beware of May. What form should his wariness take? Did not King Oedipus precipitate his tragedy by attempting to flee it? If he were to hide for the duration of each May he might be smothered in his hiding place. He granted that seers do sometimes see something of what is to come. But he had yet to hear of any case where it had been helpful.

He thought of poor, beleaguered King Saul on the eve of his ugly death, consulting the seer (whom Saul himself had outlawed) at En-dor. What comfort did that bring him?

Not a jot. All Saul obtained for his pains was a wretched confirmation of his predicament in the terrifying figure of the dead Prophet Samuel, furious to be called from the comfort of death. Saul's rejection from the next world was worse than what he was to suffer in this. But the seer-woman did cook for Saul and his men. That was a kindness. Saul took bread at the hands of the seer before facing up to what he now, helplessly, knew to be ahead.

The dyer was looking at him as if waiting for some kind of response. Gratitude no doubt. Well, he could wait on. He was a fetid little man. Ingratiating and arrogant. Wyatt pulled his dagger from his belt and enjoyed seeing the man flinch. He walked over to the basket of *cocagnes* and stabbed one of them with a violence that made the man jump. Then he broke it open with both hands like a hard-rinded fruit, to reveal its dense, dark, packed interior.

'*This* is what Fortune looks like. Stuff you can sell and deal with. I will hear of no other.'

Not that he believed a word of what he said. He could not shake off the dyer's warning, nor a conviction that his fortune might well be dark and bitter. That his *amours* might prove *amers*. So swiftly can love turn bitter.

—

Who did not love May? Who did not feel like love in May when all the trees have erupted into blossom and the whole earth is scented and new? It was a month when all things sparkled — a foam on the earth that spoke of possibility and delight. His first kiss had been in May. On May Day itself, the day when folk rise early to dance in the spring and cut down swags of blossom to deck their homes and make bowers.

He had been no more than thirteen. On that May morning he had ridden out early after some altercation with his father the night before. He could no longer remember what that had been about, only that he disputed his father's right to govern him in some small matter. So he had set out at first light, consulting no one, and had ridden across the weald and into a village he hardly knew. Hungry, he thought he would find some breakfast in the village, but he had failed to equip himself with money when he rode out. He was not so hungry that he would give his shirt for bread, but he knew it was not right to beg when there was bread enough for him at home. His scarf perhaps? Yes, he would offer his scarf in exchange for bread and a bowl of milk.

He dismounted and led his horse to the part of the village where there was some activity beyond the usual scufflings of chickens and geese (they too wanted breakfast). A girl about the same age as he came out of a house with a bucket in her hand. She wore a green jerkin over her skirt and her white sleeves were pushed up as if for work.

'Do you have some bread and milk to sell me?' he'd asked. And then he'd added quickly, 'I've got no money, only this scarf which would sit prettily on your neck.'

The girl had blushed, but she had also laughed, so he knew she was not offended. Then she had set down her pail and vanished back into her house.

Just as he was wondering whether he had after all offended her and she was sitting indoors, waiting for him to be gone and for it to be safe for her to emerge, she did come out, carrying a platter bearing a thick wedge of bread and a small can which he hoped would contain milk. It did. He needed the milk to wash down the rough dry bread which he had to tear with his teeth and chew on hard.

The girl watched in silence as he swallowed it all down. He unknotted his scarf and tugged it free of his neck. He felt her eyes on his bared throat and found himself blushing in turn.

'Here you are,' he proffered the scarf.

'I don't want no scarf,' she'd said.

'What then?'

'You can pay me with a kiss if you like.'

So he did. His first kiss which tasted of bread and milk as well as of her soft mouth and the salty dew of sweat. He tasted the kiss and would have tasted more, only the girl picked up her bucket and ran away with a laugh. It set his body ablaze. He would like to have run after her, pursued her into some barn where he could do what he now had no doubt that he knew how to do. Obvious that this was what his body was for.

But at the same time (*strange how two contrary impulses may coexist, equally weighed, the one stilling, but by no means denying, the other*) he felt shy and self-conscious. He did follow her, but not as a pursuer. Still leading his horse, he made his way to the green where others were also congregating. In fact, a crowd had gathered and he saw that there was a Maypole erected on the green. The ribbons that hung from it were red and green — the green of her jerkin.

He was not the only one who had come to watch, though the line between onlooker and reveller was thin. If he had not needed to keep hold of his horse he would have rushed forward to join his new love, for there she was now, laughing with her friends, smoothing down her skirts, and readying herself for the dance. He thought that she saw him when she glanced his way, but her smile was so fleetingly seen it could have been for

a nearer friend. Or it could be that what he took for a smile
had been a moue of irritation as she scooped back the curls that
obscured her view. He presumed nothing. Indeed it was more
delightful to watch her in a state of uncertainty, as he nursed
the warmth of that kiss knowing he would imagine it later.

The Maypole was now encircled by girls. There were six
of them. They stood to attention beside it, all facing in the
same direction, patient as dairymaids stationed by the cows
they are preparing to milk. Then six young men emerged from
the gathering. They wore brown breeches but each had a red
sash round their waists. They also took up their stations beside
the Maypole, but the men faced towards the girls. They were
equally still, though one or two seemed to bite their cheeks
to compose their expressions. Then a man hardly older than
himself came forward and took a pipe from his jacket. As he
struck up the first notes — a brief flourish such as a herald
might make — the dancers seemed to light up. Each pair of
boy and girl bowed, and then each one turned to face the boy
or the girl who had stood behind them, and bowed again.

As the dance began, others from the crowd started to join
in with the music: someone turned their bucket over and used
it as a drum. A few people began to jig about on the spot and
one mother joined hands with her children and began to dance
around in a small circle of their own. He watched as other
children turned up and were admitted to the circle which
moved with the slowness of the smallest involved. Meanwhile
the Maypole dance was warming up. It had begun cautiously
with maids and boys, solemn with the concentration it took to
remember their direction in or out. He watched as the summit
of the pole began to be clad in a chequered plait-work, the
red and the green crossing each other to make neat diamonds.

What was an openwork tent at the start narrowed to a clad pole, like a furled flag. As the weaving grew near to completion the dancers picked up confidence while the piper, responding to this, upped his speed. No sooner were all the ribbons neatly furled than the dancers began to undo their work, unstitching what had been made.

Never once did his girl look in his direction. He would like to have thought that this was deliberate on her part, that she was so conscious of the kiss she had recently bestowed that she did not dare look his way lest she betray her strong feeling. But she was going at her dance with such gusto, sometimes breaking into laughter, that he strongly suspected that she had forgotten him and was contemplating the next kiss which would not be his.

He was transfixed. He stayed as the Maypole was alternately clad and unclad, stitched and unstitched with increasing, dazzling speed. The red and the green of the ribbons and the clothes flashed past him and he felt his pulse keep time with the beat which all around him seemed to utter. It was almost as if the Maypole were itself a living creature, shifting its shape between a tent-like openness and the singleness of the erect pole. In later years when he remembered this image it struck him as like the pulse that moves between male and female, or the pulse in a verse between a long expansive line and one that contracts. He had stored this image up to take out later.

But he did not know he did this. On that day the only image he guarded in his heart was the kiss. When he rode home later that morning it was with this treasure. He guarded it carefully, like a stolen egg.

4

May 1536

There had been many other kisses since then. Other months of May. But that May and that kiss were exceptional in their light-heartedness and freedom from complication. Years later, when the door of Fleet Prison slammed shut on him one day in May, he was to remember the unsolicited words of the Maidstone dyer. Words corroborated by the court astrologer, Sephame, to whom — in the foolish spirit of a game and egged on by Queen Katherine's giggling gentlewomen — he had handed over the hour and date of his birth. The nativity that Sephame cast renewed the warning. Beware of May.

There had been good reason for his imprisonment in the Fleet. Violence had billowed out of chaos — a surge of emotion that translated too readily into act. What had it been about? Loyalty to the old religion and Queen Katherine (the only Queen of England as some then dared to say)? The conflict that threaded Wyatt's mind was ever present in the circles he frequented then. Danger was never far. Now when he tried to recall that time he saw only a mess of violent, unsteady impulse. The man who had been killed by one of his drunken party was nothing to him — a sergeant simply doing what he was paid to do: guard the King against boisterous incursions. He had deserved to be in prison then. The punishment was just and he felt shame and contrition for the tipsy heat in which a man's life had been lost. Ashamed to have so lost himself and strayed so far from his own truth. He assented to the rightness of being clapped up in that stinking place where the stench of effluent infected everything — even the food smelt of shit and he gagged on it. His clothes and his beard stank of shit too. He had burnt his clothes and scraped his face clean on his release. The punishment chastened, as had been intended. There had been a congruence between misdemeanour and punishment and he had been ashamed that his children should know of it and their mother perhaps find satisfaction in it.

That sojourn in the Fleet had been two years ago. He'd hoped then that it was the May he'd been warned against and that he was now exempt from May's dangers. But it is May again, and again he is in prison. This time it is the Tower and he does not know why he is there.

There was always a certain ambiguity about a visit to the Tower. Till now he had known the Tower only as a place of state and in a strange way it felt an honour to be conducted here, though an honour he would gladly pass on. It was well known that a man might be summoned to a meeting there and think himself privileged, only to find himself in irons, awaiting the axe. Such doubleness attended the lives of men of state.

Heavy steps up the tight spiral staircase (he would come to know these steps well — the way each foot slid towards the vertical of the next stair, as if toes must be stubbed each time before their owner would know to lift his foot again); a large, clumsy man appeared, stooping in the doorway, alongside the two men who had accompanied him earlier to his straw-strewn chamber.

'Ralph Sutton, sir. I'll be taking care of you during your stay.'

'That is to say, you are my jailor.'

The man laughed, not unpleasantly, and looked down at his large feet. With the three men stood there Wyatt almost felt that they were waiting for him, as their superior, to dismiss them; that they would take their cue from him. What he did was turn his back on them by moving across to the narrow window from where he could see the sky.

'Good position you've got here sir. There's them that would pay for such a view of the block.'

He chose not to respond. At last the men were gone. The heavy door was pulled shut and a key was turned from the other side. In addition he could hear a bolt being slid across. Just in case. He heard them make their way down the staircase; their laughter after release from recent tension: sounds of a convivial side to his recent companions. He heard them leave him behind. He heard them forget him. He was alone as, in recent minutes, he had been so impatient to be: impatient as if there were so much to be done, so much to attend to. So much that could not be accomplished while these men were intruding on his consciousness.

What had he here? He now took in at leisure what his gaze had absorbed at once when he had arrived:

Table.

Chair.

Pallet.

Bucket.

A pitcher of water and a battered beaker.

Walls. Floor. Ceiling. Window.

He put the flat of his hands against the wall to feel its

coolness; rested his brow against it; his cheek. Then, having acquainted himself with this limit, he turned and rested his back upon it and slid down, his back against the wall, till he was squatting. From this position he could survey his room — his prison — in a steady way.

Still his excitement persisted. This room, which was to be his confine for an indefinite period and which would release him either to freedom ... or to the final freedom of death, could have been a new land which he had happened upon alone and by accident. A land that could be his and he its lord. Thinking this with satisfaction he observed how a lust for dominion may persist and be gratified even in adversity.

But this room had not always been his. There were others before and would be others in the future. He began to inspect the walls for traces of his ghostly (*in many cases too much so*) predecessors. What advice might they give on life in these quarters? Now, as he scanned the walls — not just with his eyes but with fingertips, sensitive as if tracing the lips of a lover — he could discern, in addition to the roughnesses of plaster, marks that were deliberately made. What implements had been used to do this? There was no blade allowed to him in here. No point. Yet his belt remained, empty of sword and dagger, and with its buckle he might yet do something. How each of us wishes to leave his mark!

—

From his window, the sky. A bright day. Nothing sweeter than a bright day in May. A day on which to ride out; go hawking. If he were a bird like Lukkes he could fly free of this place. A little movement above and to his right makes him look up.

In a crevice in the wall a bird darts. He can hear the wheezy importunities of the young, the sudden silence of brief satisfaction. The silence interrupts the noise. The small birds — he counts three gaping beaks protruding from the crevice — keep up their pressure of noise in a way which strikes him as pitiless. When their mother returns, her beak bristling with whiskery morsels which she stuffs into a mouth, the demands stop only for the time it takes to swallow. So, he has some companions already! When he has some bread he will share it.

He thinks of his own two chicks. Their mother's word for them, in the days when they lived together as a family in something like harmony. Thom, a young man now, about to marry his Jane, fiery and keen for challenge in a way which made his own heart swell in recognition and protectiveness. Frances, no longer the cheerful chatterer; a taciturn, sullen girl these days, angry with both her parents and resisting all talk of a husband. This present confinement of their father would do them no good. Thinking of them and of the poor example he was setting them in being imprisoned yet again leaves him feeling foolish and at a loss. Who is he to direct them in their lives?

The Tower is like a great city with its various accommodation: places of state, places of prayer, places of recreation, places of torment. What of the other human inhabitants of this place? If he could know their identity he might be able to divine why he too is there. There are rumours. There are always rumours. Few are to be trusted.

In January the King had fallen from his horse and for two hours had lain unconscious. How quickly the word had spread! What treasure those two long hours had contained!

Have you heard — my lord the King has fallen and is not likely to recover.

The weight of his armour added to the impact of his fall.

No one said he had grown so fat it was a mercy the poor horse was not crushed.

During those two hours many who heard this whispered news cherished a small, spreading flame of freedom in their hearts. Of exultation.

The King is dead!

Those words, fast followed by *Long live the King*, could always inject a shudder of hope. A sense of boundless possibility hid in that small but potent silence before the sequel words had been uttered. *The King is dead*, held packed within it an explosive, transforming charge. The words themselves seemed to propel change, like a cannon-ball forcing its way into the earth with an explosion that then releases and reveals a new form. *Long live the King* (or would it, this time, be Queen?). And all is changed.

But the big man had come round and all thanked God with their lips whilst most — even the most truly loyal — felt a sag of disappointment. An opportunity had dwindled and not born fruit.

Ann had miscarried. She was to say that it was anxiety for the King that had caused this. Wyatt could well believe that the sudden reversals of those two hours had affected her — she who was so volatile, so changeable, so responsive to alteration in others. How she must have clutched at the possibility of being soon widowed, though that would expose her to many new dangers. The news that the King was not in danger of death must have plunged a dagger into her womb — though, had the child been male, that womb contained her one hope of survival as Queen.

Some were to say it was not the King's child that bled from

her that day, but if not the King's, then whose? Wyatt felt a stab of jealousy at the idea that she might have betrayed the King with anyone other than himself. Had she been willing to be unfaithful to the King, who other than himself might she have chosen? Recognising that it is jealousy he feels gives him a clue as to the reason for his arrest. If his own sense of a connection with her persists, others must sense it too. Every instinct tells him that he is where he is on account of this connection.

He quickly smothers his discomfort at the idea of her infidelity to the King with the thought that she would never have put herself in such obvious danger.

How to describe what he feels for her, what she is to him? Though he had never exactly wanted her to be his, there was something, some unmet retracted promise, that retained a place in his mind and heart. He had not loved her, but she could never leave him unmoved. Perplexity was closest to what he felt for her. Perplexity and entanglement. Once, when he had been doodling in the margins of a song, he had found himself writing — as if in the hand of another — *I am yours Ann.* He had done it, he supposed, to discover how he would feel on seeing such words: if he could believe in or wish for their possibility. He could not.

> *in my book wrote my mistresse:*
> **I am yours**, *you may well be sure,*
> *And shall be while my life doth dure.*

Untrue. She was never his mistress, except in the way of gallant language. Never his. But she continued to haunt his mind, weaving in and out of its coverts like the deer of which, on account of her slenderness and quick grace, she reminded him.

She was so sudden in her dartings — rushing out like a beast that breaks cover and then, as if bewildered by the exposure, hesitating before returning again to concealment. That was the texture of her in the days before she had attracted the King's notice. In her present situation he feared for her. For all the wild splendour and imperiousness with which she had queened it at court, he guessed her these days to be as frightened as a lost child.

Heavy steps on the stairs and the turning of a key in the lock announced the arrival of Sir William Kingston, Keeper of the Tower. Wyatt supposed this was an honour. Not every prisoner was accorded such a visit. He had met Kingston once or twice before; or rather, they had stood in the same room. There was a certain scent of death around the man, a taint deriving from his position that made all men wary of him, and Kingston — who knew he might one day be jailor to any one of them — reserved towards all men. Yet he was frank in his greeting.

'I am sorry to see you here, Wyatt. I trust it will not be for long.'

'It is none of your doing. I have known worse.'

Kingston smiled awkwardly. He knew of Wyatt's time in the Fleet two years earlier, though in court circles one seldom spoke of such experiences. The slippery ground was walked upon with apparent confidence — even nonchalance — even by those who had recently fallen. But if Wyatt's spell in the Fleet could be seen as his due — a fit punishment from which his nobility had not exempted him — this present matter was far less clear, and both men knew it.

'Do you house many guests here at the present, or am I singularly privileged?'

He did not want to hear the answer he had guessed at. He had already heard from his guards that Richard Page had also been arrested that day. Page had defended Ann in the past. Was she the link between them? Wyatt strove to imagine what crime the two of them might be thought to share. Till now they had shared only distant courtesies.

Kingston paced his reply with the skill of a man accustomed to imparting painful information.

'You will have heard something of recent events?'

Why did the bringer of bad news so often try to conjure it from the mouth of the hearer, suggesting that what was repellent to him had already found a home in his mind? Wyatt shook his head whilst holding Kingston's gaze with a firmness that would not permit evasion. His heart swooped and crashed with dread but he was not going to speak what he already guessed and feared.

'You have not heard about the Queen?'

'What about her?'

'She is your neighbour here.'

What he had heard was an account of what had happened after the May Day tournament in Greenwich where he himself had jousted, satisfyingly well. Sir Henry Norris was defender in the jousts, but Norris' famously valiant horse had bucked and reared that day as if it had seen a ghost, twisting away from the path where Norris attempted to lead him. The King, who had ever liked Norris, offered his own horse in its place (as if to say, *I will let you ride her as if she were your own*). Norris had declined, preferring his own. Rochford, the Queen's brother, was the challenger.

Attention had — as ever in these nervous days — been as much on the King as upon the two who clattered towards one another, lances poised. For all the King's smiles there was something about his appearance which made his companions more than usually uneasy. There was a restlessness which the sweating activity of the tournament did nothing to appease.

The expected — but still shocking — debacle came when the King, very suddenly, swept out and mounted his horse, declaring his intention of riding to Whitehall, ignoring the barge that was ready to convey him and the Queen. He left the Queen without a glance, taking only six men with him. Among them, Henry Norris. The next day Norris was in the Tower and so was the Queen. This was what Wyatt had heard and chosen neither to believe nor disbelieve.

'Well then, I am in high company.'

'Aye. The Queen, her friends, and her brother.'

Her brother? Rumour had not stretched to this, nor named any 'friend' beyond Norris. Wyatt looked questioningly at Kingston but knew better than to expect any enlargement from that, necessarily, most discreet of men. He did not doubt but that Kingston listened carefully to all that his charges might impart and that all might be communicated elsewhere.

Kingston seemed to sense that further conversation would be unwelcome. His manner was more that of a courteous servant than the master that he was as he nodded towards Wyatt and backed out of the heavy door. Only the turning of the lock betrayed that he had not forgotten his post.

The Queen and her friends. It was as he feared. Certain now that his friendship with Ann was behind his arrest. It was said of Wyatt that he had once filched a necklace from Ann and worn it as a trophy till the King, wearing a ring of his not-yet-wife's upon his finger (*as if to signify he could enter her should he choose*) had declared, emphatically, that the ring belonged to him. Then — so the story went — Wyatt had taken out the chain he had stolen from Ann and offered to take a measure of the ring; whereat the King grew tetchy. All nonsense. Boys' stuff. But in keeping with the atmosphere of the court where a wise gentleman would do well not to piss further than his sovereign.

Had courtesy undone him? Too many courtesies? He had played the game well yet there was something in him that found the courtships of the court repellent. He knew his genitals to be serviceable, yet his way of life made him feel emasculated. His father had warned him that the easy grace with which he moved — almost swam — between women — the compliments, the little trysts, the mock sighs (*and the real*), the games over trifles — that these were unworthy of his best self. *Now you are a man you should behave in manly fashion.* By manly fashion his father had meant a fashion honourable to a man: *virtue*, the quality of a man, very out of fashion in the English court these days where only the bravery of *virtù* was applauded.

The business with Ann had begun by way of a decoy. He had read in Dante's *Vita Nuova*, of the *donna schermo*, the screen-lady, and recognised something of his own subterfuges there. The woman he aimed at and longed for — his Dian, as he privately named her — was chastely married and unable to tolerate even a small hint of scandal. She had once indicated that she would only be his in the event of their both being widowed. There was no other way. The fact that she did this encouraged him to think she returned his affection. But he must give no sign of it. He had made up for this constraint by energetic flirtation, particularly with Ann who had the wit and spirit to respond in the manner intended. He knew that she would rally and enjoy their exchanges and that her ambitious heart would not allow her to fall for him. Of the two, he was the more susceptible.

Only once had his Dian come to him. There had been a great gathering to which they had both been invited. Both were to sleep under the one roof. Though he had danced with her — as well as with others, and for no longer than with others — he did not expect to see her after he withdrew for the night. He was already asleep when his door opened, softly. She was there. He was by now entirely awake. She came to him where he lay in his bed and leant over him, so that her loosed hair swung down and brushed against his naked chest and her dress fell away from her shoulders. She had kissed him, whispered love to him. Rapturously, he held her; flung back the covers on his rumpled bed so she could take her place with him there.

But before she surrendered to his own kiss she had pulled herself away, tugging her dress back up to cover her shoulders, retreating like a frightened creature. He was left burning in desire, erect as a broomstick, baffled. The next day she betrayed nothing of what had taken place, but he'd hoped that the encounter marked a change. It did not. He grew to realise that this had been her farewell. His love for her, which he could never quite abandon, became tainted by resentment. Perhaps that was when his complicated interest in Ann, his *donna schermo*, had quickened a little.

There had been a time when the King had appeared to relish the homage that other men paid to Ann's wit and charm. Wyatt recalled, uncomfortably, that he himself had once been roused by his own wife's flirtatiousness — the sense that other men desired her. It was only when he knew of her adultery as fact that he became, irreversibly, cold. But Henry had set so many spies around Ann during his absences, he could have no real cause to doubt her. He could savour the knowledge that she was desired along with the security of knowing that he alone had the tasting of her. Wyatt, sensing the change in the weather, had kept his distance. This was made easier by the fact that by this time he had begun to set his heart elsewhere. Not his wife, not his Dian, not Ann his *donna schermo*, but a woman called Bess, in whose company he experienced such a glad repose that he felt it might be a ground on which to build.

Not that the King would know this or behave as if he did. It had begun to suit the King's purposes if the spies he had set around Ann reported more than they had seen. Every man — not just Wyatt — who had ever paid court to the Queen was alert to his danger. This danger was made more intense by the fact that the Queen, in her felt isolation, called ever more ardently on the gallantry of her friends. How many of them were now in the Tower? Each separate, walled off, far from the hearing of one another. There was nothing companionable in the knowledge that there were others. How were they lodged? Was the Queen attended or alone? The walls of the Tower leaked a chill sweat of separation which turned a man inwards, to the warmth of his own hot breath or the quiet pulse of his soul. The thickness of the walls deterred the search for fellowship — *for fellowship is false and fleeting*. His father — though he would be sorry to know him in prison and would wish him soon home — might see this misfortune as, in some sense, deserved.

A few days earlier, while walking beside the river, he had watched as a large gull — blown inland by the recent gales — crashed, beak first, into the water, like a creature intent on ending its own life. A moment later it had emerged, an eel clamped in its beak. Wyatt had watched, amused, fascinated, revolted, to see what the bird would do next. If it opened its beak to swallow the eel there was a strong chance that the eel would drop back into the water and escape. But it was a heavy gobbet to carry. The bird could not possibly fly far with the eel twisting and encumbering its beak. Bird and eel struggled on the bank and the bird attempted to set a foot across the eel. But the eel was limber on the muddy bank and, even while the gull seemed to be in the process of swallowing one end of it, managed in one swift whip of movement to recover its freedom in the depths of the river. The great gull had flown off in search of less agile prey, prey that offered more angles on which to obtain a purchase. Wise gull. Wyatt had heard of an eel that had eaten its way through its living captor's stomach to be born again through the belly of the dying bird.

That night he slept uneasily. He dreamt he was in a thicket pierced with arrows of light but with no clear path through. He had to find the correct number of saplings and weave their branches together to form an arched alleyway down which he might escape. As he moved through the thicket he found several pairs of saplings that seemed to match one another — like pairs in a dance — and were thus suited to such pleaching. But whenever he had bound one pair, any other pair that he had already bound and lined up disappeared. He needed an alleyway of braided trees to light his way home but all he ever found was a single arch. It was as if he were in the course of building a sonnet, rhymes holding just so far, and then opening again like sprung doors, the once-held contents fleeing and disappearing.

5

When he woke his gaze rested on the low arch of the fireplace in his room. With no fire the space might serve as a sort of kennel. Wyatt experimented with cramming his back in there against the chimney back and found a comfort in creating for himself a tighter confinement. In selecting it he had exercised an element of choice. Though he had made no decision as to where his living quarters should be, their disposition was for him to arrange. He could choose where he sat, where he ate — in which direction he would face as he ate — where he shat, where, and to some extent when, he slept. In all of this he had freedom.

His previous experiences of imprisonment had taught him the benefit of order. When a day lacked all the external obligations and appointments that regulate the life of a man at liberty, it was necessary to create a rule of life, such as monks live by. Remembering the days when bells tolled the canonical hours he decided, firmly, that his Tower days must begin and end in prayer. He would ask Kingston if it were possible for his precious Psalter to be fetched and brought to him. If this confinement was good for anything it could provide him with an opportunity to know the psalms more closely; particularly those seven which King David had composed in sorrow and penitence.

Paper he had but not ink. In extremis he might cut himself with the spike of his buckle and pen a letter or a poem with his own blood. Follow the psalmist and make his tongue his pen. But he was not yet in extremis. He felt that the greatest danger presenting itself to him now was that of boredom. The next time a jailor visited him he would ask for pen and ink. For now he must rest with wit and memory.

I cannot forget — his father's motto. *Oublier ne puis.* His father's maimed body was a constant reminder of what he had suffered at the hands of King Richard. Barnacle irons had clamped his father's mouth and injured it for ever; the corners of his mouth could never quite close and his words came out mangled and mashed with spittle that could not be retained. How could his father forget? How could that father's son?

Memory can be ordered. Or it can be like the sea, washing over a man, pulling him away from the dry shore of daily duties and flooding him, drowning him. Till he becomes a bloated corpse, dragged and pummelled this way and that, like a wrecked and rotten piece of timber. No. He would order it. Instead of allowing it to be a sea he would regulate it, devising a series of dams so that the water could be contained and used. The sun would distil the salt, the clear water would fall as rain, new crops would be fed and nourished. New fruit.

Ann's symbol was a withered branch breaking into life. Roses blooming on a dry stump. She, the falcon, perched atop, her feet planted in the roses. She was like a falcon in her native wildness, and in the fact that she was captive, even before the King mewed her here. Unlike his dear Lukkes, the Ann-falcon cannot fly. *Un*-lucky falcon; *un*-Lukkes.

Even now, as one thought tugged out another — like disordered silks in a sewing basket — he felt the sea nibbling at his edges. Sitting here, in a shaft of May sunlight that streamed through the high grate making shadow bars on the floor, he saw how he might be fretted away by thought, become a lacework of land and sea, fjords and lochs fingering their way into his substance.

—

Kingston was a big man. His presence could intimidate or reassure, depending on why he was there. To his wife, his mountain breadth and height (though he was not at all fat) spelled safety. He was himself a tower as well as the Tower's Keeper. Like many a big man he had not needed to develop habits of aloofness or aggression to signify that he was not to be trifled with. His volume was sufficient to ensure respect. By nature he was amiable, courteous. Even diffident. Though his position demanded a great deal of circumspection on his part, the ability to keep his own counsel, he was remarkably honest and respectful in his dealings with his charges. No one felt any taint of irony in his courtesy — a courtesy that could extend as far as the scaffold. Wyatt perceived this when Kingston visited him again the following morning. The tall figure more than occupied the door frame. There was something comical about the Keeper stooping there, as if hesitant to intrude.

'I came to see if you have all that you need. I would be glad to add to your comforts.'

'Short of my liberty, that is.'

Kingston bowed his head with a rueful smile and stood his ground, waiting.

'I would like some writing materials.'

'They shall be brought.'

'And my Psalter, if it is possible to send for it. My man John would bring it.'

The Keeper looked down again, scratching a place above his right ear, smiling as he fished up a memory.'

'There has been talk of your writing.'

Wyatt raised his eyes in enquiry.

'Yes. The Queen — who as you know is lodged here — asked my wife if she had neighbours. On being informed that she did she enquired if there was anyone to make up their bed pallets for them (she herself is waited on by gentlewomen — they make her bed for her). When she learned that you were among those recently confined she clapped her hands excitedly and said, "Well, if they can't make up their pallets in the proper way then at least Sir Thomas can make up some good ballads." She laughed then, as if she had no other cares in all the world.'

Wyatt could picture her, as well as hear her. The laughter that could erupt out of nowhere. Like a pearl collar breaking, scattering all its beads to the ground; the decorum of the previous moment gone. Even now it could come. That laughter flashed her wildness. Though her dark hair might be parted and smoothed to a polish, though her body be held strictly in whalebones, encased in a box of damask, sooner or later the wildness would show. The tiny beginnings of a finger — like a dewclaw on the side of her hand (and which she tried to conceal with long cuffs — an action that made her look like a child, twisting in awkwardness) was further evidence of her wildness. Once, when he had lifted her hand to kiss, he had brushed his lips against this dewclaw. He had aimed at it for days, wondering how he might accomplish this delicious and delicate goal without appearing to intend it. Without, indeed, appearing to do it. He had practised the gesture in his mind, perfecting it so that it would appear no more than courtesy, his lips merely grazing the back of her hand. He would, for a tiny second, tilt the hand as if trying to recover his own balance and so catch, for a moment, that tantalising flap of flesh. And this he had done. He had brought it off. None of those present noticed anything beyond a formal courtesy. Except for Ann herself whose dark eyes — for a moment — widened in surprised awareness.

He had imagined — planned in his mind — how the next time he would, just for one fraction of a second, take this tiny finger between his lips and touch it with his tongue.

Never again did she give him her hand.

This recollection, the sweet intimacy of that little piece of her against his lips, his moist breath upon it, aroused him painfully. He would not do ease on himself now. To do so would be filthy, with her there, held in danger. Yet it thrilled him to know that she had spoken of him. That his name had been in her mouth. And that she had laughed! Though the walls that surrounded him were very thick, the imagination of her laughter made them bell out and fill, fleetingly, with light. He realised how dangerously his mind had become entangled with his *donna schermo*.

Danger. Death. I die. He had used these words carelessly. *Help me Lady, for I die*, said with a hand clutched to the heart and a fixed, supplicating gaze. At times he had almost felt he meant it, eyes turned mournfully on the eyes of some object, as if in sad reproach, as if — dog-like — begging for some scrap. It was a game played in parallel to the unvoiced innner braidings of a binding love such as he might, just possibly, be in the process of discovering. In Bess Darrell's company he would have been ashamed of any such nonsense as talk of dying.

6

Oublier ne puis. He had reached an age when there was almost too much to remember. Now with the prospect of unshaped days stretched before him he must make a plan, allocating appointed hours to certain memories so that they might present themselves like guests; and then depart. He was aware that, even in his much diminished present situation, there was more than enough; that each moment is a full bowl. This plain room for example: so many different textures in the rough plaster of its walls. Fibres of animal hair had bulked the plaster and some were now visible; palpable. So many gradations of colour. Places where fingers had scratched at the wall (it set his teeth on edge to see); a brown stain like a birthmark — perhaps where food had been thrown in disgust. And here! a series of nearly vertical lines /I\\II Were these the marks of a previous occupant, counting the days (or counting the beat)? Or were they witch marks, attempting to ward off an evil that had already descended? In his mind he flung questions at them. Were they made with buckle or nail? Even one wall — and he had four — was rich in variety and interest. He thought of Holbein — how to his eyes nothing was unworthy of attention; how he would find as much to interest him in the worn part of a sleeve as in the light of a lovely eye. He would render it with equal care. Sometimes it was better to concentrate on that worn piece of sleeve.

He wandered over to the narrow window which looked so enviably out onto the place of execution. The window itself was nothing: an innocent medium which bore no more trace of the horrors it had witnessed than a lake does of the storms it has reflected. He looked down at his own garments. The thick wool cloak that John had insisted he take with him had become another skin. He slept furled in it and when he was awake he needed it to be wrapped around himself to stave off the chill wind that whispered through the chimney. When he lifted the cloak with his arms, a gust of gamey warmth met his nostrils. He found his own smell comforting, though the first thing he would do when he was free was wash and change his linen. When might that be? Not having yet been charged, it was hard to anticipate the length of his stay. One way or another it would end.

7

They carried Ann's body away from the scaffold in a sword-chest and it was a sword, not an axe, that sliced through that slender neck and swept off her head. The sword-chest was not long enough to contain the full length of her with head in place, so they wrapped her head separately and carried it apart. He saw now that she had been surrounded by swords and knives for most of her life. They packed the air around her.

Ann watched — so he was told — as he could not, when Norris, Brereton, Weston, young Smeaton, and her brother Rochford were beheaded; in his mind he saw their mouths shocked open as their heads fell into the bran and straw. They were supposedly her lovers. Yet had any one of them loved her, other than her brother — his friend and hers? He had not seen them nor had his real eyes quite seen the Sword of Calais whip through her neck; but the imagined sight of this is with him for ever. He cannot remove it from his mind. He sees her span her neck with her hands (dear little hands with their dewclaw). 'I have a little neck,' she'd said.

> *The bell tower showed me such a sight*
> *That in my head sticks day and night*

The only way to stop seeing this is to see something else.

He will imagine the King's death. He will do this because it is prohibited and named Treason, and because by the act of imagining he will find and prove how futile the prohibition is. Wyatt can imagine any number of deaths for the King. But the King — like any — can die but once. Which manner would be the most satisfactory? The most incontrovertible?

He could fall from his horse — as he has done many times including recently when he fell at a tilt in full armour. Yet still he did not die. He might yet — if he could be winched up onto a saddle — fall from another horse. That horse could stumble on knotted grasses or shy at some billowing garments. Be spooked by a sudden thrash of leaves. How else?

He might pop his big stretched skin as a fat and silky maggot may. Yes, he could imagine the King bursting like an overripe maggot, or a puffball that had swelled to an inordinate size and then, when kicked open, revealed nothing but stale brown dust. Or he could die abed, attempting to mount one of the women who had small choice but to oblige. He would heave himself up, frot himself to a tenuous engorgement, and then, before he could approximate himself to the waiting and compliant place, expire of an apoplexy.

Rochford had said, out loud, that the King had *ni vertu ni puissance*. Now everyone has heard this. It cannot be stopped. The whole world now knows that the King can't keep it up, whatever the fancy codpieces try to suggest. Was it for this that Rochford died?

The King could die by pressing (it was a wonder some of the women he mounted had not done so). The man himself had grown as wide as a bed, fatter than the deepest mattress. Wyatt imagined mattress upon mattress pressing down. Though one man would lack the necessary weight to force it down there could be a party of them, using the upper mattress as a raft. They could make merry, stamp and dance on the top mattress, oblivious to the fat wretch who expired beneath their feet. Oblivious as that same wretch had been, feasting and wooing while the blood of his victims still trickled down the drains.

Wyatt has been tapping the uncut end of his pen upon the table whilst performing this act of treason. This extended act of imagining.

Eructavit cor meum. My heart is enditing.

'Vented' or 'vomited' would be closer.

He will not dip the cut end of the pen into ink to set down the words he thinks. His heart speaks in silence. And his head aches; fit to bursting.

Remembrance so followeth me of that face.

Not just Ann's. The faces of Rochford, Norris, Brereton, Weston. George, Henry, William, Francis — they fill his mind; familiar, living faces; good-natured, clever, amused, indignant. They had all milled together on many occasions. The one he had not known was Mark Smeaton, though he guessed he must often have heard his music. He pictured a young lutenist and heard notes in his mind, sprightly for a dance, or melancholy as now. The music always orderly.

Their heads now stuck on pikes for all to see.

He thinks, *These bloody days have broken my heart.*

A good line, but he would prefer to have had no occasion to think it.

8

Bess Darrell had been present at court a decade ago when Thomas Wyatt presented Katherine, still the Queen, with Plutarch's *Quiet of Mind* as a New Year gift. Bess knew how hard — how unquietly — he had worked at it, ready to do a favour for the Queen, though (proud man) a favour on his own terms, for it was not that particular work the Queen had requested.

Wyatt did not know then that Bess had played a part in the Queen's unusual choice of translator; unusual since his was no pen for hire. Bess, along with all the court, had read and heard many of the songs and riddles known or guessed to have been composed by Wyatt. They were passed around, memorised, commented upon. Their authorship sometimes claimed by others. He had turned Petrarch into a native Englishman with a weight and grain to his voice that touched her familiarly, like a hand. At times it was disconcerting how familiar that voice was. The voice — which she could hear when she read his words and not only when he was there to speak them — carried with them the full texture of the living man. She felt she knew what it would be like to be pressed close to him; to experience the weight and smell of him. When he talked of making Petrarch speak in *our English tongue* she burned with an imagined sense of the rasp and heat of one man's actual tongue.

None of this was evident to any other. At the times when he was present she made no particular attempt to speak to him and he paid her little attention. She did not speak about him to her friends — not one word to indicate a preference — and, when she spoke to Katherine to suggest she employ him as her translator, she spoke lucidly and with a steady voice that carried no trace of personal feeling.

She had heard the rumours about Wyatt and Ann, though she knew that it was the King Ann aimed at. Nevertheless, when Ann was in Wyatt's company Bess saw that there was a kind of enjoyment between them — an intellectual ease which made each wittier when near one another. She noticed particularly the way in which Ann's wit would fly at these times. They became like children playing word games:

Ann, *Do you not trust me, Sir Thomas?*

Wyatt, *Nay, tell me why I should?*

Ann, *You must do so, for all my wealth is trussed up and apart. Trust is all I have.*

She laughed in that slightly mad way she affected.

Wyatt, *Then I surely have not traced you truly.*

Bess had observed and listened without pleasure. She did not like him best when he was with Ann, and her love for Katherine gave her stronger cause to dislike Ann. Wyatt had caught her watching them and his eyes met hers briefly over the bent heads of the other women. She imagined there was something in his expression like a plea for her to think better of him.

Now both Katherine and Ann were dead and the King had another wife entirely. Katherine had particularly loved Bess and bequeathed her a handsome dowry in order to further her chances of a good marriage. But this had done nothing to protect her from the chill that spread to all Katherine's friends.

In the months that led up to that terrible May of 1536 she and Wyatt had spoken more with one another. Whenever they did so she had felt a simple and growing happiness and guessed — was convinced — that it was met with a like happiness. Once he had kissed her, not on the lips but on the brow, almost as if she were a child which, unfathered as she now was, she often felt herself to be. During those bloody days when nightmares were casually enacted and Wyatt was among those imprisoned, she maintained her outward reserve but listened to reports with a passionate attention.

—

Within a mere month of his release, Wyatt was required to act alongside his father as beaming host to the King and his new Queen, the simpering, anodyne Jane whom Henry had married ten days after the killing of Ann. Next, Wyatt was sent north to lead a contingent against the rebels ('loyalists' others, including Bess, would say). While he was away, his father died. Six months after his sojourn in the Tower, Wyatt had become master of Allington Castle. His son, Thomas, married a Jane of his own and joined the household. In this time of reversals, Wyatt must become the wise father and a stable centre. With no father to tether him he had turned to Bess. She was, for him, the stability which he was called upon to embody for others. He found that he loved her, and it was clear that his love was returned.

He had never known love before to be so calm or develop so stealthily, almost without notice. A sun whose warmth was felt even before it had burnt its way through a thick obscuring mist. This love was sharpened by his sense of Bess' vulnerability now Katherine was dead. Inextricably married (lacking the King's puissance), he could never be the good match that Katherine and Bess' father had both wished for her; except in one sense: that he truly and dearly loved her. Bess' father, who had lived to see the King steadily withdraw his favour from Katherine, had died despairing of his daughter ever making an advantageous marriage. She would never attract a husband of worldly ambition, for the King had made sure that Bess could not get near the dowry Katherine had intended for her.

Bess' need for protection made him serious with her in a way he had seldom been with women. After so much loss, she is his centre.

> *She hath in hand my wit, my will, and all.*
> *My heart alone well worthy she doth stay*
> *Without whose help scant do I live a day.*

But whenever anything or anyone is given to him, the spectre of its removal is present.

9

Bess had courageously — some might say, suicidally — refused to take the Oath of Supremacy after Ann was crowned. At least, she had contrived to avoid it, and had hoped the avoidance wouldn't be noticed. She persisted in her loyalty to Katherine and, even after Katherine's death, to the old religion. Wyatt loved that persistence.

He, on the other hand, had been dragged from the old faith. He had little choice but to act as a champion of the new if he were to preserve the life that had been spared him when he and Richard Page, alone of Ann's friends, were released from the Tower. He had been required to lead his own Kentish men against the northern rebellion that had aimed to place the Princess Mary on the throne and re-establish the old faith. But he must not say 'the *Princess* Mary'. To say those two words together was Treason. She was officially a bastard, born of an illegitimate union. To Bess, Mary was always Princess, as much so as Mary's half-sister, Ann's daughter, the Princess Elizabeth. This difference could never be a matter of jest between Wyatt and Bess.

Privately he too thought of Mary as 'Princess', but he no longer hoped for the old faith to be restored. This was in part to do with the intimacy with which he experienced language. Though he loved the Latin Vulgate, he wanted to know and speak the Gospels in his own tongue. To make them his own. Not just the Gospels, the Psalter too. He could not keep himself from Englishing the psalms he knew well — the Latin words flowed through the rivers of his veins and there, in the deepest rivers of the heart, sought conversion. He agreed with those who said that each man or woman who could read, should be able to read every word of the Holy Scriptures. It seemed to him wrong that the clergy alone should administer the physic of Scripture and claim sole ownership of its meaning.

He and Bess both received the sacrament with reverence and humility. If each understood in a different way what was occurring as they did so, then that was no more than an extension of what took place every day when men heard one thing and made of it two, as when one man said 'horse' and saw his horse Clarion while another saw Bucephalus. *This is what I believe*, he'd said on one occasion, resting his head upon her naked belly, idly carressing her thigh. *This*, kissing her, *is my creed*. Bess' loyalty to the first Queen Katherine was at the heart of her religion. Loyalty formed her religion, at least as much as a belief in the Real Presence.

He also loved the inky stuff of printed words. In Paris, he had marvelled at the work of the printers, the slow, diligent application of the compositors as letter was set beside letter — a long labour to make a conscientious writer curb his verbosity. The smell of the place, the serious, dark, saturating smell of ink had sunk into him. The way the ink sank into the paper — literally *pressed in* as words (or a face) may be into the mind and heart. He was humbled by the sheer industry and care of the men who worked there, selecting and setting type — such fiddly pieces, they required dextrous fingers — inking the press, setting the paper exact and square. The press transformed the room into a kind of machine with the press itself its central and hungrily demanding engine.

Without this wonderful press the Bible that Cromwell had commissioned to be installed in every parish church would never be. For himself, he had read some of the works of Martin Luther and found himself often concurring. He had read partly in homage to Ann's strong evangelical convictions, but also to satisfy his own mind. He had grown to be a convinced, if discreet, upholder of the new faith. More so than the King for whom Reform was largely expedient.

It should also be noted that he had benefitted from the re-distribution of religious properties. His new house at Crutched Friars was on the site of the monastery. Perhaps that was why Bess did not like it. When he'd teased her that she would prefer an oratory to a tennis court she was silent for he spoke the truth.

Practically, however, the differences of opinion between the two of them were few. He loved her company and she his. Her intelligence was as great as Ann's had been, but more reflective, less volatile. When necessary, she could be forthright — as when she approached Cromwell to ask him to intervene to obtain her dowry (he couldn't). Her loyalty to Katherine and Mary was evidence of true courage, quietly shown. Courage, not bravery.

She enjoyed silence in a way that he found wonderfully restful. She said her years with Katherine had taught her the necessity of quietness. While he had honoured the notion, translating the *Quiet of Mind*, Bess — at times at least — seemed able to embody it.

10

Having found his centre, he is to be sent far from it, to be ambassador to the Emperor's court in Spain. Wyatt's task: to reinforce the friendship between Henry and the Emperor Charles and, in so doing, loosen the bonds between the Emperor and the King of France.

When he strokes Bess' cheek and tells her he must be away — on embassy to the Emperor in Spain — and that she must again be patient, she says, 'What else is there for me to be? If to endure and to wait is to be patient, then I am patient. It is not what I want.'

There is a flash of fire in her manner, a fire he has found — to his great delight — when they are naked in bed, but seldom in her clothed, daily, demeanour. She has cautioned him against making too simple an ideal of her. *I am not Laura or Beatrice, but your flawed and loving Bess. I am not as good or as quiet as you think me. But I am real, and that must be better.*

Hers is at times the *de facto* quietness and submission of one who has had little choice over the course of her life. Refusing to take the Oath of Supremacy (keeping her head down, making sure she was elsewhere when necessary) had been thrilling to her.

Some weeks earlier they had read together the tale told by Chaucer's Franklin, his favourite of all the *Canterbury Tales*.

A tale of faithful love, jeopardised by folly and rescued by magnanimity. He reminds her of it now. They had laughed together at faithful but foolish Dorigen who can think of nothing but *the grisly rokkes blake* that threaten to wreck the vessel that will carry her beloved husband, Arveragus, home from his travels in search of knightly honour. Those rocks are an abomination to Dorigen — she can allow them no place in the plan of a loving God. *She mourneth, waketh, waileth, fasteth, plaineth.* Five strong beats. When they read it they laughed at the contrast between the merry beat of the sound and the meaning of the words.

'Come Bess,' he stretched out his hand to her as if inviting her to a dance, and pulled her into a clumsy Volta, chanting Chaucer's line and swinging Bess up into the air before setting her down again, rather heavily, on 'plaineth'.

But Bess pulled away. They had done this before, galumphing round the room like happy children; this time the line had lost its power to divert.

She could see his mind was already racing forwards, quickening to the task ahead. Rightly so. It would require all his gifts of discernment and tact, his good ear for listening, his human warmth, his rich intelligence, his repertoire of languages (and language), his ability to amuse. All these and more would be needed to heal the rift between the Emperor and the King, who had so injured that Emperor's aunt, the late Queen Katherine.

Her own task in the months that stretched ahead promised its own difficulties. She needed to be among friends and, with Wyatt abroad, her principal friends were in the West Country. Wyatt had tried to persuade her to stay on at Allington where his son and Jane would be her companions, but she insisted she must be with those she knew well. She would live with the Exeter family. In so doing she would, inevitably, be associated with the King's great enemy, Reginald Pole — now *Cardinal* Pole — in Rome. Communication between Bess and Wyatt could not easily be a private matter. Both acknowledged this with heavy hearts.

11

January 1541

His life seemed to shuttle between frenzy and periods of involuntary calm when he was like a ship, stuck and unable to stir on an inert, windless sea. As he had been for so long in Spain. Then he had ached to be home, at Allington, with Bess, now back in residence and expecting their child. But when he was there he found himself sometimes chafing at the quietness, wishing to be here, in London. After Ann's death he had been forced into rustication (*rus*: a rusting place) and the memory of that desultory inertia persisted; it drove him away from rural peace when he found it.

So, now he was at Crutched Friars, the dwelling he has tried to construct according to his own tastes (Allington still so much his father's). He and a few servants in a place that once bustled with habited friars and rang with their chants. The tennis court was silent and he felt less satisfaction in it than he had expected when he commanded it to be built. There was no place for such a thing at Allington and his father had not approved of the idea. Wasted ground. An empty room with a net across it. Not even King Henry's enjoyment of the game, his construction of a much finer court at Hampton, could convert Sir Henry to the notion. Men, he said, should exchange courtesies — or else blows. Not this ridiculous to and fro of a tennis game with racquets — Sir Henry had considered the old *Jeu de Paume* more manly. Now Wyatt surveyed the court he has had built and was struck by its emptiness. The plain high walls that enclosed it would look better with fruit trees espaliered across them. The net had been taken down and rolled up to await the next game. Not that there have been many games; the friends with whom he might play being elsewhere engaged. He did not like to acknowledge it, but this court was in effect a piece of costly display. *Though not so dangerous as the one at the other court!*

He goes over to a low cupboard at the side of the court — the place where balls and racquets are stored, along with a broom to sweep the court free of the leaves and feathers and general dirt that accumulate here. He selects a racquet and then a ball, squeezing it for pliancy. Then he bounces the ball along the ground a few times before slamming it into the far wall. It comes back at him, though not so close that he can meet it without running. For half an hour or so he continues, soothing his restlessness with exertion. When he sits down, his back against the long wall, he looks up at the sky which the walls frame into a rectangle. It is blue and cold. Like a pond. He would like to be home in Kent again. Out hawking, with Bess near to come home to.

> *Fortune doth frown:*
> *What remedy?*
> *I am down*
> *By destiny.*

Why do these lines — devised in his head so many years back and since penned, a motto that many have made their own — come back into his mind now? Is it the to and fro of the ball he smashes repeatedly against the wall? The sharp returns? The speed of a game has often set a pace for his verse (the slow slap of oars is quite another thing). Each empty room he comes to, square or rectangular, puts him in mind of a clean page waiting to be filled with lines. *Una stanza vida* waits to become a stanza filled with words. This empty oblong where tennis was played could represent an undivided stanza. In his mind he hangs the net across the room at various intervals. Why was it that a sonnet never fell into two equal parts (the net, as it were, half way, dividing it)? He knew instinctively that the asymmetry into which it fell — eight lines and six — was more satisfactory and created a greater adherence. It is so too when bricks are laid: a staggering from row to row was essential, enabling one to lock into another. Inequality. Inevitable? Preferable to equilibrium? Equilibrium a temporary illusion followed by imbalance. Then a fall.

12

Bess had not expected to become pregnant. She had spent so long around women who either failed to conceive or lost their developing babies at an early stage, it seemed to her no easy matter to grow a child within. She and Wyatt had done little to prevent conception. When she remembered, she would wipe herself with a vinegar-soaked cloth and allow the vinegar to penetrate where he had lately spent himself. But more often she forgot as they lay, talking quietly or in silence, luxuriating in the peace of one another's company after so many months of separation. It sometimes astonished her that such happiness could be possible in a land where so much — even certain thoughts — was disallowed.

When it had occurred to her that her monthly blood had not appeared for some time she'd found herself smiling. So *that* was why she looked so well that a great many had commented on it. She had thought it simply on account of happiness. Her body told her that this was something she could do well and she felt a kind of vindication in this.

She had returned to Allington on Wyatt's return from Spain, and enjoyed being there, even when he was absent for a few days. The texture of these absences so different from that of the months when he was in Spain when communications between them were scarce and unreliable and subject — they had always to assume — to outside scrutiny. The *grisly rokkes blake* that separated them then were the least of the dangers that threatened. But now, tranquil in the knowledge that Wyatt was nearby and safe, she rejoiced in a solitude she had seldom been able to find, and enjoyed the sensation of not being obliged to anyone as she walked and read and sewed, or wandered out of doors to look out across the Medway. The new life growing inside her was sufficient company. With young Thom and his wife Jane she was cordial, but she left them to live their lives without reference to her. She was not Thom's mother and felt no need to act as if she were, knowing he had a mother somewhere. She did sometimes wonder about the daughter, Frances. No one spoke of her and each of the few times she had enquired, a silence occurred which spoke of wretchedness and ill ease. If Frances' whereabouts were known, they were not known to her, nor, she guessed, to Wyatt. It seemed to Bess that the girl had fallen into the rift between her parents. She could not find any thread to link the ardent little girl of Wyatt's recollection to the young woman who had sunk — sagged — from view. About Frances she felt a helpless, seldom-voiced, concern. She knew what it was to feel alone and unprotected.

13

The arrest was swift and spectacular. Carefully judged to create the greatest possible degree of apprehension and humiliation. In other ways it was extraordinarily inefficient and wasteful.

Crutched Friars was but a ten minute stroll from the Tower. Absurd to be summoned from there to travel all the way west to Hampton. There was no mistaking that it was a command, not an invitation — and though he set out as a free and noble man, he knew he would not remain so for long.

The Thames was so low he might almost have walked along it to Hampton as easily as to the Tower. He could not step onto a wherry from the usual wharves but had to walk out, along some rough matting that had been laid upon the cracked mud, to the makeshift jetty. Stranded fish rotted on the mud and stank. Gulls circled and grabbed this ready food. One enormous black-back perched, wings open, on the prow of the wherry as he boarded, but flew off when the boat tipped with his weight.

The two boatmen whom Wyatt paid to row him up the narrow ribbon of water were not of the talkative kind, even between themselves. It diverted Wyatt to think of them as a long-married couple who had grown to tolerate, rather than relish, the company of one another. The younger and more nervously alive of the pair recommended that Wyatt sat at the back of the wherry where the floor carried less water; he offered him a rug against the cold which Wyatt (getting into practice?) refused, merely hugging his cloak around himself more closely. In spite of the boatman's solicitude, more water came in and slooshed around the bottom, penetrating Wyatt's shoes and making his feet even colder. He tried to distract himself from the cold by attending to the beat of the oars.

> *Fortune doth frown:*
> > *What remedy?*
> *I am down*
> > *By destiny.*

The words went on and on, in time with the slap of the water, repeating themselves, engraving themselves into his fabric.

The journey west took a couple of hours. The river was busy, as usual, but it was neither the weather nor the tide for pleasure jaunts so most of the traffic was of cargo, including some noisy, protesting livestock. The low waters were choppy. Cattle and sheep were getting their feet wet, as he had done. Would that he could bellow as they did!

When they were level with Putney the elder of the two oarsmen, who had rowed with a fixed determination and eyes that made no human contact, reached under his bench to where Wyatt saw there was a box. Lifting the lid of this with his left hand (he managed to keep sculling with his right only) he extracted a bottle which he unplugged with his teeth and swigged from. To Wyatt's surprise the man then jerked his head up towards him and offered the bottle.

'Cold day sir. You could do with some heat in you.'

Wyatt nodded his gratitude and attempted to perform a

smile with his frozen face as he accepted the bottle. He noticed the frayed wool of the man's mittens; the chapped and red hands that emerged from them. The *eau de vie* — or something like — in the bottle was fierce. It touched his stomach and flared through his veins, reviving him and rousing him from his melancholy. Whatever waited for him at Hampton, he would be equal to it and meet it as a man whose spirit was free.

For the rest of that cold journey he lost himself in observing what was going on around him. The shore life, the skeletal trees, a little dog across the water, barking and barking, the cargo of hay (so scarce after last year's drought) making its way towards London.

He stepped out at Hampton a free man. He looked around and saw no one.

Moments later he was surrounded. Twenty-four archers, their arrows pointed at him, bows taut, gaze precisely focused. It was like something from a masque. In a moment the solemnity would be exploded; they would lay down their toy arrows and dance.

But they didn't dance. They held their aim, all twenty-four of them, not even glancing aside when one of their number stepped forward to read the warrant of arrest and to bind Wyatt's hands in front of him.

When he saw the man step out with the cords to bind him Wyatt simply held his hands up, together like paws. This otiose display. Let them get on with it. He cast his eyes up to heaven — the sole place where he might find fellowship at this moment — and laughed, though mirthlessly.

The entire journey that he had recently undertaken was now performed in reverse. The twenty-four archers were now his solemn guard as he was conducted, on foot this time, a bound trophy to the Tower.

14

Cromwell had tried to warn him, but what could either of them do? The Chief Minister had been unable to save himself, his fall from favour had been so precipitate. But, vigilant and calculating to the end, he had done what he could to ensure a better fate for Wyatt. Wyatt had been there — it was the least he could do for the man who had become like a father to him. Before the butcher of an executioner began his incompetent work sawing through the short neck, before Cromwell had laid that neck on the block, Cromwell had roused himself and called out to his friend, 'Oh Wyatt, do not weep; for if I were no more guilty than you were when you were arrested, I should not have come to this.'

A final act of generosity that may have gone some little way towards keeping the air around Wyatt's head clear during the weeks that followed.

—

Of all the incarcerations he has suffered, this is the hardest. The Tower again, but this cell in no way resembles the spacious, accommodation he enjoyed here before. This cell would constrain a rat. This is worse than the Fleet, foul though that Fleet had been. Here there are no courteous visits from

Sir William Kingston — dead this half year since. Nor does Kingston's successor come.

Here his one luxury is the shit bucket. It is for him alone. At arbitrary times chosen by his jailor he is conducted to where he can empty it into the ditch: a ditch brimming with ordure and crawling with vermin. How cleanly the Fleet by comparison! Walking about is painful, hobbled as he is by heavy fetters which bite into his shins creating sores that will soon be infected. And he is cold. So very cold. The walls of this cell sweat out a chill mist that he has no choice but to breathe in. When he shivers he instinctively pulls his blanket around himself but the cold inhabits his spine. If he cups his hands and blows into them he can find a brief comfort in the warmth of his own breath. Breath warmed by the heat of the blood that supplies both lungs and throat.

He has been charged with treason on the basis of accusations made three years earlier. The charges originated in the insufferable Bonner, now — no doubt as a reward for this and like services — Bishop of London. Wyatt had known about Bonner's complaints at the time and each had been discussed with Cromwell, satisfactorily explained, trustfully understood, and put away. But the record of this process had not been destroyed and, since Cromwell's downfall, the King's rodent army had made merry among the vast accumulation of papers that Cromwell had left, bringing to light many matters long since forgotten, buried, and apparently resolved.

Wyatt had been stuck in Spain, without money, without a proper brief, without any confidence that his actions would find support at home. His situation there had been close to intolerable. He had begged Cromwell to appoint another ambassador in his place. Cromwell's letters to him had been full of paternal exasperation and impatience, chiding him for extravagance, for an excess of independence, and for neglecting his affairs at home. But he had not called him home.

The Emperor liked Wyatt — as Henry had fully expected him to do — but Wyatt had known better than to overplay his hand. He had listened far more than he had ever spoken, always keeping a close sense of the shifting relations between Spain and France, alert to any opportunity to disturb and undermine too close a friendship which could only grow at England's expense. He had judged finely the openings and closings of opportunity: when it was time to speak in earnest, when to venture a joke as between equals (for he did represent a king). He had exercised judgement about which language was fittest for the moment — Latin for matters of solemn legality, French for diplomacy, and Italian — the language of poets — for those rare moments when he and Charles might meet, not as ambassador and emperor, but as comrades — near equals — in refinement, spirit, and taste. If privately he felt himself to be the superior in these matters, his demeanour always suggested the contrary.

But without any clear instructions he was forced to improvise. For months he and his secretary, Mason — a companion without whom these months could not have been endured — had shuffled up and down the coast between Barcelona and Nice. They shuffled on horseback, in galleys, breathed-upon and crushed; and they achieved precious little beyond gossip, boredom, irritation, and debt. Would the Emperor become friends with France thereby shutting out England? Or would the Emperor ally himself with the Pope? Or, as they hoped, though without much confidence, would he unite with England against the Turk? Might that last possibility be strengthened by the marriage of Mary — the *Princess* Mary, Charles' cousin — to the *Infante*? Charles had kept all of them guessing. When he chose to be silent his huge Habsburg chin resembled a locked vault.

He and Mason had to tread carefully. The Inquisition was ever alert to accusations of heresy and they were obvious suspects. Both were adept at toning down their Englishness, and, in Wyatt's case, Protestantism, when needed. Their fluency in Latin, French, and Italian allowed them to swim easily in and out of the various companies that made up the Emperor's court. They could receive the bread of the Mass without it being known that one of them might call that Mass 'Communion', and that they might have a different understanding of what was taking place. Indeed, privately, he was far from clear on this point.

By hard-won, cultivated unremarkableness, Wyatt and Mason managed not to be forever pointed at as Lutherans. At least until Bonner and Heynes arrived from England. Henry, distrusting the very comfortableness that made Wyatt and Mason such good ambassadors, sent the two 'learned doctors' to join them in Spain, with the professed aim of demonstrating to the Emperor that the power of the Pope was imposture and that Charles, an emperor, could make or break a mere pope. Wyatt had been suggesting as much for some time, with all the considerable funds of delicacy and wit he could command. When at last the two men sent by Cromwell and the King turned up in Nice it was clear that one of them, Bonner, was an oaf and a fool whose idea of diplomatic finesse was to distribute pamphlets crudely derogating the Pope. Wyatt could not — never did — understand what the usually subtle Cromwell could have been thinking.

Wyatt had known Bonner a little in Paris when Tyndale's Englished Bible was in the process of being printed there. The worst thing about the man was that he had no sense of his own deficiency. He could not speak a word of French beyond *Monsieur, Madame*, and *le roi*, all delivered with a knowing flourish that attempted to suggest that he could say more if he chose. Wyatt guessed then that he was a man who liked to take credit for the work of others.

It was a kind of hell to be forced continually into the company of Bonner and Heynes; condemned to endless games of cards in which wit went unnoticed and the only sounds were the naming of the hands and the thump of the flushes spread out across the board. Bonner did not like to lose — even though they had deliberately altered the stakes to paltry sums. If he lost he would sulk. If he won he would pocket his winnings with a satisfied air, never thinking that this might be spent on the present company. While Wyatt stretched himself across a financial chasm in order to honour his king with a show of munificence and liberality, Bonner kept his purse close, resenting any expenditure beyond his inadequate allowance.

He and Mason thought they would show Bonner the proper way to do things!

They planned a dinner there in the galley that would surpass anything that that grudging pair had been used to. Wyatt had made sure there was enough wine for twice their number. For the food he had enquired and hired one of the best cooks in Nice (the very best had already been employed by the Pope's entourage, along with a brace of tasters in case of poisoning). They were to be served fresh langoustines — not unlike the English crayfish but much larger — fried in butter and saffron; John Dory (St Peter's fish some called it, but this was not for the Pope), baked in a pastry with apples and almonds and Normandy cider; a wild boar piglet, roasted whole and studded with cloves; after that, pastries — the lightest confections imaginable, shaped and glistening as Venetian glass, ready to dissolve on the tongue of each well-fed guest, to be washed down with the sweet muscatel wine of the region. In nothing did he stint. He even procured a woman for Bonner's pleasure.

It was always a mistake to show contempt for another, even when — or especially when — that other was contemptible. He and Mason were to regret the laughter they shared at the fat priest's expense. Remembering that meal, in his present foul cell, is disgusting. The delicious tastes of that night mix with the faecal stink around him now. At least he doesn't have to put up with Bonner in this cell.

If Bonner had complained about him to Cromwell then it was no more than he had done himself. It had been too much to expect Cromwell to laugh heartily at Wyatt's description of Bonner — the fat little priest as everyone in Nice called him, whose idea of espionage was to ask another ambassador what was new. But Cromwell had chuckled at Wyatt's description of that dinner, the way Bonner had leered at the *Señora* and played footsie with her; the way he'd raised his repeatedly replenished glass to her with a look of what he intended to be understanding. Cromwell seldom let a loud laugh escape him, but he'd chuckled; his cheeks and neck had bulged and flushed with amusement at the account with its mimicry. He enjoyed his witty friend.

Though it would seem that Bonner had had the last laugh, Wyatt can still experience a bracing repetition of the laughter he and Mason had frequently shared once Bonner was out of earshot. However, it was Bonner who was now pomping it as Bishop of London, while he was in the Tower. The charges made by that ridiculous, insufferable man — jealous, self-important, meddling, clownishly incapable of diplomatic success — showed Bonner competent at least in spite. Bonner had imputed that Wyatt had traitorously contacted Pole — *Cardinal* Pole — on account of his own personal sympathies and that he was involved in double-dealing, secretly supporting the Papist cause.

What was he, as ambassador (scantly briefed and at a time when the situation was hourly shifting) supposed to do if not work on his own initiative, keep ears open and attend, not just to what was openly made known to him but to what was concealed? How, if the King needed to know what Pole was about, was he to discover this without recourse to some kind of stratagem? How, but by taking the initiatives he had taken, was he to learn anything about Pole's intentions? His folly — which screamed out at him now — was to give voice in Bonner's hearing to the idea of sending Mason to talk to Pole, pretending to be a sympathiser. Had Bonner seemed to support the plan, foreseeing that it might provide him with an opportunity later to drop Wyatt in it? Into this present hell. Not that Mason had gleaned anything worth knowing.

Wyatt had been there because the King trusted him to act. To have the wit to act. If he were not trustworthy why had the King placed him in such a position of trust? He had not been so circumstanced as to be able to wait the month or so it would have taken for letters to be sent back to England. It was, besides, a delicate matter. Not one to be committed to writing, even in cipher.

He had been light-footed, stealthy, delicate. Bonner had been inept, absurd, and spiteful. Lord what a nasty man it was!

And now a bishop, so his nasty designs could have enduringly nasty consequences.

It is important that he remember the details of what happened in order that he may defend himself if he is given the opportunity. Even if he does not have the opportunity he wants to be able to set all down clearly.

—

Poor Cromwell; he must have sensed the moment that he began to slide, rapidly, from grace. It was his disastrous choice of the King's most recent bride that sealed it. For all his skill in calculation, Cromwell had no instinct for desire and its ways. Wyatt had sensed this lack in his dead friend. Little could have been done to save that short thick neck — the neck of a bull, he'd always thought; hard for the blunt axe to hack through.

He strokes his own neck in the knowledge that it will in all probability be severed soon. He who imagines so well finds it hard to imagine what it will be like from inside the experience, though he has watched it happen to others, seen the shocked, still-vital expressions of the snatched-up severed heads, mouths that seemed to be still struggling to utter, to describe this new state in which they found themselves. Could their eyes *see*? Would his head be boiled and dipped in tar (like an apple in boiling sugar); displayed to the curious who had not known him in life? Like those wretched bodies of crows and moles hung out by country folk as a warning to other creatures who might steal their crops? Those human heads he had seen — the failed northern rebels, Cromwell — had struck him more as full of sorrow than of terror. Limp puppets, emptied of the purposes that had driven them.

What would Sir Henry have said of his son's present predicament? If he were alive would he have written to him as when
he was in the Tower before? On that occasion Wyatt had not
been surprised to find little apparent sympathy forthcoming.
It had sometimes seemed to him that his father had expended
all his capacity to find fault with a king on King Richard. The
old King Henry — parent of the present one — had by every
account but his father's been a sour, mean-spirited creature.
But that king had known Sir Henry from boyhood and had
rescued him from Richard. That was enough for Sir Henry
Wyatt never to falter in loyalty.

If his father were alive now, would he intercede for him
with the King as he had done once before? He did not doubt
that he would pray to God on his behalf (a happy belief that
this could be effectual, a belief Wyatt could not himself quite
relinquish). But would he have risked another direct plea and
tested King Henry's sense of what was due in gratitude for past
service? His father knew very well how dangerous it is to try a
prince's patience: the scars he bore showed it. Sir Henry had
made his torment his pride, incorporating the barnacle irons
that had tortured him and for ever injured his speaking into
the coat of arms he proudly commissioned. *Oublier ne puis.* He
would not, could not, forget. Defiantly he celebrated what had
been intended to shame and maim him. *It is no more than we
Christians have done with the ugly, customary gallows cross!*

His father had endured far worse than this. Wyatt had
always known it; seen the misshaped mouth, heard the moist,
susurrating speech, and — may God forgive him — been
irritated by it. But he had never stayed long with the thought
of what his father had gone through. Instead they had told
stories. His father had made stories of his ordeal, more to

entertain than to warn. The story of his father and the cat.

This cat had once — *once* mind, not twice or thrice or per-petually — dragged a dying pigeon into the place of his con-finement. It was a poor thrashing creature, this bird. The cat must have found it already ensnared in some twine — perhaps the creature had flown into someone else's vegetable plot and got trammelled up in threads stretched out to protect some growing beans. Poor bird, she must have been struggling for her freedom before the cat came and picked her up. The cat had pushed her way into the cell hardly knowing what she did. Looking simply for a quiet place to put an end to her prey and set upon it. The twine puzzled her. Sir Henry had felt fel-lowship with the poor trussed bird. He had taken it from the surprised cat's claws and got clawed in turn for his pains. The bird was almost dead for fright, its beak opening and closing as if air were not its element; as if it were a fish drowning. Sir Henry had taken hold of the bird with the thought of ending her terror with a twist to her neck such as he would perform on a hen. But there was no need. The poor limp terrified thing had expired as soon as she felt herself transferred to the man's hands.

As for eating it, it was out of the question. A scrawny thing already and now so mangled by its own struggles and the cat's tearings there was nothing left worth consuming by either man or beast. But the tale was a good one and Sir Henry had told it with many embellishments over the years. They called the cat 'Caterer' — a word play which the young Wyatt had enjoyed. Sir Henry went along with the fiction that the cat really had intended to bring him food and it was a truth accepted by all at Allington that cats should occupy positions of privilege in the household. Every cat that lived at Allington found itself compared with this nonpareil, Kate the Catering Cat.

Wyatt had been aware of the way in which the fiction took on a life of its own. When he achieved the age at which a boy needs to break free of his father the story ceased to please him. He became impatient of the comfortableness of the pretence and indignant at its un-truth. *Why don't you say what really happened?* he muttered to the ground. It was more comment than question. The older man had shaken his head and pursed his lips, unprepared for the struggle that was on its way, intuiting that he would be required to cede space to the boisterous boy who would supplant him and not liking it at all.

Recalling how graceless and sullen he had been Wyatt was stung. He realised how Sir Henry had deflected attention from his suffering at the hands of Richard.

When Wyatt became a father himself he retrieved the story of the Catering Cat. He told it to his two with relish, embellishing it, inserting dramatic miaows and growls and cheeps. His children squealed and wriggled with laughter as he entered into the fiction, making young Fran the bird he was about to eat, pouncing on her in his role of clever cat and hungry man. The story had taken on an existence independent of the rather messy event which was the germ of it.

Why don't you say what really happened?

He asked himself this now. Is the story a shield, a carapace that obscures the truth? Or can it be like the casing of a living seed — something to protect the life of the seed until it is ready to sprout? Even a lavish and extravagant plant may carry the husk of its natal seed. On the other hand, truth can be shut up in a covering that bears no relation to it; which simply conceals and misleads.

He imagines truth as a golden seed — the origin of honour

which impels a man to action, nourishing and irrigating all he does. But when that truth directs him contrary to the way his will is pointing, will usually wins. Will wraps up a man's truth and extinguishes its life. The now-dead seed housed in a carapace inflexible and brilliant as a suit of armour fresh-minted from Greenwich. Or the King's codpiece!

Yet surface is seldom innocent of what it covers. When snow has fallen you can tell, even when you don't know the terrain, whether the white cloth spread before you covers field or lake. A suit of clothes can be flexible and follow the line of the body to show itself (*her dresses flowed, they fell like water*), but clothes can disguise — or attempt to — the inadequacy they cover. The efforts of King Richard's clever tailors to minimise his appearance of deformity were well known.

A fable can be either of these cases: a self-serving fabrication such as many feel impelled to employ, or — like the Gospel parables — a story from which truth explodes.

The kingdom of heaven is like …

It is like a man who sowed good seed in his field.

It is like a grain of mustard seed that grew to be a tree that birds could nest in.

It is like yeast, mixed into a full jar of flour, yeasting the whole quantity.

It is like treasure hidden in a field.

It is like a merchant of pearls who sells all that he has to buy the one, priceless pearl. It is that priceless pearl.

It is like a net cast onto the sea, falling across creatures of every kind, good and bad. When the net is raised up and emptied onto the shore the contents are sorted, the good retained.

It is like each of these things in different ways, whilst being greater than any and encompassing them all.

What is truth? said Pilate. Unanswerable question. Easier to know what it is not. Wyatt knows his own untruth well enough. He has dissimulated, prevaricated, equivocated. How else can an ambassador survive; or any man or woman within the King's reach? He is a respected master of those delicate arts. He has lied, to others and to himself. Unlike the scrupulous Bess, and less than her in this, he took the Oath of Supremacy, promising to bear faith and true allegiance to the King's highness.

For all his professional doubleness, he is esteemed for his truth. This is what he loves in another — in Bess, in Bryan, in all those he treasures — and it is his own truth that he values the most.

Soonest he speedeth, that most can fain;
True meaning heart is had in disdain.
Against deceit and doubleness,
What vaileth truth?

He thinks of Arveragus in the tale told by Chaucer's Franklin:

Trawthe is the highest thing a man may kepe,
And with that worde he brast anon to wepe.

There is certainly plenty to weep about.

15

With no other entertainment he can tell himself stories. He can do this in spite of the Law of Words that sought to govern what was said and, by that means, what was thought, what was conceived.

It is his illness to think in words. Here, in this hell-hole, they crash around his head like new-hatched flies. The word *conceived* startles him as if another had spoken it, reminding him that his Bess *has conceived*. She has conceived a child that will be theirs. It is probable that the child will be all that remains to her of him. He must make provision for her and the child. Pray God that his will be not thwarted in this as the late Queen Katherine's had been. He speaks her name out loud. *Bess*. Bess. Not Beth. But short for Elizabeth. *Elizabess*. Making the name end in a buss, a kiss. *My prize, Bess, is a buss*.

How that name, *Elizabeth*, dances around his destiny. The one he married; the one he now so dearly loves. Strange that the same configuration of letters should signify and summon to the mind such vastly different creatures. Depending on which Elizabeth he intends, the name sounds in his mind with a ring distinct to that person. *The King is dead: Long live the King*. The Thomas that he is, different — though related — to the Thomas of his son. So it is with words in general. The same form of sound and letters turn to diverse uses. How is it that the truth that underlies a word can shine through, making the form of a word into a casket of semi-transparent material, taking on some of the colour of its content; or a garment revealing the contours of its wearer, stained in that wearer's blood?

There is also Ann's daughter, the Princess Elizabeth. What sort of life will hers be? Will it be as soured and buried as the life of that other princess, the poor, pinched *Princess* Mary? The young Elizabeth is a fierce, determined little thing. Did she remember the voice and touch of her mother and find comfort in them? Her strange tormented and tormenting mother.

Again he sees her — Ann — spanning her neck with her hands. Again he hears her say, laughing (yes, she *would* laugh), 'I have a little neck.' The pale neck of a doe circled by a golden collar. That is how she had appeared to him when she became Queen. She had liked to see herself as the virgin who tames the pale unicorn (and for all her amorous skills she might well have remained intact for Henry). She saw herself as the one who held the chain; the one who controlled the beast. She did not see until it was too late that she was the collared creature, or that the collar was locked.

> *... graven with Diamonds, in letters plain*
> *There is written her fair neck round about*
> Noli me tangere, *for Caesar's I am;*
> *And wilde for to hold, though I seem tame.*

A tall slender neck framed by exquisite collar bones which led the gaze to the pulse of the hollow between. He had wanted to set his mouth on that place and feel its warmth. Even now, with Bess as his anchor, the thought of Ann can arouse and perplex him.

He thinks of her terror, and distances himself from the terror he feels by thinking of hers. Once she knew she was in a cage she would have crashed against those bars like any bird frantic to get out. But you can hood a bird to gentle it. Though her emblem was a falcon, he wondered if she could ever have learnt to sit patient, awaiting the moment of her release, in the way of his bird Lukkes? Did she have that stillness in her?

Now she has undergone the great transition and done so with open eyes, in full knowledge of what was to occur. Though the executioner — out of pity — had deceived her at the last, distracting her attention so that she did not see him whisk out the Sword of Calais. This image of her looking for something, interested and alive to the last, floods him with tenderness.

He strains his thoughts to put himself in this position, facing only forwards, all that he has striven for, a town diminishing at his back, himself riding away from its fading fires (as once — one rare and *lucky* May — he had ridden from Rome while the Emperor's troops ransacked it and all the roads rang with the wheels of the carts and wagons of the weary, desperate, folk escaping). Will it take courage to meet his God? He knows it will take truthfulness, simplicity, humility.

Well then, he is in the right place.

Sighs are my food, drinke are my tears;
Clinking of fetters such music would crave;
Stink and close air away my life wears:
Innocency is all the hope I have.

The thumping tread of the verse as he pushes one foot before another. He has been shuffling around his small cell with the only kind of steps that heavy fetters permit. The sound of the dragged fetters adds to the injury they impose. What freedom does he have? In terms of movement? He can move his arms around like windmill sails or clap them around his sides. He does this often to warm himself. He can move his upper body, bend from his waist. He can bang his head against his cell's damp wall and brain himself. The thundering pains in his head invite this. Perhaps if that head were cracked open those demons of pain could fly out.

—

He is sure he has not been forgotten — this cell is no *oubliette* — but here remembering is his task. He must remember not only his account of the events in Spain, in the hope that his defence will be heard, but also what will keep his mind from collapse. *Oublier ne puis.* Some memories sustain; others threaten his will to endure. He must choose. His mind is well stocked — a larder filled with preserves for a sunless winter: Chaucer (to whom he can return if he need) but also, savingly, the psalms. They are always with him. Though this time he has no Psalter in his cell, the words are spread out and imprinted in his mind. The seven psalms that David sang to the Lord in his penitence, after Nathan had named his sin, have long inhabited him. He knows the Latin and he has studied them in Aretino's Italian as well as Joye's English; but he is making these words of David his. Intimately his. He wants to understand them by weighing, turning, and tasting each word till meaning breaks free from its carriage of sound. Some men make pilgrimages across mountain ranges and dangerous terrain in order to approach an apostle's bones. The pilgrimage Wyatt makes now takes place within. He has crossed mountain ranges many times — the

Dolomites, the Alps, the Pyrenees. This present journey is at least as rocky. If he does succeed in Englishing these psalms the result will not be smooth but will reveal bumps and ruts in the road; obstacles stumbled over, fissures that catch.

De profundis clamavi ad te Domine; Domine exaudi vocem meam

Out of the deeps I have cried to you Lord; Lord listen to my voice

The figure of *gradatio*: a climbing figure which makes one word serve as the step from which to reach the next; an effortful figure. *Lord, I call to you; Lord, hear me.* A repeated word — like a repeated refrain — is never the same as it was on the previous occasion. *Lord; Lord. Domine; Domine.*

De profundis clamavi ad te Domine; Domine exaudi vocem meam

How easily these words were spoken by the King during that interlude in Greenwich. How smooth they had sounded. But the words needed to be dug out:

From depth of sin and from a deep despair,
From depth of death, from depth of heart's sorrow,
From this deep cave of darkness' deep repair,
Thee have I called, O Lord
...
No depth so deep that thou ne maist extend
Thine ear thereto: hear then my wofull plaint

—

It is not the pain of axe or sword that he fears. Even when botched or prolonged as it was with Cromwell, it would not go on forever.

Fool. Of course he fears it!

He has known men loose their bowels with the fear. The clothes, carefully chosen for one last performance, fouled with a dark and spreading stain.

Attainder, *Attinctura*: the act of staining by which, not only goods, but also lands and title are taken. He has been informed that his household goods have been confiscated. Is this the first stage of Attainder? The title gone that had been his father's and would, he hoped, belong to young Thom? What was he to be if he was no longer 'Sir Thomas'? No longer a noble man.

But a man still (and noble).

A thing of flesh and thought; a shaper of words.

Allington is to be emptied of furnishings, plate, man and maid-servants. All servants dismissed with one half-year's wages. All horses taken. Southwell to take an inventory. All to be done properly, according to law. Let it not be thought that the King's greed is behind this.

Item: One great charger embossed with the image of Vulcan at his forge;

Item: One pair of iron fire dogs. Heavy;

Item: One good quality arras, depicting Diana at her hunt.

(*Who so list to hunt, I know where is an hinde …*)

Item: One stool with clawed feet, the seat worked in blue, grey and green wools;

Each item to be scrutinised with a weighing eye.

He, tainted: like his hand stained blue that day in Maidstone.

Bess, whose condition is now apparent, is to be permitted to stay at Allington until the time of her confinement while all the other members of the household have been dismissed. Is there not one servant to care for her? Surely a midwife must attend her. She, like himself, is already, confined.

16

The King of England so honours the estate of matrimony that he has entered into it for a fifth time. He abhors the sin of adultery. He avoids the charge of it by means of perjury and murder. Wyatt has been released. He has not been found innocent, but he has been pardoned because the King's child bride, another Katherine, has interceded for him. For Wyatt the taint of his imprisonment persists. His thorough defence, composed and committed to memory while he was in the Tower, has had no public airing, though it has been privately circulated, and widely admired for its wit and honesty. But if the King has seen it he has kept quiet about it. A mere pardon is all that has been accorded: a concession, a regal favour.

The conditions of his freedom are that he resume marital relations with his estranged wife and have no more to do with Bess, due to give birth to his child any day. In spite of the earlier stipulation that she remain at Allington, she has been sent off to give birth elsewhere and has made a perilous journey to her friends in the west. Wyatt has left one prison only to enter another.

What had so recently been a pleasant and lively household is now a sad and empty place. His daughter-in-law Jane and Lady Poynings (regular and welcome residents while their husbands were abroad) have both been sent away as well as

Bess. All the servants have been dismissed and paid off by Southwell. Only Wolf, his steward, remains. He had ridden ahead to receive the keys and open the living quarters again.

———

Little had gone irrevocably from the house but Wyatt sensed — could almost smell — that Southwell had been through it all, handling and assessing for monetary worth. Yet it appears that Southwell had confined his actual residence to one room, modestly refraining from occupying the entire house as if it were his own. He was of that species who, most punctiliously, strive to avoid leaving his mark, unless it be the mark of an inventory.

The place had been empty during the coldest months of the year. No fires had been lit during most of January and the whole of a bitter February. It was now mid-March. Snow had fallen down the chimneys and settled on the uncleared ashes in the fireplaces. Melt-water had mixed with ash to form dark, soggy clumps, filthy to the handling. The place smelled of must. The stone flags and the walls were cold — cold as the high crags of the Dolomites or the Pyrenees, but with none of the exhilarating scope that those heights offer.

Wolf had done what he could: made up fires, swept away the most conspicuous cobwebs, opened windows — notwithstanding the cold — to flush out the smell of mould. He had re-engaged those household servants who, having nowhere else to go when they were dismissed, had returned to familial homes nearby. A hen had been seized and strangled; threaded onto a spit that, had it been less greasy, would have rusted from disuse. The smell of roasting fowl thinly overlay, but could not overcome, the dank scents of the abandoned home.

But it was far far better than the Tower. Relief at being at liberty again — albeit under such cruel conditions — brought real gladness as he re-entered the home of his early manhood. Just as tears can be comforting simply because they are bound to memories of the comfort they once elicited, so these desolately emptied walls were connected to deep memories of safety and love.

'We'll soon get the old place on her feet again, eh Wolf?'

Wolf looked around. He'd seen worse. He believed in taking the rough with the smooth. Working for Wyatt, which gave him pride, had brought him an abundance of both.

To sleep in a real bed again is a comfort. The linen had remained in the press (*Item:* 20 linen bedsheets with the letter W in raised stitches on the hem) — the lavender stalks that Bess had laid between them had dried out, the little seeds scattered to the floor when he and Wolf had shaken out the sheets he was to use. In the Tower he had slept fully dressed, his greatcoat tightly pulled around him, his boots still on. This was not just for warmth — though any hint of warmth was welcomed — but to be ready for whenever anyone came to his cell. *Watch therefore, for ye know not when the master of the house will come: lest if he come suddenly, he should find you sleeping.* He needed to be alert, on his chained feet. There, when he heard a key turning, he did not know who was about to enter; whether they were about to bring something to you or had come to fetch you out. That was the worst. Worse than the stink and the damp and the pain of the fetters was the uncertainty. That could destroy a man.

Now in his own high bed, shoes and greatcoat off, heavy covers pressing down, he surrendered to the exhaustion that these long days and nights of vigilance have brought. Those days were not over. They would never be over while the country was so ruled; but for this night at least he could hang his vigilance up, like a hat on a peg, to be taken down again and worn the following morning. For now he was too tired for anything else.

When he woke the next morning he thought he was still in the Tower; that the pressure of the bedclothes was from someone pressing the air from him, trying to put out his life. His limbs thrashed themselves to consciousness in a frenzy of fear and fury (*all the fs again!*). He was greeted by silence. The empty place. The full knowledge — all the fuller now his weariness was somewhat slaked — that his Bess and their yet-to-be-born child were away, he did not yet even know where, and would not be coming back.

That the blessed ordinariness he had enjoyed with Bess, in such a settled way, should now be named a crime! The ugly dancing skeleton that his marriage had been, now go by the name of true. If that was true it was a twisted, turning truth that had no truth about it. Honest love had been re-named adultery and outlawed by the King. Did the King of Heaven also judge it thus? Wyatt conceded that He might, but that was earnest matter for the soul. The King of England had no care for Wyatt's soul; he cared only to preserve and extend his foul Supremacy and stifle opposition. Wyatt's proximity to the King — his apparent friendship — enhanced the King's own sense of himself as a man of intellectual quality and refinement. The King wanted it to be known that Wyatt was his creature (to be placed in and out of prison at will). But Wyatt knew that Bess' banishment from him had nothing to do with the King's marital values. Bess Darrell had too many links with the Papists and Pole's family in particular. The King has deemed that she cannot be trusted, and neither can Wyatt if he is by her.

—

The other Elizabeth, the one he had so unwisely married and mother of his existing children, was due to arrive soon. He conceded that she probably felt as little enthusiasm for the project of renewed cohabitation as he did, though she might well find greater security in the new situation and, for that reason, welcome it. He had been little more than a child when he married her, anxious to acquire the trappings of manhood. Her brother was already a friend and it had been a short step to bring the two families together. He had entered into the game with her with all the spirit of a young man manifesting adult ways. A heartless matter, yet there had been some warmth. They had copulated with happy zeal at the start and he had been as grateful for that as any boy would have been. But he had never had any intention of restricting himself entirely to her bed. He had also — he acknowledged it — enjoyed the freedom that not loving her conferred. It left his heart whole so that he could enjoy the slight woundings that others might give it. What he had not anticipated or intended was that his lack of love would free her too. He had received the fact of her adultery with cold contempt. Had he ever loved her this contempt might have complicated itself into a renewal of desire, but this was not what he felt. He wanted her simply not to be. Certainly not to be here. The order that she return to Allington and that their conjugal relations should resume would only in part be obeyed: the part that could be verified by an outsider's eyes. For now he needs to reclaim his home for himself. To taste it, unmixed with her sour spore.

He had made his library in the eastern part of the building so that the morning sun should pour into it. He opened the door and wondered if the silent room would tell him anything of what has passed during his absence. The light on the surface of things seemed to conceal more than it showed. Would he find his book chests empty? To his sweet relief the familiar and comfortable smell of books greeted him. The smell was made up of printer's ink, sized paper, and the faint whiff of harness given off by the leather bindings. The smell was as it had always been and he guessed that Southwell has not spent time here. It might have been tact on his part, or simply a lack of curiosity.

He had long liked to begin his days in quietness, seated at this table, communicating in silence with a distant friend. Livy, Tacitus, Seneca. David, Isaiah, the Evangelists, Paul. The poets too — Horace, Catullus, Marot, Alamanni, Petrarch. He has the feeling of being in conversation with them. They speak with him and sometimes through him. (Yet, who speaks — Petrarch or Wyatt? — when he makes an English sonnet out of Petrarch's Italian? If he had drawn in an Italian breath he had surely exhaled one with the rasp of his native speech.)

This morning he sat at the table without any volume open in front of him. It was enough just to be here, allowing the voices from the past to stay quiet within their boards. Just being near them restored a ground of sanity. The light falling on the table threw the grain of the wood into relief. A whorl of concentric rings, like the whorls at the ends of his fingers. God's thumbprint in the wood? Or the wood's own signature, which might amount to the same thing. In his youth he had attempted to shape wood. Those boles were places of difficulty and obstruction.

The cat Silkin had wound herself around the edge of the door and now appeared neatly on his lap. There she sat, purring determinedly, her eyes fixed straight ahead as if she were trying to remember something. He stroked her, liking the square box of her head beneath his hand and enjoying the silky warmth of her.

'Faithful Miss Silkin! Have you been here all along? Did you miss me, Miss? Did you wonder what had become of your master? Has he been faithless and had to do with other she-cats? There was a cat in the dungeon to be sure. But he was a Tom cat with scars to prove it.'

That particular cat had been his most constant visitor during his last stay in the Tower. The narrow window was too high for Wyatt to climb up to and look from, but it was neither too high nor too narrow for the shaggy piratical fellow he named Jason to reach from an outside bough and from there drop down into the dungeon, in the hope that the prisoner might have some scraps for him. There he would wait, companionably and not restive, until a jailor's visit would allow him to slip out of the opened door and hunt somewhere else. Wyatt had begun to look forward to these visits and was careful to reserve a portion of each meal for the cat — the skin and bones of boiled fowl, mutton fat, and gristle were bolted down avidly by the starved creature. His fur was longer than Silkin's and brightly, almost crazily, coloured. Wyatt used to speculate on the places that Jason might frequent, grounding those speculations in evidence: sticky strings of cobwebs; wet, bloodstained or matted fur. Would Jason enter the annals of family story beside Kate the Catering Cat? But who would care to listen to the story now? Thom and Fran were absent and with adult concerns of which he knew little. There would be no delighted squeals of laughter as he turned himself into the pouncing cat.

'You're my confidante now, Silkin. You can keep a secret.'

The indifferent Silkin dropped from his lap and seized on a mouse that Wyatt had not even noticed. No struggle took place; just an accurate pounce and the sound of small bones being crunched. A drop of blood fell to the floor and Wyatt watched as the creature, who so recently resembled a silken cushion on his lap, drew the last of the mouse's tail into her mouth.

Alas, unwary mouse!

A country mouse was not exempt from the perils of society and cared as passionately to preserve her life as any mortal creature. When he had Englished Horace's satire about the two mouse sisters, a town mouse and a country mouse, he had enjoyed entering into a mouse's being. The country mouse had come to the door of her town sister's house:

And with her foot anon she scrapeth full fast.
The other for fear durst not well scarce appear.
Of every noise so was the wretch agast.
At last she asked softly who was there,
And in her language as well as she could,
'Peep,' quoth the other sister, 'I am here.'
'Peace,' quoth the towny mouse, 'Why speakest thou so loud?'

He had written this fable with happy fluency, knowing the moral to be true even if, in his own life, he had seldom practised the wisdom he recommended:

Then seek no more out of thy self to find
The thing that thou hast sought so long before,
For thou shalt feel it sitting in thy mind.

It was time he proved the worth of these words; to feel that thing of truth and weight. But immediately a counter-thought flashed through his mind — of something, not sitting there, but entering it, hideously and injuriously: the image of an axe, plunged into the middle of a human head as if that head were a log. He'd seen this somewhere — part of the dark panorama of sights that paraded through his mind these nights. The man whose head was so cleft might have been one of the Catholic insurgents in the north. Both sides had been guilty of horrors. Or had the head belonged to a victim of the imperial army outside Rome? Too many ghastly sights to remember exactly which or when.

17

He felt the emptiness of the stables as he passed them. They did not emit their wonted gust of warmth and horse-stench. But it was to the bird-house that he hurried — a building annexed to the stables, well constructed in brick, with a series of barred windows. The mews. He can tell, even before he enters, that they are all there. Long-suffering prisoners, tied to their perches, hooded. Would Tripp have flown them? He must have continued to take care of them, ignoring the fact that he was dismissed, letting himself in as he had always done. Perhaps the birds have simply waited, suspended in a kind of non-life, getting fatter from Tripp's feeding?

There she is. Lukkes.

You have grown plump my lady. And I have become lean. Is there a riddle here? We have both been captive.

Very gently, he strokes her feet, whispering to her all the while. She knows his voice. It has gentled her throughout the early days and nights of her young wildness. Now she shifts the weight between her feet on the perch and inclines her hooded head the better to hear him. He had been the first creature she had seen for she had lived in the dark until he had loosened the seel from her eyes. Day by day he had introduced a little more slack to the thread that seeled her lids — it was the tenderest office. When she could see him he became mother and father to her. Now he has returned he will weigh her food himself; diet her so she will be hungry to stoop. He wants her ready. While he was in prison he would picture her soaring, almost beyond the reach of his gaze. He asked her to take him with her into a realm of greater freedom. This is what he needs now.

He sees that the hood she was wearing is the one he'd stitched himself. Tripp must have decided to use this as a kind of memorial to her absent master. Wyatt had made it under Bess' laughing guidance. He had a pattern already: the basic shape of the hood — like a small casque — was formed from three separate pieces of leather which he cut out, using metal templates to guide him. It was finer work than he was accustomed to and, though his knife was sharp, he had to discard several pieces of leather before he had the three shapes. Then came the stitching. After he had pricked his finger to bleeding for the fourth time, he'd consented to try the use of Bess' thimble whose dents and welts he called the impresses of battle. The thimble he named his finger scutcheon. His stitches were not so neat as a lady's — or indeed as a shoe-maker's or tailor's — but he was determined to fashion this small thing and when it was accomplished he took pride in it. Lukkes had acquired a collection of hoods which were ranged on a shelf in her quarters, like the helmets of a miniature army. Some were magnificent, with plumed crests or delicate rosettes in a contrasting leather about the ears. All were neat and symmetrical except for this one, made by him, which sat lopsided between the others, like a loaf that has not risen properly amongst a perfect batch. Nevertheless, it was this hood that he preferred to use when he took Lukkes out on his own. It was, in its imperfect way, a gift of love from him to her and it bore the marks of his own hands — as well as some drops of his blood.

He would have liked to ride out with her today but she is not ready, nor does he have a mount. So for now he must content himself with her company. He pulls on the stiff leather gauntlet, still lying where he'd left it from their last excursion, and winds her jesses between his fingers. This process is familiar to the bird who steps calmly from her perch to Wyatt's fist from where she continues to worry away at her preen feathers and the spaces between her talons. When they step outside she lifts her head and turns it, listening to the sounds of other birds and of the wind; feeling the wind against her feathers.

Wyatt strokes the feathers of her neck where they fan out from her hood.

'Forgive me Lukkes. If I let you fly off now you might never return and I would find that hard to bear.'

He knows that her readiness to return is the trick of hunger not of loyalty. A falcon is not a dog, or even a cat! But she does know him and she trusts him to handle her. That is enough to elicit his gratitude and something like love. Together they walk, away from the castle buildings, away from the flat land by the river, to climb up towards the woodland where he has often hunted. There is a hollow tree here that he discovered when a much younger man. The lower part of this oak forms a deep canopy, a mantle wide and high enough for him to enter and stand in its shade. Bracket fungus grows in places and gives this shelter a mushroomy scent, but it is dry enough in there to make it his sanctuary. With Lukkes still on his fist, her jesses wound tightly around his fingers, he crouches down on his haunches and looks out, as if this were his cottage home. Lukkes' head turns constantly, her attention drawn by the exciting forest sounds. Wyatt feels the unfairness of taking her there and not letting her fly free.

'Tomorrow — or the day after — as soon as you are fasted — we'll come back again and you can fly free.'

He will reward her with some good pieces of mutton.

18

His wife arrived in due course. It was disconcerting to see her, so other, so separate from him, a stranger with whom he had once been intimate. He knew it but could in no way recall that intimacy. During their years apart Wyatt had felt no curiosity about her or concern for her welfare. He had turned deaf ears to the appeals that her friends had made on her behalf. Even Cromwell had asked him to provide for her, as if she were his responsibility. But the wife who returned to Allington was a pretty, brown-haired woman, not the monster that his horror and self-justification had painted during the years of their separation. She and her personal maid-servant arrived on horseback, her effects following by cart. When these arrived and were unpacked he was immediately irritated by the bulk and quantity of the stuff that was to take up residence with him in his home.

He left them to it. The less he had to do with her occupancy the better, but he was too weary to feel the passionate contempt he had so long nursed. The knowledge that she had no more sought this rapprochement than he smoothed away some of his animosity. Each gave the other leave to prefer to be elsewhere. She too had a life from which she had been forcibly removed — though it might be to her material advantage to be here.

He kept largely to certain quarters. His bedchamber — which now carried only the memory of happiness — his library, and the outside offices where he kept company with Lukkes and with the horses he had been quick to re-acquire. Though he and his wife have been commanded to resume marital relations, some things remained beyond the reach of the King's long and meddling arm. The King's spies were not above inventing details of the intimacies between a man and a woman — what had not been said about the first Queen Katherine and her child-husband? — but they would not have an opportunity to verify the details of Wyatt's relationship with his wife. He was sure of his own servants. Of those who had been dismissed and re-employed, not one would stoop to reporting on the condition of his bedsheets.

But he and his wife — he cannot bear to call her by her name, Elizabeth — were obliged to maintain an appearance of conjugality, if only for the benefit of the one new member of the household staff, Susan Holmes. Wolf had as good as told Wyatt that her appointment had been pressed upon him — there was nothing subtle about the King's method of surveillance; no attempt to conceal the fact that surveillance was intended.

They took their principal meals together — it would not have been safe to do otherwise given the terms of his rustication. The Holmes woman, present at meal times, ever ready to fill a beaker or remove a plate, did not have an offensive presence. Unusually tall and rather thick-set, she could have passed as a man. Her stance, feet often planted rather wide, did nothing to alter this impression. It reminded Wyatt of the way a prison guard would stand — the deliberate air of neutrality, the edge of scepticism, not about to be taken in by the charms of a prisoner. But there was nothing brutal about Susan Holmes; something almost touching about her vacant obedience — obedience not to Wyatt or to Wolf but to the power that placed her there, to watch and to listen.

Well let her listen.

They spoke of what was to hand: the mutton they were eating — was it one of theirs? The jellies — crab apple, quince. How long preserved down in the cool larders? Any such speculation about time brought with it the potential distress of comparison. How it had once been otherwise; how the hands of the other Elizabeth, his Bess, might have strained those jellies through muslin bags, the rosy juices dripping so slowly into the receiving bowl. Susan Holmes was attentive though without flair in waiting at a table. She was apt to remove a plate or refill a beaker sooner than Wyatt or his wife were ready for this service. She would smile in answer to a smile but never without this invitation. Wyatt did not smile at her, only nod in a civil way, but his wife, who had always liked to win a person over, was happy to smile at Susan Holmes and Wyatt can see that the woman was glad of this.

They spoke of their daughter, Frances, but if Elizabeth knew of her whereabouts she kept the knowledge to herself. He assumed she had means of support but had heard of no definite husband. They trod with caution and spoke with reserve, each conscious of a failure on their own part. Wyatt remembers the real concern that Bess had shown, her instinct that Frances might find a friend in her, had opportunity allowed. Bess had even speculated that Frances might have travelled abroad to enter a cloister — but he said nothing of this to his wife. They spoke of their son and his wife, Jane. Elizabeth mentioned them, carefully, aware that her husband might resent her speech. Thom — to Wyatt's great annoyance — had remained consistently impartial over his parents' separation. He knew that there had been letters between Thom and his mother since her return to Allington, but he had not deigned to enquire as to their contents. When she mentioned the possibility of Thom and Jane returning to Allington where they had lived until Wyatt's last arrest, Wyatt felt as if a great tree had crashed into his brain, making it impossible to think. Why did he not welcome his wife's suggestion when he loved his son so dearly; the young wife, Jane, too? The memories of the domestic harmony they enjoyed together recently, with Bess by his side, were still warm. To create a simulacrum of this household with his wife in Bess' place? She perhaps making much of being the mother — as if to suggest that *this* was how the household should be? It was not to be borne.

His wife saw only an expression of frozen affront. She remembered this expression. The meal continued in silence.

—

A great house has an existence independent of the families that live and die within its walls. Hangings change, the furniture alters, paintings come and go, but the stone flags softened by generations of feet, the thick walls, breathe a lofty breath unperturbed by the fates of those they have sheltered. When Wyatt had returned from his stays abroad it was the smell of the place that first reclaimed him. The smell of the wood, of the oil that preserved the wood, of the herbs that sweetened the closets and the water the household bathed in. Was it the same for his wife when she returned to Allington? Did smells, creaks, the sounds of latches lifting claim her with their familiarity? Or did she find all subtly altered in ways he could not guess, so gradual had the changes been in her long absence? Had Bess re-ordered the household in so many persistent small ways that now it presented an altered aspect? Her impress was light as a hare's in the grass — you'd hardly notice it but the sheen on the ground has changed.

The furniture — most of it oak — the hangings, the plate, had descended with small additions and losses from father to son. But much of it now was in other hands for not all that had been confiscated during the period of his recent imprisonment had been restored.

And yes, Bess had made changes. She had done so cautiously at first, beginning with the room he had given over to her. She liked to sit under the window that looked over the park. No one had much used this room before her and she liked this fact. It meant she was not taking this from anyone; not appropriating. (Whereas, at the old Queen's death, Ann had acquired two ivory stools that had been Katherine's. Ann who at that time could have requested their equivalent in gold, studded with pearls or rubies. That had not been an act of thrift but a kind of vaunting triumph. That was like her, he thought. Ann would have enjoyed that.) Bess had brought furnishings of her own into this room: a low stool with a design of wild strawberries that she had completed, rather beautifully, as a child; a writing stand; a work box with a marquetry lid resembling a maze. He remembered she had begun to embroider a cloth destined to become a book cushion. When he'd noticed the pomegranates, richly red, beside the pears, he had queried the wisdom of displaying the fruit that had been Queen Katherine's symbol. She'd responded with a rare flash of anger, 'Why can't a pomegranate just be a piece of fruit?

Does everything have to mean something else?'

She had asked Wyatt to provide a table and two chairs but no paintings or hangings, preferring to look out at the park. She had not wanted a mirror.

There had been times when he had gone to look for her in this room and found her sitting, not reading or sewing. Just thinking. He loved that in her, her capacity to be apart, to be roaming a universe within while outside was all placidity. Her brow scarcely bore a line. (*How is it*, he once asked her, *that you have only to go inside to find a spreading calm? See how thought and care have ploughed up my face.*)

Now when he climbed the stairs to this small room it was also to be with her. He could almost see her standing at the window, almost believe that she was there since she had a way of folding herself in to the quiet of a place, becoming part of it so she could the better see and hear what was around.

—

The King kept him busy and he was as glad of this as he was of anything. He was often from home. When Wyatt was not away from Allington on affairs of state he made sure he was occupied from dawn until late. He rode out with Lukkes whenever he was able. He worked at translation, determined, though his dearest human love could not be brought home, to bring home the poems that he loved. He was preoccupied, abstracted, tumbling phrases of Italian or Latin over and over in his mind till his mind's tongue loosened the right word.

The seven psalms continued to work their way through him. Letting the Latin of these psalms sit in his mind and remembering the narrative so tersely rendered in the book of Samuel he allowed himself to dwell on and in the story of David and Bathsheba. How the Hebrew king's passion to possess one woman had exposed all that was shabby and grasping in his nature, leading him to become a murderer and a bawd. Aretino and others had amplified their translations with linking passages that presented David, their singer, in tableau fashion. Wyatt began to think about the ways in which an internal position is reflected in a visible stance or posture. He experimented with these postures. Susan Holmes observed his abstraction and occasional strange gestures and wondered if he might be plotting something, but no messengers were despatched and she made no report.

19

He and his wife grew to tolerate one another during this enforced cohabitation. As long as certain topics of conversation were not broached, they found they could behave pleasantly enough. Inevitably the possibility of resuming physical intimacy was present. When he saw the small, brown-haired woman he had married, her brow a little low, her cheeks easily given to dimpling, he felt neither the mild desire that had once drawn him to her nor the extreme repugnance that had kept them apart. He had grown to feel a kind of weary tolerance that at times approached affection — the affection of reluctant cell-mates.

When she arrives in his bed-chamber in the middle of the night dressed only in a chemise he is startled rather than angry. He has been sleeping fitfully, waking often from anguished dreams in which Bess was travelling away from him and Lukkes was on a distant hill, refusing to stoop to the lure. The sight of his wife, irrefutably real and there, is comforting. It offers a tether to life.

Encouraged by his lack of opposition, Elizabeth goes over to his bed and lifts the covers at the side to climb in. Wyatt watches her, neither welcoming her nor rejecting her, appalled by what is happening but doing nothing to stop it. He even lifts the bedclothes further to give her space to move closer to him. When she reaches a hand to touch him she finds him hard. The familiar moves. *The old game*. He is soon inside her. So soon that she looks surprised and smiles delightedly. She begins to ride him. But he cannot bear to see her face. The face that is not Bess' face. He pulls out, turns her over and brings himself to an angry climax inside the woman whose face he does not want to see.

She felt his anger. There was no need for him to ask her to leave; she quickly gathered up her garment, holding it across her body, nor wanting him to see how it had changed from the lithe girl's body that had given birth to his children. She need not have concerned herself for his eyes were turned away. He kept his head turned away while she put her chemise back on and slipped, as silently as she had entered, out of the door of his bed-chamber and back to her own apartment.

20

The room Bess Darrell had used was empty now. No strawberry-patterned stool, no work box, no writing stand. Only the table and chairs which he had provided remained, and as he pulled out one of the chairs the very sound of its scrape across the wooden boards combined with the smell of the room's familiar dust (which must still carry her trace) nosed open a small and empty cave within his mind. A cave of utter desolation and aloneness.

As if to comment upon or correct his sense of isolation, a single sparrow begins to chirp just outside his window. He remembers the words of the psalm, spoken by David in his isolation and remorse:

> ... *sicut passer solitarius in tecto.*

A sparrow alone. He has Englished those lines:

> *Like the sparrow was I solitary,*
> *That sits alone under the house's eaves.*

Then there was Catullus' sparrow — or rather Lesbia's pet, *Passer deliciae meae puellae*. The darling of my darling.

If he were indeed a sparrow alone on the roof and not a

man condemned to something close to house arrest, he could fly to his darling, take water from her mouth.

Are not two sparrows sold for a farthing?

He considers how a sparrow has long been a trope for what is ordinary and unvalued, though again and again Scripture and verse have singled it out for value and love.

When he had been in prison he had taken pleasure in watching the small skirmishes of the sparrows who took dust baths in the yard outside. They had become as dear to him as Lukkes who first taught him to be observant of birds.

Lukkes, my fair falcon.

The messenger is so often a bird. The dove that carried to Noah proof that the waters were receding: that something grew from the earth's high places. The next time the dove was sent out she did not fly back and Noah surmised that she had found more than a temporary perch; that she had found a place to make a nest and live. Did he then send out his one male dove to breed with her? How else could there be doves in this world he now inhabits, a world in which his dove-cote chitters all day with the cool tumbling sounds of his birds? He thinks that if he had been Noah he would not have been so confident that the bird was safe. And yet what predators could there have been on an earth in which all that lived, lived with him?

Worse than any outward predators are those within. Those that torment him now are sorrow and remorse at a life squandered in compromise, complicity, evasion and unsteadiness. He who so values truth has not lived by it. At least not consistently. Because he is overly fond of his life, he is in service — *in thrall* — to a king he has come to despise as well as fear. He lives with a wife he does not respect whilst exiled from the woman he loves and is unable to help. He has betrayed her, carelessly and joylessly, and in doing so has again betrayed himself. Though he has contrived on more than one occasion to meet her in the West Country and has held his new son and kissed the adorably curved brow, he fears he may never see her again. He feels utterly unworthy of her. In his will he has left lands in Dorset to her and their son. Perhaps it will only be through his death that he will be able to help them.

—

Bess' room, as he still thinks of it, has become his preferred place of prayer and reflection. There is not the space in which to spread out folio volumes — these must rest in his library — but smaller volumes accompany him here. He has his Psalter with him now, though he has little need of a printed version. The Latin sits in his bones and he regrets never acquiring the ability to read Hebrew. (Unlike the King. Wyatt remembers the sight of the King struggling like a child to form the unfamiliar shapes of the letters, his tongue protruding between his teeth as he concentrated, and then, still like a child, attempting to pronounce the strange names for those letters, *aleph, beit, gimel.* So determined was he to pursue Leviticus *to the letter* if it would uphold his case for divorce.) He returns to the Latin of the one hundred and second psalm, sixth of the seven psalms of penitence. When he mouths these words, he feels himself in contact with the thousands upon thousands who have also mouthed them. The arched roof of his mouth becomes a small chapel, he its cantor.

He picks up his lute, which lately he has taken to keeping

in Bess's room. Once he might have painted himself as the melancholy lover and enjoyed the pathos of the role. His present sorrow is too great for such nonsense. The psalmist's words suit him better and he assumes the stance which he pictures David to have taken, left foot on the ground as he kneels with his right foreleg folded under. His lute propped on his left knee. He strikes a chord and repeats it, accompanying himself in a plangent plainsong:

> Lord, hear my prayer, and let my cry pass
>> Unto thee lord without impediment.
>> Do not from me turn thy merciful face,
> Unto my self leaving my government.

In taking these psalms into English, at times amplifying them as he struggles with their meaning, he has made them a part of his own life; he has discovered the shape of them within himself; stretched himself into new forms to meet them.

He has a deep voice which, in the past, when singing songs of gallantry, he had restrained out of a sense that his strength should not overwhelm the delicacy of his song; that song was not the place for strength. But now he gives the psalm full voice — his own English voice — and he feels his whole body become a sounding box. Now he stands by the window and the words of the psalm pour out of him. He could not have written them down — for that his memory would not have served — but in singing, each verse pulls its successor along with it. A kind of concatenation which he has often observed in his memory of verse. If the body (and his voice belongs to his body) takes part then the body with its muscular memory will fetch up what it has experienced before.

Like the sparrow was I solitary
  That sits alone under the house's eaves.
  This while my foes conspired continually
And did provoke the harm of my disease.
  Wherefore like ashes my bread did me savour;
  Of thy just word the taste might not me please.
Wherefore my drink I tempered with liquor
  Of weeping tears ...
  For thou didst lift me up to throw me down,
  To teach me how to know my self again.

His face is wet with tears he had not even known he was crying (as once, cut by a fine French blade, his arm had been wet with blood before he had felt the wounding). It is as if he had never heard these words before, as if they were fetched from the inner reaches of his being — a place where nothing ordinary would answer.

When he was young he was ambitious for glory; later he had hoped for freedom without loss of honour; most recently his ambition was for domestic happiness with the woman of his choice. All of these have been denied (though there was once glory of a kind); he is like a snake who has sloughed off one skin to reveal one so thin he feels naked. Like the psalmist, he guesses that his life is nearing its end: *He hath abridged my days; they may not dure.* The time for small personal ambitions, precious though they are, is over. He must lift himself to wish and pray for more, for a good which is not his alone or even for him to see. That is what the psalmist prayed for, the good of all, the establishment of God's kingdom, the Zion that is not a mappable place but a condition of fellowship, fidelity and truth:

Thou wrought'st the earth; thy hands the heavens did make:
They shall perish and thou shalt last alway.
And all things age shall wear and overtake
Like cloth, and thou shalt change them like apparel,
Turn and translate, and they in worth it take.
But thou thyself the self remainest well
That thou wast erst, and shalt thy years extend.
Then since to this there may nothing rebel
The greatest comfort that I can pretend
Is that the children of thy servants dear,
That in thy word are got, shall without end
Before thy face be stablished …

These words were hard won and long in the finding. Their magnanimity, which Wyatt merely follows, takes him to a place of rare peace but he cannot rest there. Soon restlessness and a habit of exploratory thought resume. From whose being did these psalms issue? Were they really the work of King David, wracked with dejection and contrition when he realised the immensity of his crime — effectively murdering his loyal servant and soldier Uriah in order to conceal his adultery with Bathsheba? For a king to translate his wishes into acts was nothing new. There are many now who would, with servile acquiescence, prostitute their own wife, sister, or daughter if the King had indicated a liking for them. Indeed he has heard that the King has an eye on his own wife. Perhaps that is why he required that Wyatt fetch her home! But, indifferent as he is to the woman, he will not be a *mari complaisant* like those men who, castrated at the King's pleasure, have limped away to the remote estate granted as reward.

It was safer for a woman never to catch the King's eye.

Bess had known that. During the years that she'd worked for Katherine she'd made herself dull. A woman can choose not to shine, can pull in her radiance so she seems almost mantled in dust. It is what a clever animal will do when it cannot make itself invisible to its enemy; it will make itself at the least too pathetic-seeming a conquest to be bothered with. His brilliant Bess, who read Plutarch and Boethius to her Queen and had lively thoughts on both, would appear reserved and almost vacant whenever the King (who in those days still liked a clever woman) was present. It was not only that loyalty to Katherine precluded the slightest flirtation with Katherine's husband. She knew that the smallest flicker of interest shown could intrigue him but there was nothing in the wilful dangerousness of the man to quicken her interest. Dull dull dull was her only resource. Wyatt had once told her that she was like the lady chaffinch; beautiful but subtly so, unlike the gaudy male. She was so adept at appearing dull, withdrawing her light when she chose, that even Wyatt had overlooked her. Perhaps that was the reason it had taken so long before he really saw her.

Ann had not been like that. It would never have occurred to her to pull in her light and be unseen. And Bathsheba? — *her whose look, alas, did make me blind* — neither did she know to cancel her radiance. What would she have looked like? Would he, if he could see her now, find her beautiful as King David had? Lovely like the straight-nosed woman in the tapestry? Could she have felt the man's eyes on her, known herself clasped by his sight without knowing the owner or the source of that sight? There are women — he has known some — who bloom under a man's gaze and ripen when desired. A look can be a reciprocal communication. As in a game of tennis, the velocity of the sent ball can explode something in the receiver which the returned ball then carries. The returned look or the avoided look can burn with summoned desire.

How weary he is to recall this game — played often and often, sometimes without considering whether in earnest or not. He remembers that he used to set his gaze as a man might rest his hands upon the bar of a spade and look long across the land he was about to work. There are women of all ages who collapse into disarray and confusion at such a look as he could frame: the calculating look which seems to combine longing with a sorrow that that longing can never be assuaged. Was the game so old that David and Bathsheba had played it? Imagining Bathsheba's body warming to consciousness in the felt gaze of King David, his own body flushes with desire.

But desire for whom? For Bathsheba whom he has never known, whose bones and radiance have long ago turned to dust? For Dian, for Ann? For Bess? For the village girl who kissed him that May morning? For all and for none of them, though there is sweetness and a tug of yearning in the thought of each. He looks out of the window at the park. The grass — kept short by the sheep — gleams after the recent downpour. A shaft of sunlight catches the moisture in the air and a rainbow appears to empty itself onto the grass. Beyond the park the open weald where he will ride with Lukkes the next fine day. Beyond and beyond; and beyond that too. Allington, Kent, England — the circle widening each time outwards till you reach the shores of heaven. Always more.

So his desire: more than an accidental engagement as blood fills his veins. It had and has its local and particular objects as well as something ever beyond them. When the local and particular are taken away (by their free will, by a tyrant's intervention, by death) there is and was nothing else for it but to go beyond. The alternative is to be left staring at an empty wall.

It has been his experience that an empty wall thwarts sight and (when the wall is in a prison) action; but it does not thwart imagination. Rather the reverse. When the Sword of Calais sliced through that little neck what had he not seen in his mind, on the screen of that plain (though pitted) wall? Though his bodily eyes had only viewed the scene from an obscuring distance, he'd seen her hands, her strange little dewclawed hands, fly up to her neck one last time, taking the measure of it; the regal way she shed her cloak, handing it to one of her weeping ladies, comforting her, showing her how it was to be done. He saw her look about her, taking in the huge crowd that had gathered to watch her last performance. He thought this would have rallied her, provoked her into some kind of stance or held her in a prepared resolve. Would there have been a friend there among the crowd (had he been there, he could have been that friend) to catch the flung posy of her last words as he had caught Cromwell's? He had seen the cloth unable to soak up all her blood. He saw the look of surprise on her face as the blade sliced through her neck as the clever swordsman distracted her gaze, dividing soul from body before mind knew.

Here in this unadorned room he could picture Bess Darrell, sitting or standing, kneeling or walking. He pictured her lifting the bedcovers to invite him in, felt the soft gust of warmth that breathed out, as from an oven opened. He heard her low laughter and soft breath.

They were fools who thought that the best cure for madness was a dark room. Darkness never quenched the imagination of anyone who had that faculty. Imagination thrived on absence.

Oublier ne puis

ACKNOWLEDGEMENTS

This book has been slow in the making and through many versions along the way. My agent, Michelle Kass, has read each one and had the tact to comment on them in ways that enabled me to continue. I am deeply grateful to her, and to all who have worked with her, Russell Franklin in particular. My friends David Black, Christopher Potter, and Samuel SSF have each helped me by reading one or other earlier draft. Thank you to them and to my editor, Philip Gwyn Jones, for their sympathetic and astute comments and to Molly Slight for her clear-eyed, thoughtful copyediting. Warm thanks also to Robert Chandler, Martha Kapos and Erwin Van de Velde whose advice and support were always there when needed, and to my dear partner, David Cash, for his support and encouragement over the many years.

I am grateful to the Authors' Foundation for a grant that bought me valuable working time.

The Wyatt section of this book is not intended as fictionalised biography. Nevertheless I was glad that Susan Brigden's fine biography, *The Heart's Forest*, came out in time for me to benefit from her knowledge and understanding. The same is true of the first volume of Jason Powell's, *The Complete Works of Thomas Wyatt the Elder*, containing Wyatt's prose. I greatly look forward to the second volume containing Wyatt's poems.

Wyatt is a haunted and haunting poet. I am grateful to Patricia Milne-Henderson for allowing me to walk around the grounds of Clifton Maybank House, near Sherborne in Dorset. It is the former home of Wyatt's friend Sir John Horsey and the place where Wyatt is said to have died. Tessa (I know only this name), the gardener who showed me round, pointed out to me the cherry tree at the edge of a huge bowling green where, she said, she'd 'seen him sometimes'.

'Who?' I asked.

'Thomas. He comes and watches me when I'm gardening.'